The Rand Conspiracy

Richard Westover

ISBN: 9798541428537

DEDICATION

for

Marie-Claire

October 1895, Witwatersrand gold fields, Johannesburg, South African Republic

Willem Leroux imagined his son striding out of the rusty haze with his slouch hat angled back, knapsack over shoulder, ready to help him.

'Good night, Mr Leroux.'

'Good night, Rory,' Leroux said, squinting west as the last of his men left for the night. Rory scratched at the stubble on his chin and pulled a neckerchief up over his nose. He cast a sideways glance at Mr Leroux and set off down the track, through the shadows stretching out from the heaps of gold ore on the scarred ridge. Rory reached the sun-bleached planks that passed for a gate and waved at two men on horseback, silhouetted in the distance. Leroux wiped his brow, smearing dirt into his gritty hair, and turned away from the sun as it simmered on the skyline.

He closed the corrugated iron door against the dust, picked up a crowbar and pried open a small crate on the top of a stack by the far wall. He looked down and tutted at the shoddy workmanship where the wicks and blasting caps joined to the dynamite. Flies buzzed lazily, where moments before the air had shuddered to the hammering of rock. Leroux cocked his head. It was the sound of men dismounting, and he darted for the entrance and the coach gun propped up beside it.

The door burst open, kicked in. A lanky man stepped through, tipped his shabby top hat, and looked down at the coach gun, smirking.

'Good evening, Mr Leroux. Yee expecting visitors?'

A younger henchman followed, and both levelled revolvers at Leroux, stranded in the middle of the storehouse.

'I told you I'm not interested,' Leroux said to the Irishman he knew as Mr O'Connell. He felt the shaft of the crowbar warm in his hand. O'Connell picked up the coach gun and broke it open, turning it to show Leroux the empty breech, sniggered, and tossed it to the floor.

'Heard the rock samples are good. Even so, the Baron's made a generous offer. I suggest you take it.'

'I'm not interested, whatever the price. I thought I had made that clear.'

'The Baron is most insistent,' O'Connell said and twitched his revolver, sending his man to Leroux's flank.

Leroux judged the distance and the heft of the crowbar - too far. He circled to his right, putting himself in front of the crates.

'Fire and you'll blow us all to hell.'

The henchman picked up a shovel and followed Leroux, six feet away.

A smile unfurled across O'Connell's face, bristly creases bracketing what remained of his teeth.

'Yee don't look the type to go to hell, and my priest reckons they won't let me in. Why I'm still alive, he says.'

He nodded at his accomplice, who holstered his revolver and brandished the shovel, closing in. O'Connell cocked his gun. 'All as stubborn as one another, you Boers. It was a lot of money, seeing as we weren't offering you a choice.'

Leroux raised his empty hand. 'Very well. Get the papers.'

'Too late for that, Mr Leroux.' O'Connell's eyes glittered behind the muzzle sight.

Leroux lunged, twisting and swinging the crowbar up at the outstretched gun. He thought he saw O'Connell step away. He felt dirt dry on his cheek and a splintering crash on his skull but wasn't sure which came first.

He was lying down, swaying back and forth, but staggering. It felt colder. He was descending. He recognised the smell, traces of rotten eggs and sweetness. Were his eyes open? It was dark. Someone was holding his feet. And under his shoulders. Must be somebody else. A heavy grunt fouled the air. He felt nauseous. They stopped and dropped him, and he landed on two bars and heard his breath forced out as he sagged between them. They were the rails, he thought. Let me rest here.

'Jaysus, this wasn't the plan.' A new voice.

'Who's to know, Finn?' O'Connell said, 'He wouldn't take the money. We'll keep it for the cause. Pull the cart to the top.'

'What about the papers, his mark?'

'I can write. Get the cart to the top.'

Crunching footsteps and well-oiled wheels receded.

Rough hands felt through Leroux's pockets. All he could do was taste the blood at the back of his throat.

O'Connell murmured, ''Tis a shame. The Boers and the Irish have a lot in common. Ourselves alone now. Yee shouldn't have made me ask twice.' He drew back and shouted, 'Let it go.'

The familiar trundle soothed Leroux. He had built this place and knew every sound, but it was fast. His head sagged to the side, and he could see a disc of light in the distance, his ear resting on the rail. So that was how it sounded. A tear rolled across the bridge of his nose. His son would not be joining him in the venture now, for the noise was loud and close, too close.

December 1895, Prime Minister's Residence, Cape Town, British Cape Colony

The Prime Minister bent his imposing frame over the map table. He gazed down with satisfaction. His company, the Chartered British South Africa Company, had annexed great swathes of territory for the Empire, equal in area to the British Isles, France, Spain, Prussia, and Austria together. The company had received the mining rights to it all for services to Her Majesty the Queen.

He moved his forefinger north from the Cape, tracing a line ever north, all the way to Cairo, and took a long draw on his cigarette. It was his dream. It gave meaning to all the power and wealth he had amassed. And it would be his legacy, a railroad from the Cape to Cairo on British territory.

His eye returned to Southern Africa, and the Transvaal region. A frown clouded his face. The Boer State calling itself the South African Republic, and its insufferable President Paul Kruger, stood in the way. The British Empire lost a war with the Boers, before his time, and before the gold, back when the place didn't matter. But now it did matter.

The Witwatersrand, the ridge of white waters on that hot and dusty plateau, held as much gold as the rest of the world. Whoever controlled the Rand's goldfields would dominate southern Africa. His plan to surround it with British territory had been frustrated. The Portuguese refused to sell Delagoa Bay, and Kruger had built a railroad to the sea there, escaping the British noose. Kruger would never treat with the British and become a protectorate now. Kruger was playing for time and sending his emissaries to Germany to purchase armaments.

No matter. He had another plan. John Hays Hammond, his right-hand man in Johannesburg, reported that the Uitlanders, who had flocked from every corner of the world to the gold mines and now outnumbered the Boers, were ready to revolt against the unjust rule of President Kruger. Hammond said the American folk would have rebelled some time ago, but the English miners were more willing to bear the yoke. It was ever thus. So, he had tasked Hammond with fomenting an uprising and proclaiming a new State.

And when the uprising began, his company's military force would dash over the border to protect the good citizens of Johannesburg from President Kruger's reprisals. He would declare them to be under the protection of the British Empire. He could rely on the commander too, Dr Jim, who had always delivered. Lord Salisbury was back in power in London. He would not concede ground to the Boers as Gladstone had done - Salisbury had already denied the Irish Home Rule. The Colonial Office had given an unofficial blessing to his plan and even started to press the urgency of the matter. A brewing dispute with the United States in Latin America meant he needed to act before Britain's relationship with America deteriorated and aggression against a sister republic would be enough to provoke war.

Yet something was amiss. Other empires were manoeuvring for power over the ridge of gold. He had received disturbing news that nagged at the back of his mind. It was too late to stop now, but he should follow it up. He stubbed his cigarette out. He was Cecil Rhodes, and it would be done.

December 1895, President Paul Kruger's residence, Pretoria, South African Republic

The President sat on the veranda puffing on a well-worn pipe. It was an ordinary residence, as were the other bungalows on the street, and the President liked to welcome petitioners here.

A gnarled Boer with a shaggy beard halted his wagon in the shade of a jacaranda tree and shuffled up the steps onto the veranda, where Kruger held his simple court. The oxen were particularly scrawny.

The Boer took off his battered felt hat and held it between his hands. He had been on the Trek with the President all that time ago when they had crossed the Vaal River and founded their nation.

'Oom Paul, I am sorry to ask. Things are not good at home. Have you thought about my request?'

'I am sorry Dirk, but all the Ministers' positions are taken.'

'Oom Paul, perhaps there is some deputy position that could be available?'

'I am afraid they are all taken too.'

'Aach, anything will do. There must be some clerk's position I can have?'

'Dirk, my old friend. We both know you are too stupid to be a clerk. Now, sit and have coffee with me. Tell me what the people are saying and what goes on in Johannesburg. Things are looking up, nee? The rains have come at last, and I hear the Uitlanders are paying good prices for food and water.' Kruger stroked his matching beard.

'Ja, ja, the rains came. It was good that we had the National Day of Prayer. The Uitlanders didn't pray. They were making great bombs in the sky. They said they would shake the rain from the clouds, but it was the work of the Devil, and it only made a little bit of rain. It was our prayers that brought the real rain.'

Kruger nodded and took a long draw on his pipe.

'Those Uitlanders shake their fist at God in all manner of ways, not just with their pyrotechnics. And they keep coming, so many there are now two for every good Burgher like you and me.'

Dirk lowered his eyes. 'Why did God put a mountain of gold on the Witwatersrand? We did not pray for it.'

'It must be a test. But with the taxes we take from the miners, the government is no longer poor. And the truth is, even us good Burghers do not like to pay taxes, so it is good that the Uitlanders do. We have built the railway with the money and are no longer beholden to the British and their ports.'

Kruger took the pipe from his mouth and expectorated into a copper spittoon. His lower lip had grown pendulous with the constant pipe use, and he wiped the back of his hand across his mouth. Dirk was still thinking.

'Oom Paul, the railways are bad. Now food comes quickly and lowers the prices for our harvests. And we don't make money any more hauling goods from the border.'

'We cannot stop it now. Maybe ten years ago, when there was nothing on the Witwatersrand, just old Oosthuizen's farm. Now, there are more than one hundred thousand souls in that Devil city. They say that half of all the gold in the world is up there on the Rand. More come every day. We must find a way to use it to our advantage.'

Dirk gazed over at the plain church on the other side of the road. 'They are godless people. Gambling, drinking, and the women! The women do not sleep in their clothes!... They say.'

'I know, and they complain about everything. Too many taxes, not enough police, too much corruption. Too much corruption! And after I made my own son-in-law the Mining Commissioner!' Kruger hawked again. 'The Uitlanders are getting ever more restless with their demands. If we give them the vote, we will lose our country. Never!'

Dirk grumbled his assent, clawing at his greasy beard. 'The farmers out by the border say there are a lot of Britisher soldiers there.'

'Trouble is coming, Dirk, and when it does, I will have need of good Boer Commandos. Such memories, nee? How the British ran!'

'You want me to get the Commando together and ride in there? I will teach them for disrespecting the Lord!'

'Not yet. Time is on our side. We grow richer with the gold, and our

German friends are sending new weapons. We must be patient. Remember! To kill a tortoise, you must first wait for it to stick out its neck.'

Dirk's face broke into a yellow-toothed smile.

'Oom Paul, I will be ready when you call.'

Friday, 20th December 1895, Cape Town

'And what is great white chief wanting with young man like you?' the Zulu coachman said, immaculate in city livery, a tall hat accentuating his rangy physique.

'Angazi,' Peter Leroux said.

'You don't know? He does not like fools. Cabanga!'

'I am thinking…'

The Zulu laughed. 'You are from the veld and white man's wars coming there. Don't worry. Nobody can beat great white chief. When you see the big house, you will feel better. Jabula!'

Yes, cheer up, Leroux thought. Speaking Zulu again reminded him of his carefree childhood scampering about the farm and far beyond out on the veld with Tom. That felt like a long time ago. The bustle of Cape Town receded behind them as they climbed rougher tracks over a shoulder of Table Mountain. The sprung suspension of the imported Studebaker Landau was much smoother than the two-wheeler Cape cart boneshakers he was used to and drew admiring glances from fellow travellers they passed along the way. He fished out the letter from his mother and reread it. The solicitor had finished settling father's estate. The mine had gone, sold to repay outstanding loans, and there was little money left over. He was not to worry. She would remain on the farm and run it with the help of Tom's family, and she was proud of him for forging his own path. Leroux folded the letter. He hadn't known there were money troubles. Was that why father had been working alone in the mine? He wished he had joined him in the business. Maybe then all this would never have happened. He pocketed the letter and pulled out the card that had arrived at breakfast:

The Prime Minister requests your presence at Groote Schuur
eleven a.m. 20th December

Cecil Rhodes was the most powerful man in Southern Africa as well as a significant investor in his employer, The Cape Argus. He had plenty on his plate. What could he want with a junior journalist? Leroux reflected on the morning papers. The leading men in Johannesburg had given speeches demanding voting rights for the Uitlanders and accusing President Kruger of putting their patience to the test. Cables reported that the Kruger Government had placed an order for two of the new Maxim machine guns. Stock in the mining companies had crashed on the Exchange. Plenty of trouble about and that was just Johannesburg. The French were on the verge of completing their conquest of Madagascar, and President Cleveland of America was rattling sabres with Great Britain over her interference in Venezuela.

Rhodes had even sent a coach to fetch him, and now it topped the ridge where a fresh breeze blew in from the Southern Ocean and the bay that sparkled below them. Before long they pulled into the long avenue to Groote Schuur. Leroux stirred from his thoughts inhaling the perfumed air trapped by the Scotch firs that lined the road, almost touching at their tops to give the appearance of a cathedral's nave. As the carriage crested a small rise and swept around a bend, the Big Barn came into view, nestled in front of Devil's Peak.

Large many-paned windows looked out beneath thatched gables in the Dutch style. Leroux brushed himself down and straightened his tie as they drew up to the white columns that flanked the wide front steps. His tweeds had seen better days, and he had to admit that his beloved slouch hat was tatty. The coachman turned to him, and Leroux looked at the dark door set well back in shadow. He felt Johannesburg calling.

'Ulindeni?' the coachman said.

Leroux wasn't sure what he was waiting for. He remembered Tom's words, a Zulu saw, that he often said, usually before doing something stupid.

'Almost doesn't fill a bowl.'

The Zulu grinned and nodded. 'Yebo!'

Leroux looked at the door again, pulled back his shoulders, and marched up the steps. A footman held the door open, and Leroux presented his card to another waiting inside. This one looked at him doubtfully but ushered him through to the anteroom anyway.

He was early and paced around the wood-panelled room, keeping a safe distance from the old colonial furniture and exquisite African ornaments. A faint buzzing came from behind the double-doors at the far end, and an official hurried out to relay some business of Empire, glancing blankly at Leroux on the way. The footman tending the doors beckoned him and announced his presence. Leroux shot his cuffs and went through into a library, where Rhodes brooded over a desk.

He was a tall man who had thickened in middle-age, and his auburn hair turned grey at the edges. A map spread out over the desk, one corner held down by a gold object, glinting in a shaft of sunlight. Leroux approached, pulling himself into a confident posture, and was surprised to see Rhodes in a grey tweed suit, not much smarter than his own.

'What did you think of the Studebaker?' Rhodes said.

'Smooth ride sir, it handled the tracks better than I expected.'

'It's much stronger than it looks. My chief engineer, an American, suggested it. Wonderful machine. What do you make of that?' Rhodes pointed at the gold piece on his desk.

It was a sundial, crafted in a native style.

'May I?' Leroux had only held something so heavy for its size on visits to his father in the mining camps. The worn-down markings were spare but beautiful.

'Must be pure gold. African craft. Looks old.'

'Very old. Missionaries and traders from the interior have often reported hearing stories of objects and carvings like this. Where that came from, in Mashonaland, there are the remains of ancient mine workings. They say that it is the lost Kingdom of Ophir, the location of King Solomon's mines. Pomegranates and lemons grow there as in the legends, but as far as I can tell the mines are all worked out. And I've no time to chase fairy tales. The real gold is here.' Rhodes jabbed a finger down at the map, looking up at Leroux and fixing him with his grey-blue eyes.

'The Transvaal – I understand you know it?'

'Yes, sir. I was raised there until I came here to the College.'

'Sit.' Rhodes gestured at one of the chairs in front of the desk, his gaze unwavering. 'So, are you a Boer?'

Leroux thought of the old-timers with their Old Testament ways and suspicion of foreigners and of his mother who taught at the small school and who counted Tom and his parents as part of their family. 'No, or at least not as they see it. My father was half-Dutch, half-French, brought up here on the Cape. He went north for work as an engineer when I was young. My mother is English, and we lived on a small farm in the Transvaal near the border, while father worked in the mining camps. She still lives there. Even now we're considered Uitlanders.'

That was an exaggeration, thought Leroux. They were entitled to vote, and he had even fought in a Boer commando. Why had he said it? Was he so drawn in by Rhodes's power that he bent his words to find favour?

Rhodes stroked his moustache. 'You look like a Boer, despite the smooth face. The hat doesn't help. I hear you fought for the Republic?'

'I went back and volunteered when they called everyone up during Chief Malaboch's rebellion. They had to conscript Uitlanders as well to raise enough men.'

'Volunteered? Why?'

The answer had not been wholly clear to him at the time. The farmers were forever wary of tribal unrest. Their families had instructions to gather at a secret location for a last stand if raiding parties came to the isolated farms. But the endless cycle of oppression, uprising and retribution sat uneasily with him. He had hoped perhaps to become a war correspondent and shed some light on the struggles to gain support for a more enlightened way of sharing this vast continent. The bitter experience of the slaughter had clarified his thoughts. War was not the answer, but that was not an answer Rhodes would welcome, and Leroux still didn't know why he was here.

'Partly a sense of duty, to protect the farms. Partly curiosity.'

'What did you make of the Boer Commando?'

Leroux wondered where Rhodes's questions were leading. He must know all this.

'An effective unit on the veld. They mobilise quickly, travel light, just their own rifles, ammunition, and rations on their ponies. They can move great distances. Expert marksmen, adept at hunting and using cover. But not used to military discipline and don't like to be away from their farms for too long. Including Uitlanders in the force did not work out well. Most lacked the skills and motivation required.'

Rhodes nodded. 'Did you know Commandant-General Piet Joubert?'

Leroux heard his mother's words gently admonishing him for painting the lily when he came back boastful with Tom from escapades on the veld. 'He was the commanding officer. I spoke with him a few times, but I don't know whether he would remember me. We called him Cute Piet for his cleverness. Popular and respected.'

Rhodes massaged the little finger of his right hand, which curled right in. He studied the map again, rubbing the finger up and down his chest. When Rhodes looked up, his eyes were warmer.

'I'm told Joubert gave you a commendation.'

'Yes, sir.'

'It's a shame Joubert keeps losing elections to Kruger. He would be more willing to come to an accommodation with the miners in Johannesburg, not to mention us.' Rhodes gave a wry smile.

'Joubert understands the inevitability of progress. But Kruger has a biblical faith in his destiny and keeps an iron grip.'

'Well, perhaps something can be done about that,' Rhodes said.

'You must know that some believe Joubert should have won the last election, that Kruger's allies interfered with the vote count?'

Rhodes nodded and rubbed his little finger again. 'Edmund Powell speaks highly of you and tells me you wish to become a war correspondent.'

'Yes, sir.' Leroux had expressed the desire to his editor when he returned from the Malaboch rising, but an opportunity had not yet arisen.

'We may be able to help each other.'

'Sir?'

Rhodes rocked back in his chair and lit a cigarette and passed a hand through his hair, leaving it confused, and then pushed himself forward and lent towards Leroux.

'I met your father once. In fact, I tried to hire him for Consolidated Gold Fields a few years back, but he was determined to row his own boat. I was sorry to hear the news. Please accept my condolences.'

'Thank you, sir. I didn't know about the offer of employment. Father kept that to himself. Maybe he knew mother would have wanted him to take the position rather than prospecting on his own.'

'Maybe her intuition was right, but he did well, and his claim had potential. Maddox Deep, if I remember the name correctly?'

Rhodes was a leading Randlord, as they called the largest mine-owners. Yet his knowledge of a small claim, one that hadn't even started producing, surprised Leroux.

'Yes, after my mother's maiden name.'

Rhodes stood and walked around behind Leroux and put one hand on his back, feeling the lean cord of muscle across his shoulder.

'There is something I would like you to consider – a proposition shall we say. I only require that you keep confidential what we discuss.' Rhodes squeezed his hand.

Leroux stared straight ahead, 'Of course, you have my word.'

Rhodes's hand brushed across Leroux's back as he returned to the desk. 'Good, good. You are no doubt aware of the situation in Johannesburg?'

'I read Mr Phillips's speech in the morning paper, although it seems unlikely that President Kruger will make any concessions. Purchasing Maxims is hardly a conciliatory gesture.'

'Quite so. Do you know what Kruger said in reply?' Rhodes quickly answered his own question, his voice rising to an odd falsetto. "'If they want their rights, let them fight for them!" The way he is carrying on, he will get his wish.'

Cape Town was awash with rumours of Dr Jim, the hero of Mashonaland. He was lionised by the public, feted by the press, and honoured by Queen Victoria for his buccaneering role in securing new territories for the Empire. Doctor Leander Starr Jameson was Rhodes's former physician and most trusted lieutenant. And now he was prowling along the Transvaal border in command of a British South African Company force.

'Even I hear the rumours of rifles smuggled into Johannesburg. It appears both sides are preparing for the worst, sir.'

'Not much secret about that. Have you heard of John Hays Hammond?'

'The best-paid engineer in the world. Works for you.'

'And well worth it. He truly understands the nature of the gold deposits on the Rand – vast, practically unlimited. The outcrop mines will soon be exhausted, but the deeps will go on far beyond my lifetime. And without proper governance and economic management, the opportunity will be squandered. I think it was him that mentioned

Maddox Deep has potential. He is a man of action and extremely well connected in the mining and business community in Johannesburg. The city is on the verge of open rebellion. Plans are in place.'

Rhodes had thrown down the statement and now paused as if to judge the ripples that emanated. Leroux willed himself not to look away and stared at the end of Rhodes's nose. It was not a surprise, but it was a big step for the miners to cross over into treason.

'Kruger will surely respond swiftly... and harshly.'

'He will, and we are ready for that. Preparations have been underway for some time. A committee is organising matters there; Hammond, my brother Frank, Charles Leonard, President of the National Union, Lionel Phillips, Chairman of the Chamber of Mines, and George Farrar, a prominent mine-owner. That is all in hand. One thing has come to my attention, though...'

Rhodes stroked his chest with the crippled finger and worked his lips as if pondering the best way to pose a question. 'Mr Leroux, do you have any reason to believe that your father's death was anything other than an accident?'

Leroux looked straight ahead, as though his eyes had been disconnected from his mind by the jarring suggestion. The memory of his mother explaining his father's death flooded back to him. He closed his eyes and took a deep breath.

'No, it was an accident in the mine. Father had been working there on his own. What are you saying?'

'By all accounts, your father was not a man to take short cuts. People I know, who had spoken to him, told of his confidence and determination, his happiness that he had taken the chance and the hope of what it would provide for his family. There was no inkling of financial distress, but when your father died the mine passed into the hands of a German company in settlement of outstanding debts. That company is called Veltheim & Co, owned by Baron Ludwig von Veltheim. One of my staff came across the transaction when he was looking into German activities in Johannesburg. However, we haven't been able to find anything more about the company or the owner, or how it came to have a lien on your father's mine.'

'Are you saying there is a connection between this company and my father's death?'

'I don't know. But the coincidence of the unexpected financial arrangement and the out-of-character nature of your father's death is troubling, not to mention the link with Germany, especially at this time.'

'Have your people in Johannesburg spoken to the authorities?'

'The authorities may be part of the problem. The person who was looking into it has disappeared.'

Leroux fought down the rising gorge accompanying the suspicions surrounding his father's death, while Rhodes continued. 'German influence in the Transvaal is increasing every day. The Kaiser pressured Portugal not to sell Delagoa Bay to us. Kruger's State Secretary, Dr Leyds, is in Berlin as we speak purchasing armaments. German banks and companies are extending their tentacles in Johannesburg at every turn. Something is going on - I can feel it.'

Anger flared in Leroux's eyes as Rhodes watched.

'You could ask questions about your father in the Republic without arousing any suspicion. Everyone's expecting trouble there. I can arrange for you to go to Johannesburg as the war correspondent for The Argus. At the same time, you can make enquiries into your father's estate and passing. Anything that you can find out about the German connection could be vital.'

Rhodes was renowned for knowing the price of everyone that he dealt with, and he had not misjudged Leroux. Dust motes spiralled up from the sundial. Their eyes met, and Johannesburg called. He thought of his father, his trips to the mining camps when he was younger, and of Tom. Nothing good happened there.

'I accept,' Leroux said.

Rhodes pinched the cigarette as if he feared letting it slip through his fingers. His eyes were piercing, even as he narrowed them. Not against the smoke, but as though he was peering at some shimmering vision.

'Good. You know, the gold deposits on the Rand are greater than anything ever seen before. Whoever controls them will have the means to control the South of Africa.' Rhodes looked back down at the gold sundial. 'There's more you need to know. Hammond and the rest of the committee are nearly ready. They are waiting for enough rifles and ammunition to arm the miners. All being well, they could rise in ten days. There is a faction of more reform-minded Boers, led by our friend Commandant-General Joubert. The Uitlanders and the Reformer Boers will form a provisional government in Johannesburg together. Then, they will invite Dr Jim and his volunteers to come to their assistance and protect them from reprisals. The British Empire will recognise the new government. President Kruger will be facing a fait accompli.'

Leroux nodded. It was a bold plan. If it could be done with speed and surprise it could work.

'Joubert may not despise the British Empire as much as Kruger, but he is no friend.'

Rhodes smiled. 'You know your man. It's a marriage of convenience, without a doubt. Joubert can see the writing on the wall. The Boers will not be able to hold back the forces of change for long. It only remains to be decided who will benefit from the change.'

There it was. Rhodes knew Joubert's price as well. Rhodes coughed, a nasty hacking cough, and took another draw on the cigarette before extinguishing it. Again, his gaze fell on the sundial.

'Take this evening's train. An old friend of mine, Sanderson, will meet you there. He's a journalist with The Star, and there is an operator in the Johannesburg telegraph office on my payroll, Miss Sinclair. You can trust her with anything. She will be expecting you. Run all communications to me through her. And I'll tell Hammond that you are coming. He will have a lot on his hands but keep him informed with anything that you uncover.'

Rhodes took a sheet of notepaper and read aloud as he jotted down, "Mr Leroux is authorised to make any purchases and has full authority," and signed it with a flourish. He rose and handed over the note.

'Here. This will be accepted anywhere in Southern Africa, should you find yourself in a hole. See my private secretary on the way out and make any other arrangements necessary.'

Rhodes pressed a buzzer, and an aide came to usher Leroux out.

'Good luck, Mr Leroux.'

Leroux stood back against the wall, near to the platform entrance but away from the glare of the electric lighting and flicked open his pocket watch. It was nearly nine o'clock, but there was time yet, the engine was still taking on water. Porters stood idly by as the lucky ones helped their passengers board the train. One approached him.

'Any bags, sir?'

'Just the Gladstone and knapsack there. But wait a while.'

The porter obliged, as there was little else going on. Rhodes's secretary had said they were expecting two German gentlemen to be taking the evening train and had booked a compartment for Leroux in the same carriage. One was Captain Karl Brandt, the military attaché from the German Consulate in Johannesburg. He was in town to meet a passenger on the Southampton steamer that had docked in the morning. Germans bound for Johannesburg usually took the Hamburg line to Delagoa Bay, unless speed was of the essence, and it was unusual for a military attaché to meet arriving businessmen. No one had heard of the new arrival. The ship's manifest had him down as Herr Heinrich Muller, listed as an executive with the Nobel company. According to the Captain, he had kept to himself during the voyage.

'Quiet tonight,' Leroux said. No one had fitted the descriptions.

'Has been the last week, sir, for departures. Arrivals are good though. Folk up in Johannesburg sending their kin away.'

Two porters pounced on a pair of last-minute passengers in a flurry of activity. They walked up the platform. The man on the right could be Captain Brandt. He was tall and strode straight-backed in high boots and cream breeches but with a rub of casualness that spoke of time spent in the colonies. His companion was shorter and nondescript in a dark wool lounge suit, but so nondescript as to be remarkable. He kept up with the taller man with small quick steps and his eyes darted about underneath a black homburg hat. Their porters stopped by a compartment door, midway up the rear carriage. It was the right one. Leroux signalled to his porter he was ready and made for his neighbouring compartment. The duelling scar low down on the taller man's left cheek removed any doubt. He glanced down at their baggage. The satchel probably belonged to the captain, but the portmanteau and briefcase were most likely Muller's. Neither had any initials or markings on them.

Leroux stepped up into his compartment, where the steward had arranged one side as seating. He prodded the banquette made up as a bed, stowed his bags and pulled down the window. The guard by the locomotive waved a green flag, and the driver released two long whistle-blasts. As the engine issued its first chuff a burly man ran through the gate, his hold-all swinging beside him in one hand, his hat held on by the other. The train gathered way, the man's legs pumped, but he was not built for speed. Guards shouted warnings as Leroux grinned and opened his door. The man leapt up, grabbing the offered arm and flung in his bag. His squat bulk filled the door frame, and then he slumped down on the banquette and gave a breathless smile.

'Much obliged, sir.'

Leroux recognised the accent of a tin man - the Cornish hard-rock men sought after for their skill at deep excavations.

'Jory. Pleased to meet you.' He thrust out a gnarled ham of a hand.

'Well met Jory, Peter Leroux. You must be the only person in a rush to get back to the Rand.'

'No rush, sir. Just be out of money.'

He had the ruddy clean complexion of a long sea voyage home, and his face was round with contentment and mirth.

'You're welcome to share this compartment. It'll be good to have some company. Were you on this morning's ship?'

'Aye, the Dunottar Castle. Made good time too, seventeen days. Just as well, I be down to my last farthing. Reckon there was some shim-shamming going on with the cards, but I'll make it back in the mines soon enough.'

Leroux warmed to Jory's happy-go-lucky manner and wondered whether it was cynical or coincidental that he might make a useful ally.

'I can stand you the ticket. Repay me in Johannesburg.'

'Thank you, sir. What's your business there then? Don't look like a digger to me.'

'Call me Peter. I'm a journalist. The paper's expecting trouble and I'm to write about it. My father was a miner, though. He had a small claim. Maddox Deep it was called, did you ever hear of it?'

'I knows of the place, near to the Simmer and Jack mine where I be. What happened there? Heard the crew left, did it change hands?'

'It did. My father died in an accident two months ago.'

'Sorry to hear that. Accidents all too common now. Was it the dynamite? Bloody scandal that be. It ain't reliable. You got to handle it like eggs.'

'Wasn't the dynamite. He was on his own and got crushed by some equipment.'

'Shouldn't be on your own with machinery,' Jory said, shaking his head. 'Sorry. I don't mean to blame. Some have to work on their own.

But it's dangerous, mind.'

'It wasn't like him, taking unnecessary risks. I don't know why he did – I want to find out while I'm there.'

'Well, you look me up anytime. Everyone at Simmer and Jack knows me. Anything you want to know about the mines, I be your man.'

'Tell me about the deep mines. That's your area, isn't it? I'd like to understand what my father had in mind.'

'The Deeps be the future. There's a great seam of ore under the Rand, bigger than anyone has ever seen. A bit of it at the surface, but most underground sloping down. The outcrops are easy, and a lot of the rock is already worn, it doesn't take much processing to get the gold out. They won't last long. The rock deeper down be more expensive to get, but there's plenty of it. Before people realised the seam sloped down, you could buy claims over that land for a song. Must be what your pa did.'

'But it would cost more to extract the gold?'

'He'd have needed more dynamite to blast the rock. And more quicksilver and cyanide to leech the gold out, and of course more men.'

'And it might cost too much to make a profit?'

'Hard to say. All about the purity of the ore. With the taxes, needs to be good. Take some to the assayer, he'll tell you. But if the mine be anything like Simmer and Jack, it'll pay.'

Leroux pulled some biltong out of his knapsack and offered a share to Jory, who took a strip of the dried meat in his chunky grasp. His hands looked as though they could crush ore on their own. They probably couldn't, but he looked entirely at ease in his own skin.

'What? You become a bloody Boer already - we ain't even got there!' Jory bent the strip into his mouth.

'I grew up on the veld. Reminds me of childhood.' Leroux smiled and put his feet up. 'Have you come across John Hammond?'

'Aye, who hasn't? He be chief engineer for the Consolidated Gold Fields Company. Big fish and knows it. They're the main owner of Simmer and Jack. He does things proper, safety-wise I mean. I'll give him that, but he be no friend to the worker. Going on about the franchise, getting the vote, all he really cares about be cutting costs.'

'Are the workers with him for reform?'

'Some are. Most of them are for gold and gambling, for whisky and women. Not for the Empire. Drifters from everywhere. Americans,

Australians, Poles, Germans, Russians, even French. They worship mammon, not Mary or Victoria. A godless crew. Reckon you could stir 'em up with promises though.'

'And you?'

'I stay out of it. I'm here to earn. Go home now and then to visit my kin. But mark my word. After he be rid of the taxes, he'll go after the workers, even those that helped him. I know men who worked for him back in America, the silver mines of Idaho. It got so bad with the unions he had to leave. And what they do with the natives here, it's a bad business.'

'Cape Smoke?'

Jory nodded glumly. 'They get hooked on it. You ever tried?'

'Once, five years ago.' Leroux grimaced at the thought of it. 'I thought there was a shortage of native workers, getting them drunk can't help.'

'They just want to make enough money to buy a dozen cattle and settle down on a kraal with some wives, and then the Randlords have to find more men and train them. So they keep 'em housed on the compound for their whole contract and get 'em hooked on Smoke to get their wages back.'

'That's an accident waiting to happen.'

'They make so much on the liquor they just hire more to make up for those too groggy or laid up.'

Leroux knew the government wouldn't do anything. The liquor concessions were probably as profitable as the dynamite. The lights of Cape Town disappeared behind them, and it was as dark as pitch outside as they talked into the night. The train climbed up the first of the mountain ranges, and they turned in with the carriage rocking and straining against the curves of the tracks.

Saturday, 21st December 1895

The train shuddered and hissed to a halt in the early morning light. A rickety sign named the place Matjiesfontein. They were through the mountain ranges and into the scrubby desert of the Great Karoo. Passengers stumbled down from the carriages and stretched their limbs, before making their way to the small canteen.

The German in the dark grey suit was uncomfortable even in the warmth of the low sun and his shirt already sported damp patches. Leroux pointed him out to Jory.

'Did you see that fellow on the ship?'

Jory considered the man. 'Reckon I did. Only once or twice, looking down from the poop-deck. Must have been in cabin class. I remember thinking he looked pretty pale. Thought it be the sea-sickness, but he still looks that way.'

'Was he with anyone else?'

'Not that I remember.'

'He works for the Nobel Company. I'm going to start a conversation with him. I'm curious to know what he can tell me about the dynamite situation. Would you listen? Tell me if you think he's straight. There might be a story in it.'

'Story?' Jory's flinty stare was a caution.

Leroux shrugged and smiled and went to sit at the long table next to his mark. Jory sat opposite him, next to the captain, who ignored him. The serving boys hopped about taking orders, and Leroux turned to the German and extended his hand.

'Am I right in thinking it's your first trip up to Johannesburg? What an interesting time to come. Peter Leroux, by the way.'

The German eyed him coldly and gave a short formal shake of the hand. 'Ja, Mr Leroux. My name is Muller. It is my first time.'

'Welcome to Africa. What are you selling?'

'Selling? What makes you think that I am selling anything?'

'People come to the Rand to dig or to sell to diggers. You don't seem like the digging sort.' Leroux could sense Brandt's eyes on him.

'Exactly, you are right, very good. Excuse me, but my English is not good. I am with the Nobel company. We supply dynamite to the South African Dynamite Concession.'

Brandt offered his hand across the table. 'Mr Leroux, may I ask what brings you to Johannesburg? Captain Karl Brandt, from the German Consulate.'

'A pleasure to meet you, Captain. I'm to stay for a while, covering events for The Argus.'

'A newspaperman! Well, you should be able to find stories in Johannesburg. Plenty of mischief going on if the rumours are correct.'

'The rumours are my raw material. I hope we will have a chance to discuss them. I also have some personal business with the purchaser of my family's mining interests, but, unfortunately, we have lost contact with him. Perhaps they are a customer of yours?' Leroux addressed the question to Muller.

'It is possible, Mr Leroux. But I do not deal with the customers, only the distributor.'

'Maybe the Captain has heard of him? He is a German national, Baron Ludwig von Veltheim.'

'I haven't heard of him, Mr Leroux.' Brandt toyed with his fork. 'A little bit strange, I must admit. If he is one of the German mine-owners, I would expect to have heard of the name, even if I had not met him. There are not so many, you see.'

'When I meet him, I will certainly suggest that he introduces himself. He may be new to the Rand. And Herr Muller, you are lucky not to deal with the customers. I hear there are complaints about the dynamite. Perhaps you could tell me something for the paper?'

Muller looked blankly at Leroux. 'Complaints about the dynamite? There is— '

A boy ran into the canteen and waved a slip of paper. 'Telegram for Mr Muller!'

Muller pinched his brow and closed his eyes for a moment. He turned to Brandt and nodded towards the boy. Brandt stood, dropped a coin in the lad's hand, and passed the message to Muller.

'If you will excuse me, gentlemen.' Muller walked in the direction of the lavatory.

The serving boys came with coffee, toast and preserves, and plates loaded with bacon, sausages, and eggs. Brandt helped himself and then turned to Leroux and said, 'Which rumours were you thinking of?'

'That the Uitlanders are arming themselves and Kruger is seeking help from friendly nations.'

'Arming themselves?'

Muller returned before Leroux could answer and said, 'Mr Leroux, you were asking about dynamite. What do you know about it?'

'The miners are unhappy. They are obliged to buy from the Government concession, which charges high prices for an unreliable product. Miners die in accidents as a result.'

Muller cut his food into neat portions. 'It can be a dangerous business. But it is an efficient way for the government to collect taxes.'

'Efficient? It's hurting the development of the gold mines.'

'Perhaps that is what the Government wants, for now.'

'And if it leads to unrest?'

Muller dabbed his brow with a napkin. 'Then, it is a dangerous business.'

Muller's eyes were cold behind the round spectacles. He set his knife and fork down and folded his napkin. His precise movements could not stop perspiration from escaping him. 'How do you find Cape Town, Mr Leroux? I had no time to enjoy it.'

'A shame. It is far more pleasant than Johannesburg, although not nearly as enterprising.'

'And the home of Rhodes, the Colossus of Africa. Have you met him?'

'Once.'

'Recently?'

'Quite recently.'

Muller forked a sausage and sawed a piece off, held it up and regarded it.

'It always amazes me how such amateurs rule one-quarter of the world's population. How can it last?' He chewed slowly and made it feel personal. Leroux sensed Jory bridling and Brandt watching him closely. Brandt's hand slipped under the table to his side.

Leroux stood and clapped Jory on the back. He was nobody's fool, but he couldn't know how dangerous these men might be.

'Perhaps we can continue this conversation another time?' Leroux and Jory walked back to their carriage, and the whistle blasted, rousing the other passengers from their tables.

'I didn't think you would be so protective of Queen and country,' Leroux said.

'It be not what he said. It be the way he said it.'

'He's a cold fish, steer clear of him.'

'That won't be a problem. He be no dynamite salesman. And I'll wager my ticket he knows that fella you asked after. I be watching him like you asked and when you said that name, he knew it.'

Jory heaved himself up into the compartment while Leroux enjoyed the last few moments of space. Brandt and Muller walked up the platform. Muller ignored him and disappeared into the train, but Brandt approached. He was a few years older and about a hand taller with a similar build.

'Captain, I hope I didn't offend your companion. I didn't mean to suggest he supplied inferior goods. If you do come across Baron von Veltheim, I would be grateful if you could let him know that I am trying to contact him.'

Brandt shook his head and felt into his jacket pocket to fetch out his card. 'You have picked a strange time to make personal enquiries in Johannesburg. But if we can be of assistance, it would be my pleasure. Where are you staying by the way?'

'I have a reservation at Height's.'

The captain looked him up and down. 'Very good, you will like it.' He had clearly decided that Leroux had not been there before. Brandt looked where Jory had clambered into the carriage and raised an eyebrow. 'Another newspaperman?'

'A friend.'

'Good friend to have if you're expecting trouble.'

'He's advising me on the mining business, nothing else.'

'Have a safe journey, Mr Leroux.' Brandt turned on his heels and returned to his compartment.

Leroux found Jory yawning, slumped down in his seat, hat placed over his eyes. The train gathered pace and Leroux pulled down the window and lent out. They drew away from the small settlement and into the vastness of the Great Karoo. Land of thirst was its name, all stony and arid. Windblown scrub and thorn stretched far away until ridged hills rose in the distance to break the monotony. Puffs of steam billowed overhead as he scanned the expanse, instinctively looking for game. After a time, the iron rhinoceros flushed out a pair of ostriches that went high-stepping away, heads held aloft. Leroux looked up the train into the dry wind. Far ahead, another two days over the horizon was the high veld and home, but it didn't feel like coming home.

Monday, 23rd December 1895

The rolling sea of grassland that had been his world rippled in the breeze and shimmered under the morning sun. Part of him wanted to jump in, run, and keep running. He inhaled the thin air, and it was sweet and fresh. Ahead the Witwatersrand dominated the horizon. Slag heaps pimpled the ridge, much further along than he remembered, and chimneys and mine-head towers clawed at the sky. As a boy, he resented the mines for keeping his father away. When he went to visit, he appreciated the ingenuity and industry but recoiled from the scarred landscape and couldn't wait to return to the veld and his carefree youth. The few trees that once struggled on the slopes had gone. As they got closer, little white landmarks like milestones littered the ground where they pegged out new claims. The air was dirty with dust and soiled the sun.

The train came around the long bend into Park Halt. Leroux pushed the window up; Johannesburg had grown more than he had imagined. Jory grabbed his hold-all.

'When you go to Maddox Deep drop by Simmer & Jack. I always pays my debts.'

Leroux's hand disappeared in Jory's fist. 'I will, and I'll remember the wager.'

Jory's face creased in weathered lines of good nature, and he lumbered away into the throng. There was no sign of anyone to greet him. Leroux hailed a white hooded cab and shoved over the rain blanket - there would be no need of that this morning. As the driver shook his reigns and pulled out into the traffic, Leroux reflected on Rhodes's generosity. Height's would be a welcome oasis from the grime of Johannesburg and make a prestigious base.

The noise and heat and dust washed over him. A fashionable lady careered past in a cart as the native groom lolled behind her, arms akimbo. They both overtook a buck-wagon drawn by a pair of depressed-looking mules whipped by an old-time Boer with an unkempt beard and wide felt hat. A smartly attired man trotted in the style of the English hunting school and called out for room to lithe Zulus barefoot between the shafts of rickshaws, while the other way came a young farmer on a half-tamed colt that tossed its head in alarm at the unaccustomed sights. It felt like all the world had business in Johannesburg. When he was last here, five years ago, the tents and flimsy shacks of the mining camp had been replaced by rudimentary buildings, all in a similar one-storey design determined by the limited supplies to hand. They squatted on the raw earth as if unsure of their future and now the gold had endured, they had been ripped down and replaced by two and three floor buildings of solid stone and red brick in a jumble of styles, none of which managed to stamp its authority on the paved ground. The town had grown up and out, but so fast it did not seem to know itself.

The hotel doors swept open before him and Leroux entered the cool of the spacious atrium, conscious of his footsteps on the polished stone, and the hotel clerk passed him two messages as he checked in. The first was an invitation from Mr and Mrs Lionel Phillips requesting the pleasure of his company at Hohenheim from eight o'clock. The second simply said Mr Sanderson was in the bar.

It was a quarter to midday, and one man read a paper at the long counter, in a crumpled jacket and a grubby shirt collar. A ceiling fan swept lazily around.

'Mr. Sanderson?'

The man looked up with rheumy eyes.

'Yes, you must be Peter Leroux. Welcome to Johannesburg, what will you have?'

'I'll join you in a whisky.'

'Hamilton asked me to show you around. Good spot this. You'll find a newspaperman or two in here most times. It's the centre of gossip after the Rand Club.'

Leroux glanced around the white-washed walls to doors which opened out on to a veranda and the hubbub outside. Fred Hamilton was the editor of the Johannesburg Star, another pie in which Rhodes had a finger. Sanderson looked in need of more than an assignment, and Leroux's heart sank.

'Rhodes said you go back a long way.'

'He's a loyal friend.' Sanderson tilted his glass on the bar. 'How was your journey?'

'Comfortable enough. I met two Germans that Rhodes was interested in, but I think they are already wary of me.'

'Who were they?'

'Captain Karl Brandt, he's from the consulate here.'

'I know of him, well regarded and respectable.'

'He was escorting a new arrival, Heinrich Muller, who said he works for the Nobel Company. An odd fish, something not right about him and the captain seemed deferential.'

'If he's with the Nobel Company he'll be here to see Edouard Lippert. He runs the dynamite concession and is close to Kruger, always whispering in his ear.' Sanderson picked up a slim file from the bar and handed it to Leroux. 'This is what we have to go on.'

'What happened to the man who got this?'

'We don't know. He was one of Rhodes's men from Cape Town. Went out from his hotel a couple of weeks ago, presumably following up on something in here, and never came back. He's been reported missing, but don't expect the Zarps to do anything.'

Leroux opened the file, which contained only two sheets. The first was a handwritten copy of a police report. Mr Willem Leroux deceased, found by one of his employees, Rory Thompson on the 22nd of October 1895. Location: bottom of mineshaft, Maddox Deep. Cause of death: Multiple injuries to head, chest and legs from the impact of a runaway minecart. Time of Death: Previous evening. Last seen by an employee at six p.m., named Rory Thompson. Witnesses: None. Filed as an accidental death. The investigating police officer was Sergeant Stefaan Bakker.

He closed his eyes. Seeing it on paper brought back his mother's words. How slowly the river of time washed away the pain. He should have been there. Leroux held out the sheet of paper.

'I haven't seen this before, I only heard from mother. Not much to go on. Is this all the police did?'

'Yes. You could try Sergeant Bakker. But the Zarps spend all their time keeping an eye on the Reformers.' Sanderson nodded towards the second sheet. 'I went down to the mine last week. It's locked up, no one around.'

The second sheet was a copy of the claim title from the mining commission, registered to Willem Leroux on the 10th of September 1894. Then on 30th of September 1895, a note had been added detailing a charge on the title providing security for a loan of 25,000 ponds. The lender was a firm called Veltheim & Co. The signatory was Baron Ludwig von Veltheim, with a correspondence address of Max Weber, Weber & Co. Solicitors, 50 Church Street, Pretoria. The firm's bankers were Dresdner Bank on Commissioner Street, Johannesburg. A final entry on 5th December 1895, showed the ownership transferred to Veltheim & Co in settlement of the loan, signed by the Mining Commissioner, Jan Eloff.

'Do you think the Zarps have looked into Veltheim? He foreclosed on the mine – he could be a beneficiary of his death. That would be a motive.' His mother had said the mine was sold, not that it had been transferred without her agreement.

'With Jan Eloff involved the police would take every opportunity to look the other way,' Sanderson said and gestured rubbing his thumb and fingers together.

Leroux cursed himself. He had never taken an interest in the mine. He knew his father had hoped that he would join him in the venture, but Leroux had wanted to make his own way and see something of the world. On his trips to the mining camps to see his father the dispirited look of the workers hauling ore out of the deep pits haunted him. The solitary excitement in the eyes of the speculator as he fingered a nugget of gold left Leroux with an emptiness that he had never felt running wild on the veld getting into scrapes with Tom. Mother had not wanted any help with settling father's affairs. He regretted now not getting involved, but it hadn't felt right to push for something he had always tried to escape. And now he had let both his father and his mother down. Leroux gritted his teeth. 'Veltheim is what we've got to look into.'

Sanderson nodded, still rubbing his fingers. 'That's it, lad, follow the money.' He pushed his thinning hair back and held his empty glass up to the barman.

'What could he have spent 25,000 ponds on in such a short time? Where did it go?'

The barman came and topped Sanderson up. Leroux declined.

'Maybe that's what Rhodes's man was looking into,' Sanderson said. 'The company, the solicitor, the bank, it all points to Germany.'

'And Rhodes is paranoid about Germany thwarting his ambitions here, although, frankly, I think he's got bigger problems.'

Leroux closed the folder and lent on the bar.

'I was thinking the same. I expected a more fevered atmosphere when I arrived. It doesn't feel like a rebellion is about to break out.'

Sanderson straightened up and smoothed down his loosened tie on the shirt that strained over his stomach.

'Plenty of people want change. The list of gripes is endless, but have you ever heard of a well-paid revolutionary? And it's Christmas for heaven's sake. Then there's the horse races, the highlight of the season, and then New Year. The timing is awful. What are they thinking?'

'Rhodes said it's planned just before New Year when they have enough rifles.'

'A week, then, to get to the bottom of this.'

'What would the Germans want with the mine? And how could it stop Rhodes?'

Sanderson gulped the last of his whisky down. 'Well young man, we're not going to find the answers in here.'

'I received an invitation to Hohenheim tonight.'

'Hamilton arranged that. Everyone will be there. Lionel Phillips is chairman of the Chamber of Mines. He's also a senior partner in the Corner House Group and chairman of their mining operation, Rand Mines. They're as big as Consolidated Gold Fields. Close to Rhodes and fully behind the Reformers. The money behind them is German, Alfred Beit and Hermann Eckstein. But don't worry they're not close to the State, they're Jewish.'

'Will you be going?'

Sanderson looked at his feet and coughed. 'I, um - no. I have, how shall we say, fallen from grace. I'm going to meet Eugène Marais later. He'll be going, a useful man for you to know. I'll ask him to go with you and make introductions. He'll want to meet you. He likes to know what's going on and work in the shadows. I'll leave a message where we are.'

Eugène Marais was a celebrated intellectual and the editor of Land En Volk, the progressive Afrikaner newspaper that pushed the Reformer Boer line. If Leroux recalled correctly, he had recently lost his wife in childbirth.

Leroux took the file. 'I'll check on this information, see what else I can find.'

'You speak the Taal?'

Leroux nodded, put the drinks on his account and left for the police station.

The cab dropped Leroux on the corner of the wide-open space of Market Square, and he looked up at the sign: Zuid-Afrikaansche Republiek Politie. All Government business had to be in Dutch, including the schools. But everyone dealt in English and the miners' taxes paid not only for everything in Johannesburg but for most of the Transvaal as well, which only increased the bitterness that the Uitlanders felt.

The Zarp behind the counter looked up from his papers and gave Leroux a tired smile and scratched at the damp patch by his armpit. The reception was hot and stuffy and buzzing with flies, the price of trying to keep out the dust.

'Ja?'

Leroux dropped into the lazy consonants of the Taal. 'Afternoon, is Sergeant Bakker on duty?'

'Nee.' The policeman looked down at his papers again.

'When are you expecting him? I would like to discuss a case.'

The policeman slowly turned a page over and raised his head again. 'Sergeant Bakker isn't coming back. He transferred to the frontier police a month ago, and I can't say I blame him.'

'Perhaps someone else can help me? It's regarding my father, Willem Leroux. He passed two months ago, and some aspects of his death trouble me. Sergeant Bakker wrote the report.'

'Willem Leroux you say. And who are you?'

'Pieter Leroux. I live out in the country near Krugersdorp.'

'Krugersdorp?'

'Ja.'

'A good place. I'm sorry to hear of your loss, what was your father doing here?'

'Getting killed.'

'Ja, it's a bad place for good people. Een moment.'

The policeman stuck his head around the door and called into a backroom, 'Jan, bring me a file. Deceased, Leroux, Willem, two months ago.'

The policeman put his papers to one side and waited for his colleague. 'What are you hoping to find?'

'Just the details of his accident. I was away at the time, but I was surprised by the circumstances. It was most unlike him.'

A shiny head with matted hair plastered down on his scalp bobbed in the doorway and passed a file through. The policeman opened the folder, revealing a solitary sheet of paper. He handed it to Leroux.

'I'm afraid that's all there is. You understand the city grows every day with foreigners who have little regard for the law, and we have very few men.'

It was exactly like the note Sanderson had given him.

'Do you have any details for Rory Thompson, mentioned here as finding the body?'

'Een moment.' He turned to face the backroom door. 'Jan, do we have a file on Thompson, Rory?'

The policeman took the sheet back. 'If he was an employee at the mine, he might still be there, or they may have a forwarding address for him. Some miners have left town - they're expecting trouble.'

A voice called out from the backroom, 'No file in the name of Rory Thompson.'

The policeman spread his hands. 'Sorry. I'll make a note to let you know if I hear anything. Where should I contact you?'

'Height's.'

The policeman looked up with a flash of surprise and a hint of anger. 'Height's?'

'Yes.'

The policeman looked down and didn't make a note.

The Mining Commission was further along the block of government buildings that made up one side of the square. Overhead thunderclouds gathered to the east, but you could never tell if they would bring blessed rain for the farmers and clear the dust for a while or just sail by. Leroux ducked into the building and through the deserted reception to talk to the clerk. The official bought out a register and opened the large book halfway, and then leafed a few pages and turned the book around for Leroux to read. Again, it was exactly as on the sheet Sanderson had given him with an entry of the charge and then the transfer with the signature and stamp of Jan Eloff the mining commissioner. And that was the problem. It looked as though someone had written the last two entries in the register at the same time.

'Thank you.' Leroux got up.

'Is that it?'

'Merry Christmas.'

Leroux slumped against the hot brick wall outside. He felt sick in his stomach. The suspicion planted in his mind by Rhodes had taken root and gnawed at the pit of his belly. The accident didn't ring true, the loan was a mystery, and the entries in the register were dubious. The mining commission had a reputation for corruption. The new owner was a German citizen. Kruger and the German Government were known to be close, and the mining commissioner was President Kruger's son-in-law. He could hardly take his concerns to the police or even the courts. Leroux was running into dead ends in the official channels before making any progress. He pushed his hat back at an angle and walked to get some air on his brow. The clouds sailed on, and the heat prickled on his skin. At the next crossroads, he hailed a cab for Pritchard Street.

Leroux hurried by the dark painted windows and gold lettering of The Johannesburg Star and up the steps to a clerk at the front desk.

'Urgent notice for submission.'

'First floor, you'll have to hurry,' the young man said.

Leroux took the stairs two at a time and found a hunched man in a waistcoat tidying away behind his counter. 'Can I put in a notice for tomorrow's paper?'

The man looked at the clock on the wall and shook his head. 'Sorry, sir. Done for Christmas now.'

'Is there no chance? I'm a friend of Mr Sanderson?'

He didn't look impressed. 'Write it out, and it'll go in the Thursday paper.'

'And Mr Hamilton.'

Leroux held up the Johannesburg Star file that Sanderson had given him. The clerk considered his options without hiding his scepticism. He looked up at the clock again and glanced at the file. Sucking his teeth, he placed a form on the counter.

'I'll make sure it's in tomorrow's paper.'

Leroux jotted down the request for information on the whereabouts of Mr Rory Thompson and Baron Ludwig von Veltheim. Contact Mr Peter Leroux at Height's Hotel for a reward of twenty-five ponds.

The clerk read through the notice, raising his eyebrows. Twenty-five ponds was an excessive amount, but Leroux was in funds.

'And I suppose you are Mr Leroux?'

'Yes,' Leroux said and opened his purse to take out payment for the notice and made sure the clerk could see some of the gold ponds that bore Kruger's image.

'Well, that all looks fine Mr Leroux.'

Leroux walked back to Commissioner Street. He removed his hat and ran his hands through his hair before mounting the steps to the telegraph office.

'I'm looking for Miss Sinclair, she is expecting me. My name is Peter Leroux.'

The receptionist eyed Leroux for a moment before replying.

'Miss Sinclair is on duty now. Wait here.'

When the receptionist returned, he showed Leroux through to the cavernous office behind. There were a dozen large desks interspersed with tall lamps. Men bent forward in concentration, their shirts clinging to their backs, their hands fluttering beside the telegraph equipment while the air hummed with rhythmic tapping and rancid odour. In a doorway in the far corner of the room stood a slim woman who saw them and retreated inside.

'Miss Sinclair will see you in the ladies' office,' the receptionist said and gestured curtly towards the doorway. The men cast sharp looks as Leroux walked down the side of the room past their desks and into Miss Sinclair's office. She was about the same age as him, dressed in sporting attire, a simple white cotton blouse with high collar and baggy mutton chop arms and grey cycling bloomers, that fitted closely at the top to accentuate her narrow waist. Her chocolate-coloured hair was up in a loose style.

'Please take a seat,' Miss Sinclair said and closed the door.

Three desks occupied the small space. Two had neat stacks of paperwork next to telegraph machines. A chessboard set out in mid-game occupied the third. Leroux sat at the indicated desk, which also had a fresh display of orange daisies in a small vase.

Miss Sinclair picked up a fly swat and moved to the window which had muslin fixed across it.

'I am one of the telegraphists here. The office manager is a Rhodes man, and he assigns news agency reports to me and another colleague, Miss Brown, where possible.' She nodded at the other telegraph machine. 'We share this office, and it's safe to talk here. I will send out any messages you have for Rhodes. Now, what on earth kept you? Your train arrived nearly four hours ago.'

'I went to see Sanderson first – do you know him? He showed me some documents, and I went to follow up on them.'

'Yes, I do. And I'm sorry about your father. I saw the records when I summarised them for Rhodes.' She perched on the desk where he sat, and a delicate scent of violets wafted across him. 'Did you discover anything?'

The telegraph machine between them buzzed before he could answer. Miss Sinclair darted around, and Leroux gave up his seat as she acknowledged the signal and noted the message. It was brief, and she giggled.

'Please go on, Mr Leroux.'

'The police station was a dead-end. But it looked as though someone had doctored the register at the mining commission. I still have Dresdner Bank to investigate and the solicitor in Pretoria. Do you know someone there that could make an appointment for me?'

Lara tore off the top sheet of the message pad and walked over to the chessboard.

'I do. Write down the details, and I'll arrange it for you.'

She advanced the remaining black knight and pressed her index finger to her lips, gently stroking her chin with her thumb. She brought her bishop out to threaten the knight and made a short note, returning to her desk.

'Ah yes, Mr Max Weber. I remember that name. I'll try and arrange it for tomorrow. Otherwise, it will be after Christmas.'

She tapped a message out from the details and then looked down at her note and continued tapping for a little.

'Who are you playing chess with?' Leroux said and admired how the deep tobacco brown of her eyes suited her.

'A friend in the Pretoria telegraph office. She will arrange the appointment too.' Lara tore the paper with Weber's details into small pieces and dropped them in the bin. 'If you have any message for Rhodes, I'll encode it and transmit.'

'For now, say I have established contact with Captain Karl Brandt and Herr Heinrich Muller. Muller likely to be an alias. I don't think he is here on business for the Nobel Company. They deny any knowledge of Veltheim.'

'What codename did you agree?'

'Starling.'

'You have talked to the Germans already?'

'Yes, on the train. I got the feeling they were suspicious of me.'

'I know of Captain Brandt. He plays the dashing officer enjoying life in the colonies. I haven't heard of Muller before.'

'He's only just arrived in Africa. I'll go to the German Consulate next to see if I can flush out anything more on Veltheim. If it appears that a German citizen is involved in fraud, they may be inclined to help me.'

'Is there anything else?'

Leroux gripped his hat tighter. 'Are you by any chance going to the Corner House Group party tonight?'

Miss Sinclair smiled. 'I'm a working girl, and I'm on the late shift. So much traffic on the telegraph these days, anyone would think something was going on.' She had the most delightful laugh.

'I'm only invited because Rhodes arranged it under false pretences. He describes me as a respected journalist with family mining interests who can help the Reformer cause.'

'I know. But there are grains of truth in there you can use. He likes you, and it will be a good opportunity to ask questions. I'll be here tomorrow after midday if there's anything you need. And you must call me Lara.'

There was a rap on the door, and a shrewish man entered and handed Lara a sheaf of paper and looked pointedly at Leroux with a pinched expression and agitated manner.

'Mr Leroux is from The Cape Argus, Mr Pienaar. We were going through the procedures for sending copy. Mr Leroux, Mr Pienaar is the assistant manager here.'

Pienaar looked around the desk and at the notepad and leaned over to look in the bin. 'Are you sending an article this afternoon Mr Leroux?'

'No, Mr Pienaar,' Lara interrupted. 'We had just finished. Mr Leroux only arrived in Johannesburg today, and he particularly wanted to know how long it would take to get messages to head office. With the amount of traffic nowadays, I thought to allow about an hour for a short article to Cape Town. Wouldn't you agree?'

Pienaar continued to look at Leroux.

'It's my fault, Mr Pienaar. I'm afraid I got carried away telling Miss Sinclair about the advantages of the Queen's gambit.'

'Queen's gambit?'

'Yes. It's by far the best opening. Do you play chess, Mr Pienaar?'

'No. Are you finished now?'

'Yes, I'll remember to allow at least an hour. Thank you, I'll show myself out.'

Pienaar held the door open. Next to him, a black fedora and a delicate white shawl hung on a hook. Leroux walked past and glanced back. Lara winked. As Pienaar escorted Leroux out, satisfied looks spread among the operators. He skipped down the steps and onto the street and headed for the German Consulate.

The brick and stone building was part of an elegant terrace. A wooden awning extended out above the ground floor supported by intricate ironwork, shading the pavement. Underneath, outside the consulate door, a uniformed sentry stood to attention as rigid as the iron columns. Above a flagpole extended diagonally up and out from where the awning met the russet brickwork and the large black, white and red striped flag of the Deutsches Kaiserreich hung limp.

Leroux presented his calling card together with Captain Brandt's to the sentry, immaculate in a white parade belt and gleaming buttons, who turned smartly and knocked on the door. It opened immediately, and Leroux walked past the footman into the cool of the lobby where just the thrum of an electric ceiling fan disturbed the silence. The receptionist sent for the captain and then left Leroux to admire an ornately framed portrait of the Kaiser.

'Mr. Leroux! Such a pleasure to see you so soon. Are we arousing such interest in the British press?' The captain smiled and gestured up at the fan. 'Do you like it? The invention of Herr Diehl, a brilliant German mind. Unfortunately, he lives in America. Such is the way of things nowadays. How may the Imperial German Consulate be of assistance?'

'May we speak privately?'

Brandt showed Leroux to an empty reception room and a pair of easy chairs.

'Iced lemon tea or something stronger?'

'Lemon tea will do perfectly.'

Brandt held up two fingers at a serving boy and then turned to Leroux.

'So?'

'It's about the Veltheim Company.'

'I have already told you we know nothing about the company or the Baron.'

'My interest is more pressing than I made clear. The ownership of the mine transferred to this company after my father died, in settlement of outstanding debts. His death was reported as an accident, but the circumstances are suspicious. My family has no record of him receiving money from the loans. I have inspected the records at the mining commission, and the entries relating to the charge on the property look suspicious. I think they were falsified.'

'That is a serious allegation, Mr Leroux. Have you been to the authorities?'

'This is my dilemma, and why I wanted to speak to you. The evidence is circumstantial. I think the authorities would not look kindly on such an accusation, particularly as the signature on the records is that of Jan Eloff. He may not have known, but even so, such an accusation would provide ammunition for Kruger's critics.'

Brandt steepled his fingers. 'And, you think, the involvement of a German company in the affair would be embarrassing for Kruger, who would not thank us for it.'

'You see my predicament. I thought you might prefer to provide some discreet assistance in locating this gentleman.'

'I can make a more thorough enquiry. But we have a problem of - how can I put it - trust.'

Leroux and Brandt fell silent. It was Leroux's move, and he needed to say the unsaid. 'Muller knew that I had met Rhodes before coming here, didn't he?'

Brandt nodded.

'The telegram?'

Brandt nodded again. 'Kruger has spies everywhere, and, if it suits him, he shares with us. So, what are you, Mr Leroux?'

'The mine did belong to my father, and I am a journalist. Rhodes knew my father and was surprised that an experienced engineer would die in such an accident. Then he discovered the German ownership. He thought I would want to investigate. And yes, he did ask to be informed about any German connections.'

'Go on.'

'I grew up here, and Rhodes thinks I will be able to investigate without raising suspicion.'

Brandt bellowed and slapped his thigh. 'Now you talk the truth for sure! Muller may have something with all that amateur talk!'

'I have nothing more to hide, but it seems to me that if you have nothing to hide, you will help me, and what I report would be of no consequence. Whereas, if you do not, that simply increases suspicion and invites more investigation.'

The boy entered with two iced lemon teas. Beads of condensation ran down the glasses to the silver tray.

'Believe me when I say I will be disappointed if one of our nationals is involved in this business. And you will find no help with the authorities. The bureaucracy and policing here are not what either of us would hope for, and of course, they will not investigate their own. Do nothing for a day or two. I will see what I can find out.'

'Thank you, Captain.'

'Write down the name and any other details.'

While Leroux wrote, Brandt continued. 'Raised on the veld, Boer name and looks, a miner for a father and working for Rhodes. We live in interesting times. Are you torn?'

Leroux looked up, and Brandt seemed sincere.

'I would prefer a peaceful resolution to the situation.'

'That does not seem likely. The Randlords are set on change. Even our Corner House Group is with the Reformers. They will go bankrupt without reform, and Kruger will not give an inch.'

Leroux knew that for Kruger, there could be no compromise with the will of God. The Great Trek was an exodus from oppression, and they took this land from the wilderness with the help of their God. It was their destiny, and you would only take it over Kruger's dead body.

'Not all the miners are as keen to fight as some say,' Leroux said.

'They would be happy with better conditions and pay. Many would go home once they had made enough money. Why would they shed blood for the vote?'

'That's not what the papers say.' Brandt stretched his long legs out before him and scratched at his thigh.

'The papers are owned by the Randlords.'

'Kruger will crush them if they rise.'

'I know. They do not have enough respect for the Boer commandos. They see the dour old men in their wagons at the market square every morning. They see the mangy mules and the cowed driver boys doing all the work. They see them ignoring the Government and even each other to live lonely lives on their farmsteads. And they forget that when there is a common threat, they come together with a bible and a gun and no fear.'

'Ja, how quickly they forget. Do you think the British Empire will intervene? Will she break the treaty and risk international outrage?'

Leroux knew the conversation was straying into dangerous waters. The Germans were aware of Dr Jameson on the border with Company troopers. The see-saw of conversation had lifted him uncomfortably high.

'The treaty protects the rights of the Uitlanders as well. Kruger should be careful not to break the treaty first.'

Brandt drummed his fingers, letting the pause extend.

'How diplomatic of you. Rhodes is a conundrum. What will he do? One moment he is a politician. The next a business magnate. But always a gambler and a man in a hurry.'

'I don't know the mind of Rhodes. I'm only a pawn in this.'

Brandt crossed his legs at the ankles. 'It seems to me that the Reformer Boers hold the key. You know some of them?'

'Some.'

'Commandant-General Joubert?'

'He was my commander for a while.'

'Do you know where he is?'

'No.'

'What did you make of him?'

'He's a shrewd man. He can bend if the wind demands it. Do you know what he said when they discovered gold and the Boers rejoiced that it would guarantee their independence?'

‘Tell me.’ Brandt shifted in his seat and crossed his legs over the other way.

‘They would do better to weep, for the gold will cause the country to be soaked with blood.’

‘I fear he is right. The positions are entrenched, and there is no trust between them. Kruger will not deal with the British again.’

Leroux took a long sip of the lemon tea. 'Kruger's refusal to negotiate is taken as stubbornness. But he is cunning. Perhaps he has a card up his sleeve?'

Brandt slapped his thigh again. 'I dread to think about what he has up his sleeve. He smells like he hasn't had a bath for a year!'

The door sprung open, and Herr Muller stood there stock-still. Brandt rose smartly and clicked his heels. ‘Herr Muller, Mr Leroux has brought some interesting information.’

Muller looked coldly at Leroux for a moment. ‘Hauptmann, come with me.’

Brandt said in a lower voice, ‘I’ll let you know what I find,’ and followed Muller up the stairs. Leroux walked out and into the late afternoon heat. He hailed a cab, and as he stepped on the running board, he looked back up at the consulate and saw Muller at a first-floor window, holding a drape back, watching him.

Leroux returned to Height’s and collected a message from Sanderson. He was with Marais at the Rand Club. In his room, Leroux placed the slim file on the writing bureau and inserted a scrap of blotting paper between the two sheets. A house boy appeared, introduced himself as David, and said Sanderson had sent him to help with anything. He duly rustled up a freshly pressed frock coat and top hat.

‘Keep an eye out for anyone coming here, and there’s a couple of shillings for you.’

David beamed and disappeared down the corridor. Leroux straightened his tie and left the oasis of the hotel, descending the steps onto the baking pavement, where a few steps away in the road a Chinaman in a circular, red-topped hat and flowing silk robes remonstrated with a hansom-driver who replied in a heated Irish accent. A thunderstorm threatened to break the sultry air and most took a cab if they could. Leroux turned and strode towards the Rand Club, and a man of medium height opposite the hotel started to walk in the same direction. He wore a sack coat over a cloth shirt and a sombrero shaded his face. Leroux waved down a cab. As he got in the man carried on around the corner without catching his eye.

The cab swung into Commissioner Street, the broadest in Johannesburg where even a sixteen-ox-wagon could turn around. Leroux told the driver to pass the brick and iron clubhouse and approach from the other direction, but the manoeuvre revealed no sign of another cab following. He looked up at the building which had just been enlarged and rebuilt in the geometrical ordered style of the Renaissance, although the ornate wrought ironwork of the balconies below triangular pediments made it look a little fussy. A turret soared out of its midst to overlook the neighbours. He searched for Sanderson's friendly smile among the faces looking down before mentioning the name to the doorman. Inside an imperious sergeant major of a porter inspected him from head to foot. He swivelled and went to the barroom door and beckoned someone.

'Preston, really!' Sanderson said to the porter, 'He's an old friend of mine.'

'That's what I'm worried about,' Preston said and having made his point let Leroux pass. The spacious bar was busy with flamboyant folk drinking champagne and whisky under the high ceilings and toasting to "Luck", but it looked more in hope than celebration, giving an edge to the festive cheer. Sanderson hailed Tempe, the Indian barman who seemed to be known by everyone and measured out whisky tots from a squat black bottle labelled "Smugglers Brand."

Sanderson guided Leroux to a corner table where a tall and angular man sat as though he was folded up, with all his long arms and legs crossed.

'This is Eugène Marais, editor of Land En Volk.'

'A pleasure to meet you, my compliments on the success of your paper,' Leroux said.

Marais nodded his head slowly and extended a hand. 'The pleasure is mine. I know your name from the Malaboch war.'

He was painfully gaunt, about the same age as Leroux, but looked older. The pain of losing a wife in childbirth had taken its toll. His delicate clean-shaven features and pale skin added to his look of vulnerability. No one would take him for a Boer. Sanderson sat unsteadily, and Leroux caught Marais's disdainful expression.

Sanderson surveyed the room and then said louder than he probably intended, 'You can talk to Marais, his paper is funded on the quiet by the Randlords. Tell him about your father.'

Marais winced, but otherwise was placid, his pupils narrowed to a pinpoint. Leroux told him what he knew, but none of the names meant anything.

'I'd be delighted to publish a notice for you, especially for a hero of the Republic,' Marais said without convincing Leroux of his sincerity. 'Finding the Baron should not be difficult - there are few secrets in Johannesburg. I was intrigued to hear that you are working for Rhodes, though.'

'My part of the bargain is to investigate the German connection. I'm surprised no one has asked you before. Rhodes had a man looking into it, but he disappeared.'

'Well, you have already done better. The man you talk of didn't get as far as meeting me. My paper investigates corruption, looking for ways to embarrass Kruger. I can ask around. But you will have no success in challenging the validity of the documents now. Wait until things settle down - preferably under a different regime.'

'I can wait for that. But finding Veltheim is urgent, for Rhodes and me. And so far, I'm looking for a man no one has heard of, without an obvious motive. The German consulate denies any knowledge of him and, if they are behind this, are already on their guard.'

'Who is the new German around the consulate?' Marais said.

'Heinrich Muller of the Nobel Company.'

Marais took a note. 'There will be many to ask at the party later. Money is always a motivation. Even if the mine is not profitable now, there are circumstances where it could be. Were Kruger to feel more comfortable about the threat of the Uitlanders, perhaps because he had German protection, he might be willing to adopt more business-friendly policies. The value of the mine would jump. They could be buying up shares in other mines on the stock exchange as well, at rock bottom prices.'

'It's a possibility,' Sanderson said. 'Anyway, Marais was just telling me about Captain Younghusband, the Times Correspondent. He's just taken the down train to see Rhodes.'

Marais gave a look of warning to Sanderson and said in a hushed voice, 'The Randlords are nervous. Leonard, Phillips, even Hammond as well, are saying that the men won't fight under the Union Jack and have sent Younghusband to tell Rhodes. Why should they? Australians, Americans, French, Russians, Poles - they want better conditions. If they rise under the Jack and it goes wrong, they'll lose their heads. And if it goes right, they'll just have swapped one oppressor for another. They'll fight under the Vierkleur. Under the Boer flag, there's no treason if they lose and if they win, they'll have a new government that will give them the reforms they ask for.'

'Rhodes won't like that one little bit,' Sanderson said. 'He's made preparations, arranging a base for Jameson down by the border. He must have received Colonial Office approval for that. I'll wager he promised them the miners would rise demanding British rule.'

'Will he listen to Younghusband?' Leroux said.

'That's why they sent him,' Sanderson said. 'Rhodes needs the support of The Times in London. Their sway with the Government is crucial to him.'

Leroux looked from Sanderson to Marais, who nodded in agreement.

'Only Rhodes is uptight about the Jack,' Marais said. 'For everyone else, this is about money. And the Vierkleur makes it a lot easier for their Boer allies.'

Leroux didn't doubt it. He could not imagine Joubert telling his men they were going to fight under a Union Jack against Kruger.

'Rhodes will come around,' added Marais, 'He's hurting like everyone else with the mining shares at rock bottom. He needs the money too. The Deeps require vast amounts of capital, even if he only sees the country as a stepping-stone for his colonial dreams and his ridiculous railroad to Cairo.'

Sanderson shook his head and pushed back his thinning hair. 'Can't see him stopping now. I think he'll swallow the flag issue to get the support he needs, press ahead and then figure out how to get what he wants later. With Kruger gone, they'll sort out the taxes and his companies will be fine. And then later he can deal with the questions of Empire. Any new state will need a protector, whether it's from restive natives or another colonial power. Rhodes will hold all the aces, the British Empire all but surrounds the Transvaal as it is.'

'Rhodes must go ahead with the Reformer Boers before Kruger is too strong,' Marais said. 'It should be enough for Rhodes to have a friendly regime, perhaps even a protectorate.'

'And then,' Sanderson said, 'the authorities will be much better disposed to investigating your father's death and any irregularities in the transfer of the mine.'

'We must make sure that the Germans are not able to foil the rising,' Marais said. 'That is Rhodes's priority.'

The crowd at the bar thinned out. Marais discretely topped his glass with a dark wine-like liquid from a hipflask. Leroux waited for him to finish and said, 'Where is General Joubert?'

'He's gone to Natal for a holiday.'

'Strange time to go on holiday.'

'Let's say he doesn't want anyone asking awkward questions until the time is right.'

'Do you think he would accept the Republic becoming a British protectorate?'

'In the right circumstances,' Marais said evenly.

Sanderson blew out his cheeks. 'Right, I'm off to Slack Alice's to find out the real gossip.' He buttoned his jacket, pushed out of his chair and said to Leroux, 'Let's follow up on the money. Meet me tomorrow at the Stock Exchange, around ten.' He held out a steadying hand as he went, swaying with practised ease as a paperboy came in with the late afternoon edition of The Star and left a handful of copies of the salmon pink paper on a side table.

'Why is Rhodes only finding out about the flag now?' Leroux said.

Marais rolled his eyes. 'We've told him, but he doesn't want to listen. He's convinced that Jameson will just ride in and take over the place just as he did in Mashonaland. But it's not the same. Kruger's commandos won't throw themselves to the slaughter in front of Maxim guns like the natives, as you well know.'

Leroux raised his empty glass and pushed the thought of that massacre from his mind.

'I need to go back to my room before the party. Sanderson mentioned that you would be going.'

'Of course, one of the highlights of the year.' Marais cast his eyes down and shook his head. 'Sanderson has fallen a long way. If it weren't for Rhodes, he'd be out of here and out of a job. Still grateful for a favour he did so long ago no one can remember what it was. Have you heard of Slack Alice's?' For the first time Marais showed a glimmer of humour as a corner of his mouth turned up.

'No, what's funny?'
'Sanderson's got a favourite up there. It's a brothel. Lord knows how Kruger's spies report that to him.'
'He must have a lot of spies if he keeps an eye on all the brothels.'
'He does, and no doubt some will be at Hohenheim tonight. Don't worry, they will see a scion of a mine-owning family dallying in journalism - and a hero of the Republic to boot – there is an element of truth in that, no?'
'I got shot in the back,' Leroux said tersely.
'You are too modest, Leroux. And now you are a journalist, what will you write?'
Leroux looked around the room. A couple of gentlemen in immaculate frock coats over pin-striped trousers went to leave, all carnations and cravats.
'I hear they are thinking of having the mass meeting of the National Union on the 27th, sandwiched between two race-days. It makes it sound more like an agreeable divergence from seasonal frivolity than the beginning of serious agitation for reform.'
'I agree, but your editor will want something more bullish. You will meet the leading men of the reform movement this evening, and they will give you more confidence. It will be quite a party - nothing but the finest for the Corner House Group. It is small compensation for working in this dusty fly-infested hole that money flows like water. I will accompany you there and introduce you. Shall we meet in your lobby, in an hour, say?'
Marais settled into a small corner table with his drink and a paper, and Leroux collected his hat and left for the hotel. The rumours were right. Marais was an addict, no doubt driven to the poppy by a combination of grief and curiosity. He was hard to read.

Leroux stepped down from the cab a hundred yards from Height's. The man with the sombrero was waiting outside in the same spot as before. David, the house-boy, came out of the hotel and took his shiny shoes off. He hung them around his neck and walked in the road. As he neared, Leroux caught his attention and waved him discretely into a doorway.
'Did anyone come to the room?'
'Yes, sir, one man.'

'What did he look like?'
'Like you. White man.'
'Taller, shorter?'
'Same. Brown hair, not gold.'
'Was it that man?' Leroux pointed at the man in the sombrero.
'No fatter, but I saw them talking.'
'Well done.' Leroux gave him two shillings. David's eyes lit up, and he turned them over in his fingers as if to check they were real. 'Do you speak the Taal?'
'Ja baas.'
'Ask that man whether he would like his shoes cleaned. Don't worry - he'll say no. But if he understands what you say, walk away carrying your shoes in your hand. I'll see you tomorrow.'
The boy hurried off, and as Leroux climbed the hotel steps, he saw the man remonstrate with David while keeping an eye on the hotel entrance. David walked away, carrying his shoes.
Leroux eased his room door ajar. No sound. The room was tidy, and as he left it. He went to the writing desk and carefully opened the file, gently lifting the top page. The scrap of blotting paper had shifted, no longer covering the name Eloff. The window was still fastened from the inside, and the man still stood opposite, watching. They either had a key or some arrangement with a housemaid.

The silver top of Marais' cane glinted as it twirled around his spindly fingers, and he nodded animated greetings to the guests in the lobby. Leroux caught his attention, and they headed north to Hohenheim in a Brougham cab lest a thunderstorm break. The man with the sombrero kicked at the dust and ignored them, and Marais did not appear to notice him.
The carriage went at a good clip, and the blessed relief of a breeze blew through the open window. Hohenheim was in Parktown, the new elite suburb away from the dust and filth of the mines to the south. Edouard Lippert had planted the Saxonwold forest on a ridge and sold off plots for grand houses. Leroux had known it as a wild and solitary spot from where you could see the Magaliesburg mountains to the west. Now it was dark, and all you could see were patches of stars showing where the thunderclouds were not.
'Phillips's folly!' Marais said. 'It's what they call Hohenheim. His wife,

Florence, found the place and they were the first to build there, in the middle of nowhere back then. Others have followed since, but the name stuck.'

They drew into the grounds past three blue gum trees and as they slowed the rhythmic chirping of cicadas welcomed them. Coaches and carriages decorated with coloured ribbons of the season, filled the driveway. The horses were immaculately groomed with not an ox in sight, and the attendants bustled back and forth in full livery.

Leroux patted his frock coat in a vain attempt to remove the city dust and looked up at the ladies escorted by the hand up the steps of the mansion. Above them turrets and balconies in different styles sat awkwardly on brickwork and half-timbered walls completed with mortar and whitewash.

'What style is that?' Leroux wondered aloud.

'I believe they call it eclectic. Forty rooms,' Marais said airily, and they were relieved of their canes and hats as Marais took a flute of champagne from a passing tray and glided through the party. Marais acknowledged his friends without interrupting his progress while Leroux followed like a pilot fish in his wake.

'Leroux, I've been thinking about our discussion, there's someone you should meet. Baroness Stein, the beautiful Katharina. A very wealthy widow, and ambitious. She was an actress and married an elderly and moneyed aristocrat. She recently arrived here, apparently to acquaint herself with her late husband's investments.' Marais skirted a circle of guests and changed direction.

'Baroness! How well you look this evening. Let me introduce Mr Peter Leroux, he is a journalist with The Cape Argus and is also here to check on his investments.'

The Baroness was a striking woman. Her voluminous flaxen hair had been rolled up into a topknot with crimped bangs that flowed down the sides of her face and caressed the sparkling earrings that cascaded down and draped on her delicate collar bone. She talked to an imperious man with an arresting red beard that Barbarossa would have been proud of, who could only be Edouard Lippert.

Leroux bowed to kiss the gloved hand. 'I am afraid my investments do not look promising, but Johannesburg certainly seems to be agreeing with you. Is it to your liking?' She wore green taffeta that complemented her sea-blue eyes and looked a few years older than

Leroux.

'The change has been diverting, even invigorating. My advisers tell me that there is opportunity in crisis and that I should look to add to my holdings. Would you not agree?'

'Of course, one must take advantage of the situation, but for me, it seems more promising as a journalist,' Leroux said.

'The Argus is a Rhodes mouthpiece is it not?' Lippert said, 'That Schwein cheated me out of concessions in Matabeleland and Mashonaland.'

'Herr Lippert, that is in the past, and now you are having such success with dynamite,' the Baroness said, placing a calming glove on his arm. Marais excused himself and joined a nearby conversation.

Leroux knew the story of how Dr Jameson had gained King Lobengula's favour by curing him of gout and then broken all convention by supplying the King with rifles in return for a concession which rendered Lippert's prior concession moot. And then Rhodes had paid Lippert a pittance for his moot claim to avoid any dispute and gained the entire Zambezi-Limpopo watershed.

'I had the pleasure of meeting Herr Muller, who also works in the dynamite business. I hope he is feeling better,' Leroux said.

'Ja, he does not travel well. He is not here. He has business in Pretoria.'

'I am sure he will find the climate more agreeable in Pretoria. Is there a big market for dynamite there?'

'The Government is the market. And, yes, he will appreciate the cleanliness of Pretoria. Perhaps one day we can clean up this place too.'

Captain Brandt approached from behind the Baroness and touched her elbow. She turned and smiled up at him.

'Dear, I see you have met my new acquaintance, Mr Leroux. I hope he is entertaining you,'

Lippert's mood seemed to darken further, and he made his excuses and left.

'I cannot complain, but Herr Lippert has lost his sense of humour. Never mind, he can be tiresome at the best of times.'

'I saw you with Marais,' Brandt said to Leroux. 'He is much harder to get a reaction from.'

Marais was holding court with three young ladies who were fanning themselves like hummingbirds.

'Erudite, successful, tall, handsome and tragically single again,' Brandt continued. 'I think he may be taking the mournful look too far. Ladies fall for it, but he is beginning to look decidedly ill. He lacks only wealth, though no doubt he has a plan for that.' He scanned the room and changed the subject. 'And what have you been up to? Smuggling in arms for the Reformers? Checking up on the activities of us Germans?'

'Running into dead-ends. The more I look, the more it looks like someone is taking great care to cover their tracks.'

'That reminds me. I asked around the consulate, and no one has heard of Baron von Veltheim – and Liebchen, I forgot to mention Mr Leroux had a mining interest. He may be able to explain better than I the prospects for the industry.'

'Well, Mr Leroux, what do you recommend? My late husband's investments have made good profits, and I am told the mining shares are cheap. Is now the time to buy?'

A string quartet struck up a classical piece, heralding the arrival of dignitary not recognised by Leroux.

'They are certainly cheap. Whether they are good value depends on the political situation. If the high taxes and restrictive policies stay, the mines will struggle, particularly the deeps.'

'So I hear. But who can tell me how the political situation will develop?' Her eyes sparkled with mischief, and her irreverent manner beguiled. Brandt looked on in admiration.

'Have you asked Marais?' Leroux said.

The Baroness looked over at Marais, still entertaining the ladies. 'I don't trust him.'

Brandt put a protective arm around the Baroness. 'My dear, there is someone I would like you to meet. Leroux, please excuse us.'

The Baroness moved with a poise born of the stage rather than the constriction of studied posture. Her eyes were quick and her smile warm but with a slight hesitancy that spoke of vulnerability.

Leroux sought out Lionel Phillips and introduced himself. He was a slight man, but everything about him spoke of quality and precision, from the cloth of his coat to the fine points of his moustache that twisted upwards in perfect symmetry.

'Mr Leroux? I heard Rhodes was sending someone from The Argus. I will be chairing a meeting of the Chamber of Mines at 3 p.m. tomorrow, where we will discuss Kruger's reply to our proposals. You should come and see first-hand the depth of feeling. We need as much public opinion behind us as possible.'

Waiters bobbed about the cream of Johannesburg society refilling champagne glasses, but there was little sign of the spirit of revolution.

'What did Kruger say?'

'Nothing. He is ignoring us.'

'It is as though he wants to provoke you. Did you know that Rhodes asked me to investigate German connections to the acquisition of my father's mine?'

'He is always concerned about German influence. The Corner House Group is German, and we are with him. He is overlooking the real problems.'

'The question of the flag?'

'Yes, and the shortage of rifles.'

'How bad is the rifle situation?'

Phillips looked over his shoulder. 'Off the record, pretty bad. We need ten thousand, ideally twenty. So far, we've only got about three. If we can't get more in, we'll have to postpone.'

A middle-aged man strode towards them. He was a head taller than most, and he peered haughtily around, the buttons on his waistcoat glittering. His aquiline nose ploughed through a full handlebar moustache below dark hair parted in the middle and pomaded.

'If Kruger wants war, he'll get it,' bellowed the man in an American accent. John Hays Hammond. Although Phillips was socially and financially senior to Hammond, it was the American who commanded the attention of the room. The waistcoat fasteners were diamonds.

'So, you are the young man Rhodes sent to help us. I hope you do better than the last one. Have you found anything?' His eyes focussed intently on Leroux

'Not yet, sir.'

'Well, I reckon it's a wild goose chase but can't do no harm, I suppose. Let me know what you find.'

Hammond escorted Phillips away into a side room, and Leroux wandered through the party dodging waiters who ferried platters and dishes out from the kitchens to a buffet in the dining room. He spoke to German businessmen from Siemens, Krupp, and Deutsche Bank but none had heard of the man he sought, shrugging their shoulders and suggesting that perhaps the rapid growth of the city was to blame.

But they all knew Captain Brandt, youngest son of Pomeranian nobility, chasing his fortune in the colonies and rumoured to have captured the heart of the Baroness. And they suggested the Baroness might be that fortune and her appearance in the Republic reflected a desire to escape her past.

The party was in full swing as Leroux sought Marais to say goodbye, catching snatches of conversation from huddled groups alive with gossip. For all the brave talk of uprising, there were precious few men of action.

Marais caught his eye and beckoned him over. 'Well, what do you make of Johannesburg society? This must be your introduction, no?'

'I can see why Rhodes is concerned at the extent of German influence.'

Marais nodded. 'They have ambitions, without a doubt.' He raised his glass in farewell.

Leroux walked back for the exercise after the cramped train journey, and the fresh air helped him to think. Everyone had made helpful sounds, but no one had delivered anything tangible. The band of revolutionaries that Rhodes had assembled seemed ill-prepared for their task. They were behind with smuggling weapons, the leaders disagreed about which flag to fight under, and they almost certainly lacked the element of surprise. Hammond was the one with the presence to pull it off and together with Dr Jameson maybe they could. But that was not Leroux's concern. His enquiries had raised his suspicions without making any progress. He felt as though he were a puppet but could not see who was pulling his strings. He needed another approach. The roar of stamp batteries crushing ore carried on the still night air as he reached the hotel and tried to raise the enthusiasm to write an article on the intransigence of the Kruger Government and the swelling support for action from the Uitlanders.

Christmas Eve, 1895

Leroux set out for Maddox Deep at the crack of dawn, catching ladies of the night returning from discreet engagements, but perhaps it was too early for the man with the sombrero. The sun swelled above the horizon, and he passed the occasional wagon as it rumbled in laden with goods for the market, the driver boys calling out and cracking their sjamboks on the oxen they knew by name. The close streets, marked out before anyone suspected the extent of the reef, gave way to little shacks, not more than a few tin crate linings fastened together and a sheet of corrugated iron for a roof. Breakfast smoke mingled with a thin morning mist as his cab went by the first slag heaps and the outcrop mines before turning south and east to the Deeps.

Leroux asked the driver to wait for him when he stopped before the Simmer and Jack mine so that he could approach on foot. As he went to the gate to ask for Jory, he saw a familiar shape in the distance lumbering up the track towards him. Three other men crossed over and stopped the man, appearing to start a disagreement. Leroux hurried towards them, sure that the man they heckled was Jory. One put his hand to Jory's shoulder, shoving him roughly. Jory's shoulder rolled back before turning square on again, not conceding but not rising to the provocation. The next pulled a handful of white feathers from his pocket and thrust them down Jory's shirt front, some going in, some clinging to the front of his shirt and the rest drifting down to lie in the dirt road.

'You tin men are all traitors, away with you coward!' one said in the accent of an English labourer. Jory said nothing and stood impassive. The men looked up and down the street, and one kicked at the dust to send a stone skittering into Jory. Leroux hailed a greeting, but Jory steadily eyed his accusers. They glanced towards Leroux and with a final volley of insults turned and walked past Leroux taking care to barge him on both shoulders and sloped off and into the Simmer and Jack mine.

'Hello Jory, been making friends again?'

'Just navvies. Can't see further than the end of their noses. Would chase a coin off a cliff.' He brushed off the feathers and looked up the street at the men disappearing into the mine. 'They deserve everything that's coming to them.'

Leroux picked a stray feather from Jory's shoulder.

'What was that all about?'

'The bosses have been in their ear, telling them that pay and conditions will improve if they get rid of the taxes. The news this morning has stirred them up. That Kruger will fight rather than give an inch. I'm not fighting for the Randlords. I've worked in mines all over and ain't never seen pay and conditions improve unless the miners force it from the owners. Don't happen by doing their dirty work for them. You here to collect your money?'

'Don't think I need to. Your wager looks pretty good. Came to look around Maddox Deep.'

'Appreciate you not looking the other way.' Jory flushed the feathers out from under his shirt and stared towards the mine. 'There's been some goings-on down there. Put a new fence up around the mine entrance inside the boundary fence.'

'You curious?'

'Will it help my wager?'

'I hope so.'

Jory smirked, turned around and started marching towards Maddox Deep. 'C'mon lad. I haven't got all day.'

Leroux gave instructions to the driver and caught up with Jory. As they walked, Jory pointed out how the reef of gold broke the surface on the ridge and then sloped continuously down underground towards them and much further past.

'The ore that Simmer and Jack pulls up be eighteen or nineteen pennyweights of gold per ton. Do you know what Maddox be?'

'No, but I want to find out.'

'We just need some of the ore and take it to the assayer.'

A corrugated iron wall, with barbed wire on top strung between the posts, enclosed the mine.

'Someone be worried about security.'

'I don't think my father put this fence up.'

'Looks pretty new. Maybe they're worried that whatever happened to your father might happen to them.'

They walked past an open gate, guarded by a sentry in a small hut, and continued around the perimeter until they came to a rise where they could see over the fence. The main building was made of brick, with a roof and door of the ubiquitous corrugated iron and was about seventy yards from the gate. Adjoining the building was an enclosure, surrounded by the new fencing that Jory had mentioned, which contained a skeleton tower poking out over the top with the winding gear for hauling up carts of ore and presumably the mineshaft entrance. In front of the door was a wagon with mules, and two horses tethered to a post.

'No tailings. The heap there is just the workings from the shaft. That building be too small for a stamp battery. They be not crushing any ore yet, nothing to protect here.'

They came around to the entrance where the guard slouched against the gate.

'What do you want?' the man said in a thick Irish brogue.

'Just looking for work, you got any need for proper miners?'

'Jaysus, a feckin' tin man. I thought you had all scarpered! We don't need anyone, least of all yellow-bellies like you.' He rested his hand on the grip of his revolver.

A stifled growl rumbled in Jory.

Leroux put his arm around him. 'Come on. We need to chat.'

They walked up the road out of earshot. The guard sidled back into his hut. Leroux and Jory sat down against the fence.

'One way or the other I'm going in there,' Leroux said.

'Something not right, lad. No reason for security and the guard be a wrong'n. I'd say he be Irish Brigade.'

'The outlaws? They're wanted men, what on earth would they be doing here? They'd be seen.'

Jory shrugged. 'Still want to go in?'

Leroux nodded. 'I can't ask you to. They're dangerous men.'

'You be not going on your own, and I won't be called a coward three times in a morning.'

Leroux sprung up and headed back to the entrance with Jory. They approached the gate with the sun low behind them, and the guard appeared and drew his revolver.

'I feckin' told you two to get lost.'

'I be just wondering if you've got any work since the last time I asked?'

The guard gaped at the insolence, strode forward and poked his gun in Jory's face, his other hand up to shield his eyes. 'Are you trying to be funny, tin boy? We'll see how you laugh out a hole in the back of your head.'

Jory was no fool. He probably knew the guard would be reluctant to shoot without being forced to, for it would only attract unwanted attention. The revolver was a long-barrelled Colt Peacemaker. The Irishman's finger hovered on the trigger, thumb on the hammer spur. One click back. Two.

Jory bent slowly forward, pressing his forehead into the muzzle and eyeballing the guard.

The Irishman licked his lips. Three clicks back.

Leroux's hand snapped on to the barrel and wrenched it upright and back, breaking the Irishman's grip on it. Jory crunched a boot into his groin. The guard gasped and reached down with both hands. Leroux brought the revolver butt smashing down on the back of his head.

Jory looked at the revolver. The hammer had dropped.

'You knew?'

Leroux drew the hammer back to half-cocked, opened the loading gate and rotated the cylinder clockwise by a chamber. He gently pushed the ejector rod back and plucked the cartridge out, showing the base of it to Jory.

'Centrefire ammunition,' Leroux said. There was a dent in the brass rim surrounding the primer. 'Chamber hadn't aligned all the way. He wasn't fully cocked.'

Jory looked down at the knocked-out guard, curled up on the ground. 'He might have to get used to that.'

A man called out inquisitively from behind the building but raised no further sign of alarm. As Leroux checked the remaining chambers, the winding gear began to turn up at the mine-head.

'I don't think they heard us,' Jory said, and they dragged the guard into his hut.

Leroux offered Jory the revolver.

'Not my way lad, I don't want to be killing nobody. Let's be having that look around.'

They ran lightly to the building. The door was pulled to, but the crossbar hung off the end bracket, and the padlock rested open. There was a small window, caked in dust, which offered no view inside.

'After you, lad.'

Leroux eased the door open a crack. It was dim inside, and distant voices emanated from deeper in the building or the adjacent structure. He stepped in. The light that came through the door revealed a storage area, with mining equipment and crates stacked around.

At the far end was another door, ajar, from where the voices came. Leroux crept up and put his eye to the opening. The room was the other half of the building, and the opposite wall had double-doors that were open and led into the area enclosed by the inner ring of fencing. He could see the mineshaft entrance with a loading cart and three men heaving canvas-covered bundles into it, all armed at the hip.

Another man, lanky with thin hair down over his collar walked to the mineshaft and called down, 'Two more loads after this.' Another Irishman. Oddly, he held a tattered top hat in his hand.

Leroux inched the door a little further open to see more of the room. Along the far wall were stacks of crates and canvas bundles until in the corner stood a desk covered with papers and lumps of rock. He motioned to Jory to look and whispered, 'The desk.'

Jory but his face to the gap, and drew back at a sound, nodded, and mouthed 'Gold ore.' Leroux moved up.

One of the loaders had entered and hauled another of the canvas bundles from a stack onto the ground. He opened it and seemed to be checking the contents. A few glimpses were enough to confirm that they were rifles. Outside the cart was lowered down into the mine.

'More Lee-Metfords,' the Irishman called out, closing the canvas cover. Another man came in, and together they carried it outside.

Leroux slipped through the door and diagonally over to the desk watching the back entrance. The rocks on the desk had the same glitter and gold sheen as the rocks his father had shown him. A scuff of dirt outside alerted Leroux, and he pressed himself back behind the stack of crates. Three Irishmen returned. The first two took another bundle from the pile and headed back. The third looked up and down the pile of canvas bundles and some nearby ammunition boxes before freezing.

His head turned to the inner door. He moved over to it stealthily, drew his revolver and reached for the handle. In one movement, he swung the door out and stepped into the opening. Two brutish hands darted out from behind the wall, clamping the man's head front and back, and yanked him through the door. Leroux grabbed two of the rocks and stuffed them in his coat pockets and dashed out. Jory had knocked the Irishman senseless to the floor.

'Come on, quick,' Leroux said and ran for the front entrance. As he closed the door behind Jory, a shout called after them. Leroux pushed the crossbar home and put the padlock in place. There was no key, but it would hold them for a few crucial seconds. More shouting accompanied heavy steps rushing through the building. Leroux sprinted for the gate. Someone was trying the door, then banging it. He caught up with Jory and was almost at the gate as he heard the tinkling of glass as the small window smashed. A round pinged through the corrugated fence next to them as the report rang out. They scrabbled through the gate and out of sight.

The driver looked back in alarm twenty yards up the road. They tore up to him, and the wild-eyed driver was already whipping his horses as they jumped aboard. Leroux covered the gate with the Colt, but by the time a bedraggled looking gunman appeared out of the entrance he was out of range, and none of them made a pursuit on horseback.

'Easy driver, no one's chasing. Pull over here,' Leroux said. They had gone past the Simmer and Jack mine.

'What did you make of that?'

Jory scratched his stubble. 'A lot of Irish. All armed. Still reckon they could be Brigade, keeping low behind all that fencing.'

'They were storing rifles down the mine, Lee Metfords, the latest design - bolt action with detachable magazine. Many more than a gang would need, and more suited to an army.'

'Smuggling rifles into the Republic be illegal. Maybe they be doing it for somebody, could be their type of work.'

Leroux crossed his arms and chewed his thumbnail. 'Ammunition crates - I reckon at least ten thousand rounds. Enough for a hundred rifles.'

'Must be for someone else. But the Randlords wouldn't deal with Irish Brigade. Didn't you say the Germans owned the mine?'

'That's what it looks like.'

'Could be on the same side. Irish got no love of the British, been fighting them forever. You be careful taking them on.'

Leroux took his slouch hat off. Perspiration ran from his plastered down hair, and he ruffled it.

'That's what I'm worried about.' He pulled one of the rocks out of his pocket and showed it to Jory.

'That be proper stuff, lad. Take it to the assayer, but that be at least eighteen pennyweights.'

'Thank you, Jory, I owe you.'

Jory put a knuckle to his brow and thudded down onto the road.

'Drive on.'

Leroux lent back and let the breeze cool him. Could the German Government be storing weapons to arm their own? Or were they preparing a supply-point in the goldfields for a fifth column to counter the rebellion? If they weren't, the German consulate would want to know about a German company storing weapons in league with a gang of Irish bandits.

A steady stream of traffic passed by as the miners went to work. In one compound, men already toiled back and forth between the shaft entrance and the stamp battery. A dozen lay insensible in a small area of shade behind a ramshackle lean-to, probably sleeping off the Cape Smoke. Leroux thought back to the last time he had seen Tom, the day before he left for Cape Town and the College. That wasn't an option for Tom, who was determined to get enough gold to settle down with some cattle. He already had his eye on a couple of potential wives. It was up on the ridge at one of the early outcrop mines where Tom had gone to work. They had toasted each other with the cheap liquor that was all they could afford. He knew when he woke up groggy-headed that Tom had a taste for it. The carriage jolted over a rock, and as the compound receded, he saw a foreman go over to them with a lash.

Leroux hammered on the door of the assayer's office until he heard bolts sliding and keys jangling. A small balding man with glasses and an apron opened the door a crack and Leroux thrust the rock sample through.

'Come back in an hour.'

'I don't have an hour.' Leroux barged in and closed the door.

'What do you think you're doing?' The assayer retreated into the room. Shelves of flasks, scales, tinctures and crucibles lined the walls. They looked valuable and fragile.

'Don't be alarmed. I mean you no harm. I just need to get this sample examined before Christmas.'

'That's tomorrow.'

'You see my problem.'

'Impossible, I have a lot of other work to do before then.'

'I have gold.' Leroux took some ponds from his purse and made sure that the assayer saw the lead slung in his belt and rested an arm on a shelf of flasks.

The assayer bit his lip and looked around his well-ordered collection of equipment. 'Show me the sample.'

He turned the rock over in his hand.

'Where is it from?'

'Maddox Deep.'

The assayer looked up. 'I don't understand why the rush–'

'I can't explain–'

'No, I mean I have already examined a sample from there.'

'When?'

'Well, about...are you the owner?'

'That's complicated.'

'I'm not sure I should be disclosing–'

Leroux stepped forward aggressively. The assayer looked at the door, perhaps wishing for another early customer.

'No one coming for a while. My father used to own this mine. I think someone tricked him out of it. I'm sure you had nothing to do with that. But I need to know the purity. Check your records. He was called Willem Leroux.'

'Was?' The assayer backed away to a bench and felt his way around to a filing cabinet. 'I think I remember him, even see the resemblance.'

He fingered through the files and pulled one out. 'Here we are, it was a few months back, October 19th.'

'Thank you.' Leroux turned to leave.

'You don't want to know the results?'

'Nineteen pennyweights?'

'Twenty, in fact. I don't understand. If you already knew, why–?'

'I wanted to know if my father knew.'

Leroux walked back through Market Square stepping through ruts and potholes and a chaos of mules, donkeys, oxen and wagons. Buxom Boer women in bonnets and shapeless dresses dealt with servants stocking up on onions and potatoes while wasp-waisted women hovered around the flower market. As the day rapidly warmed up under the cloudless sky, milkmen and newsboys made their way home, replaced by frock coats with bowlers, top hats and patent leather going about their business. Leroux reached the hotel and stood next to the watcher at his post.

'Nice day,' Leroux said in the Taal, looking over to the hotel where guests breakfasted on the veranda.

'It's always a nice day.' The man looked sideways at him, frowning.

'Why don't we make life easy for each other?'

The man folded his arms. 'Get lost.'

'You're a Zarp. But I know you didn't search my room.'

The man shifted his weight and looked across at the hotel.

'A man from the German consulate searched my room.'

The man looked back and arched his eyebrows.

'You won't be able to follow me unless I let you, but I'll tell you where I've been and where I'm going.'

The man's jaw dropped a touch.

'Like I said, let's make life easy. All you have to do is nod if I'm right so far.'

The watcher pressed his lips and nodded, staring straight at the hotel.

'I've just been to Maddox Deep mine and the assayer's office. I'm going to have breakfast now, and then I have an appointment at the stock exchange.'

'Now get lost,' the man said.

Leroux crossed over to the hotel, ordered breakfast and joined in with the rustling of morning papers. The mine-owners complained about the scarcity of labour as natives started to leave, scared at the prospect of white man's wars. President Cleveland unsettled the stock markets. He had made a speech to congress declaring it to be the duty of the United States "to resist by every means in its power any British attempt to exercise jurisdiction over territory that the United States judged Venezuelan," which the British had taken as a threat of war.

A tap on his shoulder brought him back to the veranda. David had his hand out and displayed a beautiful set of teeth. Leroux gave him his coins.

'I've got something else for you, only a shilling this time.'

Leroux made up a bacon sandwich and wrapped it in a napkin. 'That man you spoke to yesterday, take this over to him.' Leroux left for the stock exchange and saw the watcher take a greedy bite before stuffing it in his pocket and following.

Outside the exchange, between Commissioner Street and Simmonds Street, chains cordoned off a section of the road, which had been tarred to stop the dust. A babbling crowd of brokers hollered at each other and waved bits of paper as the ringmaster called out each stock in turn. Bowler hats remonstrated with boaters stood with hands on hips, while a throng of men and even women looked on flushed with excitement. Leroux found Sanderson talking to a broker and steered them between the elaborate ironwork of the columns inside to the members' bar where the Zarp wouldn't follow.

A noisy group drank at the bar. In front of each of them was a gold sovereign with a sugar lump on top. They drank their whisky sodas and waited. Before long, a fly alighted on the second cube from the end. A huzzah went up, and the lucky host scooped all the coins from the counter. A bottle of champagne arrived.

'Are we celebrating?' Leroux said.

'Celebrating you paying, dear chap. Rhodes won't stand me for anymore, but he'll pay for you. Cheers!'

'Any information in the bargain?'

'Not many buyers about and the news today is even worse. The only significant buyer is Barney Barnato, and he's just supporting his own stock.'

'That's right,' said the broker. 'And if you know any buyers let me know first. It looks like there's going to be a run on the US treasury.'

'A run on the gold reserves like in the Spring?' Sanderson said.

The broker reached for The Star, opened it, and folded the article over. It read: "To-days cable news indicates the extent of the ruin which has overtaken American securities and the paralysis which has arrested commercial activity. The draining of gold to Europe has recommenced and has already depleted the reserve by six million sterling, or nearly 33 per cent, below its statutory limit."

'Reckon that's why the President's sabre-rattling, trying to divert attention away from that, but it's killing the market,' the broker said.

'The President got a lot of criticism for the last bail-out. The press thought he sold out to Wall Street, stitched up by J.P. Morgan and Nat Rothschild. It's an election year, so I guess there'll be a lot more sabre-rattling,' Sanderson said.

'Nobody buying stock then?' Leroux said.

'That's about the sum of it,' the broker said.

'Not even the Germans? Baroness Stein?'

The broker shook his head. 'Not that I've heard.' He drained his flute and went outside in search of buyers. Sanderson topped up their glasses.

'What have you been up to while I've been beavering away?'

'I found out my father knew the mine was valuable. Also, a gang of Irish, maybe Irish Brigade, are storing rifles there.'

'Rhodes will want to know that. One-armed Jack Mcloughlin leads the Irish Brigade, nasty piece of work. Rode into town last February, murdered an informer in broad daylight and then just sat down to a meal. The front of it! The Zarps were too scared to challenge them. In the hotel three hours before they went off into the night.'

'All the men I saw had two arms.'

'There's a fair few of them, mostly army deserters from Natal.'

'You think they could be working for the Germans?'

'They've got no love for the British, especially after Salisbury quashed their hopes of home rule. But I can't see it. The German Government doing a deal with the Irish Brigade? Then again, nobody would ever suspect it.'

A bell rang, and a stream of brokers came into the bar and ordered whisky sodas.

'Elevenses,' Sanderson said. 'If you're getting involved with the Brigade, get yourself a gun.'

Leroux opened his jacket briefly. 'Can we meet at Height's later?'

'I'll be in the bar from five.'

Leroux walked out between the chains and waved at the watcher. The street was alive as businessmen hustled to the nearest drinking den for a quick whisky before heading back to their offices.

He walked around the corner and bumped into Brandt on the steps of the German consulate.

'I was blending in,' Brandt said, his voice thick with the night before.
'How rye of you.'
'Finally, I made a joke in English! Actually, someone in the bar said it first.'
'I know. I made one too.'
Brandt cursed and rubbed the back of his neck. 'Your language is impossible. Well, what is troubling you that you wish to speak on Christmas Eve?'
Brandt turned and exchanged greetings with Captain von Brandis, the Special Landrost of Johannesburg. He was responsible for maintaining order in the city, and his long white beard flowed like a peace banner as he strode down the street. Brandt showed Leroux into the cool of the consulate and laughed.
'You know he adjourns the Police Court to stroll over to Ren's and Lund's store for a nip of stout. What is it? You look serious.'
'There's something I thought that you would want to know. I went to Maddox Deep. A gang of Irish occupy the mine. They store weapons there, Lee Metfords, lots of them.'
'I see. Of course, they showed you around?'
'I broke in.'
'Well, if you want to hand yourself in, we can catch up with von Brandis.'
'Does it not concern you that a German company is breaking the law and storing rifles?
Brandt sighed. He was going to have to be serious with a hangover.
'We know the Randlords are acquiring weapons, even Maxims if they can get them, and it can't be long before they make their attempt. But I assure you this mine is nothing to do with us.'
'I believe you. Who knows? Maybe they are working on behalf of the Randlords, but to an outsider, it looks owned by Germans. That was the trail I followed, and anyone else would come to the same conclusion. What if President Kruger followed that trail? I only want your help to establish who these people really are.'
Brandt scratched his head. 'You have something in mind?'
'The only leads I have are the lawyer in Pretoria and Dresdner Bank here – do you have any relationship with the Bank?'
Brandt hesitated a moment. 'Yes, I do.' He cupped his forehead in his hand, massaging it, and seemed to come to a decision. 'I may be

able to get into the bank. I know a lady there who has access to the files. It will be closing at lunchtime for Christmas – I'll send a note now asking her to wait behind a while. Meet me at the bank on Commissioner Street at one o'clock.'

Muller was halfway down the stairs taking soft steps. 'Hauptmann, when you have got yourself together, I need to speak to you.'

'Herr Muller, I hope you enjoyed Height's Hotel,' Leroux said. 'By the way, there is a plain-clothes Zarp outside who would like a word with you.'

Muller's face flushed and he stalked outside.

'What was that about?' Brandt said.

Leroux moved to look out the window. 'Didn't seem to have any trouble knowing who I meant. You will need to handle your dynamite salesman carefully.'

'That is another joke, ja?'

Muller came back into the consulate and stumped up the stairs. 'Brandt!'

Out on the street, the watcher had gone. Leroux walked to the telegraph office to update Rhodes on his findings - an Irish gang storing rifles at the mine and Muller confirmed as a German agent working with Kruger's police. And he had some questions. Was there a known link between the Germans and the Irish? And what was the name of the agent that went missing investigating Maddox Deep?

The man on reception recognised Leroux and showed him through the thinly manned main office. He heard Lara's laugh as he reached her office door and knocked on the glazing. Another woman opened the door.

'You must be Mr Leroux.'

Kate Brown was Lara's colleague and about to end her shift. She reached for her shawl and draped it over her shoulders as Lara said, 'Mr Leroux was at the party. Do tell us what the ladies were wearing.'

Leroux's mind went blank. He could only remember one woman from the previous evening. 'The Baroness was the most memorable. She looked quite stunning in a green satin dress, with, I think it was chiffon, to accentuate her….and her beautiful golden hair was coiled up with bangs down over sparkling earrings–'

'I think Lara has heard quite enough about the Baroness. Was there anyone else?' Kate said.

'Some ladies were talking to Eugène Marais, but I don't recall what they wore.'

'Stop teasing Mr Leroux and let us get on with our work,' Lara said, and Kate winked her hand and closed the door behind her. 'Don't mind Kate. She is one of us.'

Leroux went over to the chessboard. 'You won?'

'Yes, last night while you were out with the ladies. Do you play?'

'Not to any standard. I just remembered an opening to distract Mr Pienaar. Is he one of Kruger's?'

'Yes, the deputy manager.'

'I met another earlier. Pretty much confirmed that Muller is an agent. They also have eyes on Groote Schuur. We should let Rhodes know.'

Lara took a note. Her hair was down today, curling softly over her shirt collar and her hands had an unfashionable outdoor tone that reminded him of the rolling grassland.

'Anything else?'

'I went to Maddox Deep. It's being used by an Irish gang to store rifles, enough ammunition for a hundred.'

Lara stopped writing and looked into his eyes. 'That must have been difficult, going back there.'

'I'd never been before. Father had the claim for a while but only had enough money to start work on it last year. I haven't visited here for five years.'

'Did you see where–'

'No, I didn't go down the shaft. There were too many Irish, and they were taking the rifles there. I saw what they were doing, grabbed this and got out.' Leroux showed Lara a lump of rock.

She held it in her hand, turning it so that it sparkled under her lamp. 'That's what all this trouble is about.'

Leroux nodded, sat down opposite Lara, and stared at the rock.

'Why haven't you been back?'

'My best friend died the last time I was here, and I had no interest in mining.'

Lara reached across the desk and put the rock back into Leroux's hand, her fingers smooth and gentle on his skin.

'I don't want it.' Leroux put the rock back on the desk and took the other one out of his pocket and placed it alongside.

'What happened?'

'We had been celebrating our future. Tom was going to make his fortune in the mines, and I was going to college. We got drunk. The next day Tom died in a cave-in.'

'I'm sorry.'

A figure passed across the office glazing. Leroux shoved one of the rocks on top of Lara's notepad, took a folded sheet of paper from his inside pocket and passed it across the desk. 'Don't read it.'

The door snapped open.

'Do please knock, Mr Pienaar,' Lara said.

The deputy manager walked over to Lara's desk and took a pocket-watch from his waistcoat as if to suggest there was something wrong with the time. He held out his hand to Lara, who passed him the sheet of paper.

The manager scanned down it. 'What is this nonsense?'

'It's my article for The Argus.'

'This is the sort of rabble-rousing claptrap that will cause disturbances. It's irresponsible!' A vein on Pienaar's bald scalp bulged.

'And nothing to do with you.'

Pienaar glowered at him. 'If there is a rising, it will be put down. Ruthlessly. And the people responsible for inciting it,' he said as he shook the paper, 'will be made to pay. You call yourself a journalist?'

'I have some other news.' Leroux picked up the nearer lump of rock and offered it to Pienaar.

'What?'

'I've discovered gold.'

Pienaar grabbed the rock, slammed it on the desk and thrust the article back at Lara before marching out.

'You've got a way of making friends,' Lara said.

'I'd prefer he took it out on me.'

Lara held up the paper. 'Why don't you want me to read it?'

'He was right. It's rubbish.'

'Well, I'll have to read it to send it.'

'I know.'

'I must teach you how to code. Have you anything else for Rhodes?'

'Confirmed Muller working with Zarps. Ask about any known links between the German Government and the Irish. And what was the name of his agent that went missing looking into Maddox Deep?'

'Got it.'
'If you're free over Christmas, would you mind teaching me to code?'
'I'm working early shift tomorrow and Boxing Day, finish at one o'clock.'
'Can you code outside?'
'I'm trained to code anywhere.'
'I'll be here tomorrow at one o'clock. We can take a picnic.'
'I look forward to it. Oh, I nearly forgot, I heard back from Pretoria about the solicitor, Mr Weber. His office was empty, no trace of him. There was nobody to make an appointment with, and the neighbouring businesses knew almost nothing about him. Kept himself to himself and hasn't been seen for weeks.'
'I'm not surprised. Everything about Maddox Deep is covered up. Shall I take those?'
Lara smiled. 'I'll keep your rocks as paperweights.'

Leroux was early, and he walked down Commissioner Street. He picked up the first edition of The Johannesburg Star and lent against a wall in the shade opposite the Dresdner Bank, opening the paper to the announcements. There was his notice looking for information on Baron von Veltheim and Thompson. Charles Leonard had also placed one, delaying the meeting of the National Union from the 27th of December until the 6th of January, and promising to publish a manifesto of demands. The reform committee intended to use the mass meeting as the spark to ignite the rising, so they were delaying. He turned the page. Trouble brewed in the international column as well. Cables relayed that Wall Street was blue with curses. Reports detailed nine bank failures and the expectation of a bond issue to rescue the American Government. Commentators doubted the success of this, owing to the destruction of European confidence. Telegrams from Vienna accused President Cleveland of causing widespread ruin with his threats against Britain. Venezuela held anti-British meetings, and Russia rejoiced because the dispute was likely to paralyse Great Britain in Europe and Asia. The Canadians expressed their loyalty in warm terms and took steps to strengthen their defences, announcing plans to convert paddle-steamers on the Great Lakes into gunboats. The Irish National Alliance in America offered one hundred thousand men to fight against Canada. Leroux stared blankly at the paragraph for a moment, reflecting that it wasn't just Johannesburg that was a tinderbox. The President was playing with fire in the hope of stirring up some support from voters, but he seemed more in danger of shooting himself in the foot if his posturing worsened the run on gold reserves and undermined the American economy.

Leroux looked up from the paper as a pair of Zarp troopers rode past and stopped outside the bank, followed by a smart four-horse wagon covered in Simmer and Jack livery. On the driver's bench, two armed men scanned the street and waited for another pair of troopers to pull up. The doorman at the bank rapped on the knocker and two guards came out, taking up positions either side of the door. The backboard of the wagon dropped, and a couple of men jumped down and carried small, seemingly very heavy, crates into the bank. After they had taken six, the troopers trotted away, and the guards went inside. The loaders came around to the front of the wagon.

'You two can knock off for Christmas now,' said the driver, and then lit a cigarette and sat chatting to his companion. A man garbed in rough clothes and a neckerchief over his face went up to the driver, who greeted him. Leroux heard the reply in a thick brogue, checked his pocket-watch, and pulled his hat down to shield his face. He risked missing his bank appointment in a quarter of an hour.

The Irishman got in the back of the wagon, and the driver tossed his cigarette aside and flicked the reins, turning back the way he had come. Leroux folded the newspaper under his arm and followed, walking under the awnings that reached out over the pavement.

The driver took the next turning and came to a stop behind a parked uncovered wagon. The Irishman jumped down, uncovered his face, and walked around to the wagon in front and clambered up. He retrieved a couple of small dynamite crates which the driver's companion caught and placed in the back of their wagon. They both disappeared into the wagon until a few minutes later they heaved one of the small crates down and shuffled back to the front wagon, hoisted it in, and went back for the second crate, which also seemed to have become a lot heavier. The Irishman wiped his brow and got up alone onto the driver's seat of the front wagon. He reached back and put up a small pole with a red flag and set off. At the next turning, he headed east. The driver went back to the Simmer and Jack wagon, tossing a small purse in his hand and joined his mate for another smoke. A few minutes later, he headed off in the same direction. Leroux hurried back to Dresdner Bank.

The first shops had closed their shutters for Christmas and children played out in the street in a state of heightened excitement. A carnival atmosphere prevailed, despite the storekeepers nailing up boards over the windows and the last customers heading home weighed down with additional provisions. Leroux arrived a few minutes late to see the head of a middle-aged lady appear out of the bank doorway. She raised a pair of spectacles and scanned the street, before disappearing back inside. Leroux checked his watch and the minute hand flicked to ten past.

Running down the street waving, weaving between the children, came Brandt. Sweating profusely, he held up his hand as if to say he would explain later and rapped the knocker. The lady's head appeared again, her hair scraped severely back and the spectacles balanced on the end of her nose.

'Frau Brock, fröhliche Weihnachten. I'm so sorry to trouble you with this, but it is urgent.'

'Merry Christmas to you, Hauptmann. And very irregular it is, and I don't mean being late. Quickly, come in,' she said and slid the bolts shut behind them. The guards stood to attention in the reception, the leather of their boots creaking as they shifted their weight.

'Check the rest of the building is empty,' Frau Brock said to them and turned to Brandt. 'Now, what is it that you are looking for.'

Brandt introduced Leroux to Frau Brock, the assistant bank manager.

'My friend here will explain. We need to look at the records of one of your customers.'

Frau Brock sucked her teeth and looked at Leroux, who held his worn hat and paper in his hands in supplication.

'This is against regulations, Hauptmann. The manager agreed that I could help you but helping a … someone else … is a different matter.'

Leroux unfolded the paper and showed Frau Brock the notice.

'You can see that I am earnestly seeking information about this person, Baron von Veltheim. My father died in unusual circumstances, and I believe he was the victim of a fraud.'

'This is correct.' Brandt said nodding. 'And the consulate has agreed to help.' Leroux doubted that was strictly true.

Frau Brock looked from Brandt to Leroux. 'Mr Leroux, I am sorry about your father. I cannot help you, but I can show Hauptmann Brandt the relevant records.'

Brandt shrugged and held his hands open. 'We like our rules. Let us see what we can do – what would you like to know?'

It was better than nothing, but could he trust Brandt to relay the information unadulterated? It was an open and honest face, but the steely eyes gave away nothing.

'Veltheim & Co gives this address for their bankers and apparently lent 25,000 ponds to my father on or not long before the 30th of September, secured on his mining claim, Maddox Deep. I would like to see a record of the money transfer to my father or of similar amounts withdrawn as cash. And where can I find the directors?'

Frau Brock looked unhappy. 'Hauptmann come with me. You must wait here.'

Brandt shrugged at Leroux. 'I will see what I can find.'

Frau Brock and Brandt left Leroux in silence. The scent of pine hung in the still air, and Leroux wondered how he had not noticed the giant Christmas tree in the reception. Traditional figures decorated the fir; angels dressed like miniature dolls with delicate gauze wings, cherubs with ribbons and a woodsman holding a pipe that served as an incense holder. Tiny parcels of candies interspersed electric light bulbs. A full half-hour passed with only the noise of the occasional door slamming or window rattling.

Brandt and Frau Brock reappeared, looking concerned, and sat down next to Leroux. Brandt cleared his throat and said, 'The company is owned by Baron Ludwig von Veltheim, and a man called Herr Karl Frederick Kűrtze is listed as a signatory. The only other information on record is a correspondence address - 21 Ferreira Street, here in Johannesburg. The file would normally have references and so on, but it is empty. There are no transfers to your father's name or cash withdrawals of any amount. In fact, since the account was opened four months ago, it has been dormant. Of course, it is possible that the money was paid in another way. I'm afraid that is all there is.'

Frau Brock nodded and looked down at her hands, crossed over in her lap. 'I will take this up with the manager after Christmas, but the officer who opened the account is no longer with us.'

'Thank you, Frau Brock, and I am sorry for delaying your Christmas.'

'It was nothing. I had to wait for the gold delivery anyway, and I am embarrassed by our record keeping. I hope we were of some help.'

Outside Brandt rolled up his sleeves. 'That there was little information is suspicious itself, and Frau Brock had never heard of the man.'

'Well, I have an address, that is something.'

'Let me see that,' Brandt said, pointing at the paper, folded to display the notice. 'You tell me that you have discovered a murderous gang storing rifles at the mine and you put a notice in the newspaper requesting information and give out your address? Is this some new British spy-craft technique that I should be aware of?' In the harsh sunlight and heat, the scar on his cheek stood proud and angry even as he grinned.

'Very funny, I put it in yesterday before I knew about the Irish.'

Brandt tossed back the paper. 'Would it have changed your mind?'

'Probably not.'

'What will you do?'

'I'm going to go and call at their office.'

'That's your next great idea? - save them the journey!'

'Yes. What will you do?'

'About the rifles? I'm not sure. I could report them to Kruger. But they don't seem to be working for the British, why should I try and stop them? And of course, no matter how much we deny it, people will suspect that Germany is behind it, so why bring attention to it? We should discuss this more, let me know what you find.'

'I will and thank you.'

'Well, I think I have sweated out last night, and I must bathe. I am taking the Baroness riding this afternoon.' Brandt grinned as he laced his fingers together, stretched them above his head and then bent down to touch his toes, before bounding down the street back towards the consulate.

Leroux strolled back towards Ferreira Street, taking in the new constructions. The builders imported materials from all over at vast expense to meet the whim of the day. As he walked past one newly refurbished building, two gentlemen in waistcoats stepped back out of his way and looked up with their hands on hips.

'Don't it take you straight back to Charleston?'

'Sure wish I was - would have cost me half as much.'

What had been a squalid mining settlement called Ferreira's Camp where only the roughest could flourish, was now, less than ten years later, a kaleidoscope of peoples and luxuries. Ahead lay the jewellery store that he had a distant memory of and it seemed smaller than he recalled. Either he or its neighbouring buildings must have grown. Two bare-headed Cingalese glided out of the door past the security guard, their long shiny hair tied in knots and fastened with circular combs, both in good humour, no doubt after exchanging sapphires and rubies for Christian money. If they knew they could be fined for walking on the pavement they did not show it. The armed guard yawned and seemed too bored to inspect Leroux as he passed the window display, dripping with diamonds from Kimberley and stones from around the world wrought into necklaces and bracelets of local gold. The store had flourished since his last visit, when he had gone with Tom to trade tiny nuggets of gold they had acquired, in return for services as they told the owner. Now the Randlords had extravagant tastes, and the store owner had stayed open, no doubt hoping to catch those with more money than time and more mistresses than wives.

'Can I help you?' The man behind the counter sounded impatient. He showed no flicker of recognition.

'I'm after a small charm for a necklace.'

The shopkeeper produced a tray of gold trinkets set on a dark blue velvet cloth. Stars, crosses, elephants, a clover, and even a court jester nestled before him. Leroux wondered if any contained gold from the nugget he had sold for Tom. The storekeeper hadn't asked any questions either.

'Anything in silver?'

The man sighed and took away the gold trinkets and produced another tray.

He picked through bells, owls, teddy bears, snakes and bees until he found what he sought. It was beautifully worked, a small bird in flight with short, pointed wings, but made flat like an Egyptian hieroglyph. It had an eye in the upper wing for a chain.

'Which bird is that?'

The storekeeper scratched his chin. 'What would you like it to be?'

'A starling.'

'Well, I think that's a Cape starling.'

'They're bright blue.'
'Silver doesn't come in blue.'
Leroux looked at the piece. It was almost perfect. With the flattened styling, it could just about pass for a Starling. He squinted at it. It looked a bit like a thrush too.
'I'll take it, and a chain.'

It was not much further to Ferreira Street, but Leroux hailed a cab. As they turned into the street, Leroux leaned forward and told the driver to carry on and then turn left. Ahead a man slouched in a doorway roughly where the address would be, hat tilted back cowboy fashion, probably on guard.
Leroux shielded his face from the man as he numbered off the doors of the terrace to confirm the address, and the guard looked up disinterestedly before returning to his contemplation of the pavement with a revolver on his hip. He looked cut from the same cloth as the Irish at the mine. Leroux could only see one way into the three-storied brick building, through the front door.
The cab rounded the corner, and Leroux pointed out a shop a bit further down the road where they stopped. The storekeeper nailed a board over the window from his perch on a stepladder.
'Got any Cape Smoke?'
'Inside behind the counter.' He waved the hammer as if Leroux might not be able to figure out how to get inside and put the nails back in his mouth. The door had the usual sign on it, 'Closed on account of the dust.' Leroux opened it, and a bell jingled above him. He fetched two bottles, and as he turned the storekeeper's head darted back behind the board, no doubt checking Leroux wasn't helping himself to anything else.
'Expecting trouble?'
The man shrugged. 'The quality are stirring things up. They will always land upright. Some folks are leaving. I can't. It's the likes of me that will pay for the trouble.'
Leroux paid the man far too much for a couple of bottles of smoke. It was the likes of him that doubled his prices at the first sign of distress. A couple of Zarps cantered past looking left and right. Perhaps they were trying to intimidate the Uitlanders, but they looked nervous. There were no foot police to be seen. Leroux dishevelled

himself and opened one of the bottles, splashing some over his mouth, neck and down the front of his shirt. He took a gulp, gargled and rinsed his mouth out. It was worse than in his memories, and he poured more away until half remained.

With the opened bottle in his left hand, on the building side, and the full bottle in his right hand on the street side he stumbled around the corner into Ferreira Street and slowed, swaying and humming 'Good King Wenceslas.' The guard glanced towards him. Taking a swig, Leroux launched into the verse, slurring for good measure. The guard checked down the street and then back at Leroux, smirking now, still lounging against the wall.

Leroux took another swig, only steps away, staggered and looked up at the guard. 'Merry Christmas to you!' He offered the man the opened bottle.

'Get lost,' the guard said in the brogue Leroux had come to expect.

'Aye, I'll be lost soon enough.' Leroux mumbled, raised the bottle and looking longingly after it, before taking another swig and smacking his lips, letting out a long sigh.

The guard's eyes flicked to the bottle and then down the street again.

'Scared someone will see you? No one around now. All at the boxing match I've just been to.'

'Feck. Give it, been standing here for hours.'

Leroux passed the bottle to the guard, who wiped the top of it with his shirt sleeve and raised it to his lips. He tilted the bottle all the way up as he drew his head back for a decent swig.

His eyelids half-closed as he chugged the first gulp down, and Leroux brought the full bottle crashing roundhouse into the Irishman's temple. The guard staggered sideways into the corner of the entrance, his grunt swallowed by the bottle in his mouth. Leroux dropped the broken bottle and planted his hand onto the matted mess of hair and rammed it into the wall. The guard's legs buckled, and he slumped into the doorway. A few people stopped and turned to stare as Leroux propped the man up into a sitting position, put his hat back on to cover his eyes, and gently cradled the guard's arms around the half-empty bottle. They had all seen the Christmas pay-packet spent on liquor.

Leroux filched the guard's revolver from its holster and found a door key in the man's jacket. It fitted, he pushed the door gently open, straining to hear something, and slipped into a gloomy hallway where just a little natural light filtered down the staircase. He checked the revolver. The guard had loaded all six chambers of the cylinder. Bad practice. An unlucky knock on the hammer could fire the gun accidentally. He closed the cylinder, cocked the hammer, and crept down the hallway. Two doors lead from it, one on either side. The first was a reception room with ladder backed chairs spread around, some old newspapers, and a pack of cards on a coffee table. The second was a rudimentary meeting room, with a rectangular table and more chairs arranged around it.

Leroux tested the treads as he went up the first flight of the narrow staircase. He turned on the half-landing. Still no sound. There were three doors at the top. The middle one, facing towards him had an etched glass panel in the top half through which light came, presumably from the room's windows onto the street. The fifth tread halfway creaked. He waited. He kept low to avoid looming up through the glazing. He listened at the middle door before trying the handle - locked. He stood and checked the rooms to the side, which were both empty, and then tiptoed up the next staircase.

Dust lay thick on the dado rail, and below it, the textured wallpaper had started to peel away. Both upstairs rooms lay bare. Leroux descended to the glazed door, took his jacket off and wrapped it around his arm. The glass shattered as he jabbed it hard with his elbow, but he couldn't open the door from the inside either, so pushed out the fragments and climbed through.

The room spanned the width of the building and overlooked the street. Empty shelves lined the wall at one end, while a desk and chairs occupied the other end with more shelves and some filing behind. There were two stacks of paper on the desk resembling an in and out pile.

He leafed through the left-hand pile, which consisted of letters and invoices addressed to the company for horses, saddles, guns, ammunition, and other provisions. Enough supplies to furnish a couple of platoons.

The out pile was much smaller and contained requests for cordage, food and other bits and pieces. All but one of the desk drawers were empty. Leroux took out a pad of paper, pencil, and a telegram addressed to '21 FERREIRA STREET'. The text at the bottom identified the sender only as 'HEAD OFFICE'. The body of the message made no sense, just groups of numbers that must have been code. On the top page of the pad letters and numbers were written spaced apart, 't r a i n 1 2 2 7 5'.

Leroux examined the telegram and counted the numbers. Fifteen groups of five numbers, but only ten characters scrawled on the notepaper. Leroux pocketed the message and the telegram and ran his hand along the shelves behind the desk. Some old newspapers, a couple of book-keeping ledgers, and a Bible weighting down some folded-up maps. He opened them over the desk, and they detailed the area around Johannesburg and Pretoria. He flicked through the ledgers, but there was no reference to a mine, just salaries and supplies. It was a quartermaster's office. The legal and company documents were probably with the missing solicitor in Pretoria.

The guard slumbered on in the doorway where the sun had come around and now beat down on him. He was going to have one thumping headache when he woke up. Leroux removed a cartridge from the revolver and rotated the empty chamber. But not in line with the barrel, which was safe, as it prevented accidental pressure on the pin from firing the gun. He continued to rotate the cylinder clockwise until the chamber in line with the hammer was loaded, and the empty one was next. He eased the hammer back down and put the revolver back in the guard's holster.

Leroux left to find Hammond to tell him about the Irish, the guns at Maddox Deep, and his suspicions about the gold and the wagons. The Randlords fretted about the leakage of gold from their mines. They found it impossible to stop the leakage completely and even tolerated it at a small scale, but they cracked down when criminal syndicates instigated large-scale rackets. If the Irish intended to use Consolidated Gold Fields' own money to work with the Germans, Hammond had to know.

The post office clock struck three as a telegraph boy sped past on his bicycle, the tops of little pink envelopes fluttering where they poked out of his satchel. Leroux adjusted his watch and quickened his pace. A large crowd milled in front of the Chamber of Mines building, and bowlers, kepis, deerstalkers, pith helmets and plantation hats mingled and bobbed with sombreros, trilbies, homburgs, boaters and plenty of bonnets with veils and even fedoras too. No doubt most of the top hats had business inside.

Leroux weaved his way to the doors. The crowd called out, anxious for news before they began the Christmas festivities. Some wore red, blue, and white rosettes declaring their support for Empire, but as many did not. All seemed eager to fight for something, but in the end, he knew few would be prepared to die for it. The shiny brass plaque on the double doors dazzled in the sunlight. The Chamber of Mines was the association of mine owners and related businesses, and they had moved to align their demands with those of the National Union which represented the broader citizenry. The Chamber now professed to be as interested in the franchise, sanitation and English language schooling as it was in the mining taxes. The Randlords needed the backing of the population to rid themselves of Kruger.

Three doormen held the crowd back from the entrance. Leroux showed his Argus card to the friendliest looking one, who let him through to the back of a large hall. At the far end, four men sat on a dais. Leroux recognised the Chairman, Lionel Phillips, from the previous evening, slim and smart. The man to his left must be Colonel Frank Rhodes, such was his resemblance to the Cape Prime Minister. A little greyer than his brother, he sat bolt upright but looked lost, staring out at the sea of faces. A reporter from the Star named the other two as George Farrar on the far side of Rhodes and on the near end, a vacant chair away from Phillips, Charles Leonard, with dark thick hair and a lawyerly look behind pince-nez glasses. Phillips stood and flapped his arms. The crowd ignored him until John Hays Hammond strode onto the stage with the bushiest moustache of them all and stopped behind the empty chair. The hall hushed and Hammond waited until you could hear his chair scrape back before taking his seat. The dais was now complete with the leaders of the Uitlander movement in Johannesburg, the unofficial reform committee.

Phillips gavelled the meeting to order and rose again to speak.

'Gentlemen you all know why you are here today. We are aggrieved by the State's policies and refusal even to discuss them. We must resolve to action. And in the first instance to send a list of demands, to allow them to make reasonable concessions so that we may all prosper.'

An uproar of hear-hearing rang around the packed hall. There were no working men here, but this was not their venue. Except for Hammond, each man on the dais rose to air their grievances and demand change, and each met with raucous approval.

Phillips took the floor again and looking to Hammond as if for permission, began his closing comments. When he finished, reporters shouted out questions. Hammond stood and pointed at a gaunt man. Heads turned to Marais.

'Mr Hammond, please could you give a quote for the readers of Land En Volk on how you see the Uitlander and the Boer working together.'

'Of course. We believe that South Africa has a great future and that together we can succeed. The Rand can be a shining jewel in the Republic, providing opportunity and prosperity for all of us. Those who wish to farm need flourishing markets for their produce, just as those who wish to mine need all manner of supplies. And good trade relationships with our neighbours will bring further benefits, not dangers. What we are asking of the President is not unreasonable. These are rights available to any that live in free countries from Europe to America, and many Boers also wish for this.'

It was well said and obviously a rehearsed answer to a planted question.

'Will Kruger make any concessions?' another called out. The crowd hushed again.

'We will have to see. He has never favoured the Uitlander. But remember just last October, the Drifts crisis? He backed down then. Let us hope.'

The Star reporter whispered, 'Not in this lifetime.'

An Australian voice called out, 'What about the flag? Will we hoist the Vierkleur?'

The Boer flag had become a totem for those of a republican bent like the Sydney Bulletin Australians. It had the red, white and blue horizontal stripes of the Netherlands with the addition of a green vertical band at the hoist, but more importantly, it meant that they would not be committing treason and fought for freedom, not Empire.

Phillips, Leonard and Farrar looked nervous amid the clamouring, none of them moving to address the question. Colonel Rhodes went puce and stood to speak, but a grizzled man raised his hand. The hall fell silent. The Star reporter lent over to Leroux. 'That's Poppa Mein, manager of Robinson Deep, very influential.'

He spoke in a wheezy American accent, but determined and clear. 'If this is a case of England gobbling up this country, I am not in it. Otherwise, I am up to my neck in it.'

The hall thundered harder than ever. Not one of the men on the dais attempted to counter the point. Hammond waved his arm until he could just make his voice heard above the cheering.

'We will put our demands to the President. Go home now for Christmas and rejoice, for I am sure all our wishes will come true in the New Year.'

Again, the hall shook with foot-stomping and hooting, and Hammond took the applause. As the hall began to empty, Leroux worked his way forward to the stage. Phillips lent over to Hammond and said, 'With the meeting of the National Union postponed the crowd outside are anxious, I think you should address them.'

They made their way up to the balcony. Hammond threw the doors open and went out, flanked by the other committee members, and the crowd erupted in applause. They had heard the din inside the hall and called for news. Hammond soaked in the adulation for a moment and then spoke.

'You will see the manifesto of the National Union in the paper after Christmas. We fully support it and have resolved to put our demands again to President Kruger.'

The crowd cheered. One voice managed to make himself clear.

'What of Doctor Jim?'

The city was rife with rumours. Nobody believed the official line that he was stationed at Pitsani to keep an eye on some unruly local chieftains or to protect the railway line. It could not be by chance that he lurked on the closest piece of British territory to Johannesburg.

'He is ready, and should we require his assistance, you can rely on Dr Jim - he has never failed.'

'Good old Dr Jim,' the crowd called, and the cheering began again mainly from the red, white and blue rosettes.

'When will you call up the militia?' another shouted.

'We must act in good faith with President Kruger. We will send our list of demands and await his response. We will decide on the militia once we have considered the reply. But be ready. The rifle clubs are open if you feel the need of practice! Merry Christmas!'

A wagon with two young beardless Boers plodded past.

'Make the Rooineks pay!' they called out taunting the gathering. A sullen silence spread through the mob, then angry shouts rained back. It was a sore point. The Boers paid only a few per cent of the entire Transvaal tax revenue. They should be on their knees with gratitude, not insulting them with their nickname for the English, who they thought were quick to anger and go red in the neck. The crowd, flush with fury, launched stones at the wagon and Leroux feared they would chase after the young farmers and fall on them when a pair of Zarp troopers charged dangerously close to the gathering and escorted the wagon away.

The committee returned inside, congratulating Hammond.

Leroux approached him. 'May I have a quiet word, I have information.'

'Mr Leroux, from the Argus? Hammond looked at the other dignitaries and said, 'We have no secrets between us. What is it?'

'I went to the mine. It is being used by an Irish gang to store weapons.'

'Weapons?' Phillips said.

'Yes, Lee-Metfords. I'd say as many as a hundred with ammunition.'

Phillips, Rhodes, Farrar, Leonard and Hammond all looked at each other.

'Which mine? What were you doing there?' said Leonard, the lawyer.

'The Maddox Deep mine. It used to belong to my father, who died in suspicious circumstances. I'm investigating.'

'Your father died?' Hammond said.

'Yes, two months ago. That's why Rhodes asked me to look into it.'

'I see, I see, that makes sense. I'm sorry to hear that.'

'And Rhodes was concerned that a German company now owned the mine.'

'Yes, yes,' Hammond said.

'We are short on the rifles we were expecting,' Phillips said. 'Do you think the Irish could have intercepted some of ours? Could the Irish be in league with the Germans?'

'I think they are keeping stolen gold there as well. I saw some Irish take crates from a Simmer and Jack wagon just after it deposited gold at Dresdner Bank. Afterwards, they went in the direction of Maddox Deep.'

Hammond looked alarmed.

'The Irish Brigade, you say?' Farrar said, 'Do you think they could be trying to muscle in on the illicit gold business?'

'What if the Germans are preparing a strong point in support of Kruger?' Colonel Rhodes said. 'And using our money to do it!'

Everyone now looked at Hammond. He stroked his chin and smoothed his moustache. 'This is a new development, but we must not let it divert us from our plans. I'll look into it. Thank you, Mr Leroux, that might prove to be valuable information. Will you be staying in town over Christmas?'

'I'm here until further notice to report on the crisis.'

'Keep your ear to the ground and let me know anything else you find out. You must come up to the house for our Boxing Day gathering. I'll tell Mrs Hammond to expect you. Now, we have other business to discuss,' Hammond said gesturing to his companions, 'Good day.'

Hammond led the others to a back room. Marais hovered in the background and now approached, his eyes darting around although there was no one else to be seen.

'They should be more concerned about the Germans,' Marais said and leant on his cane.

'You think the German Government could be in league with an Irish gang?'

'Sounds unlikely, I agree, but they share an enemy. The Kaiser has long sought more influence over the Boers, both here and the Orange Free State. And each day there is more activity and more rumours.'

'Muller?'

'I enquired about him, and he has no qualms. He will deal with anyone. And I've been looking into the Baroness, what did you think of her?'

'We met only briefly. She certainly catches the eye.'

'The late Baron was very wealthy and well-connected politically with the German Government.'

'What did he die of?'

'A very large smile according to the gossip,' Marais said, and the corner of his mouth lifted a fraction.

'Did she inherit?'

'Everything. Society had barely accepted her even before the Baron died, and now she has fled here to escape the gossipers.'

'Do you know anything about her investments?'

'The Baron had two mines here, which the Baroness sold to the Rand Mines Company, part of the Corner House Group where Phillips is Chairman. She also has stakes in the railway line to Delagoa Bay, as well as property.'

'I went to the Stock Exchange this morning to try and find out if she or any other Germans had been buying shares but discovered no sign of it.'

'I have heard the same. Perhaps they are expecting prices to fall further, because of some event?' Marais glanced around again, his eyes bloodshot.

'I think she's more interested in Captain Brandt at the moment.'

'And there is a man in search of a fortune.'

Leroux left Marais to his theories and went outside. The crowd had dispersed. The reform committee needed to be careful, for they had a tricky balancing act to perform. On the one hand, they had to unite the citizens behind the cause, while on the other, they had to hold them back until they were ready. He needed to update Rhodes and his thoughts turned to Lara.

The remaining telegraph operators hurried to relay the messages of seasonal greetings. Through the glazing, Lara sat bent over in calm concentration. A slender forearm rested on the desk while her hand caressed the instrument, gently tapping out a signal as her eyes followed a finger gliding delicately over a form.

She worked her lower lip with a slight frown, unaware of his presence. Her head tilted slightly down with her hair pinned up, highlighting the gentle curve of her neck.

Leroux tapped on the window and smiled. Lara started, gasped, smiled and frowned in quick order.

'Mr Leroux, you scared me creeping up like that - how long had you been there?'

'Just long enough to admire you at work, I've got some more for you here.'

'One minute, and I'll be with you.' She finished off the telegram, tidied the papers on her desk and turned to Leroux.

'Any reply to my last report to Rhodes?'

'He's pleased with you,' Lara said and showed him the telegram:

GOOD WORK STOP KEEP ON GERMAN IRISH LINK STOP AGENT CALLED ALFRED JONES LAST SEEN 15TH STOP END

'What do you make of these?' Leroux took out the coded telegram and message he had taken from the office. 'I found them next to each other in a desk draw.'

'The message looks fairly straight forward. Rail 12 27 5. That reads like a date and time.' Lara went over to the shelves and pulled out a sheet. 'There's a train service from Port Elizabeth that arrives at 5 p.m. on Friday 27th, at Braamfontein where the goods yard is, not Park.'

She put the message on the desk. 'Right?'

'Could be. Let's assume that for now.' Leroux looked at the door.

'Don't worry, Pienaar's not here. There's another, but he's junior, and I can handle him.' She picked up one of the rocks and tossed it in her hand.

'The other one's in code.'

Lara looked at the telegram, her eyes scanning back and forth.

'Not the miner's code, Bedford McNeil, or any other one I recognise. I'll need to work on it. If it's the encoded version of the message, I may be able to crack it.'

'Is there any way I can help?'

'Not unless you can find out the key.'

'I've got nothing else, but I'll ask the next Irishman I see.'

'Well, I'll have a look at it and see if I can tease anything out. I'll send them to Rhodes too. He will want to get his intelligence officer to look at it. Anything else for him?' Lara made copies of the two pieces of paper.

'I saw some Irish taking heavy crates from a Simmer and Jack wagon that had deposited gold at Dresdner Bank, and then heading in the direction of Maddox Deep. I can't be certain yet, but it looked like theft, maybe part of an illicit gold operation. It would make sense, something a well-armed gang would do. I've told Hammond.'

'I'll just say you suspect Maddox Deep Irish involved in illicit gold purchases from Simmer and Jack. Hammond updated.'

'Perfect.'

'Anything else.'

'I have an undercover mission for you.'

'Sounds good.'
'You are to pretend to be my companion at the Hammond's Boxing Day Party.'
'That's a bit of an anti-climax.'
'You'll stop me sticking out like a sore thumb.'
Leroux pushed himself off the desk and said goodbye, and she held his gaze for that extra moment that gave him hope.

He saw no sign of the sombrero outside the hotel or of another tail. They had either given him up as not worth the trouble or got a better operator. The hotel clerk passed him a card and note. An invitation to Baroness Stein's Waifs and Strays party at Gables House, Doornfontein, Christmas Eve. The hand-written paper was from Captain Brandt, which read, 'Dear Mr Leroux, please come we have much to discuss.'
David skipped up.
'Here's your shilling. Can you run another errand for me?'
'Anything sir, finish for today.'
'Any strange men around?'
'No see.'
Leroux wrote out a note asking Jory to join him for Christmas breakfast at eight o'clock.
'Go to the Simmer & Jack Mine and ask for Jory. Give him this and tell him it is important that he comes, a favour to me.' David pocketed the note and was away.
Sanderson cradled a whisky at the bar and looked like he had spent some time there. 'Didn't see you at the Chamber meeting today.'
'No point in listening to them waffle on. I can tell you what they said.'
'Hammond suggested Kruger will back down as he did in the Drifts crisis.'
'No chance Kruger will back down. Nothing to back down from. It's the Reformers who are making the demands.' Sanderson stuck his lower lip out.
'Not even a small concession to keep the peace?'
'The Drifts was a trap, and Kruger nearly fell into it. He was breaking the treaty by closing the border to trade and giving Rhodes the excuse he needed to get the Colonial Office to send in British troops. Don't forget, Salisbury is Prime Minister now, he won't back down from a

fight.'

'That's why Kruger backed down quickly then, before the Colonial Office could respond?'

Sanderson was getting more animated and indicated to the barman for a refill.

'Yes, he realised his mistake in time. Rhodes would have had clear legal justification to invade. This time he will frustrate Rhodes by not giving an inch and force Rhodes to break the treaty, getting international support behind the Republic. In his dreams, Britain's enemies would unite, and kick the British out of all Southern Africa.'

'Is it really possible?'

'Britain is isolated diplomatically and inspires jealousy. The French rival us in the scramble for Africa. Germany has always coveted Southern Africa. Combined with German South-West Africa and East Africa it would make an impressive empire. The Russians joust with us in the Hindu Kush and the Balkans and revel in our disagreements with America. Not as far-fetched as it sounds.'

'Hammond must know that Kruger won't concede anything.'

'He does. Just playing the crowd. They'll be all the more outraged when Kruger doesn't meet their demands and Hammond will have a spark for action.'

'I didn't realise you were such a cynic.'

'I have my great downward spiral to thank for that.' Sanderson swirled his drink and gulped it down with a flourish.

Leroux ordered another two whiskys.

'What happened?'

Sanderson stood upright and rolled his shoulders. His eyes were level with Leroux, watery but steady. He seemed ready to unburden himself. He lent, using the bar as a crutch. 'It began well. A silver spoon, a Guards regiment, followed by a good job at The Times. But I had expensive tastes. Before long, I was gambling. And drinking to forget about the losses. And taking short cuts to make time for the gambling and drinking. Making up quotes was the final straw.'

'What brought you here?'

'I had to leave. Debts and ignominy. I still had connections and came to Cape Town twenty years ago as a correspondent. I was able to help Rhodes a little in his early days in Kimberley. He's been very good. But you get a bad smell about you, and in time people hear you but don't listen.'

They both brooded for a moment. Sanderson's long face was well suited to melancholy, and he even seemed content in it, as though he had confronted his fate and the world still turned just the same.

'Rhodes needs to listen now. The mood in the meeting was pro-Republican. They'll fight, but not for the Union Jack. How did Younghusband get on?'

'Don't know,' Sanderson said, 'he should be back any day.'

'It's not just the flag. The whole venture is shaky. Phillips, Farrar and Leonard looked nervous when challenged. They're businessmen, not soldiers. Losing other people's money is one thing, sticking your neck in a noose is another. Hammond is solid, but he can't do it all on his own, and Colonel Rhodes seems out of touch.'

'The Colonel is a good man, but he's lost without the army.'

'What's his role?'

'Smuggling rifles. But it's just not his bag.'

'Why did they choose him?'

'Probably he was the closest to a quartermaster. And he knows the man his brother uses to forward them.'

The barman came and refilled their glasses.

'You know I want to be a war correspondent?'

Sanderson smiled. 'You'll get a story here. It'll suit you if you can stay out of mischief.'

'I nearly forgot. I saw some Irish, same lot I think, taking gold from a Simmer and Jack wagon.'

Sanderson banged the bar. 'Christ, that's all Hammond needs! I don't know what the Germans and Irish are up to, but if they're using the Company's own gold to do it, Rhodes will go berserk.'

'I was trying to see the German angle. Maybe they see the Irish as a thorn in Britain's side and are helping them unofficially, say arranging protection from the Zarps?'

'Why not?' Sanderson ran his finger around his collar. 'Kruger would love the idea of using deserters from the British Army against them.'

'And running some sort of protection racket, it's just another way to squeeze more money out of the miners.'

'It's a whole new league for the Brigade if it's them. I've not heard a whisper. What did Hammond say?'

'He said he'd look into it. I think he was embarrassed.'

'There's a wee Irish girl I can ask at Slack Alice's. She may have heard something.'

'One other thing. Brandt helped with Dresdner Bank. I got the correspondence address for the Veltheim company on Ferreira Street.'

Leroux showed Sanderson the two messages. 'Lara thinks that's the arrival time of a train at Braamfontein from Port Elizabeth.'

Sanderson's brow furrowed. 'Braamfontein or Kazerne, the goods yard next to it. I've heard Port Elizabeth is on the route they use to smuggle the rifles. The manager of De Beers in Kimberley organises it and sends them down to Port Elizabeth where they come up disguised as some new shipment from the port.'

'That must be it then. The Irish are going to intercept a shipment of rifles or other military supplies. That's what I saw them storing at the mine. And the office where I got the messages was like a quartermaster's office. All the paperwork was for equipment or rations of some type.'

'How did you get these messages?'

'I broke into the office.'

'Did anyone see you?'

'The guard. But he might not remember, I clonked him.'

Sanders pushed back damp strands of hair from his forehead. 'You're getting into deep water. Rhodes's man went missing looking into this business. These characters would have killed him if he got close.'

'I got a message from Rhodes. He was called Alfred Jones.'

'Don't know the name, but what's Brandt up to then, helping you? If the Germans are in bed with the Irish, why would he lead you to them?'

'I don't know. But he wants to speak.' Leroux put the hand-written note and the invitation on the bar. 'Marais is convinced that the German's are planning something. Thinks even the Baroness is involved.'

'He jumps at shadows. Getting worse, poor fellow.'

'He's got a laudanum habit. I've seen him topping up his drink.'

'At least I haven't sunk to that, yet,' Sanderson said.

'I'd always heard of Marais as the great intellect, destined to lead the Boer nation, and now he seems reduced to being a propagandist for Rhodes.'

'He's had a tough time. And it's easy to fall, as I know all too well.'

Leroux checked his watch. It was half-past five. He thought back to the condescension he had seen in Marais' face. He would not be happy with his current situation. 'What do you make of the Baroness?'

'I've never met her.' Sanderson picked up the paper and turned to the fashion intelligence column and the report on the previous night's party. 'Apple green chiffon dress, the big sleeves were of crepon, and the satin epaulettes were smothered in flakes of chiffon.' He put the paper down. 'I hear she's quite a beauty.'

Leroux wished he had read the column earlier. 'Charming and sharp too.'

'Popular with the other ladies?'

'I wouldn't say that.'

'Why did she invite you?'

'I think it was Brandt's doing. The note says he wants to discuss something.'

'He wants to talk to you. Or he wants you to see something. Or he wants to keep an eye on you. Or he wants to make sure you're not somewhere else.'

'Muller searched my room yesterday while we were at the club.'

'What was he looking for?'

'Just information, he went through the file.'

'You sure it was him?'

'He more or less admitted it.'

'Can you trust Brandt?'

'So far he's kept to his word. Only he was allowed to see the Dresdner records, but he did turn something up. And he wears his heart on his sleeve, at least where the Baroness is concerned.'

'Better go and see what he wants then.'

Leroux put the drinks on his account.

'There's a few of us having Christmas Breakfast here tomorrow, join us,' Sanderson said and left.

Leroux returned to his room and wrote an article, while outside a grubby man loitered across the road. His report detailed the enthusiasm for reform across the many classes and nationalities of the Uitlander. People united by an idea, not a flag. He hoped Rhodes would see it in the unlikely event that The Argus published it.

He dressed and pushed open the doors onto the small balcony. It was Christmas Eve, and the temperature had begun to drop under a clear night sky. Still, the man lingered across the road. There had been no responses to his notice, except perhaps this one.

Leroux took a cab to the Baroness's rented residence at Doornfontein without any sign of a tail and he supposed they already knew where he was headed. They jolted to a halt. The other carriages were adorned with Christmas decorations and the coachmen were dressed to look like reindeer and elves and pranced and capered as they helped the other guests down. The doorman announced him, but few took notice, and he moved discretely among the guests. A hand touched his arm. It was Muller.

'I did not know you were a friend of the Baroness.'

'I think she is courting the paper, not me.'

'Perhaps. But you seem to cause incidents, not report on them.'

'Some stories are hard to uncover. Is Baron von Veltheim on the guest list?'

'No. I would like to talk to him also.'

'Then you had better find him before I do.'

Muller's dark eyes were the hardest part of his pudgy face. They showed neither fear nor amusement.

'I do not think you will find him.'

He left Leroux standing in the middle of the room. A loud American laugh erupted behind him, and Leroux recognised Poppa Mein from the Chamber meeting and introduced himself. He stood in a corner with Victor Clement, another American and the manager of the Simmer and Jack mine.

'Your point was well received at the meeting.'

'Not by the committee,' Mein said, 'I've been telling them long enough.'

'They seem to have come around to your point of view, but they're still torn.'

'Reckon they need to un-tear themselves and quick. I won't ask anybody to fight for the English.'

Mr Clement looked uncomfortable.

'I met a truly knowledgeable miner from Simmer & Jack. A Cornishman called Jory,' Leroux said to Clement.

'One of the Cousin Jacks. Good miner.'

He looked more comfortable now.

'Saw him getting a hard time from some English, giving him feathers.'

'There's a lot of tough talk goin' on. Let's see what happens when the talkin' stops.'

'I had a run-in with a few Irish near your mine. Have you had any trouble from them?'

'Don't hire Irish if I can help it, but the few I've got are good enough.'

Two other Americans joined them, Mr Lingham of the timber company and a representative from General Electric, whose name Leroux didn't catch.

'Let me tell you the difference between the English and Americans,' the lumber man from Puget Sound said. 'There were two missionaries came here a few years back. The Englishman spent the first two years studying the natives' language and building a house for himself. In that time, he made no converts. The American rented a hut and hired interpreters. After two years he had one hundred and fifty converts and many more who were learning useful occupations and trades, so he sent home a request for more missionaries. You see, you gotta hustle in this world.'

Leroux nodded appreciatively and left them preaching the great potential of the Rand for the American brand of capitalism as he searched for Marais.

The Baroness had decorated the house in a winter theme, despite the blazing heat of mid-summer in Johannesburg. A colossal fir tree was adorned with white lace to give the impression of frosting. Tiny foil stars hung from the ceiling which had been painted midnight blue for the occasion. An ice sculpture of a snowman dripped on a table, and next to it he located Marais, pale and twitchy, attended by two society ladies.

'Twice in a day! To what do I owe the pleasure?'

'I think we share a common interest in discovering what our German friends are up to,' Leroux said.

'I saw you talking to Muller. What does he want?'

'He told me I wouldn't find Baron von Veltheim.'

Marais scanned the room. 'Do you think he knows something?'

'Hard to say.'

A waiter came by with champagne, while Marais topped his glass up with his private supply and then a man with long grey hair swept back approached and pushed into the conversation. Marais introduced him as the American consul in Johannesburg, JC Manion.

'How is the Republic this fine evening?' he said in a Southern drawl.

'Divided. But let us hope for peace and goodwill.' Marais said.

'A house divided against itself cannot stand if I recall correctly.'

Marais frowned, while Manion turned to Leroux. 'From The Argus? Cataloguing the decay of the British Empire must test the soul. This century has undoubtedly been yours, but the next will be Republican.'

He cast his gaze over the ladies with satisfaction writ large over his smug face. The women fanned themselves busily, perhaps hoping someone else would reply. Before Leroux could answer, Marais ushered Manion away for a private conversation, and Leroux left the ladies and trawled the room.

A quartet played tunes he did not recognise, no doubt aimed at the numerous German contingent. Captain Brandt was by the Baroness's side. She beckoned Leroux and dazzled even more than the previous evening in a pale blue silk dress that highlighted her eyes and complemented the wintry decorations.

'How is it that such a wise and daring and handsome gentleman as yourself is here without a lady – I must introduce you to some.'

'I don't think Mr Leroux has any trouble in that regard,' Brandt said. 'There is a beautiful young lady in the telegraph office that has caught his attention.'

'The young lady that works for Pienaar?'

Brandt smiled. 'Yes, and Mr Leroux caught our Muller in a clever trap. You have made an enemy there, Mr Leroux.'

'He already regarded me as an enemy.'

'And Mr Leroux has made enemies of the Irish too.'

'You must be in need of friends,' the Baroness said.

As they spoke, the orchestra struck up "Silent Night." At first, a few, and then everyone sang, some in English, but the most enthusiastic in German, giving a full-throated rendition of "Stille Nacht." When the singing ended, everyone made small silent clapping motions and turned back to their conversation a little brighter, a little lighter.

The Baroness made a signal. The musicians began to play another, stirring hymn. The English speakers looked around mystified as many of the Germans began to join the Baroness in singing. The rousing music built to a crescendo as they roared out the final lines.

"Deutschland, Deutschland über alles,

Über alles in der Welt!"

Muller stormed over. 'I must insist you play the national anthem at once.'

The Baroness smiled at Muller and motioned to the orchestra again. They began a dreadful dirge, which sounded at first like the musicians tuning their instruments. The English perked up, and Leroux recognised the music as "God Save the Queen," while the Germans sang their own "Hail to thee in The Victor's Crown" without any enthusiasm. The English that had started to sing fell away in confusion, and when the singing stopped, Muller strutted away. Leroux saw him approach Marais, who took a long pull straight from his hip flask

'What was that about?' Leroux said.

'Everyone loves to sing the Song of the Germans,' the Baroness said quietly to Leroux. 'It's quite new, written to tell us Prussians and Austrians to stop fighting amongst ourselves and put Germany first. But some take it to mean put your country before your sovereign. Muller thinks that it is disrespectful to the Kaiser and insisted we play "Heil dir im Siegerkranz" to show our allegiance. But if you want to stay awake, play "Das Lied der Deutschen."'

'Now, we have a lot to discuss,' Brandt said and steered Leroux through to the library and closed the doors.

'Dr Jameson is at the border with an expeditionary force,' Brandt said.

'Everybody knows that.'

'He possesses a letter inviting him to come to the aid of the Uitlanders.'

Leroux did not know that Jameson already carried the invitation.

'You didn't know?'

'I am not a part of the Randlords' plot. I am here to investigate Maddox Deep. That has led me to you.'

'But you have Rhodes's ear?'

'That overstates it. I report to him on Maddox Deep.'

'And any German role in that?'

'Yes. Who sent the letter?'

'The men on stage at the meeting today. The Reform Committee.'

'You know more than I do.'

'They must be in league with some Boers. Kruger suspects Joubert.'

'That would be logical.'

'The letter is undated. Jameson can date it when he decides to ride in.'

'That could be any day now.'

A footman appeared with cognac and cigars.

Leroux lit the cigar, which was darker than he had seen before and sweeter.

'Our man in Havana, Herr Upmann, makes the most marvellous cigars.'

Leroux swirled the cognac around his glass. 'What is it you want with me?'

'First, let us discuss more. Muller searched your room.'

'I know.'

'He is as interested in Maddox Deep as you are.'

Leroux blew a smoke ring which rolled over the decanter.

'Does Muller know who Baron von Veltheim is?'

'I believe so.'

'Who is he?' Leroux said.

'When you first asked, I checked with my staff, and no one knew the name. After we spoke this morning, I asked my assistant to go back through the records. There is an old report from ten years ago of a young man called Karl Frederic Kűrtze. He was a sailor at Wilhelmshaven and suspected of stealing a gold watch and a family seal from Captain Wilhelm von Veltheim. He deserted and is believed to go by the alias Baron von Veltheim but has escaped justice.'

'And Muller only recently found this out?'

'He has a local agent here, who you saw. He was following a British agent, Alfred Jones, do you know him?'

'I know he disappeared.'

'This Mr Jones came to the consulate and asked about Baron von Veltheim. And then as you say he disappeared. The local agent would have updated Muller, and Muller is a meticulous man and would check the records.'

'You're saying Veltheim is nothing to do with you?'

'As far as I know.'

'Do you trust Muller?'

'Now we come to my point. I do not, but I also do not think he has anything to with Maddox Deep.'

'And what is your point?'

'What I want to discuss with you must stay between us, for my safety and that of the Baroness. I must rely on your absolute discretion – can I have your word on that?'

Leroux nodded, his gaze fixed on Brandt. 'You have my word.'

'Have you heard of Abteilung 3b?'

'No.'

'Good. It is the military intelligence section of the Army, highly secret. It's fairly new, run by Field Marshal Helmuth von Moltke. Herr Muller is a Colonel there, one of the senior agents.'

'Why are you telling me this?'

'Because you need to know this to make the message I am going to give you believed.'

'The message?'

'Herr Muller is here to provoke a war between Germany and the British Empire.'

Leroux pushed himself up in his chair and lent forward.

'And you are working against the German Government?'

'There are two factions in the German Government. Those that support the Kaiser and his dreams of empire, and those that feel he is too impetuous and support Bismarck as a restraining influence on the Kaiser. The Baroness's husband was a confidant of Bismarck, and my family are also close to him.'

'The Kaiser wants war with Britain?'

'He is friendly with Kruger and sees the Transvaal and southern Africa as an ideal place for Teutonic expansion. He wants Germans emigrating here and the surrounding lands rather than to America. He will not tolerate any British aggression against the Republic and is looking for an opportunity to confront the British and increase his presence here.'

'And Muller is in the Kaiser's camp?'

'Yes, and ambitious. They believe that Russia will join them in a war against Britain, maybe America and even France too. I think he intends to create an incident that will bring international condemnation on Britain and give the Kaiser, and maybe others, an excuse to declare war.'

'The papers carried reports of President Cleveland's speech. Are they working together - Cleveland and the Kaiser?'

'I think not. But if Britain attacked the South African Republic, it would be hard for America to turn her back on a fellow Republic after all the rhetoric from Cleveland, especially as so many of her citizens live and work here. If either America or Germany declared war as a consequence, it would be an easy decision for the other to join in. Even the British Empire could not take on both at once.'

'Rhodes is being careful not to break the treaty, at least not the letter of it, precisely to avoid antagonising the Americans.' Leroux said.

'Muller is planning something, but I don't know what.'

They passed the decanter, and the cigars burned down. Leroux flexed his fingers. 'What are you proposing?'

'You have a channel of communication to Rhodes through the delightful Lara, do you not?'

'Yes.'

'There are people on your side that want war, just as there are on my side. Consider working together, you and I, to prevent a local disagreement from becoming a war that could draw in much of the world.'

Leroux thought of the slaughter of Chief Malaboch's men, the stench of the bodies piled up before the Maxims. He could still smell the wood around his rifle barrel, smoking hot from the incessant firing.

'My influence is small.'

'I also have limited influence. But there is a chance, if we put our heads together, we may be able to make a difference. We are the men on the ground. We can act.'

'I agree to think about it.'

Brandt nodded slowly. 'Don't take too long and remember I have your word.' He rose and opened the doors to a terrace and went out into the night air. Leroux followed and turned to admire the house.

'It's supposed to be a Swiss Chalet,' Brandt said with a small grin. 'With verandas. Now, what do you think of the Baroness?'

They lit new cigars, and Brandt enjoyed Leroux's praise of her. They talked on their war stories in the bush and emptied the decanter as the party drifted apart.

'There you are Karl, with your new friend. Everyone's gone, come and talk to me.' The Baroness lent against the doorframe, smiling, a few tired creases at her eyes.

'I'll see myself out,' Leroux said.

'One more thing. You're being followed,' Brandt said.

'I know.'
'Not just by us, someone else.'
Leroux bid them farewell and walked home to clear his head, reflecting on the night's events as Christmas Day dawned. The sky was clear, and he pulled his hat down, turned his collar up to his ears and balled his hands into his coat pockets. In the stillness, Leroux could hear the crunch of the dust underfoot. As he approached Height's a night-soil cart came by and the stench of the evening's collection wafted by. The elderly driver tipped his hat, 'Merry Christmas.'

Outside the hotel, a small form sat with knees huddled in, his coat drawn around them and head resting forward. It was David. Leroux shook him gently awake.
'Is everything all right?'
David rubbed his eyes and put his finger to his lips. 'No, sir.'
'You saw Jory?' Leroux whispered.
'He coming tomorrow.'
'What's wrong?'
'Two bad men. In your room.'
Leroux stood back and looked up at his first-floor room. The windows were black, the curtains open, as he had left them.
'Like before?'
David shook his head. 'Guns.'
'They speak the Taal?'
'No, sir. Maybe English, don't understand.'
Leroux checked his Colt. 'Want to help?'
'Anything.'
Leroux looked back up at the room. Dark and quiet. He had left the messages there. If it was the Irish, they hadn't just come for those. The door onto the balcony was closed, but he had left it unlocked. The maid had cleaned the room before he left, and there was no reason why the men inside would lock it, they would want an escape route.
'Take this key. Go up to my room. Make sure the light in the corridor is on. Stand to the side of the door, not in front of it.' Leroux paused to make sure David understood. 'Put the key in the lock and open it. Push the door open a little, wait for two heartbeats and then give it a big push. Don't go in, run away. Got that?'
'Yes, sir.'

'Give me time to get up there.'

Leroux took off his coat, rolled up his sleeves and silently climbed onto the awning over the veranda, and along until he was below his room. A cab trotted down the street. He paused, heard his breath and sought a handhold. As the cab passed, he pulled himself up by a baluster at one end of the balcony and over the top. He crouched under the window before the door. The room was too dark to make anything out. He muffled his revolver as he cocked it, got a grip on the door handle, and listened.

Leroux pictured the layout. The room's main door was on the far wall in the right corner, and it opened inward against the right wall. The headboard of the bed was against the left-hand wall. There was a chair and a writing desk in the right corner by the far window. The balcony door was in the middle, three-quarters of the way down the bed.

A mumble. A click. Had one of them heard a noise in the corridor and checked the other was awake?

One man would be up against the far wall to the left, firing across the door as someone entered. The other would be in the chair, able to fire out of the door as it opened, at right angles to the first man. No chance of getting caught in each other's crossfire. Shouldn't be a man in the left corner by the window. He would be visible there as soon as someone started to open the door. Leroux looked down at his gun. He wanted to speak to one of them.

A key rattled and turned in the lock. Another click. The door pushed open a fraction, and a crack of light slit the dark. He waited for two beats and just as David shoved, Leroux yanked the balcony door and dived low and left onto the floor, revolver aimed at the desk.

The man in the chair was caught in the light and had no chance. Dazzled, he turned from the corridor to the new danger, but his arm couldn't traverse nearly fast enough. A bullet snapped his skull back. Under the bed, the other man's feet swivelled, and a shot blasted out above Leroux, wood splinters bursting from the balcony door. Leroux squeezed again, shooting the man in the ankle. A yelp and the man fell.

Leroux drew back the hammer. 'Stop!'

The man scrabbled on the floor, fumbling with his gun.

'Stop!'

He was young, lying on his side. Whimpering in pain, he raised his gun. Leroux closed his eyes and pulled the trigger. The youth rolled onto his back, and his fingers released their grip.

No, no, no, Leroux leapt over the bed and pressed a pillow to the man's chest. He couldn't have been more than twenty and clung to it as the stain spread out. A sorrowful expression adorned his delicate features, framed by dark curly hair. He was still alive, but blood bubbled from his lips.

'Who are you?'

The eyes moved. He coughed and winced, blood trickling down his chin.

'It should never have happened.'

'What?'

He grunted. 'Your Pa.' He was bleeding heavily. Leroux pressed the pillow harder.

'Why?'

The man sighed. 'He got greedy.'

'Who?'

'We're after the same thing you and me.'

His eyes closed, a mournful smile weighed on his lips and he murmured,

'Too long our Irish hearts we schooled
In patient hopes to bide,
By dreams of English justice fooled
And English tongues that lied.
That hour of weak delusion's past –
The empty dream has flown:
Our hope and strength, we find at last,
Is in ourselves alone.'

His callow life had ebbed away, and his mouth formed a crimson crescent. The words meant nothing to Leroux, other than the man was Irish.

David's head poked through the door, and when he saw that Leroux was unharmed, he bounced in. Hotel staff called along the corridor, checking on the commotion.

'You did good. Tell them to go and get a doctor,' Leroux said and then searched the two bodies. The man in the chair had taken the messages, the file and the keys to the office. He felt through his own pockets. He still had Rhodes's letter. But what did the young man mean? Who got greedy? Did he mean his father? It didn't sound like father. Who else could he mean?

Christmas Day, 1895

Leroux awoke with the sun streaming into his room. He reached for his pocket watch on the side stand, which showed half-past seven. He wound it and reflected on the previous day and his father's mine. He had poked the nest. Muller was an enemy, for sure. But how was he linked to the Irish? Brandt claimed to want to stop Muller and had been helpful with Dresdner Bank, but he was close to the Baroness and Marais suspected her. She seemed to sense that and distrusted Marais in turn. Brandt knew Rhodes suspected the Germans. Was he trying to divert him somehow? And if so, why? Either an Irishman or Veltheim was responsible for his father's death - he was sure of that. The reaction that he provoked indicated he was at least making progress.

He roused David, curled up in a blanket on the floor. The hotel had attempted to clean up the room, but there were still bloodstains on the rug, where the young Irishman had died reciting poetry. He had seemed different from the others, more of an idealist than a killer. The Zarps had come, but it was clear that it had been self-defence and they had just taken a statement from Leroux. He left out the bit about coming in through the balcony.

The dining room was busy, and in the middle, a long table heaved with a dozen newspapermen. Sanderson had kept a place at the end of the table free, and Leroux joined him. As he sat Sanderson whispered, 'Be careful what you say in front of Barbarian Brown over there, he reports to Kruger.'

Leroux asked the waiter to lay another place at the end with them, and as he did, the barrel-like Jory made his way across the room, a broad grin on his face despite the quizzical looks that greeted him.

'Merry Christmas Peter, this be a right nice surprise.' He sat down, and the chair creaked.

Perched at the end, they were too far away for Barbarian Brown to overhear.

'You were right about Muller. Breakfast on me. I wanted your opinion on something else. Yesterday I saw the Simmer and Jack wagon taking gold to the bank.'

'That be right. Once a week usually, takes it there for safe-keeping.'

'I'm sure they didn't drop it all off. After they deposited six crates in the bank, the escorts and the wagon guards left, just leaving the two drivers. They went and met another wagon and one of our Irish friends. They took some empty dynamite crates into the wagon. I couldn't see what happened inside, but when the crates came out, they seemed very heavy - must have been gold.'

Jory scratched his chin. 'Security be very tight at Simmer and Jack.'

'There would be a discrepancy in the manifest,' Sanderson said. 'A difference between the amount the mine said they were delivering and the amount the bank signed for.'

'Could the wagon be loaded with more gold than is on the manifest?' Leroux said.

Sanderson thought about it a moment. 'But then there would be a discrepancy in the mine's stock-take, more gold would leave than was being recorded.'

'I be not involved in the records, but I know they keep a close eye. Every miner that leaves the shaft be searched – and I mean everywhere,' Jory said, grimacing.

'Could the discrepancy be at the bank end?' Sanderson said.

'But why?' Leroux said, 'Firstly you'd have to assume they were in league with the Irish, and if they signed for more gold than they received they would just owe Simmer and Jack a lot of gold. It must be at the mine end.'

'Has Hammond found anything?' Sanderson said.

'Not yet.'

'Mr Clement manages the mine. He's a good friend of Mr Hammond, from back in America, and well thought of,' Sanderson said.

Jory nodded. 'Victor Clement be a good man.'

'I met him last night. Doesn't seem the sort to be involved in something like this,' Leroux said.

Sanderson rubbed his scalp. 'But it could be someone in the office.

High enough up to have access to the records.'

'Are there any Irish at the mine?' Leroux said.

'A few diggers,' Jory said, 'but none with access to the records.'

'One, if not both of the drivers of the wagon were Irish. And they were the only ones left with the wagon when they switched the gold. Do you know them?'

'No. The security for the delivery comes from head office. The drivers and the guards in the wagon. And they get an escort of Zarps.'

The waiters brought breakfast out, and the table conversation died down. Leroux lowered his voice and changed the subject. 'Why do they call him Barbarian?'

'He was one of the editors at the Coeur d'Alene Barbarian, a mining paper in Idaho. He opposed Hammond there. Still writes occasionally for the Standard and Diggers News, pushing Kruger's line that the Randlords are no friends of the workers.'

'Sounds about right to me,' Jory said. The conversation around the table built up again and Leroux leaned forward. 'Last night two of the Irish tried to jump me in my room.'

'What happened?' Sanderson said.

'I'm still here, but one of them said some strange things before he died.'

Sanderson's head was in his hands, but Jory grinned from ear to ear.

'He said, "It should never have happened" with my father. When I asked him why, he said, "He got greedy."'

'Who got greedy? Your father?' Sanderson said.

'I'm not sure. Maybe. Father had just got a report from the assayer confirming the purity of the ore, just as you said, Jory. Maybe he had agreed to sell the mine and tried to increase the price?'

'Or maybe your man was talking about the buyer. Maybe he didn't want to pay a fair price?'

'I tried to ask him, but all he said was, "We're after the same thing, you and me."'

Jory shook his head. 'Irish be always speaking in riddles.'

'Then, as he died, he recited a poem. It was about the Irish. The only words I remember are, "Our hope and strength, we find at last, is in ourselves alone."'

Sanderson looked up beaming. 'I know those words!'

'You recognise the poem?' said Leroux.

'Not the poem, but the phrase "Ourselves alone." It's the Gaelic League slogan.'

'Who are they?'

'They are for a free Ireland, and willing to fight for it.'

'You think the gang at Maddox Deep are Irish nationalists?' Leroux said.

'The man who died saying those words was.'

'What did he mean by "we're after the same thing"?'

'Gold? Maddox Deep?' Jory said.

'No, I think this man was an idealist,' Sanderson said. 'They're called Fenians and have been active again since Salisbury and the Tories won the election last summer. The Home Rule legislation for the Irish is well and truly dead with them. Your man is fighting for independence from Britain.'

'But I'm not after that.'

'What if he thought your father was a Boer?' Jory said.

'The Boers want to keep their independence from Britain, that could be what he meant,' Sanderson said.

'It's possible,' Leroux said.

'They're ruthless men. I'm not surprised they came for you. Ten years ago, they were bombing stations in London. They hit Victoria and Paddington, called themselves the dynamitards.'

'What do they want with Maddox Deep?' Jory said.

'They want to hit the British anywhere they can,' Sanderson said. 'And they need to finance their operations. Maddox deep could help with the money end of things. It looks like they are operating some type of protection racket as well as a smuggling operation.'

'The Randlords need rifles.' Leroux said.

'But they have their own supply routes and mines to store them,' Sanderson said. 'And why would they steal money from themselves?'

Waiters bought out more coffee and champagne for the table, but Jory got up to leave.

'I be getting back. I'll ask quietly about the gold deliveries, one of the lads might know something.'

'If you find out the day of the next delivery,' Leroux said, 'we might be able to catch them in the act.' Jory nodded and shambled out of the room.

'The Irish Nationalists have one enemy, Britain,' Sanderson said.

'This points to the Germans again, despite all their denials. I couldn't imagine the German Government, or even Muller, dealing with the Irish Brigade. But an Irish Nationalist group, that's different.'

'I saw Brandt last night. He said something interesting. Until I know whether he is acting in good faith or not, don't repeat this to anyone.'

'Understood.' Sanderson's eyes were sincere with the earnest look of someone who yearned to be trusted with something important again.

'Brandt claims there is a division in the German Government. The Kaiser and his supporters, and Muller is one of them, want to challenge British aggression against the Republic, even if it means war. Maybe even bring in America, France or Russia with them.'

'The Germans would be natural allies for the Irish. Maybe the Irish are preparing a base in Johannesburg for them and act as a fifth column.'

'Brandt had an unusual proposition. He wanted to work together to stop such a war.'

They moved outside to a quiet table on the veranda.

'That's an admirable aim. But if the Germans think you're onto them, they might be trying to distract you.'

'Or worse. If they're in league with the Irish and Brandt's lying, I'd be walking straight into a trap.'

'What about the Baroness?'

'I'm sure she is on whatever side Brandt is on. But she doesn't like Marais, and Marais thinks she is up to something. His condition is getting worse. I saw Muller corner him at the party last night and I thought he was going to faint. He's jumping at ghosts, and if he's not careful, he could let something slip. He's not right.'

'I'll see if I can find anything out. If there's a problem, Rhodes will want to know. Marais is crucial. They need Land En Volk to get public support for any move against Kruger, and his ally Joubert to lead the men.'

'I met JC Manion last night with Marais.'

'He's the US consul here, well connected and likes to let people know. He's close to Senator John Morgan of Alabama, Chairman of the Senate Foreign Affairs Committee. He'd be the person to ask about the risk of war with America.'

'He was in a bumptious mood. Marais took him aside for a conversation, maybe that's what he wanted to know about.'

'I might have a new lead on the Irish as well,' Sanderson said.
'Go on.'
'I was at Slack Alice's last night. I have a friend there, Daphne. She said that yesterday some Irish turned up. Not the usual ones who provide the bouncers, a new lot, keep themselves to themselves. They've taken to using one of the big rooms there as a private meeting place. It seems that they couldn't use wherever they used before.'
'If they're from Maddox Deep or the Ferreira Street office they might think someone is watching those places.'
'Exactly, my boy. Now, my Daphne saw some of them arriving. A right mixture of rough and smooth, clean and dirty. Her boudoir is above that meeting room. She couldn't quite hear what they were saying. And when they left, they went in one's and two's, some out the front, some out the back, and went different ways.'
'Is there any way she can tell if, or when, they will come again?'
'Alice normally uses the room for soirees, but it's been reserved during the day for all next week, probably by them. She has no way of knowing when they might come, but she should know as soon as they arrive, either coming in one of the entrances or hearing the activity from her room.'
'Would she do that? It'd be dangerous.'
'We are old friends. She's not getting any younger and wants a life away from Alice's. I'm happy to assist her. She will help if she can. I asked her whether we could lift some of the floorboards to see if we could hear them.' Sanderson's eyes were bright now.
'We need someone to keep watch.'
'David will do it. There is a chandelier in the room below. If we remove one of the fixing bolts, I think we may be able to hear through the hole.'
Leroux drained the last of his coffee.
'When do you want to do it?'
'Right now. It'll be quiet. And if it works, what a story! The scoop of scoops!'
Sanderson scrunched up his napkin and tossed it in front of him. He got up and stretched out, and for a moment, the yellowish tinge left his skin.

Leroux went to the concierge to collect a hamper and met Sanderson at the front of the hotel. He lifted a jar of preserves showing Sanderson the heads of two monkey wrenches lying underneath and hailed a cab.

'They rustled that up quick,' Sanderson said.

'I already had it on order. I'm taking Miss Sinclair for a picnic later.'

A few minutes later, they pulled over outside a church before the end of Plein Street. The congregation spilt out, and children played and ran among the departing folk who chatted as if for a day everyone had agreed to forget a revolution was in the air. Leroux and Sanderson walked up Plein Street and approached a bouncer who tipped his hat at Sanderson.

'Merry Christmas, Mr Sanderson. A bit early for you. Who's your friend?' The accent put Leroux immediately on edge.

'New gentleman in town, I'm showing him around, and I have a gift for Daphne.'

The bouncer eyed Leroux up and down. 'Any weapons?'

'No.'

'Plenty to choose from today, but you might have to wake them up. Nobody else around.'

The bouncer stepped aside. Inside, the gloomy reception had benefited from an early morning sweep, but no one attended the front desk, and the lamps were cold. The stale smell of forgotten nights hung in the silence.

'Don't mind him. He's part of the furniture. I doubt he's connected with your friends.' Sanderson picked up a bell from the desk and rang it.

'I'll say you're here to see Maggie. She's a friend of Daphne's in the next room. She won't say anything.'

Movement stirred above, and shuffling footsteps descended the stairs. Leroux and Sanderson waited with their hats held over their groins as a middle-aged lady appeared, clenching a ruby satin dressing gown close around her. She squinted at Sanderson. 'Is that you Harry? What are you doing at this hour? It's Christmas Day for heaven's sake!'

'I have a gift for Daphne. My friend here is new in town. A long journey and I thought of the perfect Christmas present. Is Maggie around? Leroux this is Alice, the most important lady in Johannesburg.'

Alice eyed Sanderson.

'Giving my Daphne ideas is what you're doing. Don't you go getting her hopes up. Go on then, you know where they are. And settle your account before you go, it's been running up.' Alice laboured back up the stairs, retying the cord around her gown, her bright red curls bouncing with every step.

Sanderson led Leroux to the second floor and knocked gently on a door. The runner in the corridor was sticky, and the odours of cologne lingered for want of airing.

'Go away,' came a muffled plea from inside.

'Daphne, my dear, it's Harry.'

The door cracked open, and a puffy-eyed lady stood before them. Her skin was clear of make-up, and her hair scraped up. She looked in her mid to late thirties.

'What are you doing here so early?' She rubbed her eyes and flinched back. 'Is there someone with you?'

'Please don't worry, you remember what we discussed yesterday? The meeting room downstairs?'

'Yes, oh come in, I didn't realise it was that urgent.'

Leroux followed Sanderson in. The room was tidy with a small double bed, a chest of drawers with a pitcher of water on it, and a long narrow brass framed mirror hung on the wall opposite the bed. The one extravagance was a coromandel screen. A tree, birds and flowers were intricately picked out in gold leaf on black lacquer in an oriental style. A red silk night dress hung over the top of the middle panel, and behind in the corner of the room was a small stool and desk with a newspaper, pen and ink. Daphne drew back the curtains. The sunlight silhouetted her figure through her cotton shift, and Leroux proffered the basket as she turned back around.

'I'm very grateful for your help. I know it's asking a lot.'

Daphne set the basket down. She was childishly pleased, and Leroux wondered how long it had been since she had received an innocent gift from a man.

'Well, I'm nearly finished with this place. Harry has been teaching me to read and write. Every day he goes through the paper with me.' Daphne smiled and rested her head on Sanderson's chest. 'I've enough saved up, and I'm going to open my very own coffee shop next year. Harry will help me.' She draped an arm around him, and Sanderson squeezed her in return and nestled his head down on hers.

'I paced out the chandelier. It's six steps in from the window downstairs which is in line with the window here. I haven't heard anyone this morning.'

Leroux and Sanderson got to work. They rolled back the rug and lifted the floorboard which was in between the bed and the chest set against the corridor wall. Underneath were four bolts rising through the ceiling in a square arrangement, two on each side of a joist. The bolts passed through angle brackets screwed into the joist, with nuts to hold them in place.

'You loosen one here, and I'll go with Daphne and pull the bolt through from below.'

Leroux took the monkey wrenches from the basket and saw the small look of disappointment on Daphne's face as she left. By the time Leroux had worked one of the nuts loose, he could hear the door closing in the room below. He twisted the bolt to show Sanderson the one he had freed. Leroux heard furniture move and then scrabbling, and finally, he felt the bolt gripped from below.

'I've got it,' hissed Sanderson. Leroux gently tapped on it, and between them, they worked it free.

Daphne and Sanderson returned to the room as Leroux put the floorboard back.

'How does it look?'

'I don't think anyone will notice.' Said Sanderson. 'No one ever looks up, apart from sailors.'

He went to the window, which was over an alley at the back of the building. 'We'll get David on lookout down there. As soon as you hear anyone in the room, give him a signal, and he'll come and fetch us.'

'What kind of signal?' Daphne said.

'Just wave until he notices.'

'What happens if I have a customer? It's not often busy during the days, but, you know, it would be awkward.'

'How about if Leroux pays for what you would normally get, Alice will get her cut and won't fuss, and you say you're not feeling well.'

Leroux and Daphne looked at each other.

'Don't worry Leroux, stick it on the account, Rhodes will understand.'

'I'll say I've got an itch, that'll scare 'em off.'

'Good,' Sanderson said, 'Let Maggie know she was supposed to have been with Leroux for the last half an hour. We'd better get going.' He indicated to Leroux to provide some cash and then ushered Leroux out and gave Daphne a modest peck on the cheek. The house slumbered on as they stepped out into the bright daylight.

'Merry Christmas.' Sanderson lifted his hat to the doorman, who smirked and raised his eyes skyward, and they walked back towards Height's.

'We'll have to make sure one of us is at Height's in case David comes. I'm happy to volunteer. Let me know where you're going to be, and I'll set up camp in the bar,' Sanderson said.

It was a motley team thought Leroux, but they were making progress now. He ought to let Hammond know about the new Irish angle.

'Do you know where Hammond is?'

'The talk at breakfast was of a meeting at Colonel Rhodes's house on Saratoga Avenue. They expect Younghusband to return from Cape Town.'

'I'll go there.'

Leroux felt uncomfortable without his revolver and collected it from Height's on the way to Saratoga House, Colonel Rhodes's mansion. Younghusband's train was due at eleven o'clock, and he would be arriving at any moment. The grounds bustled in anticipation, guarded by Captain Roland Bettington and a dozen men in plain clothes. He recognised Leroux and waved him through. Judging by the security, the Reformer leaders had already gathered inside. At the front door, a sentry with bright pink cheeks that clashed uncomfortably with the burnt red brickwork stiffened to an interpretation of attention and opened the door.

Hammond, Phillips, Farrar, Colonel Rhodes and Leonard waited in silence in the library. Hammond gazed out of the window. Rhodes stood rigidly as if waiting to be told what to do. Phillips, Farrar and Leonard fidgeted and paced up and down.

'Leroux? What are you doing here?' Hammond said.

'It's about the men at Maddox Deep. They are not just outlaws. They are Irish Nationalists. They attempted to kill me last night.'

'Those bastards bombed London a decade ago and murdered Lord Frederick Cavendish,' Colonel Rhodes said. 'I'll take some men and go and give them a damn good thrashing.'

'I know you would love nothing better. Frank, but we must be careful,' Hammond said. 'If we start a fight with them, it will attract attention. Kruger would claim that he had to send troops in to restore public order, and that would be the end of the flotation.'

'But the Fenians are terrorists!' Colonel Rhodes said.

'I agree with your sentiment, but it's not our country - yet. Leroux has been investigating the links between Maddox Deep, the Irish there and the Germans. He has a theory that they are working together, isn't that so?'

'It's possible sir, the German consulate denies any connection, but it does look like the mine is German-owned. And they would be natural allies, although I have yet to find anything other than circumstantial evidence.'

'Which makes sense,' Hammond said. 'And what Kruger and the Germans would dearly love is for us to attack the mine and give them the justification for crushing us before we are ready. It would bring down international condemnation on our heads and take the Transvaal out of our reach. I believe it is a trap. We must be patient. I have sent some men from the Simmer and Jack mine nearby to observe.'

Phillips, Farrar and Leonard looked relieved that a calm head was prevailing.

'So, what are we to do?' said Farrar. 'Dr Jameson is getting restless. He fears the Boers know his position. If they start to call up the Commandos, he will have to move quickly or face a tough fight just to get here.'

'Jameson must be patient too,' Hammond said. 'On no account can he start before we are ready. The Colonial Office will disown any blatant violation of the treaty, and we'll be on our own. We must stick to the plan. A rising by the citizens, declare a new government with our Boer allies and then appeal to Dr Jameson to protect us from retaliation by Kruger.'

'But we don't have enough rifles yet,' Phillips said. 'Without them, we won't be able to fight off Kruger's men.'

'Frank?' Hammond said.

Colonel Rhodes cleared his throat. 'We have more shipments coming in this week, another two thousand rifles at least. Williams is arranging for them to be smuggled by train from Kimberley.'

'That will be enough,' Hammond said.

'This plan is changing as we speak,' Farrar said. 'I fear we are moving too fast. We said we would need at least ten thousand rifles to deal with the Commandos. From what I've heard we'll have at most four thousand. We must delay!'

'Together with our Boer allies, four thousand will be sufficient. We may not be able to beat Kruger, but he won't be able to take Johannesburg. In that event, the Colonial Office will step in with the threat of British troops and demand free and fair elections. With one man one vote, Kruger will be gone.'

'We will be putting the civilian population at serious risk,' Leonard said, 'if Kruger thinks he can take Johannesburg.'

'I will also have Marais publicise that there are twenty thousand rifles and a dozen Maxims on the Rand,' Hammond said.

Colonel Rhodes grunted. 'That should make Kruger think twice.'

The atmosphere was tense, and Hammond was struggling to maintain the conspirators' confidence. Leroux thought the better of raising his suspicions about the Irish and the train shipment from Port Elizabeth.

'There are more rifles at Maddox Deep.' Leroux said. 'I've seen them. When the time is right, I would like to volunteer to lead a party to seize them. I know my way around the mine.'

'That's a good idea,' Hammond said. 'But not until we're ready. Understood?' He seemed relieved that someone was searching for solutions rather than problems. A commotion outside prompted Hammond to move to the window.

'Good. Younghusband's here.'

The small gathering turned to the library door in expectation. Captain Younghusband cut a determined figure despite his long journey, but he looked worried as he entered the room.

'I am sorry to report that Rhodes insists on the British flag. I believe that the indications of support he received from the Colonial Office depend on it.'

'We must delay until this is resolved,' Phillips said.

'He must see that the Uitlanders will not risk their lives for the British flag,' Leonard said. 'And our Boer allies will certainly not fight for it.'

'We will have to change his mind,' Hammond said. 'There is no alternative. We all understand that he wants Kruger gone and the Transvaal under the British Empire. But he must also see that it can't be done in one step. The second step will naturally follow in time.'

The group all nodded and muttered their assent.

'Leonard,' Hammond said, 'catch the next train to Cape Town. Explain this to Rhodes. You are the best man for it, and it must be in person. Take Fred Hamilton with you, Rhodes respects his views too.'
Phillips coughed. 'Given this uncertainty and the shortage of rifles, surely delay is the prudent course.'
'We must look at all the factors, gentlemen. Jameson is raring to go. He is concerned that the Boers have discovered his location and wants to move before they raise the Commandos. It is all we can do to hold him back. Just as Jameson must not jump the gun, we must not lose heart.'
'So what date are we going for?' Colonel Rhodes said.
'There is, ah, one more thing,' Younghusband stammered, 'The Times requests that the rising not take place on a Saturday.' He looked nervously at his audience. Leroux looked down and bit his cheek to prevent himself from laughing, and then glanced at Hammond, who was shaking his head in frustration even as a smile seemed to spread across his lips. Would he accommodate the lack of a Sunday edition of the Times?
'The National Union Meeting meets on the 6th,' Hammond said. 'Kruger will expect that to be the trigger for the uprising. We must act before then to gain the advantage of surprise. Jameson will need it. I propose the 3rd of January. A Friday.' Hammond inclined his head to Younghusband.
They all looked at each other. Leroux judged that Phillips and Farrar were the most uncomfortable, but neither spoke against it. Younghusband wiped his brow. Hammond had just managed to hold the group together.
'Leonard, you will have had time to convince Rhodes by then. We have Jameson's word not to act until we give the nod.'
Leroux doubted Jameson would hold back. He was not a by-the-book army type. He had never actually served in the army and had been spectacularly well rewarded for not holding back during buccaneering private expeditions. Queen Victoria had even given him the Order of the Bath. It would take more than an order to deny him an opportunity of death or glory. If he thought the Boers were mobilising to block his path to Johannesburg, it was an even chance he would jump the gun.
'I'm worried about Jameson,' said Phillips. 'He has that letter and can put whatever date he likes on it. It's all our names at the bottom. We

need to make sure he follows the plan.'

'Agreed,' Hammond said. 'We'll send two messengers to remind him in person. One can go cross-country, and the other can take the train to Mafeking and ride from there. They'll make it in plenty of time.'

'Friday 3rd then?' Colonel Rhodes said.

The reform committee all looked to Hammond.

'Gentlemen, we have a date. Frank, make plans for the militia to form. Leroux, you will take Maddox Deep. But we must be discreet until then.'

Leroux collected another picnic hamper from Height's and hurried to the telegraph office. Mrs Beeton would have been proud, although it was far too much for the two of them. A small joint of cold roast beef and a pigeon pie. Sandwiches of salted meat with cress, lettuce and celery. Grated cheese mixed with chopped nuts and a miniature sweet steamed plum pudding. To drink; sherry, champagne, brandy and ginger beer, all in a sturdy wicker basket with a blanket on top.

Lara waited after her shift. If she was pretending to be cross, she stopped when Leroux brought her up to date with events.

'Are they still following you?' she asked.

'I haven't seen anyone today.'

'This came in last night. I didn't bother sending it to the hotel as I knew you were coming. Just as well.'

'You must take care too, Lara, the Fenians are ruthless. What does it say?'

'It's from Rhodes. He is not aware of any Irish involvement in the "flotation." That's the term he uses when referring to the plot.'

'That's a relief. Better reply that we suspect the Irish are Fenians. Also, Baron von Veltheim is an alias for Karl Frederic Kűrtze, a deserter from the German Navy in Wilhelmshaven. I believe Muller plans to provoke the Reformers and Britain into breaking the peace treaty and draw international condemnation or worse from Germany and potentially America, Russia and France.'

'That's quite the update. But Rhodes can't take that to the Colonial Office without some sort of verification. How do you know?'

'For now, say I discovered Muller is a Colonel working for Abteilung 3b, the military intelligence section of the German Army, highly secret. It's new, run by Field Marshal Helmuth von Moltke. That should give credibility to the information.'

Leroux watched her write and hoped she was impressed.

'And I think your idea about the message being the arrival time of the train from Port Elizabeth is right.'

'I haven't got anywhere with the code. My best guess is that it's a book cypher, where both sender and receiver use the same passage in a book to decipher the code. I've worked with them before, but you can't get anywhere unless you have an exact copy of the book they're using.'

'How long would the text have to be? Could it be a poem?'

'A long poem maybe, but a book is much more likely.'

Leroux fished a few items out of the hamper for Kate and then led Lara to the cab. She was beautiful in a simple yellow cotton dress and had foregone her usual fedora for a straw boater with a blue ribbon. He helped her up into the carriage and sat back and looked up at the clear blue sky, happy for the first time that he could remember.

They were out of Johannesburg and heading north, away from the mines to a spot he knew well. A steady stream of traffic left town, but as he directed the driver down smaller tracks, they soon had the path to themselves. He found his spot, by a solitary tree, overlooking a stream.

'What do you use for protection on the highway?' Leroux said to the driver. The man reached back and produced a coach gun. 'Come back in two hours. Keep a watch at the top of the track there. If you see someone approaching, come and get me.'

He gave the man some sandwiches, ginger beer, and a good tip and then walked down from the track, through the long grass to the old tree, and laid out the picnic.

'It's wonderful.' Lara said, 'Have you been here before?'

'I used to roam all around here. But this was my favourite place. Watch down at the stream and you'll see game come.'

As they sipped champagne on the rug in the shade, Leroux's cares melted away.

'What kind of tree is this?' Lara asked.

It was a good question. Leroux had only ever known it as the shady tree.

'It's a shady tree.'

Lara rolled her eyes. 'Did you come here alone?'

'I came with my friend, Tom. We'd fish and fight and dance.'
'Fight?'
'Like cubs. Except with spears and sticks.'
'I'm not doing that. What about the dancing?'
'He taught me the Umsanzi. It's a Zulu war dance.'
'I'm not doing that either.'
'How about fishing?'
Lara looked down to the stream. 'Is that a Zebra?'
'Yes, look how well their stripes blend in with the reeds. They prefer it out in the open where they can see any threat. But when they come down to the bank, their stripes keep them hidden.'
They watched the animal drink its fill and then move off.
'Here,' Leroux said, giving Lara a small gift box. 'Merry Christmas. I'm not sure how I would have coped here without your help.'
She opened it and dangled the little bird on its silver chain and laughed.
'What type of bird is it?'
'Guess.'
'A dove?'
'No.'
'A thrush?'
'No.'
'An Ostrich?'
'Are you teasing me?'
'It's so easy! I'm sorry, and it's gorgeous, and I haven't got anything for you.'
Leroux topped up their flutes, and they ate under the tree.
'You must be getting used to the champagne lifestyle in town,' Lara said. 'What was the gossip from the party last night?'
Leroux tried to remember something. The only woman he could recall was the hostess. 'The Baroness was in a pale blue silk dress, with diamonds dripping down. The effect was quite stunning, like melting ice beneath her golden hair.'
'The Baroness again. Were any other ladies there?'
'Not that I remember.'
Lara lent back on the rug. High up in the sky, a bird circled.
'What's that?'
'An aasvogel, you call it a vulture.'

'What's it doing?'

'Looking for food. Somewhere a lion will have taken a springbok. And when the lion has had its fill, the hyenas dine. When they finish, the aasvogel will eat.'

Her face tilted up, radiant in the dappled sunlight, one hand shielding her eyes, her lips just parted. 'It goes round and round. What is it waiting for?'

'The right time.'

'Well, the aasvogel should read Voltaire and not let the perfect be the enemy of the good.'

Leroux looked up at the aasvogel, soaring free. Lara would never see anything in a farm boy like him. A movement caught Leroux's eye. The driver had returned, and they packed up and walked to the track. Leroux held out his hand for Lara as she stepped gracefully into the carriage.

'No sign of anyone on the road, sir.'

They came back into Johannesburg with the sun low to their right, the slag heaps on the distant ridge marked by shadows.

'Is it safe to go back to the hotel?' Lara said.

'I'll be careful, but the Irish coming after me could be my best way forward.'

'Won't you find them at Maddox Deep? They wouldn't leave the gold or the guns unguarded.'

'Hammond doesn't want any trouble there. If it escalated into a shoot-out, Kruger could exploit it.'

'What about their office?'

'I think they've abandoned Ferreira Street and started using Slack Alice's. Sanderson is watching there.'

'I'm sure he is. What will you do?'

'If someone is waiting for me at the hotel, I'll try and lure him away somewhere quiet, where we can talk.'

Leroux gave the driver the bottle of brandy from the hamper, the fare, and Lara's address. He couldn't risk the Irish seeing Lara with him and waited to walk the final hundred yards to the hotel behind a portly couple who had evidently enjoyed a good lunch. Leroux smiled to himself and crossed over the road before the man in the doorway opposite the hotel noticed him. With a felt hat pulled down over straggly hair, he was not there to celebrate Christmas, and Leroux bounded up the steps.

Sanderson sat in the bar, looking in remarkably good shape.

'Food agrees with you!' Leroux clapped Sanderson on the back.

'I'm sure Miss Sinclair agrees with you. How was the picnic?'

'As good as I could have hoped.'

'She's turned down grander than you and not given them as much time.'

'Any news from David?'

'No, he'll be back soon. They don't have the room booked for the evening.'

Leroux sat on the stool next to Sanderson. 'Something's been nagging at the back of my mind. The Baroness and Marais seem to dislike each other. He thinks she is connected with Veltheim in some way, perhaps trying to acquire assets secretly. And she has an aversion to him.'

'Did she say why?' Sanderson said.

'No. I don't think they know each other very well. It came across as a woman's intuition.'

'The brokers at the exchange didn't think much of his theory. And he looks worse every time I see him. That habit is making him paranoid.'

'Paranoid, yes, but he looks under stress as well.'

'I'll go and see him tomorrow,' Sanderson said. 'I've known him for a long time. He's had a rough spell, and there might be something he wants to get off his chest.'

David arrived. 'No signal at the window.'

'Can you get me a knobkerrie?' Leroux said, 'A small one, like a walking cane.'

'No problem, know many places.' And he was gone. Sanderson raised an eyebrow.

'It's my turn to do the ambushing,' Leroux said. 'I think there's an Irishman outside. They've got some explaining to do.'

'Can I help?'

'Don't worry. Get some rest, and let's reconvene tomorrow.'

David came to Leroux's room with the knobkerrie. It was perfect. It would pass for a cane, but the solid sphere on one end had a good heft without being too conspicuous. It was carved from a single piece of blackwood and, in the right hands, could be an effective club as well as a useful throwing weapon. Leroux tapped his hand with the knob end and remembered hurling one end over end to bring down small game out on the veld with Tom. Leroux put on his frock coat, best shoes, and top hat and strode out of the hotel like a gentleman into the dusk.

Over the road, in the darkened doorway, the watcher straightened up. Leroux walked north towards an alley he knew. As he approached the first crossroads, a piercing whistle blew from behind, and two men emerged from the shadows ahead. The odds had risen.

A low-slung two-wheeler Hansom came up from behind him. He let the horse pass and then darted out and jumped in the front, ignoring the driver's curses. He drew his revolver and spoke to the driver on an elevated seat behind him through a trap door in the hood. Leroux urged the driver on with a show of coin, and they sped past the two men at the crossroads who waved down a cab coming the other way. He looked back. A fourth man came up behind the watcher, and they also hailed a ride. They were all in similar cabs, but Leroux's had the marginal advantage of a lighter load, and the horse looked in good condition. It was uncomfortable seated above the axle at this pace, but the alley was just three streets further on the left. Leroux instructed the driver to slow a touch after the corner, then carry on and keep turning left until he arrived back at the alley to pick him up. The driver looked unsure, but some more gold ponds encouraged him, and he cracked the whip over the hood again. They raced to the corner. The cab turned and slowed. As soon as Leroux lost sight of the chasing cab, he leapt down, leaving his hat and coat behind. He scrambled along the pavement and ducked into the alley. Pressing back against the alley wall, Leroux glanced around the corner just as the first cab turned the corner. He waited, shrinking into the brickwork. The first chasing cab charged past, the whip cracked, and the axle squealed. If they kept up that pace, they would catch Leroux's driver before he completed the circuit. Leroux walked out of the alley, casually swinging his cane and staring after the cab, even as he heard the second one rounding the corner. He whirled around, feigned surprise, and dashed back down the alley. With a little bit of luck, the men ahead had not seen him, and the men behind would not be able to stop their comrades from chasing Leroux's cab.

The second cab stopped, and the two men jumped down and

appeared at the head of the alley. He could see the head of the cab's horse tossing behind them and flecks of frothy spittle caught in the streetlight. The men each took a side of the alley and started feeling their way in, peering into the dim recesses. Leroux crouched behind a stack of crates filled with rubbish. A little indirect light seeped into the alley from the windows and the street, revealing the moving shapes.

'Stop there,' Leroux said as though issuing an order to a commando.

'Give yourself up. We've got you outnumbered,' came the reply, harsh, but a tiny modulation in the tone hinted at uncertainty.

The shapes were still. Leroux had the better cover. The 7.5" barrel of the Colt Cavalry model was deadly accurate at fifty paces, and fewer than twenty-five separated them.

'Put down your weapons before I count to five,' Leroux said, as calmly as he could. He inhaled and waited. The men adjusted their stances to the sound of his voice.

'One.' No movement.

'Two.' Nothing. He aimed at the man on the other side of the alley, to the right. The angle gave Leroux more of a target. The man squeezed into a doorway, but a good chunk of shoulder protruded behind the sheen of gunmetal. The men muttered to each other.

'Three. I only want to talk.'

Two flashes flared out as the reports reverberated in the passage.

Leroux shielded his eyes, dazzled, and one round thumped into the crates while a metal pipe clanged behind him, shaking against its fixings.

Leroux opened his eyes, the shape in the doorway formed in front of him, and he squeezed. A satisfying grunt coughed across the ally. Leroux ducked back behind the crates as the other man fired and the bullet ricocheted off the brickwork above him. At the head of the alley, the horse bolted, the cab surging away as the driver struggled not to tip off the back.

A metallic rattle drew Leroux's attention back to the man hunched in the doorway, clutching his arm, his hand limp and empty at his side. The odds turned in Leroux's favour, but time was against him.

'Four. I know you're Fenians. Drop your gun, or your friend gets another. I just want to talk.'

'Wait.' Leroux let them mutter, but not too much, they would want to play for time.

'Five.' A thud as the second gun hit the dirt. Leroux peered around the crate and stepped out. He had four rounds left and the knobkerrie.
'Back up.'
They shuffled backwards away from their guns.
'Why are you trying to kill me?'
They looked at each other. 'Donal told us to,' the injured one said.
Leroux propped up the knobkerrie, picked up the first revolver, and threw it as far into the alley as he could.
'Who's Donal?'
He threw the second revolver after the first.
'Donal O'Connell.'
'He's your leader?'
'Yes.'
'Do you know who I am?'
'Your Pa owned the mine.'
Leroux walked past them and then backed towards the street.
'Why come after me?'
'You were sniffing around.'
'How do you know it was me?'
They looked at each other again.
'Donal told us.'
'Who told Donal?'
'We don't know. He goes somewhere with Finn, the young lad you killed last night.'
'Does he meet Veltheim?'
'Who?'
'Baron von Veltheim.'
'Never heard of him.' The injured man shook his head blankly.
'The gold you store in the mine - what is it for?'
'The cause.'
So, the gold transfers were being taken to Maddox Deep.
'The Fenian cause?'
'A free Ireland.'
'Who killed my father?'
The sound of hooves, wheels and traces reached into the alley. The men looked at each other, differently now.
'Who killed my father?' Leroux shouted from the end of the alley.
'Donal,' the injured one said in a low voice and looked behind Leroux

to the street. 'Would you like to speak to him?'

Leroux's driver reigned in the sweaty horses. The second cab appeared at the corner.

'Go get your guns,' Leroux shouted, staring down the long barrel as they hurried into the darkness. The torso of the chasing cabdriver stood proud of his carriage, tempting Leroux to try the knobkerrie. It would take the man down, but the fall at speed might kill him. He hadn't done anything. Leroux leapt into the cab.

The chasers had a dilemma. They had seen him, but if they chased their odds were now half as good. Or even worse as he had bested their comrades. The cab behind slowed and stopped. A lanky man with a top hat alighted gracefully and looked towards Leroux. It felt an age as those dark eyes bored into him before the man turned and strode into the alleyway.

'Thanks for coming back.'

'They pushed hard, but she's a good'n. Blowing a bit now, though.'

'No hurry, take the next turning.'

Leroux directed the driver to Lara's lodgings and kept watch behind. When he rapped on the door, the landlady opened it smartly and lectured Leroux on the importance of appearances as she led him up the stairs to Lara's set.

'Well, don't you look dandy!'

Leroux was conscious of his stained shirt and heavy perspiration and had forgotten he was in a frock coat, top hat and wielding a crude cane. He mumbled a reply.

'Is everything all right?' Lara asked and ushered him into the parlour.

'I underestimated them. But I managed to talk to a couple. They pretty much confirmed what we know.'

'They're Fenians?'

'Yes, and the gold is for their cause.'

'And your father?'

'Killed by their leader, Donal O'Connell.'

'Why?'

'I didn't have time to ask that. More of them were coming. But the odd thing was they had never met or even heard of Veltheim.'

'What about the other name he goes by, Kűrtze?'

Leroux cursed himself, he'd forgotten.

'Didn't have time to ask that either.'

Leroux looked down at his hat.

'It's lovely to see you, but why did you come?'

He worried about her safety. 'I need to send a message to Rhodes.'

'Of course. I can go in tonight or send it first thing.'

'Tomorrow's fine. Tell Rhodes their leader is Donal O'Connell. Scotland Yard may have some information on him.'

Lara noted the name and twisted a curl of hair. 'There's something very strange about this Veltheim or Kűrtze. There are just rumours, nobody knows him.'

'He's like a ghost. The Irish have never seen him. Muller told me I'd never find him, and Brandt swears that whoever he is, he's nothing to do with them.'

'What if Muller said that because he knew Veltheim is an alias?'

'Maybe. He seemed to be laughing at me. Perhaps because he thought I didn't know it was an alias, which I didn't, then.'

'Rhodes will turn something up on Kűrtze.'

Leroux got up to leave. 'Please take extra care. These men will do anything to get at me.'

'Don't worry about me, Kate'll be back soon, and the landlady can scare anyone off. You're the one that needs to take care.' She smiled and brushed down his shirt. He tensed as her hand glided down his chest.

'But if you don't, I'll have something to remember you by.' She lifted the chain out from under the neckline of her dress and the silver bird swayed below her chin as he turned for the door.

Leroux skipped down the stairs and back towards the main street and its electric lighting. As he walked, he could hear Lara's voice, feel her skin and smell her fragrance. Lost in his happy imagination, he turned the corner.

And straight into a fist, with a knuckleduster.

He crashed back against the brick wall, stunned. And the fist came again, in the same place, on his temple. He felt his knees buckle, and he slid down the wall. He tried to cover his head with an arm.

'Gotcha, yee bastard.'

Leroux struggled to focus his eyes. He heard a scrape on the floor and a smack on his ribcage. The spasm of pain sucked all the air out of him. That felt like the knobkerrie. He curled into a ball on the floor and looked up from behind a shaking hand.

'I thought it was yee,' the man said. The guard from Ferreira Street stood over him.

'Think you're funny? Well, Merry feckin' Christmas.' A boot found its way into Leroux's groin, and he gagged in agony. He lay on his side, gasping and straining to get up. The guard whacked him down again with the knobkerrie and then dropped it and drew his revolver.

He bent down, cocked the gun and shoved it along the ground and out of sight into Leroux's ribs. With his top hand, he searched Leroux's pockets.

'Where are the messages?'

Leroux's mind reeled, and he mumbled, 'What messages?'

The man shoved Leroux's head into the filthy pavement, pinning him on his side and leaned in with foul breath.

'From the office, yee took 'em.'

Dirt pressed into the cut, stinging, bringing him back to his senses. The guard's hand thrust into Leroux's coat and tossed his revolver aside.

'They're here.' Leroux took them out of his inside pocket with his free hand before the man found Rhodes's letter. He reassured himself that Lara had copies.

The Irishman glanced up and down the street.

'What do they say?'

'What?'

The muzzle of the revolver dug into his ribs. 'I can't read. Tell me what they say.'

'Rail, one, two, two, seven, five.'

The guard repeated the numbers to himself. 'Is that it?'

'The other's in code, just groups of numbers.'

The guard snatched them. 'Yee tell anyone else? Your German friend? Your lady friend?'

'No.'

The guard smacked the palm of his hand into the side of Leroux's head and ground his face into the street again.

'I'm going to ask yee once more. Anyone else?'

'No, nobody.'

A low whistle blew across the road. The guard glanced up. A young lady walked towards them from the south, about twenty paces away. The Irishman looked towards the whistle where another man stepped out of the shadow of a doorway. Leroux recognised the angular frame and top hat of the man in the second cab. He was the one in charge at Maddox Deep. Was he O'Connell? The guard turned to the sound of a horse and carriage trotting down the street from the north.

Leroux sensed a movement of the muzzle in his ribs as the guard adjusted his grip. Leroux's bottom arm was trapped under his body. The guard looked back at the girl. Leroux rolled forwards on to the revolver and smacked the guard in the face.

He felt the guard squeeze the trigger.

Click.

Bad practice. He hadn't checked his gun. The chamber that rotated into line as the hammer cocked was empty. He'd struggle to cock it again now. Leroux kept rolling into him, his body on top of the man's gun hand. The guard was trying to grab him with his top hand, but Leroux was inside, upper-cutting viciously and kneeing him in the groin. The girl let out a piercing scream and shrank into the wall. Across the road, the Irishman drew his gun and stepped out, and the carriage driver cracked his whip in alarm.

The guard's grabs at Leroux's face became feeble as his blows took their toll. Leroux pushed himself up, retrieved his gun and scrambled around the corner. A shot rang out from over the road, harmlessly wide. Leroux glanced back where the Irishman leapt onto the coach seat alongside the driver and lined up to fire again. The guard stumbled and reached for the side of the carriage, scrambling to get his feet on the running board. Leroux ducked back, breathed, and stepped out. He braced his revolver in two hands as the carriage drove away. The guard held on, and the man in the top hat had his gun aimed at the driver, who lashed his horses. It was a tough shot at the man who might be O'Connell. Too risky. The moment passed and the chance had gone. Leroux could feel those dark eyes staring back at him as the carriage receded.

Leroux checked on the young lady. She was shaking and reaching her hand out to his face. It was Kate. The adrenaline subsided, and he remembered. He felt his right cheek and temple. Blood and grit. Throbbing and stinging.

Along the street, windows opened, and curious heads popped out. Leroux picked up his knobkerrie and hat, and Kate walked him back to the lodgings where Lara already had the front door open.

'Kate, what on earth has happened? You look like you've seen a ghost. I heard a shot. Oh, Peter! It's you - look at your face!'

Leroux slumped in an easy chair and winced as his ribs protested. Lara fetched cloths, carbolic acid, and water while Kate went to see the landlady and make some soup for them all.

'What happened?' Lara said.

'The Irish either followed me, or they knew where you lived and gambled that I would come here.'

'The gunshot, are you–?'

'It was a knuckleduster that got me.'

Lara cleaned the wound with water and a solution of the carbolic acid. It hurt. Wincing hurt even more.

'It's opened a cut from the top of your cheekbone to the temple, but it's clean now and stopped bleeding. I'll put a dressing on, and a doctor can stitch it tomorrow.'

'They got the messages.'

'I took copies, don't worry.'

'I know. But there was something about them. The man couldn't read and asked me to say them out loud. I can't quite place it, but we're missing something.'

'Rest now and sleep on it. I'll make a bed up here.'

Leroux thought about the landlady. 'I should go back to the hotel.'

'And leave Kate and I to those outlaws?'

Lara settled the argument by preparing a bed on the sofa. Leroux got up gingerly and felt his ribs.

'Show me.'

Leroux took off his shirt and turned side-on.

'What on earth have you done?'

'I got a whack on the ribs.'

'No, not that, your back.'

'I got shot.'

'That's quite a scar.'

'The bullet hit my shoulder blade, and the surgeon struggled to get the fragments out.'

'When?'

'Just over a year ago.'

'What were you doing?'

'It was during the Malaboch rising. We were on patrol and got caught by a war party. They shot my commanding officer in the hip and chest. We'd nearly made it back to the wagons, and some men came out to help with him when one of the warriors got me.'

'Is that what the commendation was for?'

Leroux nodded. 'How did you know about the commendation?'

'It was in the report I sent to Rhodes. You don't like to talk about it?'

'Bad memories. It all seemed wrong. The warriors tried to attack the wagons. They didn't have a chance, and we slaughtered them. Cut down by the Maxims. The officer died later that day of his wounds. And I got a commendation for being shot in the back.'

'The report cited your bravery and deeds throughout the patrol.'

'All those men fought bravely, and they gave more than me.'

Kate returned with the soup.

'There's not much we can do about the ribs other than rest,' Lara said.

'I don't think they're broken,' Leroux said tentatively prodding them.

'Was that a knuckle duster?'

'Knobkerrie.'

'I thought you were supposed to be the expert with the knobkerrie.'

'Ouch, don't make me laugh.'

They ate the soup in silence. Leroux sucked the last from his spoon and said, 'I was sure they didn't follow me here tonight. I watched all the way.'

'Then how did they know to find you here.'

'They've been watching me for days, but I've never been here before.'

'What about the driver that dropped you off?'

'I don't think so. I was only here ten minutes before I went back, and they were waiting around the corner. What are the chances of them finding the cab driver so quickly? None, I'd say.'

'Were they just looking for the message?' Lara said.

'That's all they asked about. And I think they'd had enough of me poking around.'

'Did he say anything else?'

'He didn't know what the message was. It wasn't that he couldn't read it and wanted to check it was the right message. He didn't seem to know what it said. Maybe they weren't just trying to keep it secret, maybe that was the only copy they had, and they needed to know what it said.'

'How did they know to come here?'
'Wait. He asked if I'd told my German friend or my lady friend.'
'Who–'
'You must be the lady friend,' Leroux said, a little too quickly.
'–is the German friend?' Lara said with a hint of a smile.
'Must be Brandt. He's the only one I've had any real discussions with. And he took me to Dresdner Bank, which is what led me to the office and the messages.'
'Well then, they were told by someone who knows you, me and Brandt, and knows where I live or how to find that out.'
'Somebody or somebodies.'
'Muller?' Lara said.
'Together with Pienaar, a definite possibility.'
Leroux shifted on the sofa and grimaced. 'Wish I hadn't given that brandy away now.'
'We have some.' Kate went up to the sideboard and poured out three tumblers.
'Every time,' Leroux said, 'that I want to believe Brandt, that there is no connection between the Germans and Maddox Deep, something like this happens which points right back at them.'
'Maybe he's not in on it? Who else could it be?' Lara said, 'Any names, however unlikely, that would know to come here.'
'I tell everything to Sanderson. I just trust him. Everyone dismisses him as a has-been, but he's wise in a way, and well-meaning.'
'He's down on his luck,' Lara said. 'Maybe susceptible to inducement. But I've always thought of him as sweet, albeit a little seedy.'
'We keep Rhodes and Hammond informed on everything.' Leroux ruffled his hair and regretted it. 'But that makes no sense, the Irish are working against them.'
'The Baroness? Could she know through Brandt?'
'Possible. Marais is suspicious of her. But I would swear she's with Brandt, and Brandt led me to Ferreira Street and the message. And if he's the German they asked about it wouldn't make sense.'
They sipped their brandy.
'Marais?' Lara said.
Leroux thought back. 'I've only told him a few things. I don't think he knows that we meet.'
Lara raised an eyebrow. 'You might not be the gossiping type, but

Marais is.'

'And he looks like he's going to fall apart under the pressure of the flotation. They're relying on him and his paper to bring the Reformer Boers with them.'

'Who knows that we think the message is a train arriving from Port Elizabeth?'

'Just Sanderson. But he was the one that made the connection with the rifles.' Leroux stifled a yawn.

'Sleep on it now,' Lara said. 'But Muller looks the most likely.'

Leroux knocked back the rest of his brandy.

'I think I know what Donal O'Connell looks like.'

'How?'

'It's just a guess, but earlier I saw a skinny man in a top hat jump down from one of their cabs, and he looked in charge. He was there again outside, in charge. And I think I saw him at the mine. Didn't have the hat on, but had the same way about him, the way he moved, lithe. And he was giving the orders there as well.'

'Can you remember anything else about him?'

Leroux closed his eyes and pictured the times he had seen him. 'Tall, slim. The hair was longish, over the collar and dark and thin. The top hat was tatty. I can't see the face, I was always at a distance, but it was unshaven, and the eyes were dark as night.'

He rested his head back. Lara perched on the edge of the sofa and adjusted the light dressing on the wound.

'I had the chance to shoot him.'

'Who?'

'O'Connell.'

Lara looked him in the eyes. Her lips just parted.

'Why didn't you take the chance when you had it?'

'There was someone in the way.'

'I'm off to bed, goodnight.' Kate said.

Lara stroked the dressing and brushed his hair back with her fingers. Leroux's eyes were closed.

'We never did get to do that coding,' Lara whispered and kissed him on the forehead.

Boxing Day, 1895

Dawn broke quietly in the spotless parlour. Leroux rubbed his face and remembered where he was. He stretched and wished he had not. Lara and Kate emerged into the soft grey light and fixed breakfast and plenty of good Boer coffee from the Magaliesburg mountains.

'Have you had any more thoughts?' Lara said.

'Just questions. The Irish seem to be running a protection racket or just stealing gold to raise money for their cause. But somebody else must be helping them. And what are they doing with the guns? Too many for their own use.'

'What will you do?'

'I've got to find out one way or another if Muller is with them. Rhodes is relying on me to follow up any connection with the Germans.'

Lara nodded. She seemed to approve. 'I'm going in for the early shift now. Why don't you go to the hotel and get a doctor to put in some stitches? I'll send any replies from Rhodes to you there. You need to rest. I'll come and see you when I finish work, and if you've got something to tell Hammond we'll go and find him – they're hosting a reception later today, aren't they?'

'Is that a yes?'

Leroux followed Lara down the stairs. She fetched a bicycle from the back hall, and he watched her all the way to the main road, when she turned, waved, and was gone. Leroux followed in the same direction to find a cab as the town began to wake.

The clerk at Height's reception avoided Leroux's eyes. He hesitated to say something and seemed worried. 'Mr Leroux,' he said finally, 'there is a message for you.' He fetched an envelope from the pigeonholes behind him. Leroux opened the envelope, while the clerk fidgeted with his gloves and finally blurted it out. 'The manager would like to see you.' The clerk disappeared before Leroux could reply, presumably to inform the manager.

The message was from Jory. The delivery drivers on the Simmer and Jack wagon had changed about two months ago, about when his father died.

The manager bustled out from a back room.

'Mr Leroux, we have a serious problem. This cannot continue.'

His tone did not show much deference to Leroux's top hat and coat, although the overall effect was more crumpled and beaten than smart.

'This what?'

'First, we have police and two dead bodies. Blood everywhere. And now your room has been ransacked, turned upside down.'

'When?'

'I presume last night, the maid reported it earlier this morning. I'm afraid we must ask you to leave.'

'I wasn't here. Somebody else has done this. Was the room broken into?'

The manager stammered. 'No, I'm not sure, but that's not the point. You attract trouble, and we have other guests and our reputation to consider. You will leave this morning.' He stared accusingly at the wound.

Leroux had not wanted to use Rhodes's letter, but moving now would interrupt his communications just when he needed them. He pulled the folded note from his coat and passed it to the manager.

'I am sorry for the trouble. I hope this will smooth things over.'

The manager shook it open and scanned down it, blinking. And then reread it, his lips moving. He removed his glasses, folded the paper with care and politely returned it.

'I see. This does change things. I hope I was not too hasty. Perhaps while we are repairing the room, we can offer you the Empire suite on the second floor? It's on the corner and has particularly good views.'

'Thank you, and please send for a doctor.'

Leroux checked on his old room. Someone had had a thorough rummage. Cotton stuffing spewed out of slashes in the mattress, and the desk lay in pieces. This felt more like Irish work than Muller's. Maybe the unscathed one from the alley had come back to the hotel while the other two had ambushed him. The office keys had gone and his file too, but no matter. He knew everything in it, and so did they. He picked up his old slouch hat from the floor. It didn't look any more battered than before. A maid came in and fussed, and Leroux left for the Empire Suite.

He walked through the sitting area and admired the adjoining bathroom, before opening the double doors onto the corner balcony. It had a clear view of both streets and over the lower rooftops across Johannesburg. The air, just this extra floor higher, was cleaner and clear of dust. He soaked in the bathtub until an elderly doctor arrived with a large bag. As he stitched the wound with silk, a message came from reception saying that Sanderson was in the dining room. The doctor gave him a bottle of laudanum for his headache and left.

Leroux went down and found his friend tucking into a late breakfast. Sanderson looked up and gulped the mouthful down. 'What on earth happened to you?'

'I had a disagreement with the Irish, but here's the news. The leader is called Donal O'Connell. They're using the gold for some scheme to free Ireland, and they were very keen to get those messages back. I think they needed to know what they said.'

'You rest here this morning -- you look like you need it. David's watching Slack Alice's, and if you're staying here, I'd like to follow up on our chat yesterday. I've known Marais for a long time, and he doesn't look well. Maybe something is bothering him, and maybe he can explain his suspicions about the Baroness.'

'Good idea. Try and find out what Muller was asking him about, it certainly made him look nervous.'

'The Land En Volk offices are in Pretoria. It's less than an hour by train, and I'll drop by The Star as well. There was some reporting on the Irish troubles a few months ago. I can't quite recall the details, but it might be useful. Should be able to dig out the back issues.'

'Good. I'll wait here, then. I want to check Muller out later. I can't think of any other way than just getting into the consulate. Maybe tonight.'

'Will Brandt help you?'

'I don't know if I can trust him yet.'

'What do you need?'

'If I can get onto the roof, I think I can get in. Do you know anything about the layout or where Muller would keep information?'

'Rhodes has been attempting to get a mole in there for years. Keeps trying to bribe the cleaners, but they're very cautious who they hire. The only thing I've heard is that the library on the first floor is off-limits.'

'I've seen Muller in a room on the first floor, looking out the window.'

'That could be it.'

'What about neighbouring buildings?'

'Three doors down you'll find the Burlington House Store. I know the owner. I'll let him know you'll drop by. You should be able to get on the roof from there.'

'Good, anything I can do while you're gone?'

'It's the Summer Stakes today at Turffontein. If you can get anything on Gauteng Lad, I'd appreciate it.'

'Consider it done.'

Breakfasted, Sanderson set off with a boater on his head, and a paper and fraying umbrella under his arm, while Leroux went to the clerk on reception.

'Mr Leroux, good to see you up and about and looking much better. Is there anything I can do for you?'

'Yes, there is. Please send someone out for twenty yards of rope and a grappling hook and put ten ponds on Gauteng Lad in the Summer Stakes. I'll need the rope by two p.m.'

'Right away, sir.' The clerk rushed off with his notepad.

Leroux returned to his room, took a slug of laudanum, and went to sleep on the crisp cotton with the windows and balcony doors wide open, and the curtains flapping softly in the light breeze.

He woke to the tinkling of glass and sat bolt upright. He heard a scream but couldn't tell if it was from the hotel or outside. He leapt out of bed and onto the balcony in just his drawers and scanned both streets. There was a carriage making haste away from the hotel. The hood hid the occupants, but the driver was working the horses hard. A man over the road was pointing at the carriage talking to his neighbour.

BOOM!

A shower of glass and debris blew out from the hotel, one floor below, where his old room was. Yellow smoke billowed out. Feathers and fragments of cloth floated down towards the street.

Passers-by stopped and stared up at the blown-out windows. Two Zarp troopers galloped around the corner, and the passengers on a horse-drawn tram pressed up against the glass to peer up. Leroux recognised the sound and the smoke. Dynamite.

The manager would want another word, and he needed to write another article. He pulled the bell for room service, and a wild-eyed house boy appeared in moments.

'Don't worry, sir, building is strong. No fire.' He looked terrified.

'I heard a scream before the explosion. Was there a maid in the room?'

'Yes, but she got out. She said a brick came through the window and it was smoking. She ran.'

'Sensible lady. No-one else hurt?'

'No, sir. Manager upset. Big light fell down in dining room.' Leroux stifled a grin and waited for the knock on the door which came half an hour later, as he lay on the bed, propped up on cushions, his article nearly finished.

'Come in. It's open.'

The manager entered, huffing. 'Mr Leroux. Really! This is the final straw!'

'Is there something wrong?'

'Yes!' He waved his arm in the direction of the window. 'The explosion. It's destroyed the room. The guests are most alarmed–'

'*I* am alarmed - men getting into my room to search it or assault me. Your security is atrocious! There are two Zarps outside. You should pay them to stay there!'

'You must pay for the damage. And there's the chandelier in the dining room.'

'Me? Because a bomb went off in your hotel?'

'In your room!'

'This is my room.'

'Mr Leroux, we both know that bomb was because of you.'

'And we both know that you helped people get into my room.'

'Those three incidents were nothing to do with me.'

'I would believe you, but I only reported two of them.'

The manager's jaw kept moving, but no words came out. His head cocked sideways as though he was trying to think something through.

'You can put the damage on my account if I have no further trouble in this hotel. Remember, Rhodes and Sam Height are good friends.'

The manager nodded, wrung his hands and said, 'I'll make sure the maids and porters are all reminded of their responsibilities.'

He turned to leave as someone knocked on the door. It opened slowly, and the reception clerk shuffled in, carrying a length of rope and a grappling hook. The manager scowled at him and turned to Leroux. 'And what is this?'

Leroux thanked the clerk, tipped him prodigiously and turned back to the manager. 'I noticed earlier that this building doesn't have a satisfactory method of escape from fire.'

Leroux finished his article, and a message arrived from Sanderson. He had arranged for Leroux to see Mr Roberts at Burlington House at four p.m. That would give him time to scout the nearby buildings. Then see Hammond, and then when it was dark, and the consulate staff had gone for the day and were either celebrating after the racing or at Hammond's, he would go in. He owed Brandt an answer, but he had to know what Muller was doing first.

His article described the atmosphere of a phoney war. Like Johannesburg thunderstorms, the clouds often gathered, but you never knew if they would break. Both sides were entrenched in their positions and distracted by other events. The Uitlanders gambled on the Summer Stakes, while the Boers celebrated Nagmaal, their quarterly gathering for Communion. There was a light tap at the door, and Lara came in.

'You didn't mention you were staying in the Empire Suite!'

'I've just moved.'

'The guests downstairs are talking about an explosion. They said it was a water heater.'

'It was my old room. Dynamite. Must have been the Fenians.'

'I leave you on your own for a few hours, and you're already in trouble! I've got a message from Rhodes.' She handed the note to Leroux. It simply read:

NO FURTHER INVESTIGATION UNTIL FLOTATION STOP END

Leroux cursed. 'Well, I can't help it if they investigate me.' He screwed up the message and threw it in the bin. 'I watched you cycling. You were really good.'

'Oh, I love the bicycle. There's a torchlight parade tonight at the Wanderer's Club. Why don't we go? I can arrange a bicycle for you.'

'I'm going to break into the consulate.'

Lara saw the rope and grappling hook on the table.

'What are you looking for?'

'I'm not sure. Something that tells me whether the Germans are connected to this or if I can trust Brandt.'

'What about Rhodes's message.'

'If anyone asks, say you sent it here and that you haven't seen me today.'

Lara chewed her lip and looked down. She picked up the article, as if to change the subject, and read it. 'You write beautifully, Peter.'

'I've got my mother to thank. She's a teacher.'

'You weren't just running around with your sticks and spears then?'

'Not all the time.'

'I'll take this to Kate when you're gone.'

Another knock at the door and Sanderson entered.

'How was Marais?' Leroux said.

'I couldn't find him. He wasn't at his office, and they didn't know or wouldn't say where he was.'

'He might be at Hammond's later. I'll look out for him there.'

'There was something odd, though. There was a visitors' book for the directors' offices. I looked back through it to see if Muller or somebody else that Marais might be worried about had signed it.'

'Was there anyone?' Lara said.

'Nobody I recognised. But someone had torn a page out. Between the 10th and 16th of December.'

'Muller wasn't here then. We arrived on the 23rd,' Leroux said.

'It could just be that Marais didn't want Kruger's spies to know who he was meeting,' Sanderson said.

'They would be looking for ways to accuse him of treachery and acting in the Randlords' interest.'

'I was thinking on the train back from Pretoria,' Sanderson said. 'If Muller provokes the Reformers and Jameson to commit an act of aggression and break the treaty, Kruger, with the backing of Germany, and maybe the Orange Free State and the Cape Dutch could kick England out of South Africa.'

'Muller might be using the Irish to create an incident.' Leroux said. 'Maybe that's what the guns are for.'

'Rhodes and Hammond would be walking into a trap,' Lara said.

'I've spoken to Hammond. They're taking care not to cause an incident that could provoke war. They've sent messengers to Jameson to remind him to wait for the rising, and they're holding back from attacking Maddox Deep. Not to mention that telegram from Rhodes, warning me off.'

'What if the Irish aren't waiting to be attacked?' Sanderson said. 'What if they plan to take the initiative?'

'Maybe that is what the message is - the time they plan an attack. You said Port Elizabeth is where the Randlords' guns come from. Maybe they're going after the arms shipment?'

Sanderson leaned forward, his hands animated.

'A false flag operation. Muller tells the Irish to intercept the guns and act as though they are British. They overpower the smugglers, but even if they don't, there'd be a firefight. They capture the guns and then get arrested by the Zarps, caught red-handed smuggling weapons for insurrection and committing an act of aggression. The Germans profess outrage and declare that Britain is in breach of the treaty, and offer to protect Kruger, possibly with the support of other allies. The Randlords lose their weapons, and Muller kills two birds with one stone.'

'What's in it for the Irish?' Leroux said.

'Money? Striking a blow against the Empire? Support for their cause? Kruger would quietly release them when everything calms down.'

'If that's what Muller is planning, there must be some evidence in the consulate.'

'You had better get going to Burlington House. I'll wait here in case David reports,' Sanderson said.

Leroux gathered the rope and grappling hook in a bag and left to meet Mr Roberts at Burlington House. Three doors further down, the sentry stared rigidly ahead in the shade, guarding the front door of the consulate. Roberts welcomed him and showed him to back of the top floor, where Leroux could see along to the rear of the consulate. The buildings of the terrace looked similar in construction and Leroux made a mental note to collect a knife and a crowbar on the way back. After a few tries, he succeeded in snagging the grappling hook on a chimney stack. He climbed up and secured the rope around the chimney before returning to the hotel.

Lara wore a beautiful lilac silk dress, and she had wrapped a length of matching material around the hatband of her fedora as a puggaree. She cut a risqué figure, the effect heightened by Leroux sporting a black eye and swollen cheek below his top hat.

The two Zarp troopers stationed outside Height's cast admiring looks as Lara descended the hotel steps with her dark curls caressing her shoulders. When they entered the Hammond's mansion, heads turned hungrily at the mysterious new addition to their insular world. The party brimmed with guests, and many arrived straight from the racing at Turffontein and laughed a little too loudly. Leroux and Lara moved through the gathering looking for Hammond. Footmen attended to every need, with crystal goblets for champagne and gold plate for food. A solid gold replica of a mine-tower dominated the table decorations in the main reception room, and green damask adorned the walls. Only the library, which led off the main reception room, had been cordoned off. A feeling of fin de siècle permeated the room as the guests sprawled over the sofas, continuing to imbibe with abandon, and entertained by a talkative parrot in a gilded cage.

They found Natalie Hammond singing to the accompaniment of a piano, her reputation deserved. She flitted about the Steinway like a songbird in a pale green dress with yellow piping. The audience whispered that she had trained in Paris, and just as she trilled the final lines, John Hays Hammond marched in to lead the applause, snapping his hands together. He looked sober and irritated by the whole affair.

It would have been the last thing Leroux would have wanted either in the final stages of preparing a coup, but Natalie Hammond was in her element. A southern belle, Mrs Hammond hailed from Mississippi, her uncle a renowned Confederate General. She curtsied and touched her hand to her crimped hair and porcelain skin. She drank up the acclaim, and her laughter tinkled high notes.

Leroux guided Lara to John Hammond and introduced her. Hammond's eyes drew away from Lara at the sight of Leroux's injury.

'Everything all right, Leroux? I heard about the explosion at Height's.'

'The Irish have taken exception to my enquiries.'

'No trouble with the police I hope,' Hammond said and steered them outside where a small orchestra tuned up to the backing sound of cicadas.

'Let's try not to set anything off before the flotation. The reports I've had from the mine are that it's been quiet. Locked up and guarded. I'm keeping it under observation.'

'Sanderson has a theory that the message from the office is the arrival time of a shipment of rifles from Port Elizabeth and the Irish are planning to intercept it.'

'When is that?'

'5 p.m. tomorrow.'

Hammond thought for a moment. 'How sure are you about this?'

'It's only a guess. But they took desperate action to get the message back. It must signify something important, and it matches the train times at Kazerne.'

'And the production figures from Simmer and Jack are a little light. You could be right about the Irish.'

'How much below your expectation are they?'

Hammond grimaced and scratched his moustache. 'Five to ten per cent.'

It was probably closer to ten thought Leroux.

'Sanderson has another theory. If the Irish are working with the German Government, they will do more than just intercept the weapons. They will start a firefight, and the Germans will present it as proof of aggression by Rhodes. That will be the excuse Germany needs to offer Kruger protection from the British or worse.'

'He could be right. Intercepting our rifles could be the incident they want. I'll check with Colonel Rhodes and see if that is when the shipment is, and what we can do about it. But if they get some of the rifles, so be it. We must not start before we are ready. Not before the 3rd, Friday, everything is planned around that.' Hammond pulled distractedly at his moustache.

'But if the Irish succeed, and Germany offers Kruger protection, it will be too late to start.'

'This is just speculation, Leroux. It could be another trap, like us attacking the mine. We must stick to the plan.'

Leroux ground his teeth, but he could see from Hammond's hard-set jaw that there would be no swaying him. At least Colonel Rhodes might take some precautions.

'I'd like to keep an eye on Maddox Deep.'

Hammond looked keenly at Leroux. 'Captain Bettington is raising his horse militia on Monday at the Wanderers Club. They will drill there discreetly without weapons. I want you to go there and hand-select a troop and then keep a close eye on Maddox Deep.'

'That's another four days.'

'My men are watching it for now. We have another week to wait. Putting a troop of cavalry there before would be too risky. Kruger could take the fact that we have organised a militia as provocation enough.'

Mrs Hammond sashayed across the lawn and put her arm through her husband's. Her storied jewellery glinted in the last of the day's sunlight. The chunky amethyst ring had once belonged to Walter Raleigh, a gift from a grateful Queen Elizabeth I, while the gem-studded gold necklace that hung heavy around her delicate neck had reputedly been Marie-Antoinette's.

Leroux took Mrs Hammond's proffered hand and bowed. 'I see you are a fan of adventure and revolution.'

Natalie laughed, 'Well maybe that's my husband - he bought them.'

Hammond continued. 'Bettington's men will continue to parade at the Wanderers. They can be passed off as volunteers preparing to keep the peace. But you must be careful not to provoke any incident at the mine before the 3rd – is that clear?'

'Yes, sir.'

'We won't summon the other militia until then. We'll have different Uitlander Brigades – English, Scottish, Irish, Australian, Dutch and Americans – I'll call them the George Washington Brigade, as well as Bettington's Horse.'

The orchestra finished their warm-up and played Hail Columbia, a slow march that the Americans often used as a national anthem. JC Manion joined their small group and greeted Mrs Hammond.

'Why, my dear, you look as pretty as a yellowhammer.'

‘I’m sure you’re too kind, can we get some fine old music on?’

Manion went to speak to the musicians and when he returned the orchestra struck up “Dixie” as the sun bled out on the horizon. Natalie Hammond clasped her hands together at her chest and swayed softly singing the words from her childhood.

“I wish I was in the land of cotton,
Old times there are not forgotten,
Look away, look away, look away, Dixieland.”

Hammond stood dutifully staring at the players and flipped open his pocket watch. As the last notes faded, Manion raised his glass.

‘To new beginnings.’

‘Amen,’ Natalie sighed.

‘So must it be,’ Hammond and Manion murmured in unison. Hammond turned to Leroux, ‘Now there is something else that you can do. The time is coming, and we need to start stirring up the public and stoking the anti-Kruger flames. Support from the Cape Dutch will be important. We need a rousing article. Let me see, I think I could write it myself. Something like: ‘The Transvaal is today the last refuge of patriarchal despotism. The termination of the present system is evidently approaching, as a party is forming amongst the Boers to oppose the domination of the least advanced section of their society. Mr Lionel Phillips’s recent speech outlined a political manifesto on the part of the Uitlanders. Nothing less will satisfy them than purity of administration and an equitable share in the conduct of the affairs of the country, which they intend sooner or later to obtain. President Kruger was born one hundred years too late. The Uitlanders have hitherto been orderly in their conduct and have endeavoured to avoid resorting to violence. But President Kruger is putting their patience to a severe test, and he would do well to listen to their grievances. Soon, the Helot system organised for the exclusive advantage of a privileged minority will no longer be able to resist the force of enlightened opinion.’ There that should do it, did you get it all?’

Leroux nodded, his heart sinking. He indicated to Lara that they should leave, and as they turned to go two horsemen appeared out of the dusk and cantered up the drive to the house. Mrs Hammond gasped in delight.

'I do believe that it is Mr Marais. Why, he is the most charming man, the finest flower of civilisation of any man I have known. We are fortunate to have him on our side.'

When Leroux saw Marais, something nagged at his mind, something that felt wrong. Hammond excused himself and walked to greet the arrivals. The other horseman rode erect in the saddle, uniformed, and with a huge head. Leroux recognised him as his old commander, Commandant-General Piet Joubert. Sweat streaked his horse, and he patted its neck as he dismounted and caught his own breath. He exchanged greetings with Hammond and opened a leather saddlebag and drew out a portfolio.

Leroux scanned the other groups. Muller stood with a group of German businessmen but was not engaged in their conversation. Instead, he seemed focused on Hammond, Joubert and Marais, and must have sensed Leroux's gaze, catching his eye and holding it with a chilling look. And then Leroux realised what was bothering him about Marais. Someone had removed the page of visitors covering the 10th to the 16th of December. Alfred Jones had gone to the German consulate asking about Baron von Veltheim, and then he disappeared on the 15th. Could he have gone to see Marais? Did the Germans follow him and know?'

Joubert and Marais passed their horses to a footman and walked with Hammond towards the house as dusk fell and the first guests drifted away from the party. Leroux took Lara's arm and led her to the reception room next to the library, where he assumed they would go for a private meeting. Leroux tried the door, but it was locked. Hammond would arrive at any moment, and they slipped out onto a deserted terrace. Above some shrubbery, some twenty feet away, was a window looking out from the library.

Yellow light bathed the guests inside the reception room who turned to see the tall General with a full white beard stride through after Hammond. He was deep in thought and still wearing his slouch hat as Marais hurried to keep up with him. Muller slipped unobtrusively into the room after them, and Lara shivered and clasped her hands about her arms despite the warm evening air.

'Watch Muller,' Leroux said and slipped off the terrace, along the wall, and into the undergrowth beneath the window. He tried to ease open the window, but it was fastened, and he moved to the far side, flat against the brickwork. Two sofas faced each other, with a large desk behind one of them. A sideboard decorated with decanters occupied the only wall space not covered by books.

Leroux looked back to the terrace and Lara, her face lit by the pool of light spilling from the reception room. She had never looked more beautiful, her drink tilted in her hand, still hugging herself.

The library door opened, and Hammond entered, followed by Joubert. Hammond turned and locked the door while Joubert took a document out of the portfolio and set it on the desk. He glanced up at the window and Leroux froze. Joubert looked away and said something to Hammond and Leroux inched to the side and slid down the wall and into the bushes. Even if Joubert had seen something, he could not have recognised him. The window rattled as Joubert tested it. Leroux peered through the leaves. Muller had joined Lara out on the terrace and was looking over towards the window. He seemed to be searching for something but then talked to Lara. Leroux kept his head still, his eyes moving back between Lara and Joubert standing at the window. Joubert glanced left and right into the darkness and then stared left at Lara and Muller before drawing the curtains closed. Lara and Muller reacted to the change in light, both looking towards him. Muller hopped from foot to foot as he talked and then walked towards Leroux up to the edge of the terrace. Leroux held his breath. Could Muller see him in the shrubbery without the light from the window? Lara raised her voice and walked to Muller's side, touching his arm. He frowned and turned to talk to Lara while watching over her shoulder back into the reception room. Lara rubbed her arms, as though she were cold and moved to the reception doors and looked in. Muller glanced back at the library window, and abruptly went inside, leaving Lara on her own.

Lara continued peering into the reception room and discreetly beckoned Leroux.

'Muller watched Hammond and Joubert go into the library,' Lara said, 'but when the door shut, he came out here. I think he had the same idea as you, but I tried to keep him talking. He gives me the creeps.'

'What was Marais doing?'

'He stood outside the library door.'

'Hammond locked it from inside. They weren't taking any chances.'

'I saw Joubert looking over towards us before he drew the curtains.'
'I just saw Joubert take a document out of his wallet. I couldn't hear anything.'
'Marais left with Joubert, and Muller went in and followed them.'
They walked around the side of the house to the front, where two grooms provided Joubert and Marais with fresh mounts. They trotted out of the gate and into the night.
'What did Muller talk to you about?'
'He tried to ignore me at first, but I reminded him that we had met at the telegraph office. He asked me who I recognised. I pointed out Marais, and his lip curled. I don't think he likes him. He didn't say much else. He seemed distracted and irritated.'
'Let's go in.'
They found Mrs Hammond to thank her, and she was talking to JC Manion, who cradled an empty champagne flute in one hand and flourished the stump of a cigar in the other.
'An unexpected pleasure to see the General,' Leroux said.
'I hear he was summoned back urgently by Kruger,' Mrs Hammond said.
'Kruger is a wily old fox,' said Manion. 'Keeps his enemies close, right where he can see them.'
'You think he ordered Joubert back to Pretoria?' Leroux said.
'That's the word,' Manion said, prodding the air with his cigar. 'And taking Marais with him. A whole lot rides on those two.'
'The mining shares could certainly do with some help. I understand the American market is suffering too?'
'Only speculators betting, Mr Leroux. Look around you. The compressors, drums, electrical hoists, power drills, pumps, even the wheat and timber come from these businessmen and bear the nameplates of New York, Philadelphia and Chicago,' Manion said gesturing with his arm at groups of Americans. 'Hell, most of the chief engineers on the Rand are Americans.' Mrs Hammond looked sharply at Manion after the cussing, but he continued. 'Gardner Williams introduced American methods and machinery back in Kimberley. He earns twice what President Cleveland does.'
'I don't doubt the success of the businessmen,' Leroux said tiring of Manion's haughtiness, 'but will it come quickly enough to prevent the drain on gold reserves and another bail-out from the financiers?'

'The President will be damned if he goes begging to Wall Street again, not in an election year,' Manion bellowed with a blast of stale breath and cigar smoke. Mrs Hammond scowled harder, tutted and led Manion away, rolling her eyes at Leroux over her shoulder. Leroux turned to see Muller watching him again as he left with Lara and took a cab to drop him at the hotel and then take Lara home.

Leroux changed and collected his revolver, knife and crowbar and concealed them under his coat. Outside Burlington House, Leroux surveyed the terrace. The sentry kept his lonely vigil, but all the windows in the consulate were dark, not even a glimmer of light crept out from behind a curtain. Roberts, the storekeeper, was waiting and hurried him inside.

'All quiet?' Leroux said.

'The few staff left at six. No one has come or gone since then.'

'Does the guard stand out there all night?'

'No, he usually goes in at seven. There's a staff room on the ground floor at the back.'

'Just the one?'

'I think so.'

'But he's still out there, it's after seven now.'

Roberts shrugged. 'Sometimes he stays out there later. I think when he knows somebody is coming.'

'Well, better out than in.'

Roberts led Leroux up to the back of the top floor again and opened the window. Leroux reached for the rope and hauled himself out and up. He unfastened the hook, coiled the rope, and slung it across his shoulder and chest. Overhead, clouds blotted out most of the stars, but it didn't smell like rain. Leroux traversed the intervening houses. The grip on the roof was good enough, and he felt his way along, his hands reaching over the top of the ridge tiles. Above the second house, his foot dislodged a loose tile. It skittered down over the edge, glanced the rim of the iron guttering with a clang and then disappeared into the darkness. A second later, he heard a dull scratch as it landed. He focused on his breathing, looked over his shoulder, and listened for any response.

Only the faint rumbling of the stamp mills carried on the breeze. A light came on inside and cast a brighter patch on the building opposite.

A window opened. A cat meowed, and then the window closed, and the light went off. Leroux shuffled further along until he was on the consulate roof, rigged up the rope around another chimney stack, and tied two loopholes, one at the end and one five feet up. He lowered it down so that the end was to the side of and level with the first window. Leroux made it fast and climbed down, standing on the lower loop with one foot and putting his arm through the higher loop, allowing him to lean over and look in. All dark. The construction of the window was identical to Burlington House. He took his knife and inserted it between the upper and lower sash and worked it along to release the catch and push the lower sash up. He swung his feet in and wriggled through.

He listened as his eyes took in the surroundings. Boxes of papers and supplies lay about the floor. He drew his revolver and moved to the door, opening it a crack. The top floor was still with no sign of light through any gaps at the bottom of the doors. He crept out and down the dark stairwell at the back of the building, stepping sideways on the treads, covering the flight below with his gun. Two doors faced him on the first-floor landing, one to the left and one to the right. It was in the second one that Leroux had seen Muller. He tried the handle - locked. The off-limits room. It was a solid wood door that opened away from him. He worked the claw of the crowbar between the door and the frame above the lock and paused. All still. He braced his weight on the bar and chewed his lip - there was no quiet way to do this. He shoved, and the wood splintered and cracked, snapping in the dark as the door sprung open. Quiet again. The sentry must have heard something. Better to move quickly now. He closed the door and struck a match. It was an office, with a solid mahogany partner desk to the right, one chair behind it and two in front. Shelves and maps covered the walls, with a large portrait of the Kaiser hung on the far-left end. The largest map showed southern Africa, with the German colonies highlighted in light blue. German South-West Africa, a vast arid expanse to the north of the Cape, had British Bechuanaland and Rhodesia to the east in pink. German East Africa sat on top of Rhodesia and Mozambique.

Leroux checked the curtains were flush to the walls and lit a lamp on the side table. He lifted one side of the portrait revealing a steel safe. The casing was an inch thick and impenetrable with the tools and time that he had, but it did confirm this was the right place. The desk had three drawers along the top and doors in the pedestals. The right-hand drawer was locked. He set to work with the crowbar, and it gave in quickly. It contained only a folded map which Leroux opened over the desk. It showed the western half of the Transvaal, and Johannesburg was circled in pencil, as was a small place called Pitsani, just over the border in Bechuanaland. From there someone had inked a dotted line, marking a route to Johannesburg. Pitsani was Jameson's base, the closest British territory to the goldfields. The dots passed right by his mother's farm, a reasonable route for the invaders to take, but not the one he would have chosen.

A creak.

'Have you seen enough, Mr Leroux?' That voice.

Leroux hung his head. How had he not noticed? He straightened to face Muller, standing in the doorway, pointing a Reichsrevolver, already at half-cock. Single action. Exceptionally reliable. He wondered whether the safety-catch was applied, as it usually was at half-cock. It might give him a split second.

'Hands Up!'

Leroux raised his hands. The tip of Muller's tongue flickered over his lips. The round lenses of his glasses glinted, reflecting the lamplight.

'You're very quiet,' Leroux said.

'You are very predictable. Stand in front of the desk.'

Leroux moved around. 'Your English is improving.'

Muller smiled. 'Slowly, drop your revolver on the floor.'

Leroux drew his revolver with just his finger and thumb and let it fall. Muller's eyes darted to the portrait of the Kaiser.

'Kick it to me.'

Leroux complied.

Muller moved closer, staying between the door and the desk, the gun levelled at Leroux's centre.

'So, Mr Leroux. What are you doing here?'

'You must know that my father was murdered at Maddox Deep. The more I look into it, the more I think you have something to do with it.'

'Why?'

'The ownership. And you followed me and searched my room.'

Muller placed his homburg hat on a side-table. 'Yes, you have been so busy. Tell me, what have you discovered about the mine?'

Leroux sought the eyes behind Muller's glasses. Still beady and glistening. He was a professional, extracting information, giving nothing away.

'It's a base for a gang of Irish. They are storing guns there.' He had already told Brandt as much.

'I think you have found out more than that.'

'They are stealing gold from the Simmer and Jack Company and keeping it there.'

'For what purpose?'

'They are Fenians fighting for a free Ireland.'

'And what do they plan to do?'

'Why don't you tell me? What are the Kaiser's plans for South Africa?' Leroux said, nodding at the portrait.

'I tell you this. If that is all you know, you have outlived your usefulness.' He released the safety catch.

Muller's voice was even and calm, without emotion. Leroux clenched, sensing Muller's finger squeeze on the revolver, imagining each piece of the mechanism pressing hard up to the release point.

'I am a British agent.'

Muller snorted.

Leroux hung his head. 'Your map is wrong.'

'Wrong? How?'

'I know the country well. I grew up in Krugersdorp. You have Jameson marching that way, but that is not where they will resupply.'

Muller's eyes narrowed. 'Show me.'

Leroux turned to his right and reached back for the map with his left hand. He held the near corner and started drawing it towards him and lifting it off the desk. Sliding his right hand back along the surface of the desk, he grasped the crowbar. He turned back around holding the map one-handed in front of him, then whisked it away and hurled the crowbar with his right, spinning end over end.

The crowbar clattered into the doorframe behind Muller, who ducked to the side.

As the map floated to the ground, Leroux leapt to his right, parting the curtains and smashing shoulder-first through the window. He tried to grasp something of a curtain, and he felt the material ripping from its fastenings as he crashed down onto the awning and managed to get a hand on the flag that hung limply down above him. He rolled and scrabbled for purchase. His feet hit the framework on the rim of the structure. It slowed him enough, and he rolled over the edge and on top of the sentry, just as he stepped out to check what was happening.

They collapsed in a heap to the ground. Leroux twisted on top of him and glanced up but couldn't see the window. Which meant Muller couldn't get a shot at him. The sentry looked up at him with a strange expression somewhere between astonishment, fear and anger. He tried to rise, but Leroux smashed him on the chin, and he slumped back, limp. Leroux rolled over and onto his feet and darted under the awning to sprint in cover along the street. At the corner, he turned to see Muller hurry down the front steps and berate the guard as he struggled to his feet. Leroux jogged down the next road back to Height's, trying to make sense of Muller's behaviour.

With a heavy heart, Leroux read through his notes and wrote up the article that Hammond had dictated. He resented the task and made hard work of it. There were real issues to resolve on the Rand, but Rhodes and Hammond planned a rising for their own benefit and for that of the British Empire. They stoked the divide between city folk, reliant on mining and commerce, and the pastoral settlers, who led devout, albeit antediluvian lives. Leroux felt inexorably drawn into the reformer's plot as he tried to pursue his father's killers. From being aware of it but staying silent, he would write an article gaining support for it, become an enabler of it, and then finally he would be on the front line, in Bettington's Horse, and fight tooth and nail for it. He felt sick. And Hammond did not even seem concerned at the danger of it spiralling out of control, spawning a far bigger conflict, destroying many more lives, although doubtless Hammond's would not be at risk.

Was Leroux imagining or exaggerating the dangers? If Rhodes pulled it off, would the German Empire really go to war to reinstate Kruger? That was unlikely if the British had done it without breaking the treaty, however affronted the Kaiser may be. Cecil Rhodes would have pulled off another brilliant coup to bring the Transvaal further under the British sphere of influence and solidify Britain's domination of southern Africa. Through commerce and geography, the Transvaal would slowly slide into a British United States of Southern Africa, and Rhodes's dream of a Cape to Cairo railroad would be realised, creating a continuous land route dividing the African continent from top to bottom with the Union Jack. With luck, the Uitlanders and Boers would avoid a bloodbath and flourish under the protection of the British Empire. Leroux doubted Tom would think much of it. Still, maybe that was a better outcome than the other alternatives - Kruger's Government hanging on by its fingernails, repressing a fabulously wealthy country with the backing of a small minority, which would ultimately lead to bloodshed - or the Kaiser getting the justification he required to declare war. Joubert was right. With so much gold at stake, nobody would let the people decide. Leroux turned the article over and stared at the blank side. He had made little progress. He had learned the identity of his father's killer, but he had made dangerous enemies, and if Rhodes and Hammond found out that he had ignored their instructions, he would have some more.

Friday, 27th December 1895

Leroux awoke with a start and took a moment to recall where he was. His bruises reminded him. He cleared his eyes with cold water and discovered new cuts and scrapes as he dressed before gingerly descending the stairs to breakfast. The clerk handed him a stuffed envelope and a message, mentioning that the message had just arrived as he entered the salon. Who would be sending one so early?

Go to 21 Ferreira Street 9 a.m. today for what you seek.

Unsigned. In an hour and a half. Was this a response to the advertisement for information on Veltheim and Thompson? It could be from anybody, but it was most likely a trap. Still, it was not as though he had any better options.

Muller was inscrutable. Leroux had discovered a heavy-duty safe, but they would increase security now. Had Muller come back by chance, or had he known Leroux was there? And had Muller been grilling him for information about Maddox Deep or was he checking how much Leroux knew and might have reported? Either way, Muller wanted him dead. As did the Irish, but were they working together?

Sanderson's theory had an arms shipment arriving this afternoon at five o'clock, and the Fenians would be keen to make sure Leroux did not interfere. He weighed the envelope in his hand and slit it open. It contained winnings from the Summer Stakes. Well, Sanderson had been right about that.

Leroux stretched back in his chair, blew ripples across his hot coffee and took a sip. It must be a trap. But is a trap a trap, if you know it's a trap? It felt like an opportunity he had to take. He had an hour to decide and turned to the fashion intelligence column, which eulogised Mrs Hammond's dress. A few minutes later, Sanderson arrived in good spirits, soon followed by more steaming hot coffee.

'How did it go at the consulate?'

'Badly. Muller caught me. Had to jump out of the window.'

'You didn't find anything?'

'Only that he knows Jameson's route and there's a big safe.'

'What do you think he plans for Jameson?'

'He's probably shown it to Kruger so they can prepare an ambush.'

Leroux passed Sanderson the message.

'It's a trap.'

'I know.'

'You're going to go, aren't you?'

'Considering it.'

Sanderson looked at his watch. 'Think it over. Did you see Marais yesterday?'

'I saw him, but no opportunity to talk. He came with Joubert, spoke to Hammond and then they left again. Seemed to be in a hurry.'

Sanderson sipped his coffee. 'Word is Kruger ordered Joubert back to Pretoria.'

'I heard the same. How do you think that will affect Rhodes's and Hammond's plans?'

'As long as he remains Commandant-General and leader of the Reformer Boers, he will have the credibility they need to form a provisional government and call on Jameson for help. But they'll have to make sure Kruger doesn't arrest him beforehand.'

'Hammond confirmed that gold is going missing from Simmer and Jack, he said their production numbers were five to ten per cent lower than they should have been.'

'That must have been embarrassing for him.'

'It's a lot of money.' Leroux did the calculation. 'The Rand produces about two and one quarter million ounces of gold or just over $40,000,000 worth in a year. Nearly half the world production. Ten per cent of that is $4,000,000. Let's say they are skimming from a third of the Randlords' mines. That's over a million dollars.'

'Or fifty thousand rifles if the Irish are buying,' Sanderson said and eyed the packet next to Leroux's plate.

'But they've only been operating a few months, if it started when the delivery drivers changed, which is about the same time as they took over Maddox Deep.'

'Still, enough to start a war.'

Leroux drummed his fingers on the table next to the envelope. 'We have to let them be for the moment. Hammond doesn't want to stir things up before the flotation.'

'Have you decided to go?

'My head says, don't.'

'And?'

'My heart says, go.'

'Rhodes would quote scripture at you, Proverbs, chapter sixteen, verse nine.'

'I don't know it, and I'm surprised you do.'

'I'll try not to take that the wrong way. The heart of man plans his way, but the Lord establishes his steps.'

Leroux knocked back his coffee and nodded for some more. 'You think I should go?'

'Your heart is telling you to go. And a message out of the blue like that feels providential.' Sanderson shrugged and smiled. 'Still, my life is not exactly a shining example of great decisions.'

'Can I borrow your gun?'

Sanderson tutted and took a small gun out of his coat pocket. 'It's supposed to be discreet.'

'It's certainly small.'

'I've just started carrying it and only fired it on the range.'

Sanderson handed it to Leroux, who turned it over and flipped the cylinder open, revealing five chambers. It was an old Webley British Bulldog revolver, with a stubby two-and-a-half-inch barrel, designed as a pocket gun. It looked in good enough condition.

'This is yours.' Leroux handed him the envelope and watched him crease with delight. 'Any news from Slack Alice's?'

'I saw Daphne last night. No sign of the Irish, but they reserved the room until the 29th. Must be waiting for something, maybe this shipment. Any reply from Rhodes?'

'Not yet.'

Leroux walked to Ferreira Street. He would be rudely early. A small cart stood in front of the office and the donkey snuffled in the dirt. He waited across the street. Nothing stirred. He went up to the cart which had boxes of papers in the back. The front door hung ajar. There was no movement or sound from the open window above. Someone was there. He drew the small gun out of his pocket and nudged the door. The air was fresh. The doors on the ground floor were closed. He took the stairs sideways, one by one, back to the wall. As he reached the half-landing, he felt a light breeze on his cheeks coming through the open door with broken glazing. The tread halfway-up would creak, and Leroux paused after four steps. The doors to the side rooms were shut. He skipped the next tread. Some papers rustled softly, strewn on the floor of the office. The donkey bayed outside as he crept up the last steps.

Leroux slid into the doorway, holding his breath. The desk stood unoccupied, not a soul to be seen. A draught tickled his neck. He spun. Facing him, a guard pointed a Colt, smiling, one hand gripping the side room door that partially covered him. Leroux recognised the man, with a fat lip from their fight outside Lara's that made his thin face comically lop-sided. Leroux's temple throbbed.

'Well, well, well. What in Jaysus's name are you doing here? Drop the bean shooter.'

Leroux let it fall.

'I couldn't believe me own eyes when I saw you out there.'

He waved his gun, motioning to Leroux to enter the office.

'I thought to myself, wonder if he comes in here looking for more messages?'

The office had been half-emptied. They must have sent the guard to clear it out, a small punishment for failure.

'And in you come.'

The shelves lay bare, and a couple of sheets of paper fluttered down from a stack on the desk.

'Pick up those and put them on the pile.'

Leroux retrieved the papers and took them over to the desk. The guard pocketed the Webley and moved into the centre of the room, still covering Leroux.

The stair creaked.

The guard jerked his head toward the doorway.

'Who the feck are you?'

There was no reply, but the guard looked concerned.

'This is none of your business. Get lost,' he said to the doorway while keeping his gun on Leroux.

A click of a heel and the barrel of a revolver came slowly through the door.

'I said, get lost… what do you want?'

Another step and an arm appeared, and then a man, Captain Brandt.

'I have orders to kill him.'

'Be my guest. Stop pointing your gun at me.' The guard's eyes darted back and forth between Leroux and Brandt.

'Drop it,' Brandt said.

'I have no quarrel with you. Kill him and go,' the guard said, his gun still on Leroux, but now looking at the revolver Brandt aimed at him.

'Drop your gun now.' Brandt had not even glanced at Leroux. His eyes bored into the guard, his distinguished features made menacing by the scar. The guard's arm wavered and then lowered, and he let go of the gun.

'You're messing in business that is nothing to do with you,' the guard said.

'I will be the judge of that.'

Brandt turned his gun on Leroux.

'Well, Mr Leroux. Muller has ordered me to kill you. I would need an exceptionally good reason not to. Do you have one?'

The guard looked confused, for the third time in as many minutes.

'Is it too late to take you up on your offer?'

Suspicion crept into the guard's face. His arms hung casually, but his right hand inched towards his pocket.

'It does not feel like a fair trade now,' Brandt said.

'The Irish are going to meet a train at five o'clock in the goods yard, Braamfontein. I think that's how they're getting rifles in, and I think they plan to start a war.'

The Irishman flashed a look of alarm at Leroux, and his hand slipped into his pocket. Leroux dived at him, wrapping his arms around the guard's body and drove him into the wall and down to the floor. The guard fumbled for the gun. Leroux could feel the shape of it in the guard's trousers and kept one hand clamped on it, pressing the short muzzle flat against the guard's leg and tried to jam some cloth in between the hammer and the pinhole with his thumb. The guard struggled to free the gun as Leroux's other arm gripped him as tightly as possible while attempting to butt him. Brandt stood back watching. The guard's other arm wrapped around Leroux's head, clawing at his face and eyes.

'He's got a gun,' Leroux shouted.

'What are you waiting for? Kill him!' the guard shouted at Brandt.

Leroux was losing. The guard had a firm grip on the gun and gouged his eyes. Leroux rolled off and pulled the material out from the gun mechanism. It fired. A hole smoked in the guard's trousers, and he wriggled to prop himself up on his elbows, pulling the gun out, but it snagged. The guard gritted his teeth, and then a bang and the wet slap of a bullet punctured him. His head lolled to the side and stared blankly at Leroux who lay panting next to him. Brandt had shot him in the heart.

'I wanted to talk to him,' Leroux said.

'He was just a foot soldier. And he had seen too much.'

'You sent the message?'

'No, Muller. Then he ordered me to shoot you. He's cunning. He's testing my loyalty. I'm sorry, but you are going to have to die too.'

Leroux looked up at the smoking barrel. He was prone. The guard still staring stupidly next to him, his mouth hanging open. He could reach the small gun in his pocket. But not in time. He followed the line of the gun's shape and the hole in the guard's trousers to a mark in the opposite wall where the bullet lodged. It must have come close to hitting Brandt. Not close enough.

'How would you like to die?' Brandt said and aimed his gun at Leroux's heart, between his eyes and back again. There was a glint in his eye. His mouth began to widen and crease. His teeth showed, and he roared with laughter.

'Your face! So serious! Come on, Leroux, we must make a plan.'

Leroux sweated profusely. It ran down his forehead and back, and he bought his hand to his pulsing cheek. Adrenaline coursed through his veins and the breeze through the window sent a shiver down his spine.

'What have you got in mind?'

'Everybody wants you dead, Leroux. The Irish, Muller, maybe others. I want to stop Muller. You want to stop the Irish. They may be working together, but either way, we both want to stop this developing into a catastrophic war. We need to find out what's going on. And that will be easier if they think you are dead.'

Leroux brushed himself down and sat on the edge of the desk. Rhodes had shackled him from investigating Maddox Deep, the Irish or anyone else. The timetable of the rising was slipping, and that would only benefit the Irish and Muller. This was the opportunity, today, with Brandt, to get at them. He could not bear the feeling of letting his father down again. And he would never forgive himself if he passed up the chance to prevent war engulfing his home. Sanderson and Lara would escape any blame if it went wrong. It may even prove difficult for Muller or Kruger to claim he was acting on behalf of the British, or the Randlords, if he was with Brandt. Being dead might be the perfect cover. And it would undoubtedly make things easier for Brandt.

The dead Irishman still stared vacantly. 'We can call the Zarps, and you tell them it's me.'

'He doesn't look anything like you.'

'They don't know that. Whoever's waiting for the Irishman is not going to report him missing. And if somebody identifies the body as me, the Zarps won't go looking for extra work.'

'Who do you trust to identify the body as you?'

'Miss Sinclair, Sanderson.'

'Sanderson?'

'You may think he's unreliable, but I trust him. And he's watching an Irish meeting place with me, which could be important. He has to know.'

'Just those two.'

'I'll need to tell Jory too, the big fellow from the train.'

Brandt accepted it and pulled Leroux's old Colt from his waistband. 'Here, you left this at the consulate. Have you got anything on you, that we can put on the body?'

'He's got the gun in his pocket. And the message from Muller will do. It's addressed to me and places me here.'

They searched the Irishman and put the message in his pocket before dragging him down the stairs to the front door. Leroux went back and looked through the papers, but there was nothing of note.

'Time for you to disappear.'

'I'll go to Lara's. It's on Bree Street, number fifteen. You'll find Sanderson at Height's. Tell him I said not to spend all the money at once and he'll know to trust you and let him know where I am.'

'What then?'

'The train arrives at the Kazerne goods yard at Braamfontein at five o'clock, from Port Elizabeth. I think there'll be a shipment of arms on it. I want to know what the Irish are doing. They might intercept it or attack it. Can you come?'

Brandt puckered his lips in thought. 'Shall we meet at Miss Sinclair's at three? I'll bring transport. You ride like a Boer, I assume?'

Leroux nodded and tied a neckerchief around his mouth and nose. No one would look twice, many wore them, or some other type of veil, against the interminable dust.

'You should do something about the black eye too.'

Leroux pulled his hat forward, went out and stepped up onto the cart's driving seat. He flicked the reins, and the donkey plodded on obediently. No one paid him a second glance as he looked back to see Brandt raising the alarm about his corpse. The cart creaked and rumbled along the dusty streets to Lara's lodgings, where Leroux explained the ruse. She made an eye patch, and he gave her the article he had written the previous night.

'Hammond wants this published. Say you received it first thing this morning.'

'What will you do now?'

'I'm going to watch Maddox Deep. I told Brandt I'd meet him back here at three and then we'll go to Kazerne and see who shows up.'

'I'll go to the office,' Lara said clutching the article, 'and I'll let Kate know you might be here.'

'I'm sorry to put you in this situation. You know Rhodes ordered me not to intervene, and I will do my best not to provoke anything. But this rendezvous is my best chance. Not only to get at O'Connell but to find out what they are doing.'

'I know. I won't lie to Rhodes if he asks, but I won't tell him if I don't have to.'

Lara tied the eye patch on and adjusted his hat. From most angles, it was hard to tell that he had an injury. Leroux drove the cart towards Maddox Deep and bought a selection of newspapers on the way. As the donkey picked its way over the ruts on the tracks outside of Johannesburg, Leroux willed an Irishman to recognise him and try and stop him.

By the time he went past Simmer and Jack, it was late morning, and he stopped at a roadside canteen just before Maddox Deep. It was more of a shebeen with sawdust on the floor, and he expected that the coffee would taste of it too, but at least he could see the entrances to both mines. He ordered coffee. Behind the small bar were shanties, roughly constructed from the zinc linings of packing cases and flattened out paraffin cans. They were windowless and too low for a man to stand upright. The air held a stench that even the smoke of the dagga pipe couldn't cover. The flies buzzed incessantly as if angered by their putrid surroundings.

Leroux called to a boy sat listlessly in the shade.

'Go to the mine there and give this message to a man called Jory, no one else.'

The boy nodded gratefully and scampered off. Leroux watched Maddox Deep. The gates were chained shut, and nobody came or went. The boy returned saying Jory would arrive soon after midday. Leroux crossed his palm and got back onto the cart and drove alongside the fence next to Maddox Deep, passing the gates and the padlocks on the chains. He stood on the driver's seat. New barbed wire ran along the top of the inner fencing that enclosed the mineshaft opening. They had replaced the little window, and the bar across the door rested in the open position. They weren't that sloppy. Someone was inside.

He stopped the cart, took a box of papers from the back and placed it on the ground next to the fence. Standing on it, he peered over the corrugated iron. Leroux selected a stone the size of a plum and launched it in the direction of the building. He jumped back up onto the papers to see it fall just short and skitter into the brick side of the building. Slightly further and surely the guard wouldn't ignore a clang on the iron roof. But before he reached for another stone, an urgent scrabbling and growling emanated from behind the building, and two huge dogs tore around the side and then stopped, heads high, sniffing the air. They couldn't pick up Leroux's scent, downwind. He picked up another rock and tossed it at the dogs. They sprinted to investigate, snarling and panting in the hot sun, only thirty yards away now. They were Boerhunds, a cross between the ferocious hunting dog used by the Khoikhoi people of the Cape and the Great Danes brought by settlers. Along the top of their backs, the distinctive ridge of hair grew in the reverse direction. Leroux stood proud of the fence and tossed another stone towards them. They spotted him now and came tearing at him, with full-throated barks and straining on their hind legs, tearing at the fence, stretching their forelegs up almost to the top. He ignored the snapping and slathering and watched the window. Something moved behind the glass, but Leroux could not make out any detail.

He stepped down, and one of the dogs snorted and sniffed around the base of the fence while the other still pawed and scrabbled at the top of it. The growling increased to baying as he stepped back up. No response came from the mine. Whoever hunkered inside lacked the curiosity of the hounds.

Leroux checked through the papers and finding nothing of interest threw them over the fence. It set the dogs off again, thrashing around and shredding the paper. He would at least get the Irish thinking about what had happened to their man. He drove the cart around the perimeter and saw no one other than the dogs. He turned back to the shebeen and waited for Jory with the newspapers, more execrable coffee, and one eye on the entrance to Maddox Deep.

Jory came at a quarter after midday, all smiles and sweat.

'Well look what the cat dragged in, who have you been scrapping with?'

'Irish. And they think they've won. I'm officially dead.'

'Is that what the eye patch is about?'

Leroux nodded. 'You remember Brandt from the train?'

'The tall one with manners?'

'Yes. I've made common cause with him, to go after the Irish. One of them tried to kill me, Brandt shot him, and the authorities think it's me.'

Jory put his hat on the table and sat at the bench, scratching his head and waving flies away.

'I'll not pretend to understand what be going on, but all be quiet here. No comings and goings from Maddox Deep, apart from those dogs making a row every now and then.'

'Have any Simmer and Jack men been watching the mine?'

'Not that I've seen. Business as usual.'

'I couldn't see anyone about either.'

Leroux tilted his coffee mug and threw the dregs on the floor.

'The Irish must have another hideout. They're not at their office in town, and they're not here apart from one or two lying low inside.'

Jory shook his head. 'I haven't seen them, but I found out the time of the next gold shipment. Next Thursday, the 2nd.'

Leroux jogged his knee and tapped the table. 'That's a long time to wait. The Irish have something planned for this afternoon at Kazerne goods yard. There's a chance they may come back here afterwards. Will you keep an eye out? Won't be before six.'

'No problem. And good luck. I've a feeling you'll be needing it.'

'If anyone asks, you haven't seen me.'

'No one asks me.' He laughed and walked back to Simmer and Jack in his familiar style, his body rolling from one step to the other. Leroux returned to the newspapers for another hour, but nothing stirred at Maddox Deep.

Frustrated, Leroux headed back to Lara's, where he found Brandt and a groom tending two horses. Brandt sent the groom away with the cart.

'He works for the Baroness. He doesn't know you and, in any case, can be trusted not to talk.'

'How is Muller?'

'He has taken a great dislike to you and couldn't get enough of the details. I was worried at one point he would go to the morgue just for the satisfaction, but he took the train to Pretoria.'

'What's he doing there?'

'He didn't say. He is not the type to reveal information unless he sees a clear benefit. On the contrary, he hoards it as though it were gold and will only tell you something when it helps you do something for him.'

'I told him the route he had marked out for Jameson's force was wrong. He may want to discuss that with Kruger or Joubert.'

'Was it wrong?'

'I don't know. It's not the route I would have chosen.'

'I saw Sanderson. He's quite happy at Height's and had no news. And I saw Miss Sinclair. She asked me to give you this.' Brandt handed Leroux a telegram. It read:

KURTZE KNOWN CRIMINAL STOP WANTED BY SCOTLAND YARD FOR MURDER IN LONDON STOP END

'It doesn't make sense,' Brandt said, 'that Muller would use a known criminal as a cover for a German operation.'

'No, I agree. But Kűrtze could be the sort of person the Irish Brotherhood come across. Who knows how their Machiavellian minds work? If they are in bed with Muller, maybe they thought that establishing a German-sounding connection would protect them from being double-crossed.'

'From what I have seen of them, I reckon you're over-thinking this.'

Leroux screwed up the telegram. 'You're probably right. I'm new to all this. I'm over my head and suspicious of everything.'

'You are still alive, which is better than Rhodes's last agent. Whoever is with the Irish knows you were on to them. They will be on their guard. Even if they believe you're dead, it will keep getting harder, until you succeed. Keep pushing.'

Leroux gave Brandt an appreciative nod and took solace in methodically checking over his horse and gear and cleaning his Colt, of which he had grown fond. He swung himself up into the saddle and rested his hands on the blanket roll and cape tied across the pommel. He looked up at Lara's window, but she was not there, and he turned the horse's head in the direction of Braamfontein and clicked his tongue. They set off at an easy walk. It felt good to be back in the saddle again, and his confidence in Brandt had grown. He had been good to his word and had a calm competence to him that would be an asset in a fight. Brandt had dressed down for the occasion, in moleskin trousers and a well-worn beige coat and felt hat. He could have passed for just another prospector, but his ramrod posture and scar were too proud.

'How does it feel to be dead?'

'So far, it agrees with me. But there hasn't been anything to see. Maddox Deep was quiet, although I'm sure there were men inside.'

'Muller was curious about the Irish,' Brandt said. 'He said he didn't know they were fighting for a free Ireland or that they were running some sort of protection racket on the Rand.'

'I couldn't tell whether he was asking me because he didn't know or because he wanted to know how much I knew.'

'I don't think he knew. It might have saved your life. I think he was surprised that there was so much about Maddox Deep that you had found out, and he hadn't. So, when you said the route he had for

Jameson was wrong, there was doubt in his mind as to whether you were bluffing.'

Leroux thought back to the moment. Muller was usually arrogant in his manner and sure in his tone, but just then he had hesitated. He had not been in command of all the facts and was uncomfortable. Maybe he did not know about the Irish, which left a big question. Who, if anyone, was helping them?

Leroux forced himself to think through the muddle again. He had assumed that the Irish were running guns on behalf of somebody. The man in the alley had said the gold was for their cause, perhaps the guns were too, and it was just a coincidence that they were doing this in the middle of the Randlords' plot to take over the Republic. Maybe O'Connell had used Veltheim as a ruse, to cover their real purpose. It had certainly confused Leroux. That would explain why the men in the alley had never met Veltheim or knew who he was. They were well informed, though. If the theory about the rendezvous was right, they were getting information on the Randlords' rifle smuggling operations. There were many republicans on the Rand who might sympathise with their cause and sell or even pass them information. The Irish also knew he had been investigating them and waited for him in the hotel, although they could have deduced that from the newspaper notice.

If the Irish were working alone, then Muller was not waiting to pounce on any incident involving them as justification for his plans. Leroux suddenly worried he had given him the idea.

The easy gait of his horse soothed his mind. The moving parts looked simpler under these assumptions. The Randlords were planning a rising for the 3rd, and Muller would try to provoke an incident before then. For now, Leroux could concentrate on the Irish, and Brandt seemed happy to help him.

'I think you're right about Muller,' Leroux said. 'How will you explain your interest in the Irish?'

'You've established they're up to no good. It is my duty to investigate whether they pose a threat to an ally of the German Empire.' Brandt raised his eyebrows in innocence and shook his reins.

'Do you know Braamfontein?'

'A little. There is a separate goods yard. We should find a place to observe who goes in and what they collect.'

They reached the yard and dismounted, handing the horses into the care of a boy. There was an hour until the train arrived. In the yard, a gang of labourers unpacked wagons and carts with goods for the train. Dust swirled around, ever more kicked up with each new arrival. Leroux squinted out from behind his neckerchief while Brandt shielded his face with an arm. Furniture and ornaments to be sent away for safe keeping were stacked up alongside the usual assortment of hunting trophies, tallows, ostrich feathers and aloes.

They found a spot where they could watch the rail wagons unload and keep an eye on the yard entrance. The porters sat chatting, and Leroux recognised the clicks and tones of the Tswana. Standing separately, the Zulus oversaw the pack animals. As the hour approached a steady stream of empty wagons entered the yard with their long trains of mules and oxen. On most wagons two local drivers sat upfront, one held the reins and a short whip, while the second worked the longer whip, for reaching the beasts at the front.

Leroux approached a solitary driver, hollering to offer his services to anyone there to collect cargo. He had an uncovered wagon and had treated the mules' backs well. They had a brief discussion, and Leroux returned to Brandt.

The yardmaster and two assistants appeared with schedules tucked under their arms and positioned themselves along the track. In the distance, small blots of smoke and steam heralded the arrival of the train, and the little dot of the engine grew bigger until the hissing and chuffing and screeching roused the porters to action. The couplings of a dozen wagons clunked a final time as the train shuddered to a halt. At the back was a tanker car, a large cylinder on its side emblazoned with Standard Oil Company lettering. A small yard engine approached from the rear and connected to it. Two railway men then uncoupled the car from the train, and the oil tanker was pulled away and shunted into a separate siding, where it disappeared into a shed.

The yardmaster barked instructions, and porters shuttled to and fro with freight, but nothing looked out of the ordinary. Stacks of crates and sacks grew in front of the wagons, containing all manner of supplies for industry and luxury. Paperwork passed back and forth between the wagoneers and porters.

At a quarter past five the Simmer and Jack wagon pulled into the yard. It had a larger team of horses than before, eight in total, and two company troopers rode alongside. Leroux did not recognise the drivers and the wagon trundled past the main goods area and over to the shed where it pulled up by a side door and waited in the shade.

'Everyone seems very relaxed,' Brandt said.

Leroux looked around the yard. 'No sign of our friends. Do you think my knowledge of the message has spooked them?'

Brandt sucked his teeth and concentrated on the wagon. After ten minutes, Brandt tapped Leroux. The shed door opened. Four men bought out large packages similar to the bundles of rifles Leroux had seen at Maddox Deep and loaded them into the wagon. There were no Zarps in sight, and the yard manager had taken no notice of the oil tanker. The Simmer and Jack wagon trundled towards the entrance.

'I thought you said the Irish were coming to meet the rifles. Simmer and Jack is part of Rhodes's operation.'

'I'm not sure what's going on. It looks as though they have converted that oil tanker to conceal weapons. But we should follow the wagon. Maybe they will intercept it on the way back.'

The wagon turned out of the yard in the direction of Simmer and Jack. The driver Leroux had spoken to earlier had not secured any business, and with a last doleful look around the almost deserted yard, he clambered up onto his perch. As Leroux rose to collect their horses, a new covered wagon arrived. He felt a chill down his spine. One of the drivers was the Irishman from the gold transfer.

'Don't look. This is them, I'm sure. I recognise the driver. Leroux turned his face away and crossed over to the solitary driver as he prepared to depart and hired him. It would look strange, two horsemen following the Irish wagon. They would naturally be faster and conspicuous if they held back.

The Irishman steered his wagon over to the shed, and the side door opened again. Two men jumped down from the back of the wagon. They carried three bundles out of the shed and then half a dozen small crates followed by a larger one. The two men climbed back into the wagon, and the Irishman promptly flicked the reins and headed for the exit. Leroux made a show of examining some aspect of his wagon's undercarriage and looked up just in time to see the Irishman turn out of the yard. Not towards Maddox Deep, but north towards Pretoria.

Leroux let the Irish go a few minutes ahead. He took a red flag from the back of the wagon, unfurled it, and slotted it into hoops fitted on the sideboards to indicate that they carried dynamite. He turned to the driver. 'Qhubeka!'

The driver clicked his tongue and cracked the whip. The wagon lurched forward, and they turned north after their quarry, who had picked up an escort of four riders. Leroux waved at Brandt who brought up the two horses and tied them off the back of the wagon and climbed aboard. It was not the most comfortable, but they fashioned makeshift seats opposite each other where they could watch fore and aft. They passed through the woods of Parktown and left Johannesburg behind. The road became rougher, and the wagon jolted and rocked along, and Brandt moaned that it was worse than being at sea. The wagon ahead came in and out of view as the road straightened and curved. The day was ending, and there were no other travellers on the road.

'The Simmer and Jack wagon headed for the mines,' Leroux said. 'They must have picked up the rifles they were expecting and then headed home to store them. After they left, our Irish friends arrive and collect what looked like rifles and ammunition from the same shipment. They didn't want to be seen by the Simmer and Jack boys, which suggests they're not in it together. But it seems odd that two separate groups of smugglers would use the oil tanker at the same time. Maybe they're paying off the porters to hold some back, or it's part of a protection racket.'

Brandt checked his watch. 'Where do you think they're going?'

'I hope it's not Pretoria. It'll take all night at this rate, but at least that wasn't the ambush or incident we feared.'

Overhead clouds gathered and glided like a squadron of galleons across the sky, with dark hulls and white topsails billowing. The setting sun flashed fire and gold on the swollen bellies. A storm threatened. Brandt rescued their capes from the horses, and the wagon rolled on through the sultry air. As the sun slowly sank and darkness enveloped them, the driver lit a paraffin lamp, and ahead pools of light spilt out to the sides of the canvas tilt covering. They wobbled and flickered and sometimes took sharp diversions as the wagon navigated a rut or a large rock marooned in the middle of the track.

Leroux measured the time from when the Irish disappeared behind a small kopje or mound until they arrived at the same place to estimate whether they were keeping pace. The driver knew the road well and called his animals by name, coaxing them when they shied at sounds only they could hear. Occasionally he had to wield the long leather sjambok, and when he did, he did it deftly and accurately touched the offending beast. Leroux had seen many mules so abused by the harsh whip of rhinoceros or hippopotamus hide, that they became stubborn and surly until finally, they had to be led behind the wagon or abandoned. They would have no such trouble this night.

'Where do you think they're going with the guns?' Brandt said.

'The Irish may have set up another base. They know that Maddox Deep and the office are compromised. According to Sanderson's friend, they're using a room at Slack Alice's for meetings. Perhaps they need somewhere larger out of town away from prying eyes.'

'But to what end? If they were gathering gold and guns for their cause, I would expect the Irish to ship them out, nearer home where they can be of use.'

'Unless they are waiting for something and see the Republic as a haven where they can operate away from the eyes and ears of Scotland Yard.'

Brandt considered it. 'Well, there is almost no law enforcement for them to worry about here. But if the Randlords are successful, then the British Empire will have much more influence.'

'Which means they can't be planning on waiting long, or they are part of trying to stop the Randlords.'

'Ja, maybe we will find out tonight.'

Leroux searched the sky for familiar constellations, but cloud covered much it, and only a few patches of stars pierced the inky firmament. As they rumbled gently down an incline he looked to where the Crux would rise over the horizon later in the year, and something caught his eye, a star blotted out for a moment, behind them on the crest of the hill.

'I think someone is following us,' Leroux said. Brandt watched behind, and Leroux opened his timepiece.

'Nearly five hours, we must be half-way to Pretoria by now.' He settled into the routine of checking his revolver.

'Two. They come up and then drop back,' Brandt said. 'I don't think they're friends.'

Leroux asked the driver to slow down. 'We'll put some more space between us, in case there's a problem.'

'Is there a bend in the road soon?' Brandt said to the driver.

'Another mile, they will disappear around a kopje.'

They waited hypnotised by the pools of light bobbing ahead. Finally, first one side dimmed and extinguished and then the other.

'He go round corner now, behind little hill, we don't see until we get there,' the driver said.

'Just before we get to that bend put the lamp out. Before the bend, understand? The wagon ahead must not see our light appear and then go out,' Leroux said.

The driver nodded.

'What's your plan?' Brandt said.

'We douse the light and let the horseman come up. They won't see us until they are close. One of us will wait in the wagon, the other on their rear flank.'

Brandt scratched his chin, fingering his scar.

'Good, you take the flank.'

He got to work moving the empty crates to one half of the wagon to provide cover he could duck behind and pulled the canvas buck-sail over them. A cooler downdraft from the storm clouds blew up dust around them. Rain was coming. The sky was black as pitch, and the first fat drops spattered down. The driver tapped Leroux on the shoulder and snuffed the lantern out while pulling in gently on the reins. Leroux led their horses forward and tied them up behind a bush to the side of the road. The rain fell heavier, insistent drumming on the wood flatbed and the softer sound of the thirsty track. Leroux and Brandt donned their capes, and the first flash of lightning was followed just a second later by a clap of thunder that startled the mules.

Leroux warned the driver that the horsemen could be highwaymen, but they would ensure that no harm came to him and that he would be well rewarded. The driver grinned and turned to calm his animals, who tossed their heads and showed the whites of their eyes. The road turned to mud as the rain pelted down and made a ferocious tattoo on the wagon. Leroux hurried twenty paces down the track and secreted himself to the side with a good view of the approach and the wagon. He saw a lantern light up behind them. It first bobbed and then swayed from side to side as the pursuers upped their pace. They trotted past Leroux, crouching unseen, scrutinising them through the sheeting rain. He recognised neither man.

The first held a lantern in one hand and his reins and a revolver in the other. Water ran off the rim of his wide-brimmed hat, and he was soaked to the skin. He screwed his face up against the elements, and his grimace shone in the glare of the lantern. The second man held his gun up, pointing skyward, as though to ward off the threat from the heavens. His dark beard glistened, his mouth hung open, teeth bared on the edge of screaming out. Just after they passed, the man with the lantern yanked on his reins. The horse turned awkwardly to the left and stopped, and the man lurched forward, perhaps unbalanced by the lantern that he held forward, illuminating the back of the wagon. The caped outline of Brandt's side was visible, crouching behind the crates on the right side of the wagon. His gun pointed at the lantern, rivulets of water streaming off him. The bearded man veered right and stopped alongside his companion. Leroux stood and stole up to their rear quarter. The driver was bent down below his seat back, his arm along the back of it, and one wide eye peeking above his hand.

'Who goes there?' Brandt called out, his face yellow and glistening in the wet lamplight.

'We're with the wagon ahead,' the rider said in a thick brogue, peering around his lantern, 'and it looks to us like you're following them and armed at that.'

The bearded one leaned over to his companion and said, 'Where are the horses? There were two horses earlier.'

'Where are you headed to?' the man with the lantern said and Leroux marked him as the leader.

'Pretoria,' Brandt replied, squinting into the glare. Another flash of lightning framed the two riders, eerie silhouettes holding their pistols levelled at Brandt. The picture vanished and thunder cracked and rolled away. Leroux had the men covered at ten paces. Brandt didn't look for him, no doubt taking care not to tip their hand.

'On a night like this? Got some urgent cargo there?' The man raised his lantern higher and lifted himself in the saddle to get a better look at the contents of the wagon. He waved his pistol at the small pile of cargo under the canvas in front of Brandt, indicating that he should uncover it.

'Don't see how that's any of your business,' Brandt said and nodded at the sodden red flag that hung bedraggled from the pole. 'The wet will ruin it.'

'Show us.'

A gust of wind and rain swept over Leroux. He wiped his face and crept further forward to five paces, bent down out of Brandt's field of fire.

'Drop your weapons!' Leroux shouted to make sure they both heard him clearly through the din. They whipped round in their saddles. The bearded one's face twisted in anger.

'You don't know who you're dealing with. You had better get out of here while you can.'

'I won't say it again,' Leroux straightened his gun arm at the man with the beard, nearest to him.

They faced off. The two men's guns still aimed at Brandt while they glared at Leroux.

'And I told you,' the Irishman said, 'you don't know what you're getting into.'

Lightning forked across the sky. The leader moved first. He flung his lamp at Brandt and fired just as the thunder crashed around them. Brandt instinctively jerked behind the cargo and fired back as he hit the side of the wagon. The lamp smashed, and paraffin blazed over Brandt's arm and the canvas, spitting and flaring. The Irishmen's horses reared up, spooked. Leroux fired at the bearded rider, missing as the man flailed, grasping the reins with one hand and shooting wildly at Leroux.

Brandt flapped at the scorching blaze, cornered against the side of the wagon. The leader had brought his horse down and hunched behind its neck and had Brandt dead in his sights. Leroux circled, staying behind the bearded man as he struggled with his horse, and fired again at the Irishman. The leader's face twisted into a cruel grimace, and Brandt froze at the sight of the gun through the dying flames. Leroux's man slumped forward and slid off his mount, but Leroux's attention was already on Brandt and the sudden movement behind him. A dark flicker snapped out, and with a sharp crack, the leader's gun hand recoiled and fired aimlessly. Lightning flashed again as the storm reached its crescendo, and the thunder echoed the shots. The driver had cracked his sjambok on the Irishman's hand. The rider frowned stupidly at his hand, and his thumb slipped on the wet hammer as he tried to cock the gun. Brandt scrambled to one knee and shot. The Irishman jolted back, but brought his gun round to bear, just as Brandt fired again. The man swayed in a small circular motion as if drunk and then slumped forward, doused like the flames.

The driver jumped back from his seat into the wagon, wiped down the cargo with a sodden blanket and checked for damage. Leroux stepped over the bearded man. He lay pale in the mud, staring unblinking into the rain. His neck rested at an awkward angle. If the bullet through the chest hadn't killed him, the fall from his horse had.

'You're not very good at taking prisoners, are you?' Brandt said as he inspected himself and found a bullet hole through the scorched cape. Leroux pulled the leader out of the saddle, and he too was stone dead. He searched the bodies and gave the few coins and tobacco to the driver and then dragged the bodies off the road and into the scrub. The hyenas would finish the job. Brandt tied the Irishmen's horses to the back of the wagon and went forward to collect their own which they added to the menagerie aft of the wagon.

The driver lit his lamp again and carried on around the corner. With luck, the rain and thunder had masked the gunfire sufficiently to avoid causing alarm in the party ahead, but as they caught sight of them, they could see that a light had separated from the group and came back down the road.

'Damn, they must have heard something,' Brandt said. 'You cover yourself under the canvas in case one of them recognises you. Shall we try and take this one for questioning?'

'It'll spook the wagon. We may not get anything out of him, and the wagon will know we're following them. I'd rather find out where they're going. Only take him if he smells a rat.'

The summer rainstorm subsided. Brandt made himself comfortable in the wagon and pulled the damaged cape off over his head and screwed it up under the cover just as the rider approached.

'Who goes there?' Brandt shouted out.

'A friend,' the rider said, a thick brogue again.

'How can we help you?' Brandt said, keeping his revolver out of sight.

'Be careful on this road. There are highwaymen around. Have you seen anyone else out tonight?' The rider peered behind into the wagon and to the horses beyond.

'No, we're headed for Pretoria. We're late on a delivery needed for the morning. Wouldn't be out in this otherwise.' Brandt jerked his head at the red flag. 'If you're going that way we can close up and go together. That should deter any brigands,' he continued, in what

Leroux thought was an excellent attempt at sincerity, and the driver angled the lantern to illuminate the flag. The rider eyed it warily and then, wheeling his horse around, said, 'No, we're turning off soon. You keep your distance.' He trotted ahead, his lantern swaying as it moved back up to join the lights in front.

Brandt watched him go. 'Those Irish were expecting to be followed.'

'It won't be long before they miss their comrades.'

'I've read about the Irish troubles. They have much to complain about,' Brandt said.

'And they're passionate about it. One of the men who came to my room died reciting a poem about the cause. He must have thought I was a Boer because he said we have much in common.'

'Because you are both trying to be independent of the British Empire?'

'I think so.'

'Why does the British Empire want Ireland? From what I hear, they make poor subjects and worse rebels.'

'Good question. I'm told they can't let go. The English landlords get rich exploiting the land and are well-connected. But the people are left in poverty. Many starve. Many emigrate to America.'

'They say so many left, their largest cities are Chicago and New York. Many Germans leave for a better life too.'

'I don't oppose their cause, but they killed my father.'

'Do you know why?'

'As he died, the lad said, "He got greedy." But I don't know if he meant my father or someone else, maybe a man called O'Connell. He was the murderer.'

'I doubt it was your father.'

'So do I.'

'What would O'Connell be greedy about.'

'The purchase of the mine. I wasn't aware my father wanted to sell. Maybe he wouldn't or was asking too much for it. I don't know, but I'm going to find out.'

The driver turned to Leroux and said, 'Hey, look there, they turn off. Road is straight now, but they turn.' Leroux peered forward into the dark. Stars shone across the sky now, and the thunderstorm had rinsed the air, but how the driver could tell they had taken a side road at this range was a mystery.

'Is there a turning there?'

The driver rubbed his head. 'Small track only.'

'When we get to it, you carry on for an hour with the light on, and then you can go wherever you want. You can keep those two horses too. Sell them in Pretoria, don't bring them back to Johannesburg.'

The driver thanked him effusively and gave his sjambok a celebratory snap just over the head of the lead donkey. They would have missed the rough path without the driver, and they parted ways in friendship. Leroux and Brandt walked their horses along the dark track, occasionally catching glimpses of the party ahead in the distance. Their friend carried straight on, slowly diverging, his lantern rocking gently back and forth.

Brandt was in a talkative mood and seemed to want to get something off his chest.

'It's a crazy world we live in. The Kaiser is determined to have an empire. Bismarck thinks it's a waste of time and money. Most of the colonies cost more to pacify and administer than you can ever make from them.'

'Not the South African Republic.'

'Ja exactly, that is the problem. It will pay for the whole of southern Africa, which is why the Kaiser is so keen.'

'And Rhodes.'

'I have fought two wars in Africa. The Abushiri revolt six years ago in Dar Es Salaam and the Khoikhoi rebellion two years ago in South West Africa. You learn nothing from the second one. I don't want to be part of another.'

'I've only fought in one, but I feel the same. The Malaboch rising left me sick in the stomach. There is more than enough land here for everyone.'

'I could live here one day.'

'With the Baroness?'

'Ja.'

'You look comfortable in each other's company, as though you have known each other for a long time.'

Brandt coughed. 'We met in Windhoek three years ago.'

'When her husband was alive?'

'Yes, they owned estates there. We fell in love. When the rebellion broke out, she had to return to Germany with her husband.'

They remounted and plodded on down the track, slowly drying out, splashing in puddles as they went. Insects emerged from the dripping foliage, and the whine of mosquitoes accompanied the patient walk of the horses and the swish of their tails. They gradually closed on the wagon, the shapes of the escort riders sharpening and further ahead a light flickered but remained stationary. Another light appeared alongside it and blinked three times. One of the lamps on the wagon blinked three times in response and continued to converge with the flickering light. As they neared, it transformed into flames from the top of a brazier and Leroux and Brandt led their horses off the track.

The wagon stopped by the brazier. A man approached, and then the wagon moved forward again. The man returned to the brazier and picked up his lantern and directed one long flash away from them. A little further along came a brief glow in reply.

'A guard post, and there must be another further along.' Brandt said.

They tethered their horses a short way into the bush and crept parallel with the road towards the brazier. As they squatted, the buzzing and chirruping of the night chorus crowded in on them and filled their senses. Leroux wondered whether the flimsy hut set back from the brazier was sturdy enough to protect the men from hailstorms. Once he had seen lumps of ice, the size of cricket balls, fall from a summer storm. Fence posts, with barbed wire strung between, extended either side of a gate into the darkness. They had cleared the bush back twenty yards from the wire, while inside the fence the ground looked flat and grazed. Two men talked by the brazier.

The wagon had continued to the front of a large building, from which a vertical sliver of light escaped. And smudges of light seeped out from the shutters of another lower building to the left.

'Looks like a barn and a farmhouse,' Leroux said. 'Two guards at the gate, four riders with the wagon and the two drivers, as well as whoever lives at the farm,' Leroux said.

'We've come all this way, let's at least look. How would the Boers do it?'

'I'll crawl in further along the fence. I should be able to get close to the barn without anyone seeing me. You cover the gate guards, in case I need to make a quick escape.'

The two sentries sat on stools and played cards by the light of the fire. Men milled outside the barn unloading the wagon. Leroux slunk along the edge of the bush until he was fifty yards away from the gate. He crawled through the wet grass to the fence and rolled under the wire. Leroux slithered forward on his belly and rested forty yards from the wagon. The barn and farmhouse were both more extensive than he had first thought. The doors of the barn were open, and six men opened the bundles and checked rifles on a trestle table. Behind them stabling for at least thirty horses took up the rest of the barn and the heads of horses protruded from most of the stalls. Two men lifted the large crate from the wagon and set it down. They pried off the top and lifted individual components out and unwrapped them from their grey cloth covers. One assembled a tripod, and Leroux knew what was coming next. The second one lowered the fat barrel of a Maxim gun on top and then stood back to admire the fearsome weapon as his partner unspooled a belt of ammunition. They rejoined the others checking and storing the weapons. Leroux crawled to the left, in front of the farmhouse.

It was a single-storey wooden building with steps up to a shallow veranda and front door. The sound of revelry and a little light emanated from the shuttered windows on either side. The indistinct chatter of at least half a dozen men ebbed and flowed. Leroux continued crawling to the left. The room extended for the whole depth of the building and was probably the main living area.

Further round was a backdoor and towards the end of the rear wall were windows to what he assumed were living quarters. When he crawled back to the front, he saw a swinging light approach the gate. The sentries and the wagon signalled to each other and then back towards the barn, as before. Leroux crawled back to the barn and lay flat in the dark as close as he dared to the doors. The men had finished storing the weapons and took the first wagon away around the far side and stabled the horses.

The new wagon approached, and its lantern illuminated the faces on the driver's seat. A gnarled man with a great shaggy beard and bulbous nose held the reins. His cheeks were so chubby that his eyes just peeped over them like currants on top of a bun. Next to him, a much younger man wielded the whip, thinner and yet to grow a beard, but with similar features, most likely the old-timer's son. They shouted Boer greetings as three men came out from the barn and replied in a brogue.

They talked haltingly in heavily accented English, and Leroux struggled to hear. He crawled nearer keeping the wagon between him and the light spilling from the barn. The men loaded five bundles of rifles into the wagon, having to repeat nearly everything they said. Through the wheels of the wagon and the legs of the oxen, Leroux watched as the men finished their loading and stood expectantly as the conversation ran dry. Someone came out of the barn holding a map. The hair on the back of Leroux's neck rose. He could only see the bottom half, but he was sure it was O'Connell. The rangy lope, his trousers cinched in at the waist. He came closer and Leroux adjusted his position to see straggly hair framing a thin face of stubble with a hawkish nose. Leroux's finger itched, and he felt the grip of his revolver. O'Connell stopped between the other men who made way for the angular limbs and bony shoulders.

The older Boer got down and looked at the map. He put a stubby finger on it.

'Here. He will be here the day after tomorrow. Understood?'

O'Connell nodded. 'Good, well done. We'll come back here, after. When will you know the time?'

'Soon. We will let you know, ja, like before.'

'Yes.'

'Good. We will see you then, kamaraden.'

O'Connell whistled at two men in the barn, who came running over and said to the Boers, 'Take these two with you.'

The light from the Boers' lamp shone on O'Connell's rotten grin, and his eyes glittered as the two men jumped up into the back of the wagon. Leroux's tongue stuck dry to his palate in anticipation. The wagon would draw away, and he would have a clean shot at O'Connell, and, with more than a bit of luck, he would disappear into the dark, over the fence and into the bush. They would not catch him there for he knew its ways far better than them. He drew his revolver. The old Boer hauled himself up into the driver's seat and took up the reins. He clicked his tongue and flicked his wrists. O'Connell abruptly turned and walked back to the barn, followed by his three countrymen. Leroux cursed under his breath. The chance had gone, and when the wagon moved, he would be stranded, caught in the light from the barn.

If he ran back, the young Boer would surely notice him in his peripheral vision. Leroux stole forward, into his blind-spot, and stepped lightly alongside the wagon as it trundled away and turned for the gate. The young Boer's forearm stuck out in front of the canvass tilt as he drew the sjambok back to crack it. Leroux rolled under the wagon between the wheels and stretched up to grab the timber connecting the axles. For a moment, his heels dragged as he pulled himself up and wrapped his feet around the beam and clung on. Behind the grease bucket that swung from the rear axle, O'Connell closed the barn doors. A burst of fiddle and light escaped the farmhouse as a bandy-legged man staggered onto the veranda in a haze of smoke. 'Donal! You in for the next hand?'

'I am, wait.'

'We're dealing.' The man disappeared back inside, leaving the door open. O'Connell and the other men bolted the barn doors and walked back to the farmhouse. Leroux muttered promises to himself, and O'Connell stopped and looked over to the wagon, as though he had heard. The dark eyes seemed to follow Leroux for a moment before O'Connell ducked into the warm glow. When the wagon was halfway to the gate, Leroux lowered himself down and dropped to the grass. The wagon passed over him, and he lay still until it reached the sentries, when he crept away and under the fence.

'I was beginning to get worried.' Brandt said.

'It's a big operation. Thirty to forty horses stabled in the barn. O'Connell's there. I'm sure he's the boss. I counted eleven different men, including the sentries, and there were more in the farmhouse. They're planning something for Sunday, and they've got a Maxim.'

Brandt whistled under his breath. 'Shall we take the guards? Find out what they're up to.'

Leroux looked at them through the foliage. The flames flickered, and shadows played on their faces as they hunched near the brazier still playing cards.

'The men I questioned in the alley only knew that they fought for their cause, and those men aren't any higher up. We know O'Connell will be here on Sunday. And whatever he's planning sounded important. Let's keep the advantage of surprise.'

'They'll know those two men are missing, not to mention the guard at the office.'

'They won't know what happened to them and they may already believe I'm dead.'

Brandt concurred, and they fetched their horses. They led them through the bush until they came out into grassland and found a small group of rocks where they laid out their bedrolls for the few hours of the night that remained. Leroux lit a small fire that threw shapes on the boulders, and in the distance, a lion roared. An answer to the challenge bellowed from the other side of the darkness, and then there was just the rhythmic chirping of cicadas. Leroux rested his head in the crook of his elbow and remembered Tom and wondered if he would have grasped the chance to get O'Connell.

Saturday, 28th December 1895

The tendrils of dawn brushed Leroux and he stretched out his stiff limbs. He turned to the warmth of the sun swelling over the horizon and peeled off his damp shirt and laid it over a rock. The kopje where they camped stood in a sea of grass, undulating away to the south, parted only by a few other mounds or marooned thorn bushes. The farmhouse lay more than a mile away to the north beyond a low rise and some scrub. They mounted and returned to the path, noting the landmarks. The long grass waved in greens and yellows, and a herd of long-horned cattle drifted through. The easy gait of his horse seemed to sway in time with the veld, and as Leroux breathed the rain-washed air and basked in the golden glow, he reminisced about his friend Tom and what it was like to be carefree.

'Does Muller know you met the Baroness in Windhoek?'

Brandt lent forward in his saddle, pushing down on the pommel to readjust his seat.

'Yes.'

'And that the Baroness supports Bismarck?'

Brandt nodded glumly. 'He has made it clear that if we oppose him, he will reveal our relationship and accuse her of murdering the Baron.'

'Is there any truth in it?'

Brandt looked dismayed. 'No, nothing. Yes, we were lovers. That side of their relationship was over. But she cared very much for him. She respected and adored him for his values and bravery, and she supported him in everything he did. She had made her choice to stay with him when she left Windhoek. But Muller does not need the truth. The perception is enough for him, and the accusation alone will be enough for the Kaiser's supporters and the Baron's family to tear her down. They have already made her life unbearable back home. That is why she came here.'

'To you?'

'Yes, I know it looks bad, but where else could she go?'

'Does she know that you disobeyed Muller's orders?'

'No. We must go and see her.'

'There are few secrets on the Rand. Best to tell her before she finds out from someone else.'

'Just so. And the Irish have been masters at keeping their activities concealed. Not a whisper until you poked around.'

'Sanderson tells me they have had plenty of practice over the years with Scotland Yard spying on them and sending infiltrators and agent provocateurs.'

'If you needed to operate covertly,' Brandt said, 'they would be useful men to work with.'

They caught each other's eyes in recognition of that truth as they reached the main road. They made sure they could pinpoint the turning again and then spurred the horses on to Johannesburg. The sun was still low when the chimney shafts and mine towers up beyond the city came into sight, and they reached the outskirts. Leroux strapped on his eye patch.

'Do you think the Baroness will like it?'

'I think she might give me one when I tell her about you.'

They stopped by Lara's lodgings. Leroux hung back in case the landlady recognised him, and Brandt updated Lara. He returned with Sanderson.

'Dear boy, how are you?'

'Been chasing Irish around the veld. They've holed-up out there. I guess Slack Alice's has been quiet.'

'Not a dicky bird. Miss Sinclair and Miss Brown have been looking after me very well.' His face was pink and hale in the sunshine. 'Although they told me you drank all the brandy!'

'The Irish have got themselves a farmhouse off the Pretoria Road, rifles, horses and a Maxim. I overheard them planning something for tomorrow. They're waiting on some information. Any idea what might be going on tomorrow?'

Sanderson smoothed his shirt, and his hands came to rest in contemplation on his potbelly.

'No. But if they're going to use Slack Alice's for a meeting, it will be soon. David's still there.'

'Does Rhodes know I'm dead?'

'No. Nobody's asked me, and I haven't said anything. I was the only one to identify the body. Officially Miss Sinclair doesn't know. And as far as most people are concerned, you've just stopped causing trouble.' Sanderson lent backwards, gripping his lapels and chortling at his joke.

'Any sign of Muller?'

Sanderson turned serious and shook his head.

Brandt and Leroux rode to the Baroness's house. They trotted up the drive under the gum trees and found her sitting out on the veranda reading. She kept her expression neutral as she sent them inside to refresh and ordered a late breakfast for them.

'You look well,' she said to Leroux when they returned.

'I had no chance to tell you yesterday,' Brandt said, holding her hand and sitting next to her.

'Muller came by last night looking for you when he returned from Pretoria,' she said, and then looked at Leroux. 'He told me you were dead.'

'Officially, he is dead. Muller tricked Leroux into meeting the Irish, hoping they would kill him and sent me to make sure. There's an Irishman at the morgue called Leroux.'

The Baroness looked down the driveway.

'Muller ordered you to kill Leroux?'

'Yes.'

'He could turn up at any moment. If he sees Leroux alive, it will wreck our plans.' Her hands fell to her lap, and she looked from Brandt to Leroux.

'This is my fault. I owe the Captain my life. I will make this right.'

The Baroness looked about the grounds, a tear welling, as though it might be the last time she would see them.

'I'm not upset.' She stared up at the crowns of the gum trees and sniffed. 'Muller was in a good mood last night. He may be about to make his move. Karl and I, and many others in Germany, are concerned that we are headed for war. A war that we do not want. A war that could escalate and suck in all the great powers. The Kaiser is an impetuous man. Since he dismissed Bismarck, he has been playing his hand with increasing recklessness. He does not listen to the advice of experienced counsellors. Bismarck warned that just as the catastrophe of Jena came twenty years after the death of Frederick the Great, the next European war will come twenty years after his departure, if the young Kaiser carries on this way. We are not radicals. We believe in a strong Germany, but a peaceful one.'

Leroux saw the Baroness in a new light. Not as the beautiful host of extravagant parties, but as a compassionate woman, wise beyond her years. She seemed prepared to risk her fortune, maybe even her life, for her ideals.

'Many agree with us,' Brandt said. 'Napoleon's crushing victory at Jena and the subjugation of Prussia haunts the German consciousness. We cannot risk it again.'

'Do you have any idea what Muller is planning? He knows the route that Jameson plans to take to Johannesburg,' Leroux said to the Baroness.

'Yes, I heard you destroyed the consul's desk. He is letting Muller use his office while he is here. Was there nothing else in it?'

'No, but there was a safe there.'

'I don't think he would use the safe,' Brandt said. 'I have access to it, as does the consul, but the desk drawer he could lock.'

'Knowing the route would make it easy to set an ambush,' Leroux said.

'That helps Kruger, but not Muller unless he can show that Jameson broke the treaty first,' Brandt said.

'Then he must have a plan to make the Reformers or Jameson break the treaty,' Leroux said. 'What has he been doing in Pretoria? As far as I know, Kruger has been away, touring the countryside.'

'I know he sees the Ambassador,' Brandt said. 'And they are in close contact with Berlin, the Political Secretary of the Foreign Office, Baron von Holstein. He is something of an eminence grise to the Kaiser. Relations with Britain have cooled. The Kaiser was greatly insulted by Lord Salisbury in Cowes last August when they failed to come to any agreement on the partition of the Ottoman Empire. The Kaiser and von Holstein have a vision of expelling the British from southern Africa and all of it falling within our sphere of influence. If Muller returned in a good mood, it would seem logical that they have agreed to whatever scheme he has.'

'We should assume Muller has the Kaiser's support,' the Baroness said.

'But Kruger is fiercely independent, even of the Kaiser,' Leroux said. 'If this is just about keeping the British out of the Transvaal and becoming a German Protectorate, Kruger would not be in favour of it. But driving the British out of South Africa completely, uniting the Orange Free State and the Cape Dutch, perhaps with German backing, that would appeal to him.'

Brandt sawed an end of sausage off. 'If Jameson invaded and the Germans protested would Rhodes back down?'

Leroux sipped his coffee and looked down the drive. 'If it was down to him, I doubt it. He is not well, and I think he knows time is running out for him. He may not get a better chance to achieve his dream. But the Colonial Secretary may overrule him, especially if they are facing diplomatic pressure from both the German Empire and America.'

Brandt pressed his hands down his thighs and looked up as a thrush flew from one of the trees. 'It's hardly believable that the disputes of some miners and farmers on a hot plateau in Africa, which no one was interested in ten years ago, could bring the world to the brink of war. A wrong move by a junior officer in a remote dusty town could be all that is needed to convulse the world in conflict.'

A cab drew up at the end of the driveway, and a young lady alighted. Leroux's pulse quickened. It was Lara. She walked with grace and purpose, her fedora at a jaunty angle, a cream cotton shawl over her shoulders. Leroux and Brandt rose to greet her.

'I came as soon as I could, I've brought messages you must see.' Lara toyed with her shawl.

'You can talk freely here, we're on the same side,' Leroux said.

She hesitated and chewed her lip. 'This could be awkward, are you sure?'

Leroux wasn't sure, but he was committed. 'I'm sure.'

She drew out a clutch of papers and laid them on the table. 'These are copies of two telegrams. This one Muller sent last night to the German Foreign Office, Berlin. And this came from Berlin just now.' Lara pushed the two sheets to Leroux. Underneath the telegraph office header, both pages were full of groups of four or five numbers. The first had 'FOREIGN OFFICE BERLIN' above the numbers and 'MULLER' below. The second had 'GERMAN CONSULATE JOHANNESBURG' at the top and 'FOREIGN OFFICE BERLIN' at the bottom. Leroux passed them to Brandt.

'You are a very resourceful lady, Miss Sinclair,' Brandt said. 'I won't ask how you got these. Before I decode them, is there anything else?'

Lara looked to Leroux who nodded. 'Peter, a message came from Rhodes in response to your question.' She paused as if inviting Leroux to interrupt. 'Donal O'Connell is known to Scotland Yard. He is a senior member of Clan Na Gael, the American sister organisation to the Irish Republican Brotherhood.'

'They're Americans?' Leroux said.

'Irish Americans, but they are fierce supporters of Irish independence - they mostly left to escape the British.' Lara said.

The Baroness stood and went over to Lara. 'You are the most interesting visitor I have had all week. Let me show you around the house,' she said and led Lara away.

Brandt went inside and returned a few minutes later with some folders which he set on the table. He rummaged through his pocket, pulled out a cigarette case and offered one to Leroux before lighting one for himself.

'Filthy habit, I know. I try not to. So bad for the teeth, but they help me concentrate.' He worked methodically through the messages.

Leroux looked down the drive again, expecting Muller to arrive at any moment. He wondered what on earth he thought he was doing. A week ago, Leroux was a journalist, with an ambition to report on world events. Now he was stumbling around a situation where one mistake could cause a catastrophic war.

'What's wrong?' Brandt's pen hovered over the pad.

'I feel as though life or death depends on our every action, and I'm not sure I know what to do.'

'We do what we can, Peter. What we think is right. You must do what is right by your father. And neither of us want war, that is enough.'

Brandt finished decoding the first message and passed it to Leroux, and turned immediately to the second, referencing back and forth between the folder and the slip of paper. Leroux studied the first message:

BRITISH INVASION IMMINENT STOP REQUEST SMS KONDOR AND SCHUTZTRUPPE PUT ON STANDBY FOR

IMMEDIATE DEPLOYMENT STOP END

Leroux wondered what caused Muller to believe that the "invasion" was imminent. If he knew the Randlords plans he would be expecting Jameson to move on the 3rd of January. That was six days from now. Soon, but 'imminent' made it sound sooner.

Brandt finished the second message, handed it over and blew out his cheeks. Stretching back, he signalled a footman and asked him to call the Baroness.

'Well, what do you think, Peter?'

The second message read:

SMS KONDOR AT ANCHOR LOURENCO MARQUES DELEGOA BAY STOP AWAITING FURTHER ORDERS STOP SCHUTZTRUPPE SW AFRIKA DEPLOYING GRIQUALAND BORDER STOP COUNT HATZFELDT PREPARING TO BREAK OFF DIPLOMATIC RELATIONS STOP PROCEED STOP END

'Who is Count Hatzfeldt?' Leroux said.

'The Ambassador to London.'

'The High Command is backing whatever Muller is planning. To the best of my knowledge, the Randlords have decided on 3rd January for the rising. But it feels as though Muller intends to move before then.'

'I agree, but I have no idea what or when.'

'The map suggests he plans to ambush Jameson. How significant are the forces mentioned in the messages?'

'The Schutztruppe are the colonial troops in German South West Africa. They could spare maybe one thousand to come. It would take them weeks cross-country to Johannesburg, but from the Griqualand border, they can threaten the diamond mines of Kimberley and block the most direct route of British reinforcement from the Cape. They do not pose an immediate threat. However, SMS Kondor is a cruiser and carries a company of Marines, only a day away by train.'

Leroux reread the messages. 'But they wouldn't be strong enough to stop Jameson.'

'No, but they don't need to stop him. They just need to be attacked.

Suppose Jameson's raiders came over the border and got into a fight with the Marines. That would effectively be declaring war on Germany. Berlin would say they had been invited by Kruger to help protect the Embassy and German interests from rebels.'

'It'll take Jameson three days to reach Johannesburg. The marines could meet him before he got to Johannesburg and linked up with the Reformers, especially if the Boers held him up.'

The Baroness and Lara returned arm in arm.

'Lara, have you seen anything that suggests that Rhodes has brought the flotation forward?' Leroux said.

She shook her head.

'If I were Muller, I would try to trick Jameson into an early departure,' Brandt said, 'before the Uitlanders rise. He will be an invader, not a saviour. And the Uitlanders will not be ready.'

'How would you do that?' Leroux said.

'Misinformation. Make Jameson think the Uitlanders are in danger, or that the Boers are on to him and if he doesn't leave soon, they will ambush him. Maybe that's the purpose of the map. To give him proof of an ambush.'

Leroux looked at Brandt. 'That makes more sense than anything else. But it would take Muller days to get to Jameson out at Pitsani.'

'He must have a contact nearby - someone who can approach Jameson as soon as they get the instruction. Mafeking is the nearest town. They may already have a copy of the map.'

Leroux slapped the table in frustration. 'We could spend all day guessing at Muller's plans. We should just try to stop him from sending any message.'

'He's at the consulate,' the Baroness said, clearly supporting the idea.

Brandt waved one of the telegrams. 'He'll try to set his plan in motion as soon as he gets this message.'

'He'd have received those at the same time as you,' Lara said.

'There's no time to lose if he was just waiting for confirmation from High Command,' Leroux said.

'I'll go to the consulate,' Brandt said and looked at Leroux. 'You go to the telegraph office.'

They sent for their horses, and Leroux agreed with Lara that she would stop by her lodgings on the way to tell Sanderson. If Brandt could not find Muller at the consulate, he would come to the telegraph office as well, and they would reassess. Leroux swung up into the saddle, donning his eye patch and slouch hat, and galloped into town.

He flew by wagons leaving Market Square and dropped down to a canter. Long ox-trains impeded the traffic, and businessmen and farmers swarmed over the pavement. Women bustled and chatted, and there was not a revolutionary to be seen. The lively Chamber of Mines meeting before Christmas was a distant memory, and life had slotted back into its customary track. A church bell struck noon and still tolled as Leroux dismounted outside the telegraph office and engaged a boy to look after his horse.

He had to stop Muller from getting inside and sending a message. He waved down a sturdy Landau cab directly in front of the office. If Leroux could get Muller inside the enclosed four-seater carriage, he could spirit him away. The driver up front could not see what went on in the cab, nor could anyone in the street. The consulate was across the square behind the Landau. Leroux said that he was waiting for an acquaintance who was late and told the driver to be ready to go. He removed his coat and folded it over his right forearm, covering his revolver, and then crossed his left arm over the top. Not ideal, but discreet enough on a busy day.

He opened the door of the Landau and scrutinised the approaching carriages. A handful of Victoria cabs, a couple of Hansoms, a Brougham, and an open Phaeton sped past him. Suddenly a Victoria cab swung out of the traffic. He could not see the occupant behind the horses and the driver, perched on a high seat in front of the hooded cab. Leroux took a step back to look around him as the horses slowed. The occupant had pushed himself up, ready to step out of the open buggy. It was Muller. Their eyes met. Muller was not deceived for a moment by the eye patch or the neckerchief, and Leroux recognised the alarm in his eyes. 'Drive on,' Muller shouted at the driver, who responded with alacrity, cracking the whip and swerving adroitly back out into a gap in the traffic. Muller threw the only thing to hand - a rolled-up blanket - just before he passed behind the Landau. Leroux dodged it and ran to his horse.

The cab raced around the square and north up Rissik Street. Leroux gained on them without difficulty and kept fifty paces behind. He could see Muller, bareheaded, looking around the side of the hood, clutching his Reichsrevolver. He had the advantage for the moment and scanned the street, no doubt hoping to attract the attention of a Zarp. But they were few and far between, especially when needed, and the cab sped on in the direction of the Wanderers Club and Pretoria or Park Halt. At least the police station was behind them. Muller must have received and decoded the same messages and now wanted to reply or activate his plan. He had seen Leroux alive and must assume Brandt was either dead or dead against him. Muller could send any message he needed to from Pretoria, and from there he could set the Zarps onto him. They had already helped him follow Leroux. Now they would accuse Leroux of the murder of the Irishman at the morgue and feigning his own death.

The cab turned right on Noord Street. He was going to the station. Leroux closed on the cab, but the closer he got, the more he sensed the barrel pointing right at him. The driver's hat flew off and tumbled past, but now the cab slowed down. To his dismay, Leroux saw two Zarps checking the papers of new arrivals at the station. He kicked on, only to be startled by the flash and crack of Muller's revolver. It was an impossible shot and went harmlessly wide but hitting Leroux would have been a bonus. Muller disappeared behind the hood as the Zarps on the entrance steps looked around. With his revolver in one hand, Leroux hauled on the reins.

Muller leapt into the throng outside the station and pushed his way towards the approaching police. He pulled a paper from his pocket and presented it to them, talking animatedly and gesturing at Leroux. Leroux holstered his gun and stood up in the saddle, to better see Muller and could only grit his teeth as one of the policemen bought a whistle to his mouth and blew. Both Zarps drew their weapons and advanced towards Leroux with Muller skulking behind them. Pedestrians scattered from their path. There was nothing for Leroux to do but turn his horse and bolt. He crossed to the far side of the street and back towards the centre of town chased by shouts and further blasts of whistles. As he turned left into Rissik Street, he twisted in his saddle. No one followed, but it was only a matter of time before they circulated his description. Another few minutes and he was back in Bree Street.

Lara opened the door on her way to the telegraph office, but Leroux ushered her back up the stairs. Sanderson awoke bewildered from a nap in the easy chair. He cradled an old pith helmet in his lap, to which he had fixed a green puggaree to protect the nape of his neck

'Dear boy, I thought it was David for a moment, you startled me. I've got a feeling we're about to see some action, sit down and tell me.'

'I found Muller on his way to the telegraph office. He fled to Park Halt and found some Zarps. He must have told them that I'm responsible for killing the man in the morgue and that I've faked my death. They came after me. I don't think I can stay here long - he will have told them where they can find me.'

Sanderson yawned and moved over by the window to look down the street. 'Lara told me about the telegrams, what do you think Muller will do?'

'He will keep trying to send a message, from Pretoria probably. He can safely send anything from there. The last telegram he received said "awaiting further orders." We think his next move is to trick Jameson into departing early or fake some incident which he can report as the raiders invading.'

'Jameson is under explicit instructions from Rhodes and Hammond not to move unless specifically ordered by them,' Sanderson said.

'I know. But Jameson is not regular army. He's an adventurer and headstrong and has been mightily well-rewarded for it. If Jameson learned that the Boers knew his position, were raising the commando and had discovered his intended route and were moving to ambush him, would he sit and wait? If he thought that the civilians of Johannesburg were under threat, and it was now or never? I'm not sure. He might back himself to win the day, as he has in the past. Muller might have something that pushes him over the edge.'

'I don't see there's much we can do about Jameson from this end. You've already warned Rhodes and Hammond about the danger of Muller precipitating a conflict and Jameson jumping the gun,' Lara said.

Sanderson fiddled with the Webley that he had retrieved from the morgue. 'The other possibility, that he is planning on faking an incident, feels more likely,' Sanderson said. 'It would make sense of the Irish activity, and I've got news on that. I had a junior go through the back issues, and he found some articles.' He looked down at his notes. 'In September there was a convention in Chicago of the Irish National Alliance. The Chairman was John Finerty, and he declared, "We'll circle England with a wall of fire, which shall never be extinguished until all Ireland is free." That fits the bill.'

'Rhodes confirmed that Donal O'Connell was from Chicago and known to Scotland Yard as a member of an American sister organisation to the Irish Republican Brotherhood,' Lara said.

'They're Irish Americans then?' Sanderson said.

'Looks that way,' Leroux said. 'The young Irishman in my room was called Finn. It could be short for Finerty, maybe some relation.'

'There's one more mention, again from September. "There is a discerned attempt by the Democratic Party to muster as many Irish Societies as they can beneath the banner of their Presidential Candidate." They'll be relying on Irish votes next November. Grover Cleveland can't stand again, but he'll be doing everything he can to help the new Democratic nominee.'

'This ties in with Brandt's idea. He thinks Muller is trying to provoke a war between England and Germany with America taking the opportunity to come in on their side. British aggression against the South African Republic might be too much for the President to ignore, given his belligerence over Venezuela and the popularity it would gain him with the Irish.'

'Back in the Sixties,' Sanderson said, 'after the American Civil War, Irish veterans launched raids on Canada. There was even an attempt at a rising in Ireland.'

'That could be happening again,' Leroux said. 'There was a report in the Star last week about the Irish Americans offering one hundred thousand men to invade Canada if war broke out over the Venezuela Crisis.'

'Perhaps the guns are to fight the British here?' Sanderson said.

There was a knock at the door. Brandt arrived, flushed and perspiring.

'No sign of Muller at the consulate–'

'–He escaped me. I think he took the train to Pretoria to send a message.'

'But while I was there, I did some digging. The farmhouse we went to last night, I found it on a map. It's called Irene and belongs to Alois Nellmapius or used to - he died two years ago.'

'Who is Nellmapius?'

'He was an Austro-Hungarian. Good friends with Kruger and close to the Corner House Group. His estate is still being settled. And by someone you know.'

'Who?'

'Lionel Phillips.'

'Phillips? I don't understand.'

'There's more. Muller left me a message before he realised that I had crossed him. It said, "Alfred Jones is a Rhodes Agent. He came to the consulate asking about Veltheim. We followed him, and Jones went to see Marais. Then he disappeared. Find Eugene Marais and what he knows about Veltheim."'

Leroux bent forward, head in hands, massaging his temples.

'Phillips controlling Irene suggests a connection between the Irish and the Randlords, which makes no sense. Rhodes asked both Jones and me to look into Maddox Deep and Veltheim.'

'Marais is with the Randlords,' Brandt said, 'and it looks like he could have something to do with Veltheim unless Jones's disappearance was a coincidence.'

'We're going around in circles,' Lara said.

'Somebody is playing both sides,' Leroux said. 'And if Kruger and Muller know about the force at Irene that would be all the justification they need.'

'I can ask Phillips about Irene. Maybe there is some explanation,' Sanderson said.

'Nobody at the consulate knows where Marais is,' Brandt said.

'I saw him with Joubert two days ago. They left together.' Leroux said.

'Shall I ask Rhodes?' Lara said

'Wait until we hear what Phillips has to say,' Sanderson said. 'Everyone is tense. We should be careful about making accusations.' He checked again down the street.

'We know the Irish are planning something for Sunday,' Leroux said. 'And we know they are waiting on a message, confirming the time. We also think they have a meeting planned at Slack Alice's sometime today or tomorrow.'

He swung his eyepatch like a propeller as he paced the room. 'We must keep the Irish under observation. The Zarps won't think to look for me at Maddox Deep, so I'll check there. Sanderson, why don't you wait here for a message from David and then find Phillips after?'

'Will do. Hang on. A Zarp's coming down the road, two of them now.'

'Peter, Captain Brandt, follow me,' Lara said and led them up to the landlady's rooms and asked for her help in sheltering two high profile Reformers from the Zarps. The landlady looked impressed, especially with Captain Brandt, and took them in.

The Zarps hammered on the front door, and Lara went down. Leroux strained to hear. They had agreed with the landlady to lock the door as though she was out and stay quiet. If the Zarps broke in, Leroux would say he had taken her hostage, and tie up the Zarps and escape. Lara's door opened and closed below them. And then opened again, followed by heavy footsteps on the staircase. But they didn't come up. A few minutes later, Lara collected them.

'They've gone, but they are suspicious. They asked about your horse outside.'

'That's your one Peter. I came from the consulate by cab.'

'They tried to bluff me, saying someone had seen a man entering the building. But I showed them into my rooms and introduced them to Sanderson. He had a bit of fun with them.'

They went back down where Sanderson peered out of the window. 'I don't think they've fallen for it. They're both watching the front, and they sent a boy off with a message. Could be for reinforcements.'

'Do you think they are only after you?' Lara asked Leroux.

'I don't think Muller would tell the Zarps about me,' Brandt said, 'It would reflect badly on the State, and I haven't done anything illegal here.'

'Apart from killing that Irishman,' Leroux said.

Brandt shrugged his shoulders. 'They think you did that.'

'I suggest you divert them before reinforcements arrive.' Sanderson said.

'I've got an idea,' Lara said. 'I'll put this eye patch and Leroux's hat on you, Captain, and then you run outside and take the horse. Without a coat, it's clear you're unarmed. Distract them as long as you can.'

Leroux smiled. 'Sounds good so far.'

'And I'll put my bonnet and shawl on you, and when we see the Zarps going for Brandt, you take my cycle and go as quick as you can the other way.'

Brandt smiled. 'I'd like to see Leroux's disguise before I go.'

'Bravo,' Sanderson said. 'I'll stay here and wait for word from David.'

Lara got Leroux and Brandt ready.

'I'll go back to the Baroness's,' said Brandt. 'Muller might try to threaten her to get at me. You should join me. I don't think it's safe for you to return here tonight.'

'Thank you, but I'll stay here,' Lara said, adjusting the bonnet on Leroux. 'I'll put this flowerpot in the window if the coast is clear.'

Brandt, more or less fitting Leroux's appearance, if a little taller, waited for some traffic to obstruct the Zarps on the other side of the road. He dashed to the horse and launched into the saddle, urging it on, as the closest Zarp shouted a warning. The other policeman sprinted up the pavement, and as the horse kicked on, the first Zarp fired a warning shot. Brandt raised a hand in surrender and made a meal of reining in his horse one-handed, swerving over, causing the oncoming carriages to careen out of the way or screech to a halt. The second Zarp grabbed the reins and ordered Brandt to dismount amid the chaos. Zigzagging through the confusion, the other Zarp arrived, ignoring the screams of irate drivers and the protests of shaken riders to question Brandt.

The other way, Leroux wobbled along on the bicycle and took a last look back as both Zarps escorted Brandt to the side of the street. Leroux turned the corner and stopped. He stuffed the bonnet in his trouser pocket and wrapped the shawl around his head, turban fashion, as a sunshade. He let the loose end of material hang down the injured side of his face and pedalled towards Maddox Deep. His mind turned all the information over and over as the wheels went round. Somewhere there was a connection that would make sense of this.

He propped his bike against the old shebeen overlooking Maddox Deep. It had been a good six- or seven-mile cycle, and he needed a drink. The other patrons huddled around their dagga pipes and jars of cape smoke and eyed him suspiciously as he ordered an iced lemonade, but let him be, with his revolver and his brutal wound. He sent a boy with a message for Jory. With everything spinning in his head, Jory's refreshing straight talk would be a welcome change. Leroux knocked back the drink and cycled around the Maddox Deep perimeter, jerkily negotiating the ruts, freewheeling down the slopes and rising from the saddle for the inclines. It couldn't compete with a horse, whose iron shoes were much sturdier than the inflated rubber and canvas rings marked Dunlop, but bouncing down the tracks was a lot of fun. The two Boerhunds picked up his scent and charged around the building, but no one came to investigate. He flew back past the chained gates to the shebeen where Jory had just arrived.

'I went to Kazerne yesterday. The Simmer and Jack wagon arrived with the same driver to meet an oil tanker. They had adapted it to store weapons. I didn't follow them, but they headed in this direction.'

'The wagon arrived just afore eight last night. They asked some of us to wait and help. They had bundles of rifles which we stored in the mine.'

'Maddox Deep looks quiet.'

'Has been. Occasionally see a light from there at night.'

'Any Zarps.'

'No Zarps, no anybody. Like the place has a bad smell. I've had a lad on our gatehouse keeping an eye out, but he's seen naught else apart from the odd wagon arrive, I think just food and water. Could be a few of them in there.'

Jory cracked his knuckles, and Leroux looked back at the chained gates and weighed the consequences of breaking in again.

'Are you working tomorrow?'

'Don't stop for Sundays. Be going all the time.'

Leroux settled the bill and cycled west, into the rusty sun burning low through the haze. On the way to the Baroness's, he stopped to buy an assegai, a light Zulu throwing spear, and another knobkerrie, and when he jounced up the drive and skidded to a stop in front of the veranda, Brandt rose to greet him. A footman appeared and served pre-prandial gin and tonics.

'How did you get on with the police?'

'They refused to take my word and insisted on going to the consulate to have an official vouch for me. Still, it occupied them for a while.'

'Jory saw the Simmer and Jack wagon from yesterday. He helped them unload the rifles and store them.'

Brandt scratched his head and took a sip. 'Then the weapons Clan Na Gael took were part of the same shipment that went to the Randlords?'

'Looks that way. While it makes no sense, Phillips administers their base at Irene and Marais may be connected to Veltheim. And the Irish are planning something for tomorrow.'

'We need to go back there. I'll have the horses prepared for first thing.'

The sun slipped below the horizon, and a footman showed Leroux to his rooms where a valet drew a steaming-hot bath. Leroux sank beneath the surface and tried to wash the fog from his mind. As Joubert had predicted, the mountain of gold called the Rand would bring nothing but trouble. The British Empire needed it. Without the Rand, they would slowly but surely lose their South African colonies, which would fall under the sway of whoever controlled the gold. The Germans saw the opportunity to challenge the British Empire on attractive terms, with Kruger as an ally, the moral high ground and international backing. The Irish were operating beneath the surface using the chaos to weaken the British in any way they could and loosen the chains on Ireland.

The trekkers had tried to get away from the schemes and machinations of empires and live a simple life with the bible and the plough, but control of the Rand would shape the destiny of empires, and no one would let Kruger and his small band of devout farmers stand in the way. And the local tribes too, who wanted nothing to do with white man's wars, would continue to suffer, forced off their lands and offered the bitter compensation of a job in the mines. He thought of Tom and how he hoped to make enough in the mines to settle down out on the veld. But once the mines had gotten hold of him, they never let him go.

Rhodes delegated everything from far away in Cape Town. In theory, his plan could work, but in practice, the reform committee had prepared inadequately and almost certainly lost the critical element of surprise unless they had a closely guarded trick up their sleeve. The Irish had nonchalantly collected part of the Randlords' shipment of rifles. Either they were working together, which Rhodes denied, or the Randlords tolerated the Irish activities, whether it was a protection racket or some other scam. And there was no reason why the Randlords would tell him or publicly admit to working with avowed enemies of the Empire. With Johannesburg such a melting pot of ambition it was almost impossible to keep a secret, and the Irish would be a logical choice of partner if secrecy were paramount. They had spent their life dodging British spies. Could this really be a Rhodes scheme to recruit additional off-the-books help? Hammond had seemed oddly unperturbed by the idea of the Irish intercepting the rifles.

Eugène Marais - what to make of him? He was paranoid and not just from the laudanum. He had something on his mind that worried him. Leroux had seen it in his face when Muller cornered him. Muller clearly suspected a connection with Veltheim, and Marais had never printed that notice in his paper. He could have forgotten with so much on his mind. But if Marais had Veltheim on his mind, he was unlikely to forget someone asking him to print a notice seeking information on the very same person. He was part of the Reformer Boer movement that the Randlords were confederates with, but could he be trusted?

Phillips was business-like and precise and next to the others timid. Leroux could not see him in the same room with Donal O'Connell. What would he say to Sanderson about Irene?

Jameson was a wild card. Capable of the most audacious of exploits in the native wars, did he genuinely believe he could accomplish such feats against the Boers on their home terrain? And were Rhodes and Hammond relying on him to do that?

Hammond was Rhodes's best hope. Of the reform committee members, he was the one who kept calm, acted decisively, and had the respect of the miners and the charisma to bring them with him when the moment came. Hammond remained focused amid all the distractions. Maybe he could carry the day. They planned the flotation for the 3rd, but that was still six days away. Somebody, maybe Muller or the Irish planned on lighting the fuse before then.

Muller. Professional and dedicated. Determined to win glory for his Kaiser and no doubt himself, which was the only route for someone from a modest background to advance far in Imperial Germany. He would not let anything get in the way of his ambition. And Leroux had only a general idea about what Muller was planning.

The Baroness. She too had reason to fear Muller. Already regarded as a parvenu, he could destroy her reputation by revealing the affair with Brandt and had threatened to accuse her of murdering her husband. She faced losing her reputation, fortune, and perhaps liberty.

Captain Brandt. Leroux owed him his life. Unless Brandt could expose Muller's reckless plans to provoke a war, Muller would destroy his career. Brandt and the Baroness may get their wish of making a new life for themselves out here, but not as they had intended.

O'Connell, the dynamitard. Depending on your perspective, a

revolutionary or a terrorist, but maybe a greedy one, and definitely a murderer. He wanted to hit the British where it hurt and free Ireland. But it didn't matter which side he was on. O'Connell had murdered the wrong person and Leroux realised he did not care who won the fight for the gold - people would fight over it as long as they breathed, and the Earth spun. It had ended his father's life and Tom's and would ruin many more. The only meaning lay in justice for his father, and he would not let him down again. He pictured Tom raising his spear and charging into the bush with no idea what lay in wait for him and happy about it. Leroux smiled.

He pulled himself out of the bath, towelled down and went through his bag that Lara had sent over from the hotel. She thought of everything. Laundered and freshly pressed, crisp and dry. He ran the palm of his hand over a shirt and thought of the caress of Lara's skin. His black eye had faded a little, parts were still dark blue or violet, but much of the bruising was now sallow or green. He made a mental note to ask Brandt for the eye patch back. It reminded him of Lara.

He descended the sweeping staircase and onto the veranda where Brandt and the Baroness chatted quietly.

'You look refreshed,' the Baroness said.

'I feel much better and relieved that we have made common cause.'

The Baroness cocked her head, and Brandt put a reassuring arm around her waist.

'We are all in Muller's sights,' Brandt said. 'And I believe the solution to both our problems runs through the Irish at Irene.'

'Muller is vindictive,' the Baroness said.

'I know,' Leroux said. 'But if we can show that he is risking the German Empire's reputation by concocting false justifications for war, he will be lucky to survive, let alone attack you.'

'How can we do that?'

'I don't know, but, like Karl, I'm sure Irene and the Irish lie at the heart of it. All roads lead there. Karl and I will go tomorrow. If we can find out what they are planning, we may be able to work it to our advantage.'

The Baroness looked at Brandt.

'I cannot think of a better plan, darling. I don't know what the Irish are doing there, or what Muller's part in this is, but if the Irish are planning something illegal, which they almost certainly are, you will be justified in going there - the Government will want to know that.'

'I'll go to Lara's first thing to check on her and Sanderson and then come back,' Leroux said. 'From here, it should be just over three hours if we ride hard.'

'I'll send a messenger to the consulate to see if anyone has seen Muller,' the Baroness said. 'One more thing, I've heard rumours that Kruger is considering making concessions. Small ones, such as allowing English schooling and the removal of tariffs on foodstuffs.'

'Concessions that will be welcomed by the working man,' said Leroux, 'and which will take some of the wind out of the Reformers' sails. It will make the whole affair look like a capitalist coup.'

'He's a cunning fox,' Brandt said. 'I'll wager he makes the offer just before the Reformers announce a rising.'

They sat to dinner and talked about their love of Africa. Tired and replete Leroux repaired to his room for an early night, but sleep wouldn't come. He sat at the writing desk and penned what might be his last article for The Argus. He detailed the crisis in Johannesburg for his readers as his editor would wish. The heady excitement of the Uitlanders whipped up into righteous indignation by economic and political oppression. They were without the vote and ruinously taxed while the Burghers paid next to nothing. As he wrote, he realised the picture he painted for his readers was more Boston Tea Party than a cry for Queen and country. The expeditionary force, led by the dashing Dr Leander Starr Jameson, the Lion of Africa, pawed at the border poised to rescue the Uitlanders if President Kruger put upon them anymore. The lack of policing was inviting trouble and if Kruger would not protect his citizens, then someone else should. The world was watching, and the prize was enough gold to fund an empire.

Leroux put his pen down. He scarcely believed in a word of it, but it was what his editor demanded. Perhaps one of Rhodes's papers was not for him. They were just a tool for the Randlords to stir up conflict in the Transvaal. Nobody was genuinely working towards a peaceful resolution. Their thoughts had become too twisted and fevered by the possibilities that controlling the mountain of gold offered.

The people who lived in the Transvaal had everything they needed. Enough for everybody, gold and coal, pasture for cattle and land for crops. But they were divided between liberals and traditionalists, and it was all too simple for outsiders to stoke the division for their own ends, encouraging the people to seek foreign help rather than reach a compromise with each other. He laid his head back on the pillow and wondered what tomorrow would bring. He would have no regrets.

Sunday, 29th December 1895

Leroux cycled over to Lara's at first light, freewheeling down from the grand mansions of Saratoga Avenue, over the crossing and along Noord Street by the train tracks. Leroux cut a lonely path through the damp air, and no Zarps disturbed his progress to the corner of Rissik and Bree Street. Johannesburg slept like any other Sunday. The flowerpot waited in the window, and he knocked gently on Number 15 and stood back. A movement flickered in the window, and Lara ran down to open the door. She stood coyly in a white cotton dressing gown with intricate blue lace edgings and cascades of flounces adorning the front, but it was the smile that mesmerised him. He would have cycled across Africa for it.

'You're a wanted man.'

'The Zarps came back?'

'Searched the whole building last night.'

They went up to her rooms and the aroma of freshly brewed coffee, and Leroux kept an eye out from the window.

'What are you going to do?' Lara handed Leroux a steaming cup.

'Going back to Irene with Brandt. That's where O'Connell will be. They've got something planned. For Brandt, uncovering that may protect him, and the Baroness, from Muller.'

'Is Muller still here?' Lara clutched her arms around her.

'I don't know. Watch out for messages but keep clear of him. He will stop at nothing. Sanderson will be here with you, and you can ask the Baroness for anything.'

Leroux sipped his coffee at the window and Sanderson came hurrying along the street, with quick urgent steps and his puggaree flapping from his helmet. Leroux went down to meet him, and as they climbed the stairs Sanderson stopped halfway, wheezing and flushed, and said,

'I saw Phillips late last night. Difficult to track down. I told him it's about the administration of the Nellmapius estate. You're never going to believe this,' he gasped for breath, bent over.

'What?'

'It was rented out by Hammond as a staging post for Jameson just a couple of days ago. He was most concerned that I knew about it. It's all supposed to be hush-hush.'

Lara poured another coffee for Sanderson.

'Then the Randlords know about Irene,' Leroux said. 'O'Connell looked in charge. The Randlords need manpower, and fighters, and people who can keep a secret. But even so, it would be a huge embarrassment to the British Government if it became known that they were working with Irish terrorists to overthrow Kruger – what is Hammond doing? Imagine if Muller found out? And does Rhodes know about it?'

Sanderson raised his hand and waggled his index finger. 'This could be about funding the uprising. The British Government wouldn't pay for it, at least not upfront. Rhodes and the Corner House must be doing that, but the companies have other stockholders. They can't have gone to them for approval. Maybe they are using the Irish protection racket to siphon funds for their scheme. And Hammond and Rhodes are keeping it quiet from the Government.'

'Rhodes did send that message saying not to investigate further,' Leroux said.

'But why was Rhodes concerned about Veltheim if he knew what the Irish were doing?' Lara said.

'Could be he didn't know. Maybe he delegated the details, and things began to go wrong.' Sanderson said.

'The young Irishman said that killing my father wasn't intended, that someone got greedy.'

'Murdering your father can't have been part of the plan,' Sanderson said. 'And then when Rhodes investigated, he saw the name of a German company. Perhaps he worried that German intelligence had infiltrated the operation, and then his man Jones goes missing. After all, the Corner House Group is German-owned too, and while they are allies of Rhodes, they could easily have had a spy in their midst.'

'And so, then Rhodes sends somebody completely unconnected to look into the Veltheim connection?' Lara said.

'Me?'
Lara and Sanderson nodded.
'Should I tell Rhodes what you have found?' Lara said.
Sanderson picked at his moustache. 'Rhodes has denied any connection with the Irish and instructed you to stop any investigation. Hammond has told you to not stir anything up before the flotation. I don't think Rhodes will thank you for putting this business down in writing.'
'Rhodes was worried about a German connection. Apart from Veltheim being a German name, I haven't found anything that links the Germans to this.'
'I won't send anything then,' Lara said. 'If there is a link you may find it at Irene later.'
'The shipment of guns on the train was divided between Simmer and Jack and the Irish. It's reasonable to assume that the Randlords shipped the guns and sent the message to Clan Na Gael telling them when the train arrived. Who organises the guns for the Randlords at the other end?'
'I spoke to Phillips about that last night as well. I told him the Irish took some of the guns to Irene. He looked a bit concerned but said Gardner Williams organises it. He's Rhodes's General Manager of De Beers Mines in Kimberley. The guns come up from The Cape. They've adapted a Standard Oil tanker to take fuel in the top and bottom in case anybody checks or turns on the spigot, and the middle is a dry storage section for the weapons. They send the wagon through De Aar Junction down to Port Elizabeth. Then it comes here on a regular service through Bloemfontein, like any other oil tanker.'
'But the message to the Irish used a code that Lara didn't recognise, and Rhodes denied knowledge of,' Leroux said.
Sanderson pushed the curtain back from the edge of the window.
'Hang on, David's coming. It looks like we're going to see some action.'
Leroux and Sanderson grabbed their coats.
'Send a message to Brandt to say I'll be a little delayed.' Leroux held Lara by her arms, and then remembered himself and let her go. She adjusted his hat and shooed him down the stairs. 'Take care, Peter.'
They made an unlikely trio. Sanderson strode with the occasional skip to keep up with Leroux while David scampered along, carefree.

Sanderson had dressed in a safari jacket and his pith helmet, anticipating adventure, and the neck flap bounced on his nape as his face reddened. He looked happier than Leroux had ever seen. They went north up Eloff Street to the corner of Plein Street, and they could see the single guard the door of Slack Alice's, scratching his beard.

Sanderson panted up. 'No guns. You won't get in the door with that.'

Leroux gave his revolver to David, who thrust it in the back of his waistband and slipped off to the back alley. Sanderson and Leroux sidled toward the guard as nonchalantly as they could for a couple of men approaching a whorehouse at eight o'clock on a Sunday morning.

'You still got some money left?' the guard said, and one of his teeth popped out through his lopsided sneer.

Sanderson removed his pith helmet and smoothed the stands of hair scraped across his balding scalp. 'It's early, I know. I've come to say goodbye to Daphne. I'm leaving town for a bit.'

'Other people after you for money?'

'No, no. Just going for New Year's.'

'I've been told not to let you in 'till you make a payment on your account.'

Sanderson rummaged in his pocket and pulled out a thin fold of notes.

'Now I see why you bought your friend.' The guard looked at Leroux, who dug into his inside pocket and produced his money clip. Sanderson eyed it and wiped his sweaty hands on his trousers. 'Thirty ponds should do it.'

'Fifty.' The guard thrust out his hand.

Leroux feigned grievance and counted off the notes. It was a ridiculous sum. But the stakes were high, he wasn't paying, and the person that was could more than afford it. Whether Rhodes still wanted his help or not was a different matter.

The dim interior looked the same, but the air was not. People had passed through this morning. They crept to the first floor where the meeting room door was shut. The commotion of people arriving disturbed the silence, and they heard steps below them along the corridor as they reached the second floor. Daphne's door was ajar, and Sanderson gently pushed it open. She stood in her nightgown against the window, half turned towards him, angelic in the morning sun.

'I've seen three arrive at the back. Maybe some more at the front, with all the banging of the doors.' Daphne had already lifted the floorboard.

'You're a treasure, Daphne, well done.' Sanderson looked at Leroux. 'You should listen, better ears than mine.'

Leroux knelt, placed a notebook and pen down and lowered his head between the floorboards, turning his ear to the bolt hole. He caught snatches of chairs shifting and indistinct conversation. The door opened, and the room quietened. Leroux strained to get closer. Beads of sweat formed on his neck and forehead. The door shut, firmly. They welcomed each other, and he became accustomed to the speech. In between the harsh brogue was a voice he had heard before, a softly lilting voice.

'Here we are then, gentleman. Y'all ready?' It was the voice of JC Manion, the United States consul in Johannesburg, cocksure and supercilious.

'We have the gold. We're ready.' It was an Irish voice, low and slow. Leroux thought back to Irene and Maddox Deep and O'Connell directing operations and was sure it was him.

'Good. We'll consider that a deposit. I'll tell y'all where to send it later. Ten thousand Springfield Rifles and passage for two thousand men. Have you confirmed the destination?'

'Derrynane, County Kerry. The ships will need to anchor in the bay at night, and we'll ferry the men and guns ashore.'

'The voyage from New York takes six or seven days. The ships will be ready by New Year's Day. Your men should be ready to embark. By then we'll know if you have delivered on the rest of the bargain,' JC Manion said.

'We'll deliver, as long your friend's information is correct.'

'Good. Make sure they're ready. When we're done here, Britain will threaten war. You don't want to be at sea if they really mean it, you'll have the British Navy to deal with.'

A new voice spoke. It was a Boer accent, but not one that Leroux recognised. 'Our information is correct, but I hear troubling things. There was a robbery at your office, and they took a message. We are risking our lives here. This is treason. Who took the message?'

'We've dealt with it,' said O'Connell, and now louder. 'And brother, you do not tell the Clan about secrecy. Scotland Yard has been planting informers and sending agent provocateurs against us all our lives.

These men here have been tested and are trusted. If your life wasn't at risk, we wouldn't be talking.'

The American spoke up. 'I heard you killed the owner of the mine. We gave you funds to buy a safe location discreetly and to make sure nothing led back to us. I got a feeling you endangered that to line your own pockets. I want to be reassured you understand the priorities here.'

A hand slammed on the table. 'You deal with us because we get the job done and keep our mouths shut,' O'Connell said. 'Your President wouldn't even be in power if it wasn't for Irish votes, and this will give you another victory.'

Leroux's mind raced to process the information, and he suddenly remembered to take a note and scribbled down, "Guns and passage to Derrynane for Gold, Clan Na Gael and JC Manion."

'Gentlemen. Let's not pitch a hissy fit. We are on the verge of success,' said JC Manion.

Sanderson read the note and straightened. 'Of course, Manion! A good old Irish name and an American Consul like–,' he whispered, raising his hand in realisation…

'All the pieces are in place,' Manion had continued, 'You will let us know when–,'

…and knocked the water pitcher off the chest. It thudded to the floor. Sanderson lunged, grabbing hold of it, but not before half of the water splashed over Leroux and down through the floorboards to the lathe and plaster of the ceiling. Leroux instinctively put his finger over the hole, but the dust had darkened around the opening.

'Upstairs now,' O'Connell roared.

'You've got to get that information out,' Sanderson said, clutching his hands by his side in despair. Daphne fumbled with the floorboard as Leroux got up and helped her place it down.

'I'm sorry, but I suddenly remembered - Gardner Williams is also the US consul in Kimberly as well as the General Manager for De Beers. That must be how they knew about the rifle shipment. Go, go.'

Footsteps thundered on the stairs.

Leroux levered himself out of the window. It was a long way down. Sanderson pulled the rug over the floorboard and tipped the rest of the water over it. He looked up at Leroux and pointed with determination. 'I want a by-line out of this lad, now go.'

Sanderson donned his pith helmet, dropped his trousers and clambered on to the bed.

'Daphne! To me!'

Leroux reached for an iron gutter pipe to the side of the window, swung out and got both hands on it.

The door burst open, and Daphne screamed. Leroux fought for a foothold. No time to go down, he scrambled up the pipe. The lintel protruded a couple of inches above the window, and he got one foot onto it.

'Be quiet!' an Irishman shouted. There was a harsh slap, then silence.

Leroux pushed himself away from the downpipe and got his other foot onto the corner of the lintel. He held himself leaning out from the lintel against the ironwork, pressing into the wall. He looked down and saw David, mouth open, startled. Leroux put his finger to his lips as a revolver and a greasy head stuck out of the window. It's strange, thought Leroux, the scalp didn't look menacing, even as the gun swept left and right along the alleyway.

'Hey, you!'

David looked up. One hand covered his eyes, and the other went to the small of his back.

'Anyone come out of here?'

'No, sir.'

'What are you doing there?'

'I'm here to make sure no one goes in!'

Good lad, Sanderson had chosen well. The Irishman took one last look and then disappeared. They were interrogating Sanderson now. A shot. Daphne screamed again. Another shot. No one screamed.

Leroux waved his arm at David to run away, but he shook his head. The room was quiet now. Tears ran down Leroux's cheeks. He hung on to the pipe, waiting, cursing, swearing they would pay. He couldn't go back to the room - there was no point - they wouldn't leave witnesses. He scrabbled down the pipe. There was no time to lose, the gold at Maddox Deep was part of the deal, and the Irish weren't there. David returned the revolver and fleet of foot he kept pace with Leroux as they ran grim-faced to take a cab to the Baroness's mansion.

Leroux found Brandt with a couple of grooms preparing their mounts for the journey. The horses were saddled and fully equipped with nosebags of grain slung to the side, blankets across the pommels, rifles holstered in buckets, axes in leather holders and nets with grocery rations and water bottles. On the ground lay bandoliers, cloaks and two haversacks. One groom filled a wallet with a patrol tin and ammunition, while the other held two bare remounts by their bridles.

Brandt tightened a girth strap and looked up.

'What's wrong?'

'They killed Sanderson. There was a meeting at Slack Alice's between Clan Na Gael and an American, JC Manion. He was with a Boer I couldn't identify. They discovered us and the Irish shot Sanderson and his friend. He sacrificed himself - I only just got away.'

'Schweine! I'm sorry, I know you liked him. We're nearly ready. You still want to go?'

'Not to Irene. I overheard some of what they said. The Irish are planning a rising in Ireland with American help. I've been wrong about them and Muller.'

'O'Connell plans to start a war with Britain?'

'They're using the gold to buy passage for two thousand armed men from New York to Ireland.'

Brandt's eyes widened, and he straightened and handed the reins to the groom.

'JC Manion is the American consul, a diplomat!'

'I know.'

'Why would America risk that? Was he there in an official capacity?'

'Given what he's organising, I think we have to assume that he is. There's another part to the deal, something the Irish are going to do, which they said would give a victory to the American President. Manion called the gold just a deposit. O'Connell said he could do it if the information was correct.'

'What information?'

'I don't know, but there was a Boer there who vouched for it. Must be the information O'Connell was waiting for when I overheard him at the ranch. And Manion said that what they were planning here might make the British declare war.'

'Something else apart from the guns and men to Ireland?' Brandt said.

'Yes, he told the Irish to hurry because they wouldn't want to be at sea and face the Royal Navy when the British threatened war. It would explain why they are stockpiling rifles here.'

Brandt looked over to the veranda where the Baroness had come out. She rested her head against a wooden column and held one arm across her stomach, watching them.

'Muller is going to report me for insubordination. He's a Colonel. They won't listen to my side.'

Leroux saw the sadness is Brandt's eyes. Muller would destroy Brandt and the Baroness if he didn't get what he wanted, and Muller would want this information.

'Muller isn't aware of any of this, is he?'

Brandt looked down. 'I just don't know. I have seen nothing to make me think he is involved, but he would certainly welcome America and the Irish being at war with Britain.'

'I have suspected him all the time. But not of this. I'm sure he would like to know, though, and would be extremely grateful to whoever told him.'

'Are you suggesting I–'

'–No, and I know you wouldn't. There's something else going on. I've been so wrapped up with O'Connell that I've seen everything through that. My father, Maddox Deep, the Irish - that has been my viewpoint. But the more we find out, the more it looks like a sideshow, a small part of the picture.'

'You mean America and Britain at each other's throats over Venezuela, the President trying to whip up the public with a war before the election?'

'No, not that either. I mean what is going on here, on the Rand. Manion said the British would threaten war "when we're done here." Not over Venezuela, not over the Irish, something else, something here.'

'Something bad for Britain?' Brandt said.

'If Muller already knows about this, he won't reward you for telling him, even if you would. My guess is he doesn't know. Which means the chances are that Kruger doesn't know about it either. Whatever is happening here, it's probably not good news for Kruger either.'

'You have an idea?' Brandt said.

'If it's bad for Kruger and we can uncover it, that will reflect poorly on Muller, and his accusation against you will look like spite.'

'What do you think is going on?'

'I don't know yet. O'Connell is involved in Maddox Deep and Irene.

Sanderson told me that Irene was rented a few days ago by Hammond as a staging post for Jameson.'

'Are the Irish helping the Randlords or fighting them?'

'Good question. Somebody is playing both sides. O'Connell got the information he was waiting on, but we can wreck their plan if they're still at Slack Alice's and we move fast. If we can get the gold at Maddox Deep, it will scupper their deal with Manion. Then go to Irene for O'Connell, he's got some questions to answer.'

The Baroness walked up to them, looked into Leroux's eyes, and put her hand on his forearm. 'What happened?'

'They killed Sanderson. Will you tell Lara?'

She raised a handkerchief to her mouth and looked at Brandt. 'A message came from the consulate. Muller is looking for you - it won't be long before he comes here. What will you do?'

'We're going to Maddox Deep and then to Irene,' Brandt said. 'We'll leave the remounts here and pick them up on the way back from the mine.'

Leroux collected his knobkerrie and spear and inspected the blade head.

'A Lee-Metford not enough for you?'

'Not for what I've got in mind.'

'I'll go and see Lara, we'll look after each other,' the Baroness said, as Leroux and Brandt wheeled their horses. Leroux pulled David up behind him, and they galloped away in a cloud of dust. They headed south and east as the sun rose higher. Out through the shanties they charged, past families shepherding their children to church, who stood back to gawp as they thundered by.

They went past Simmer and Jack where the stamp presses still pounded, and smoke poured from the chimney stack. From high in their saddles, they could see the barren land beyond the fencing around Maddox Deep.

'Head straight for the building once we're over. We want to get to the door before they can see us.'

David jumped down as Leroux slowed his horse to a walk and stood in his saddle. He threw his weapons over and leapt and rolled in the dirt. Brandt followed suit, and they scrambled to their feet and ran for the door. 'Watch out for the dogs!'

'What?'

The Boerhunds tore baying around the corner.

'Stay behind me,' Leroux said and dropped the assegai to the floor beside him. Just thirty paces away, both dogs bore down on Leroux. They moved fast, at full stretch, focused on their target, teeth bared, not barking anymore. Leroux raised the knobkerrie two-handed behind his head. The lead hound now only twenty paces from him, snarling, gums glistening. Leroux flung his arms forward and released the knobkerrie. It flew end over end. The dog's jaw widened, perhaps instinctively to catch it or in anticipation of clamping onto Leroux's throat. The bulbous end of the stick came round again and struck the junction of the dog's skull and spine sending it sprawling dazed in the dust. Leroux dropped to his knee and raised the pointed end of the assegai. The second dog was already in the air, leaping for Leroux as he braced the butt into the ground. The dog filled his view with hair and teeth and coal-black eyes as it impaled itself slavering and yelping. Its breath and saliva and frothing blood spurted over him as he rolled with the spear and the beast to the side. Brandt went for the door. Leroux and the first dog staggered to their feet simultaneously. Leroux had seen Boerhunds continue to attack even when severely hurt. He stood sideways, avoiding direct eye contact, offering no threat and edged away with his hand on his revolver just in case. The dog staggered, holding its head low and looked from Leroux to the other dog which floundered on its side, its pitiful whines fading into wheezy gasps.

Leroux left them and ran to the building. He flattened against the wall the other side of the door from Brandt, who bought his finger to his lips. Someone moved inside. Brandt turned back to the door and, pointing at the handle, held his revolver up by the muzzle.

Someone lifted the latch from inside, and as the handle rattled, Leroux grabbed it and yanked hard, pulling the door open sharply, and bringing a guard with it. Brandt smashed the butt of his revolver down on the man's skull, knocking him senseless.

The Irish had cleared out most of the stores apart from a few tools and lengths of chain and rope. There were four rudimentary cots, one along each wall, and a washstand with a water jug and basin, while white powder had been scattered on the floor around the beds to ward off sand-flies.

'Hey Connor, what was it?' A voice called through from the next room.

Steps approached the door at the back. There was nowhere to hide, and they both covered the opening with their revolvers. The guard walked into the room,

'I said–'

Leroux put his fingers to his lips, and the Irishman raised his hands.

'Turn,' Brandt said and removed the revolver from the Irishman's holster. They bound his hands and feet.

'How many others?'

'One.'

'The man outside?'

'Yes.'

Brandt acted out counting the four cots and looked back to the guard and raised the butt of his gun. 'One?'

'Make that two, in the mineshaft.'

Brandt stuffed and tied a sock in the guard's mouth. 'Any noise…' he drew his thumb across his windpipe.

They moved through the backroom. The crates had gone too. Either they weren't using Maddox Deep for the weapons anymore, or they were all down in the mine. The desk remained with some paperwork, and there were some files left on the shelf. Leroux inched the double-doors open and went out into the deserted yard. A machine ran in the background, probably the pump, and a loading cart waited empty at the top of the mineshaft. Leroux gently released the brake, and they descended, holding the iron cart in front of them. They trod lightly and peered into the depths as the paraffin lamps shimmered yellow light on the walls. The slope and the receding lights disorientated the senses, but the cart steadied them as they passed concrete pillars and occasionally a wooden support.

They reached half-way when a call came up.

'What are you doing?'

Leroux and Brandt descended steadily, water dripping off the walls, oiled wheels turning on the rails.

'Hey, what are you doing?'

'It's Connor,' Leroux shouted back in a poor attempt at brogue. They kept going down, not trying to muffle their noise now, footsteps crunching on the loose rock chips, shielded by the cart.

'Connor, what the feck are ye doing?' Heavy footsteps stamped up towards them. The man was only twenty yards away now, wiping his brow and they could see behind him another man in a waistcoat bent over, his long hair hanging down, lifting something into a crate. Brandt showed himself and his revolver. 'Hands up!'

Leroux held the cart with one hand and covered the man further down.

'Who the hell are you?' the man nearer to them said. He had raised his arms just enough to bring his right hand even closer to the handle of his gun.

'Hands–'

The man at the bottom went for his weapon, turning and drawing in one movement. Leroux fired into his body, just where the top buttonhole of his waistcoat hung open. The report was deafening and shuddered around the mineshaft. The man staggered, blinked and looked down at his chest and the spreading blot of blood. He bought one hand up to the wound with a look of confusion and then seemed to recover his senses and snarled and swung his arm up. Leroux fired again into his chest. The man collapsed backwards, arched over a crate. His arms splayed out, and his gun slipped from his grasp and clattered to the rocky ground. Brandt stayed focussed on the first man, who thrust his arms up as high as he could.

Brandt tied him up, and Leroux went to check the bottom of the shaft. Past a small stack of empty wooden boxes, the Irish had built an iron lattice into the tunnel to cage off the end. The gate hung open. Inside, a few canvas bundles leant against the wall, fewer than Leroux had seen on his previous visit. Right in the middle, a small pyramid of gold ingots lay on the floor. A pile of treasure, roughly cast and duller than in the fables. The bars were small, less than a hand long, a couple of inches wide and not even an inch deep but weighed about five pounds apiece. Each one worth well over a thousand dollars. There were eighty of them. The uneven surfaces and malformed shapes of the bullion made the little bricks look like the worn playthings of an ancient child king.

Leroux gazed at the pile and knew then that he didn't have the gold bug and could never have followed in his father's footsteps. Down here, deep underground was the best place for it. No amount of gold could bring back his father or Tom, and it would only cause more trouble. The gleam of the gold took him back to the veld, stalking through the tall yellow grass with Tom, the time they came upon a lion. Their gaze met, Leroux transfixed, gripping his rifle tight. He held his ground and saw the light in the lion's eyes, and perhaps the lion saw the light in his. And the moment passed, the lion dipped its great head and turned away and vanished into the grass. Those were the times he treasured.

'What do you want to do with the gold?' Brandt said, looking over his shoulder.

'It belongs to Simmer and Jack.'

'Shall we lock it up and tell them to come and get it?'

'I don't think we can take the risk. The Irish could be here soon.'

'Let's give it to them ourselves. It won't take long. We can use the cart and the wagon outside. I'll fetch David and the horses.'

'No, we need to make sure they can't make the payment today or in the next week, and we don't know for sure that there is no connection with Simmer and Jack. Can you fetch some dynamite from the store?'

'You're going to cave the mine in?'

Leroux nodded. 'I'll deal with the body.' Brandt loped up the mineshaft while Leroux hauled the dead guard to the cart and tipped him in. He pulled the other guard to his feet and pointed up the shaft with his gun and prodded him along. As they trudged, Leroux thought he heard a rumble. He stopped and listened.

'Faster,' Leroux said, and the guard jogged awkwardly, his hands behind his back, towards the light at the surface. At the top, a tall figure staggered into the opening as though propelled from behind. It looked like Brandt.

'Leroux!' The familiar voice sent a shiver down Leroux's spine. It was O'Connell, and the lanky figure in the top hat stepped out into the light, putting a gun to Brandt's head.

'Give up. There's no way out.'

Leroux grabbed the guard by the scruff of his neck, using him as a shield.

'I've got one of your men. Let the Captain go, and you can have your man and me.' He knew O'Connell would never let him go, but he might free Brandt, and Leroux owed him his life.

'Shoot the idiot for all I care.' O'Connell drew the hammer back at the side of Brandt's head. More men appeared behind them.

Leroux dropped his gun and shoved the guard forward. O'Connell prodded Brandt down the slope followed by five of his men.

'It's the Leroux boy, isn't it? You've caused me a lot of trouble.' He put his face into Leroux's and breathed open-mouthed as though trying to taste the fear.

'Who have we here then? Captain, is it?' O'Connell spun around and pressed the muzzle into Brandt's cheek. He drew it up the length of the scar to his temple. Brandt turned his head against the muzzle until it pressed against his forehead and stared directly at O'Connell.

'I am Hauptmann Karl Brandt of the Imperial German Army. This mine was acquired in the name of a German citizen who is wanted for theft and murder. I am investigating under the authority of President Kruger. Baron von Veltheim, or rather Herr Kűrtze, as he is actually called, is also a suspect in the death of Willem Leroux.'

O'Connell looked dumbfounded. He blinked and looked from Brandt to Leroux and his men. He let out a snort of laughter. He threw his head back cachinnating, ever louder, finally howling in the cavern, filling it with nightmarish mirth.

'Jaysus, Mary and Joseph! Baron von Veltheim is wanted for murder! What kind of a feckin' cover is that? I'll give you murder,' he said, tapping the muzzle of his gun against Brandt's skull.

O'Connell moved over to Leroux and pressed his gun into the bruising.

'Seamus did that to you.'

Leroux thought about the guard that ambushed him outside Lara's. The guard that surprised him when he returned to the office. The guard that Brandt shot.

'Where is he?' O'Connell's face twitched as his eyes glittered.

'He's warming up the morgue for you.'

O'Connell glared at Leroux and drew his hand back and whipped him with the butt of his revolver, taking care to strike the raw wound. The stitches gave way, and the skin peeled apart. O'Connell turned to his men.

'Aidan. You, Tyler and Liam stay here. Tie 'em up. Find out what they know and then kill them. Show him what happened to his Pa. Box the gold and get it to the top. A wagon will come. Pick up's at six.'

Leroux recognised Aidan from the alley. The one he had not shot. Yet.

O'Connell turned to Leroux. 'You're as stubborn as your old Pa. I admire that. I'd ask you to join us if you didn't have to die.' Leroux looked up. A trickle of blood ran down from his cheek, and he had a strange sense of déjà vu as he focused on the gleam in O'Connell's eye.

'Make sure the bodies aren't found. Rest of you, with me.' O'Connell turned and climbed the slope, his men hurrying to keep pace with his long stride.

The three remaining Irishmen tied them up and shoved them to the bottom of the mine and sat them down on crates, their hands bound behind them.

Aidan spun around and punched Leroux.

'That was for Jimmy in the alley.'

He punched him again.

'That was for Finn.' There were going to be a few more. Leroux's head hung forward, spittle and blood dripped to the floor.

'I shot Seamus,' Brandt said.

Aidan nodded to Tyler who stepped forward and hammered Brandt with his fist, snapping his head to the side, and Aidan belted Leroux again.

'That was for Micky.'

Presumably, he was the other one in the hotel room. He heard Brandt receiving a beating, the smacks of fist against face, and the duller thuds of body-shots.

Leroux spat to clear his mouth. 'Get it over with. I'm not saying anything.'

'I haven't asked you yet. You think this is the first time I've questioned someone?'

Aidan slammed the butt of his revolver against Leroux's right shin.

So, this was how it all ended. He'd bitten off more than he could chew in a vain attempt to make his father proud - a father who couldn't be proud because he was dead. Leroux chuckled darkly to himself. At least Tom would have admired the recklessness of it. He tasted blood and looked over to Brandt, who was having a hard time of it. Past Brandt, the top of the tunnel was just a small disk of light. The shimmering paraffin lamps like two lines of stars converging on the moon. And a cloud passed across it.

Aidan grabbed a fistful of Leroux's hair and jerked his face round.

'Were you at Slack Alice's?'

'I've got something valuable.'

Aidan stopped. His ferrety little eyes narrowed.

'What are you on about? More valuable than that heap of gold?' He sneered, tugging Leroux's head over in the direction of the little pyramid.

'In the right hands.'

Aidan's eyes looked from the gold, sideways at Leroux. 'Go on, then, tell me.'

'It's in my inside pocket.' Leroux glanced down at his chest.

'Liam, watch him.' Liam drew his gun and stood next to Aidan, covering Leroux. Just past him, Tyler had stopped hitting Brandt and watched too.

Aidan reached forward, and his hand felt inside Leroux's coat. Leroux looked down and rolled his head to check on Brandt. He was bloody but still alert. Behind him, one of the lamps winked about halfway along the tunnel on the right side. Then another, the next one down. Aidan's fingers delved into the pocket and found the letter. He pulled it out and stepped back. He held it up so that the paper unfolded and squinted at the handwriting in the lamplight.

'What is it?'

'That is written by the richest Randlord of them all, Cecil Rhodes.'

Aidan thrust it in front of Leroux's face. 'Read it.'

'It says "Mr Leroux is authorised to make any purchases and has full authority." Signed by Cecil Rhodes. If we go into a bank together, we could withdraw as much as you want. Captain Brandt, how much credit do you think Deutsche Bank would forward on this?' Leroux looked over at Brandt, and past him, another lamp winked, near now. He could make out a bulky outline.

Brandt blew out his cheeks. 'For Cecil Rhodes, as much as they had.'

Aidan showed the letter to Liam. 'One of us could take the letter to Donal. Keep 'em down here until he decides.' Liam shrugged. 'I wouldn't go to Donal until we found out what they know.'

'Are you going to talk?' Aidan said.

Leroux gave a resigned nod and spoke clearly and slowly. 'I was at Slack Alice's. I heard about the shipment to Derrynane. I told Brandt.' Leroux looked deliberately at Brandt, into his eyes. 'There's another who knows - a man called Jory. He's not far from here. I'll take you, Aidan. Leave him with Brandt. There's one more thing…' His voice trailed off, his head nodded forward, and he spat out some blood.

Aidan moved closer. 'What?'

Leroux looked up at Aidan, blinking and Aidan slapped him. 'One more thing - what?'

Leroux's head lolled back, he arched his back and dug his heels into the base of the crate and whipped his body, neck and head forward, butting Aidan brutally in the head. There was a blur of bodies. A huge figure barrelled in from the right like a buffalo and flattened Liam. It was Jory. Brandt launched himself forward into Tyler. He buried his head in Tyler's chest and drove him, legs pumping, backwards into the wall. Leroux fell back on to the crate, and Aidan roared, stood straight and reached for his revolver. Jory scrambled to his feet and grabbed Aidan's head from behind in one hand and propelled him into the side of the mineshaft, crushing his skull into the rock with a sickening crunch. Leroux struggled to his feet. Tyler beat down on Brandt's head and wrestled him off, throwing him to the ground where he floundered, helpless with his hands still tied behind his back. Tyler drew his gun and then crumpled, shot in the stomach, as the thunderous noise engulfed the mine. Tyler looked up, astonished, still raising his revolver while his other hand went to his belly. Jory fired again, and Tyler fell back and slid down the wall. Jory looked at the gun in his massive hand, as though he was surprised such a small thing could make such a noise and he placed it down on the crate beside Leroux and untied him.

'You move quietly for a big man,' Leroux said.

'I'm from a long line of smugglers,' Jory said and handed the gun to Leroux. 'David came and found me. He said you were in trouble, so I knew he was telling the truth. He's outside with the horses.'

They checked on the guards. Only Liam was alive and still unconscious. They carried him to the top and tied him up with the one O'Connell left behind outside. The one they had bound inside had gone.

Leroux brought a crate of dynamite from the stores. 'Jory, can you set enough to cave in the mine? Make sure that no one can get to the gold for a good while.'

Leroux and Brandt searched the building looking for any scraps of paper with a code on it or a message. Brandt ran his hand along a shelf in the office until he got to a sheaf of documents weighed down by a bible. Brandt looked through the papers, scanning each one and tossing them to the floor. 'Nothing here,' he said and put the bible on the desk. 'Don't suppose they had much use for this.'

Leroux looked at it. 'That's the Statenbijbel of the Reformed Church. It wasn't my father's. What on Earth are Clan Na Gael doing with that?'

Brandt flicked through the Bible. 'It's in Dutch.'

Leroux searched the papers on the desk. He had seen one of those Bibles before, recently. Leroux rifled through the drawers, and then Brandt said, 'Look here.' He held the Bible open, two-thirds of the way through was a slip of paper.

'Don't lose that page,' Leroux said. 'The coded message I found before, Lara couldn't crack it, but she thought they could be using a book code where both parties use the same book as a key to decipher the message. I know where I've seen that Bible before, there was one in the office on Ferreira Street. I just didn't think anything of it - I see those Bibles all the time.'

Brandt handed Leroux the slip. It was a telegram, and in code just like the other one, groups of five numbers set out between the header and footer. At the top, it was addressed to Maddox Deep, Johannesburg and at the bottom, the sender was Max Weber.

'Lara's got the other message and the coded telegram. With these, she might be able to break the code and decipher this message. This could be the information they were waiting for.'

Jory came in, rubbing his hands and grinning from ear to ear. 'All set.'

'We're going to find the rest of the Irish. Can you take the guards to the infirmary at Simmer and Jack and make sure they stay there all day?'

'That be no problem. But I want to come with you. Reckon you need some help.'

Leroux clapped Jory on the back. 'There's no one we'd rather have helping. O'Connell's got a head start on us, and we've got to go to Lara's first. You catch up with us there. David will guide you.'

Jory went to light the fuses while Leroux and Brandt searched the rest of the office. They dragged the guards down to the gate where David was overjoyed to see Leroux and capered about singing in Zulu. He had their horses ready and had rounded up three Irish mounts as well.

'You did very well David, Sanderson would have been immensely proud.'

'I saw the bad men from Slack Alice's go on their horses to the mine.

I go get your friend.' David pointed to Jory, who was charging towards them, waving his arms.

'Get down!'

'How much of the dynamite did you use?'

'All of it,' he said, holding on to his hat.

It started with a sharp crack, followed by a deep rumble, and a great whoosh of air and dust exploded out of the mine shaft. And from out of the billowing cloud, the iron cart smashed through the fencing and tumbled end over end towards them, coming to rest halfway from the building.

Jory clambered to his feet and dusted himself down. 'Always wanted to do that.'

Leroux and Brandt mounted up.

'Can you ride?' Leroux said.

Jory eyed the spare horses suspiciously. 'Are those Irish horses?'

Leroux laughed. 'I pity the horse that has to carry you. David will show you what to do.'

Leroux and Brandt rode to Lara's. The flowers poked out of the vase in the window, and Leroux slid down from his horse, relieved that the Zarps seemed to have lost interest in searching for him. Or maybe they preferred not to work on a Sunday.

'Look at you two, have you been fighting? I'll get some ointment,' Lara said.

'No time for that. I think we've found the key to the telegram code.' Leroux showed her the new message and the Bible. She retrieved the old, coded telegram and the corresponding note.

'If this is the book, we need to work out which part of the text they are using first.'

'I found the telegram on this page, the Gospel of Mark,' Brandt said.

Lara took the book and scanned the page. 'It's in Dutch, and the message is in English. Rather than use the whole word, they may just use the first letter or the last of particular words. The first word of the message is Train, and on the telegram, the first group of numbers is 11602. Let's say they are using the Gospel of Mark. The numbers could refer to the chapters, pages, lines, verses, or the number of words in the verse. There are ten letters or numbers in the decoded message and fifteen groups of numbers. If the message is the decoded telegram, the extra numbers could be a signature which they haven't bothered to write out.'

Lara set to work. In her theory, the first group of numbers represented a "T". After a few attempts, she found a path that worked. 'If I take the first number to be the chapter, assuming they use only the first nine and then the next two digits are the verse, and the final two digits are the number of words into the verse, I get a "T." Chapter one, verse sixteen, the second word is "Terwijl".'

Leroux looked at it. 'Terwijl is the first word.'

'I think they count the verse number as the first word. That way, they can use the verse numbers as numbers.'

She quickly completed the rest of the message to confirm her understanding. 'Yes, that's how they write numbers. See, twelve is written as 90101, chapter nine, first verse, first word, which is one. And then 60201, which is chapter six, second verse, first word, which is two. The telegram is to 21 Ferreira Street, from Head Office and reads "TRAIN 12 27 5 EAGLE." The signature Eagle was missing from the original decoding.'

Confident in the code, Lara started on the new telegram.

'Does Eagle mean anything to you?' Brandt said.

'Apart from the Imperial German Eagle?' Leroux said.

'That's not Muller's codename. I know that for sure.'

'This was a message to Clan Na Gael, alerting them to the delivery of weapons. Sanderson told me that Gardner Williams organised the smuggling operations for the Randlords. He is the De Beers General Manager and US consul in Kimberley.'

'Americans have an Eagle too,' Brandt said.

'That's it - that's what bugged me about the message. The date order is month, day - not day, month. The train arrived at five o'clock on the 27th of December, and they wrote it as 12 27. That's the American style.'

'And Gardner Williams is American.'

'As are the Irish,' Leroux said. 'Someone codenamed "Eagle", at "Head Office" sent the Irish a message telling them when to pick up the guns. They then took them to Irene, which Phillips said was rented by Hammond for Jameson.'

Lara put down her pen. 'This message is to Maddox Deep, from Max Weber & Co and reads:

KRUGER TRAVELS FROM PRETORIA BY DOORNKOP ROAD 3 PM SUNDAY 29 STOP LIGHT ESCORT STOP SPRINGBOK STOP END

'They're going to kidnap Kruger,' Brandt said.

'I think they already have,' Leroux said looking at his watch, it was a few minutes after three.

'Who is going to kidnap him?' Lara said.

'The Irish are working with the American Government,' Brandt said.

'And the Randlords, if Phillips is telling the truth,' Leroux said.

'Certainly doesn't sound like Muller,' Lara said.

'The Kaiser will not take this well, whoever is behind it,' Brandt said.

'This must be the other part of the deal that Manion and O'Connell discussed this morning. Kidnapping Kruger is the rest of the deal,' Leroux said.

'Wait,' Lara said, 'the Irish are getting guns and a base from the Randlords and are doing a deal with the Americans to kidnap Kruger. We're missing something here. Are the Irish playing one against the other?'

'Somebody is,' Leroux said.

Leroux rubbed his scalp with both hands. 'Can you show me that telegram again?' He read the new telegram from Springbok, using Weber's office as cover. 'Weber's office was cleared out about a week ago. This telegram is dated yesterday, so the address must still be working as a post box. And for someone that knows Kruger's movements.'

'They could have someone watching out for telegram boys,' Lara said.

Leroux looked at Brandt. 'This doesn't change anything for me. I'm still going to Irene to get O'Connell.'

'Nor me. If we can free Kruger, Muller won't be able to touch me.'

'And we may be able to stop war breaking out over this. I've got an idea.' Leroux started to jot a note down while Lara fetched ointment to clean the cuts on their faces.

'There's a messenger outside.' Brandt moved away from the window and went to meet him.

Leroux handed his message to Lara. 'Can you encode this using their Bible code and address it to Max Weber, from Head Office?'

SPRINGBOK PRESENCE REQUIRED AT MEETING IRENE ESTATE FIRST LIGHT TOMORROW STOP EAGLE STOP END

Lara started on the code.

'Have you had any inkling of this?' Leroux said.

'None. Removing Kruger is good for Rhodes. The next in command is Joubert, and he is their ally. But I don't think it's Rhodes,' Lara said.

Footsteps raced up the stairs, and Brandt burst into the room breathless. 'Jameson has set off.'

'What?'

'A messenger just arrived from the Baroness. Muller must have had someone near Jameson's base. A telegram arrived at the consulate from Mafeking to say the force had set off. They'll cross the border in a few hours.'

'Does Muller know?' Leroux said.

'He will soon.'

'There's no way of anyone contacting Jameson now. Let Rhodes know if he doesn't already,' Leroux said.

'Muller has caused this,' Brandt said, 'This is what he has been planning. When Berlin finds out, the Kaiser will declare war. Should we inform anyone else?'

'It will cause panic,' Leroux said. 'But if Rhodes reacts in time, and we can free Kruger perhaps we can stop Muller.'

Lara had finished on Leroux's message. 'What shall I send to Rhodes?'

'Reported that Jameson left Pitsani heading for the border. No sign of uprising in Johannesburg. Sources in German Consulate say this will precipitate war if not officially denounced and ordered to withdraw. Send a copy to the High Commissioner as well.'

Leroux pulled out the article he had written and amended it to include that Jameson had set off and the world waited with bated breath.

'Send this last thing tonight to Sanderson's editor, with Sanderson's name on it. Send a copy to the London Times. They'll get it in the morning.'

Lara read it, and her eyes moistened as she bit her lip and squeezed Leroux's hand.

Jory and David rode awkwardly down the street, and Brandt excused himself to meet them.

'I'd better get to the telegraph office,' Lara said and collected her papers.

'Can you arrange to forward any messages for me to Irene through Pretoria? Any news or developments. They should get there pretty quickly, starting at dawn?'

'Of course. What have you got planned?' Lara drifted closer to Leroux.

'I'm going after O'Connell. Little of this makes sense. Someone is playing a dangerous double game and risking war. I'll try to flush them out before it's too late.'

Lara caressed his cheek, her eyes searching over the wound. 'Take care, Peter.'

'When Muller finds out that Jameson is about to cross the border, he will contact Berlin.' Before he could continue, Lara put her hand on his. 'Rhodes placed me here to deal with exactly this type of situation. I am indebted to him. When my parents died, he made sure I was educated and found me work. I will be careful. I want to see this country with you and without war.'

Leroux held her tight and kissed her with overwhelming tenderness, before resting his forehead on hers. 'I have to go.'

'We'll pick up the fresh horses at the Baroness's on the way,' Brandt said. The street was quiet. Not a hint of unrest or revolution, and yet they had just heard that Jameson had ridden, the plan was in motion. It was an ordinary Sunday afternoon as the unlikely trio rode out of town. Jory looked uneasy on his horse, and bounced along grimly, uncomplaining, but not as uncomfortable as the horse.

They picked up the spare mounts and took the road to Pretoria, alternating walking and cantering. A pair of field glasses hung from Brandt's neck which he used to check whether there were any Irish on the road ahead. He turned to Leroux and said, 'You believe me that the Baroness didn't kill her husband?'

'Yes.'

'Muller does not care for the truth. It may be convenient or inconvenient, and he decides the truth accordingly. Because she came back here, it looks like that was her plan all along. But she had no choice. Society in Berlin shunned her. To come here where she had investments, and a friend, was logical.'

'Perhaps not wise, so soon.'

'I was happy for her to come as well. But now it makes it easy for Muller to accuse me of being a traitor as well. It fits into the same story.'

'Let's see what happens. By the end of the day, we may find other people to play the role of traitor.'

'Marais?'

'He is hiding something. Jones went to see him about Veltheim, then Jones disappears, and someone removes the page showing his visit. I asked him about Veltheim, and he denied any knowledge. I saw Muller talking to him at the Baroness's party, and he looked terrified. Perhaps Muller had said he knows Jones came to see him?'

'The Reformer Boers could be involved in the kidnapping of Kruger, they would know his movements,' Brandt said.

'I agree. And Joubert would certainly know the security arrangements.'

They reached the turning as dusk fell.

'There's a lot of men at Irene.' Brandt said.

Leroux looked across at Brandt. 'I don't need O'Connell alive. I just need an opportunity. If there's too many for us to be able to free Kruger, then we can let his people in Pretoria know where he is.'

They kept to a walk as darkness enveloped them and the entrance to the farm lay just over a mile ahead. They dismounted and took the horses in hand until they could see the brazier flickering in the distance. Leroux found a spot off the track where they picketed the horses and crept through the scrub and grass to the fence line fifty yards along from the little gatehouse. Two guards sat on crates set well back from the brazier for it was still warm from the day. Shadows played on the hut, and occasionally the glow illuminated one of their faces.

In front of the barn, three guards tended a dozen saddled horses next to a cart. They had increased the security, and another guard patrolled the perimeter, about twenty paces in from the fence, pacing slowly back and forth. There would be more on the other sides of the property. The barn door opened, and light flooded out. At least two dozen men led out more horses.

'They're preparing to leave,' Brandt said adjusting his binoculars.

'How many?'

'A lot. Thirty horses outside now, maybe some more still inside.'

The farmhouse door opened. The familiar gaunt figure stood in the light, peered out into the dark, put on his top hat, and strode to the barn. Leroux followed him in the sights of his Lee Metford. Even at night, at a hundred paces, he was confident of the shot. A guard walked into the line of sight. Brandt lowered his glasses.

'Can you see Kruger?' Leroux asked.

'No. The men by the barn all look like O'Connell's men. He's just talking to some of them now.'

'Where do you think they're going?'

Brandt turned on his side and shrugged his shoulders, as Jory lay behind them taking forty winks. The moon emerged from behind a cloud. Brandt and Leroux pressed their faces down as one of the guards trudged past. Leroux took the glasses as more horses came out of the barn, and a dozen men emerged from the farmhouse and checked them over. One by one they mounted and formed up into something approximating a column. The guard prowling the perimeter stopped to watch. The horses obscured the barn entrance, but the top hat of O'Connell appeared by a horse's head at the front of the column, where he talked to the troop's leader. The rider flicked his horse into a slow walk. Leroux followed the top hat, appearing momentarily between the gaps in the horses as O'Connell walked back towards the farmhouse. It would be suicide to shoot now.

'What's happening,' Brandt said.

Leroux adjusted the binoculars. Rhodes would have received the message by now, and the High Commissioner. What would they do? Did Berlin know yet? Leroux passed the glasses back to Brandt.

'They're about to leave. But maybe not all of them. No sign of Kruger, he must be in the farmhouse, and O'Connell's just gone back there.'

The troop moved out in double file, forty-five riders in total. O'Connell disappeared into the farmhouse and the barn doors closed.

Brandt passed the glasses to Leroux. 'Do you recognise anyone in the column as they pass the brazier?'

'Some look familiar from Maddox Deep. Nobody important. Kruger's definitely not there, and O'Connell went back into the farmhouse.'

'Let's give them time to get out of earshot.'

They crawled back from the fence and checked their weapons. Leroux had his Colt, a rifle and a spear. Brandt a revolver, a knife and a couple of sticks of dynamite. They showed Jory the workings of a Lee-Metford rifle. If he was close enough to use a revolver, he wouldn't stand a chance.

Monday, 30th December 1895

The activity at the farm died down until just smudges of light filtered out from the buildings. The perimeter guard changed over. Leroux and Brandt decided to go for the sentries at the gate first. Then the perimeter guard, the barn and finally the farmhouse.

'Can you shoot like a Boer?' Brandt said.

Leroux nodded.

'Are you sure you're not a Boer?'

Leroux picked at the grass and threw a few blades in the air, watching them fall with the light breeze. He rose to his feet.

'There's a part of me that belongs to this land. But there's another part that needs to escape.' He swayed subtly from foot to foot in rhythm, remembering the war-dance that Tom had taught him, not far from here. In the moonlight, Brandt's scar was livid against his pale skin. He put his hand on Leroux's shoulder.

'What are you thinking?'

'Remembering an old friend.'

'What does he say to you?'

Leroux looked at the farmhouse. So close now. 'Almost doesn't fill a bowl.'

'What?' Jory said.

'It means it's not enough to try. You must do - It's time to go,' Leroux said.

'I'll provide the diversions,' Brandt said. You pick them off. Jory, you fire at anyone you see shooting at us. Keep it up, even if they're in cover.'

Leroux and Brandt approached the gate on each side of the track. The two sentries were on the far side of the path from Leroux, by the brazier. Leroux waited until Brandt got into position behind them.

Leroux stalked in the long grass, only thirty paces away now. The guard patrolling this side of the perimeter had turned and walked away. Leroux rose slowly from his crouch and cocked his arm back. With his other hand, he tossed a stone. One of the guards cursed and got to his feet to peer towards the sound. Leroux froze, and the breeze murmured through the grass. The guard walked over the track towards him. Brandt loomed behind the other Irishman. He would know the signal.

Leroux pivoted over his front foot, unleashing the assegai and the guard twitched to the motion. A frown flickered on his face, and then he gaped and widened his eyes at the swoosh of the spear as it sliced through the air. It ripped into his chest, knocking him from his feet. Brandt cupped a hand around his man's mouth and drew a knife hard across his throat.

Leroux stood over his kill. The sentry drew his last rasping breaths, and Leroux silenced him with the butt of his rifle and retrieved the spear.

'We're not going to have the advantage of surprise for long.' Leroux said. 'The guard will be back in a minute. There'll be another on the right side. You take him, I'll take the one coming back here. Then we'll go for the barn. If they get lights on, there's no cover. Jory, you go for that cart, try and turn it over on its side.'

Brandt nodded and stole off into the night to find the sentry patrolling the right side of the farm, while Leroux and Jory waited by the brazier for the first sentry to come back. They looked nothing like the dead guards. Leroux moved away from the brazier and opened the magazine cut off on the Lee Metford and cycled the bolt. Leroux kept the sentry in his sights as he walked past, a bored expression just visible in the glow. A sharp crack from the right cut through the night as Brandt found his man. Leroux fired. Point-blank range. The guard dropped.

Jory sprinted for the cart, and Leroux ran towards the barn, where the door tentatively opened, and a golden pillar of light widened. A head poked out as Jory reached the cart and put his shoulder into tipping it. The barn door swung fully open, and Leroux's stomach sank. He fired, hitting the guard pushing the door and dropped to the ground. In the middle of the doorway was the Maxim gun, already mounted. Two men scrambled behind its small shield and loaded a belt. Leroux hit the gunner, but more men came to the entrance, and one replaced the gunner and cranked the first round into the chamber. Leroux fired again hitting the belt feeder. The gunner targeted the cart, which disintegrated into matchwood. Jory lay flat on the ground, one hand grasping his rifle the other over his head as splinters of wood showered over him.

Where was Brandt? Leroux shot again winging the gunner and knocking him back. Another man replaced him, and more men fired out from the barn into the darkness. Bullets zipped past or thudded into the ground, attracted by his muzzle flashes. Someone else fired from the side of the opening ripping up turf just by his elbow. He saw a light flare to his right and Leroux drew his revolver and sprinted left towards the remnants of the cart, firing into the doorway. He threw himself to the ground as the Maxim opened fire again like a demented carpenter hammering nails. The rounds smashed into the remains of the cart and zipped inches overhead into the darkness. Only the surviving timbers of the frame, wheel and sideboards protected them.

The belt had more than three hundred rounds, enough for thirty seconds of continuous fire. It already seemed an age but could not have been ten seconds yet. And then a panicked scream and the dreadful metallic hammering stopped. Leroux lifted his head and saw men scrambling back into the barn, a little wisp of smoke curled in front of the Maxim and then the boom, the beautiful boom of dynamite.

The machine gun lay on its side, smoking. One of the barn doors hung askew on a broken hinge as Brandt ran to the side of it and lobbed in a second stick. A window smashed over in the farmhouse as the dynamite exploded.

'Jory, fire at that window.'

Jory blinked and then snapped out of the terror of his first encounter with a Maxim gun. He pushed his hat down and rolled over, aiming for the window. Leroux sprinted further left, away from the light of the barn. The man at the window took a shot at him as he disappeared into the dark. Jory fired back, deliberate and slow but accurate enough to bother them. Brandt fired the odd pot shot into the barn, in a stand-off with the men inside, who seemed content to keep undercover.

Leroux dashed for the door of the farmhouse. Someone smashed the other window, to the left of the door, and Leroux fired instinctively at the shape, which grunted and disappeared. A gun protruded from the right window in Jory's direction. Leroux made it to the veranda, and Jory fired hitting the frame of the window. The gun flinched and then stretched forward zeroing in on Jory. Leroux shot the man's hand, re-cocked and barged through the door.

The iconic Old Testament features of President Kruger greeted him. He sat on a stool, a face like thunder, puce with a thick white fringe of hair around his chin and cheeks and he nodded to the back door where a tall thickset man slipped out. Two men were bound in the corner, presumably Kruger's bodyguards. A man clutched his ruined hand by the window.

'Two of them. Go!' barked Kruger assuming command. He would be able to manage the injured man on his own. Leroux charged across the room and out the back.

'Stop!' Leroux fired in the air.

The large man was already past his injured accomplice but stumbled to a halt and raised his hands. He turned slowly, the faint light from the doorway falling on his face. It was Hammond, panting and sweating in his immaculate attire. A lean hunched man clutched his blood-soaked shoulder, his shirt stained black in the moonlight. A gun hung down in the hand of his limp arm. He lurched around. Donal O'Connell had lost his top hat.

He breathed raggedly and sneered at Hammond. 'You said he wouldn't be a problem.'

'It was your damned greed messed everything up when you killed his father.'

'My greed, is it?' Donal raised his arm, growling against the pain as he strained to point his revolver at Hammond.

'Who was Veltheim?' Leroux said.

O'Connell looked back to Leroux with tired eyes and a tremor in his rotten grin. 'I'll not tell you anything, you Sassenach loving bastard.'

Leroux squeezed the trigger. He wasn't going to give the Irishman the pleasure of making him ask twice. The weeping hole, where the Irishman's right eye had been, gave his face an astonished appearance as he stared up motionless at the firmament. Wherever he had gone, he seemed surprised to be there.

Hammond stumbled backwards, ashen faced, his mouth twisted in a rictus of terror as he cleared his throat and stammered, 'Well done,

Leroux.'

There was no hint of the buccaneering braggadocio that had bought him to this place. Hammond looked to his raised hands and tentatively lowered them. 'Who are you with?' Are Kruger's men with you?' His eyes flicked to the door.

'Who was Veltheim?'

Hammond swallowed and looked down at the last man asked that question. His eyes pleaded. His head quivered in denial. 'Nobody. A nobody. A conman used as a front. Your father...it was a terrible mistake. O'Connell's mistake. Please believe me.'

'Jameson has crossed the border.'

'What?' Confusion compounded the fear in his eyes. 'How?'

Leroux savoured the sight of the little remaining colour drain from his face.

'That can't be…' Hammond gulped, and his eyes cast about hoping for an answer.

'I must get back and form the provisional government. Rhodes is committed. We can still win the day.'

'We?' Leroux said.

Hammond edged back towards the corner of the building.

'Yes. You work for Rhodes, don't you?'

'I do. Do you?'

'I understand you're upset. But there is much more at stake here. You've got to let me go, while there is still time.'

Leroux lowered his pistol. Hammond seemed unaware that his plan had been discovered. He had a long way to fall. Why deprive him of the slow sink into the stew of his own corruption?

'Go.'

Hammond's mouth twitched in a grin, and he shuffled back and turned and ran to a horse tied to the rear of the barn. Leroux smiled to himself. He had guessed right about "Eagle." He should have listened more to Jory, who had never trusted Hammond. Now to see if he was right about "Springbok."

Leroux went back into the farmhouse where Brandt was with Kruger, and the bodyguards dealt roughly with the wounded Irishman.

'Pieter Leroux. I have heard your name before, I think,' Kruger said. 'Was it the Malaboch campaign?'

'Yes, sir.'

'And you are wanted by my police, I hear?'

'That is a misunderstanding,' Brandt said.

Kruger raised an eyebrow. Even in old age, he was a powerfully built man. Ungainly, and ugly to most, even those that loved him, he had fine dark brown eyes that penetrated the most guarded of veils.

'Did Hammond get away?'

'Yes. The Irishman, O'Connell, is dead.'

'What game do they play? Where is Rhodes in this? Does he think he can get away with it? That he can beat me? The racehorse may be quicker than the ox, but the ox can bear greater loads. We shall see who will be the winner.'

'The men who left earlier do you know where they went?' Leroux said.

'They are planning to storm the arsenal in Pretoria just before dawn. We must send word. Dirk, come here.'

A burly Boer, one of the bodyguards, walked stiff-jointedly over and clapped Leroux around the shoulder.

'Oom Paul, what can I do?'

'Send your son to the arsenal and alert them. Those Uitlander devils will try to storm it before dawn. And tell him to send some men back here.'

'It will be done.'

Dirk turned and went outside, kicking the injured Irishman as he went. There were still a few hours before sunrise.

'The Reformer Boers are up to their necks in this business I can smell it,' Kruger said. He sat back and sighed. 'But we must stick together, God willing, if we are to have any chance.'

Kruger looked at Brandt. 'Your countryman, Colonel Muller. He told me about the Irish. He told me they were storing arms to fight against the English. That Britain would break the treaty and Germany would declare against them, and maybe America too, and we would run the English out of all of Southern Africa. What a fool! Was he born yesterday? They're just mercenaries working for Rhodes, the Reformers and the Randlords.'

Leroux coughed. 'Did you know that Jameson had crossed the border?'

'What, already? You see! Those treacherous English. I knew they were behind it. Finally, the tortoise has stuck his neck out!' He rubbed his hands together, and his dark eyes sparkled, as though he were young again, riding down the veld and picking off redcoats.

He lumbered over to the window. 'Dirk! You hear that? Doctor Jameson is coming. You will get your wish!' He turned to Leroux. 'The scouts will pick them up. The commando will shepherd them to Doornkop and finish them there.'

Leroux checked his watch and left Kruger and Brandt discussing the consequences of Jameson's incursion and walked out to the gate. He imagined Lara at her desk, waiting for a reply from Rhodes or the High Commissioner. Time was running short.

Leroux fetched their horses back to the barn. Jory had been shot in the arm and fiddled with a temporary dressing while he guarded three Clan Na Gael men bound on the floor. Leroux returned to the brazier and stoked it and moved the bodies of the sentries out of sight. The fainter stars disappeared from the sky, and he could distinguish the contours of the horizon. The sound of horses travelled with the rustle of grasses and movement down the track caught his eye. First one, then three shapes appeared rising in a trot. Leroux reloaded his revolver. The familiar outline of the leading rider approached, tall and erect in the saddle, broad in the shoulder and with a massive head adorned with a slouch hat. The sky to the east was blue now, and Leroux signalled three times with the paraffin lamp. He pulled the brim of his hat down a touch and stepped into the light of the brazier.

The lead horse pulled up. Leroux advanced and saluted.

'Good morning, sir.'

The man bent forward in his saddle. Leroux looked up at Commandant-General Piet Joubert. Behind the General was a man with an equally impressive Boer beard, that he recognised but did not know. Abraham Malan, Joubert's son-in-law. And slumped in the saddle at the rear was the clean-shaven and gaunt Marais.

'Is that you, Leroux?' Joubert said.

'Yes, sir.'

'What are you doing here?'

'Reconnaissance report, sir.'

Joubert twisted and looked back at Malan and then turned slowly to Leroux. 'Go ahead.'

Leroux drew his revolver and covered Malan.

'President Kruger is at liberty, sir.'

Joubert stiffened and looked over to the farmhouse.

'Anything else?'

'He requests the pleasure of your company, sir.'

Malan's right arm moved slowly back from the reins. Joubert must have sensed it. 'Leave it, Abraham. You'll be dead before you've touched it.'

'Hammond has fled. O'Connell is dead, and the arsenal has been alerted. It's over, Springbok.'

Joubert worked his jaw and looked down at his saddlebag. 'You sent the telegram?'

Leroux stepped up to the horse's flank and opened the saddlebag one-handed. He pulled out a neatly bound document. 'I don't think the President will be interested in this.'

'Kruger will lead us all to disaster, you know it.'

'When the Boers trekked, it was to protect their families from tyranny. Family and freedom came before the State, nee?' Leroux said.

The General's shoulders sagged, and he pursed his lips.

'They killed my father. They killed Sanderson too, and a young lady called Daphne.'

'Ja, Leroux, I know. We should never have broken bread with the dynamitards.'

'That degenerate journalist and his whore?' Malan spat into the dirt. 'What do you care about them?' It was the Boer voice from the meeting.

'He was my friend, and she had nothing to do with it.'

'The Uitlanders will still rise,' Joubert said. 'With my followers, that will be enough.'

Leroux shook his head. 'Jameson has crossed the border–'

'What? How can that be?'

'I don't know. But, if you join him, you'll be a traitor, no one will follow you.'

'And Kruger knows all this?'

'He doesn't know your part in this. He knows Jameson has invaded and suspects you and the Reformers of complicity with Rhodes. He has no idea that you and Hammond double-crossed Rhodes.'

The first rays of the morning lit the farmhouse.

'Well, we had better not keep the old crocodile waiting.'

'Good luck, sir.'

'What should I hope for?'

'When this is over, Rhodes and the British will want the Reformers to retain some sway in the Government. And Kruger knows he has to keep the Boers together.' Leroux stepped back and saluted his General again. He watched them pick their way up the track and took a lamp to the document and turned over the first page.

It was a treaty between a new Republic of Transvaal and the United States. America would recognise the new Republic and guarantee its sovereignty. They would establish Johannesburg and the Witwatersrand goldfields as a free city within the Transvaal, to be known as The Rand. The Rand would pay a royalty in gold each year to America in return for its protection. It would commit to free trade and democracy, with the Uitlanders entitled to vote. Joubert signed it on behalf of the new Republic of Transvaal, John Hays Hammond on behalf of The Rand and JC Manion for the Americans. It was a clever plan. For the United States gold and exports to help with the financial crisis, a popular move in support of a Republic, and millions of Irish American votes for the President. It may even have provided the Boers with an independent future, free of the British Empire. He could have supported it.

He fed the document page by page into the brazier. The edges curled and blackened before flickering yellow and vanishing. He walked back up the track to the farmhouse lost in thought and stood in the open doorway.

Kruger, Dirk and Brandt sat in the middle of the room while Joubert, Malan and Marais huddled just inside the door by the smashed window. Malan stared rigidly straight ahead. Marais squirmed in the early morning sun. Only Joubert stood as though he intended to be there.

Kruger beckoned Leroux into the room.

'There you are! General, this is the young man you gave a commendation to you. How right you were. Go on …'

Joubert nodded and smiled thinly at Leroux. 'Thank you. We are all indebted to him. As I was saying, I learned late last night that you had not returned. I sent out search parties, and then Marais here said he had heard rumours of unusual goings-on at old Nellmapius's estate.

We came in-person to investigate.'

Leroux turned to the sound of horse riders galloping into the farm. Dirk's son had returned with a troop of Boers. Kruger sucked on his pipe and eyed Joubert. 'Jameson has invaded.'

Joubert wrung his hands and glanced at Leroux. 'The pirate! We will run them down like the old days!'

'I thought you would say that. Take the State Artillery and join up with the commando at Krugersdorp. Dirk and his son will go with you. If you see any Irishmen, shoot them.'

Joubert saluted and left. Malan marched after him, and Marais slunk surreptitiously out of the door. Kruger spat across to the spittoon.

'You think I am mad to trust Joubert?' Kruger asked Leroux. 'Don't answer that. He is a politician. Who would trust them?'

A messenger arrived at the door, flushed and covered in dust. 'Telegram for Mr Leroux.'

Leroux took it and unfolded the pink paper and presented it to Kruger.

'The British Government has denounced Doctor Jameson and ordered him to withdraw,' Kruger said, looking up with a rueful grin.

'Sir, I understand that the German Government has offered to send men in assistance against any invasion,' Leroux said.

Kruger rubbed the stump of his left thumb which he had reputedly amputated himself. 'I won't be needing their help.'

Brandt bowed his head. 'You are most wise. I take the British message as a signal that they wish to avoid raising tensions and any misunderstanding.'

'Then you had better speak to your Colonel.'

Kruger turned to the messenger who gawped at him. 'What was happening in Pretoria when you left?'

'The soldiers from the arsenal had captured some men and were taking them to the gaol.'

Kruger heaved himself up.

'I must return to Pretoria before people wonder where I have been.'

He went outside where a young Boer helped him into the saddle. The troop had collected the prisoners from Jory and formed up to escort their President.

'You will not be popular in Johannesburg, Mr Leroux. Where will you go?' Kruger said.

'Away, but there's someone I need to see there first.'

Leroux and Brandt fetched Jory and their horses.

'You knew it was Hammond, Marais, and Joubert?' Brandt said.

Leroux smiled. Looking back there had been so many little things he wondered that he had not seen it sooner. But even as the suspects emerged, he had not fathomed their plot.

'More of a guess. The Baroness's intuition about Marais was right, and Jory never trusted Hammond.'

'Their plan was brilliant. They nearly pulled it off under the noses of Muller, Kruger, Rhodes and the Randlords. They just didn't account for Rhodes's paranoia about a German name.'

'And an awkward bugger like you,' Jory said to Leroux.

'The Veltheim connection threw me for a long time. I guess they intended it as a red herring. Anyway, you're in the clear with Muller. Kruger will vouch for you.'

'Maybe we've done it,' Brandt said, 'Maybe we've found some peace. How does it feel?'

Leroux closed his eyes for a moment. He could see and smell the nightmare of the slaughter in front of the wagons. He heard his father's voice too.

'I'll let you know after I've slept.'

'I need to find Muller and make sure he knows that Kruger has refused outside assistance. He would have telegrammed High Command as soon as he heard about Jameson. They may already be reacting.'

'Lara will know what's been happening on the wires, let's go there first.'

They rode hard for Lara's, and it was after breakfast time as they clattered through the town. There was no sign of revolution, and Bree Street was up and about like any other day, but closed curtains crowded against the flowerpot. Lara must have overslept. She had probably worked most of the night, and Leroux rapped the knocker and stood back. He rapped again. Hesitantly the door opened, and the landlady peered cautiously through the crack. She recognised Leroux and opened the door.

'It's you. Like Piccadilly Circus this morning,' she said.

Leroux bounded up the steps followed by Brandt. The door to the lodgings was ajar. He pushed it open and froze.

'No! Please, no!' Lara lay on the floor next to the sofa, with one arm extended above her head, the other curled over her chest, her legs pulled up. A hideous gash across her neck led down to a pool of blood soaking into the rug. Leroux sank to his knees and wept. Brandt stood in the doorway, aghast.

'Why?' Leroux cried out. He cradled her head and felt the last traces of warmth.

A carriage drew up outside, and the Baroness hurried into the building. She appeared behind Brandt, pale and clutching a paper.

'She stopped the war, Peter.'

'What?' Tears streamed down his face as he rocked, groaning.

'The telegraph lines to the Cape went down shortly after you left. But the raiders missed one. Pretoria's connection to the Cape still works, and they could still send international cables via there. With everything going on the operators worked shifts through the night. Muller must have sent a message to Berlin about Jameson - this arrived a few hours ago. It's a reply from Berlin asking for re-transmission. The message they received was incomprehensible. The consulate also received a message saying the British had denounced the raiders. The clerk who brought me this said Muller left in a rage. I don't know how, but I think Lara interfered with the transmission.'

Leroux stroked Lara's hair, brushing it back from her face. That sounded like Lara's work. If she hadn't been in a position to alter it herself, she would have requested her friend in the Pretoria office to do it. As each relay station forwarded Muller's telegram, no one would have realised that it had been scrambled until they tried to decode it in Berlin many hours later. And now the opportunity Muller had sought for the Kaiser to declare war had passed. The landlady stood behind Brandt, and she too was in tears. Leroux looked down at Lara one more time, held her hand and felt the chain and the little bird clutched within it.

'I thought she knew the man,' the landlady said, dabbing her eye with a handkerchief. He said to "say Starling was here". Lara laughed and called him up.'

'My height, round face, dark eyes and a homburg hat?'

'Yes. Do you know him?'

Leroux stared blankly as Brandt knelt and put his arm around him.

Two weeks later

The Great Karoo passed in a nightmare of grief. Leroux had never told Lara how he felt, and he had much to say to her. She was the kind you would marry in both lives and not regret it. He looked out the window at the bleak expanse, and his mind drifted. Muller had fled to Delagoa Bay. Brandt had promised help. He did not know Muller's real name but did reveal his codename, "Luchs," - the Lynx. The reform committee in Johannesburg learned of Jameson's foray. They armed the miners, but pitifully few and the British High Commissioner forbade them to assist the raiders. The rebels raised the Vierkleur and sent Kruger a list of demands. Kruger ignored them and cornered and captured Jameson's force. The High Commissioner came to negotiate with Kruger and, squirming with embarrassment, issued a proclamation to the Uitlanders demanding that they lay down their arms to spare the lives of Jameson's men. The Reformers sent a party to negotiate. Kruger said he couldn't negotiate unless he knew with whom he was dealing. The Reformers sent him an impressive and comprehensive list. Kruger rubbed his hands, arrested them all and sent for a hanging judge.

The train hammered on. Two Springbucks bounded through the scrub making impossible leaps, and he hoped Lara was in a better place. The thought gave him small comfort, and he looked at the other passengers in the carriage. People from all corners of the world seeking a better life. Didn't they know that nothing good ever happened in Johannesburg? He wondered where they were going. Heading home to visit a loved one? Giving up on their dream of striking gold? Or just escaping for a few days the feverish and dusty place that only existed because it sat on a bloody great big heap of gold? Gold that drove men mad and could pay for all their madness. Could it really have ended in a war of the world? His thoughts wandered again with the rocking of the train. And what on Earth was he going to tell Rhodes? Right then, he could not care less.

Rhodes emptied a drawer and added to the jumble on top of his desk. 'What a shambles!' He tugged on his cigarette and stomped around the room in his flannel trousers and tennis shoes. 'It's not official yet, but I shan't survive this. I've been called to London. Time to face the music.'

'Sorry to hear that, sir,' Leroux said.

'If it weren't for you, it would have been a lot worse. I owe you my thanks.'

Leroux shifted in his seat. Rhodes did not need to know the whole story.

'What will you do now?' Rhodes said.

'I don't think journalism is for me.'

'Yes, well. Powell was a bit miffed that you got beaten to the Jameson story by Sanderson - of all people!'

'He was invaluable in uncovering Muller's plot.'

'No, no, you did very well to flush out the Germans. And I understand you're the only man who can identify their top spy. They were even more audacious than I expected. Ha! The Kaiser has been reduced to sending pompous telegrams. War is averted, and the Transvaal is still within our grasp.' Rhodes stubbed out his cigarette. 'I have a contact in Whitehall who could use your talents. I'll speak to him. You have the fortunate gift of getting out of trouble marginally quicker than you get into it.'

'Thank you, sir, but Miss Sinclair should take the credit. She knew that Muller was on to her, and she stalled his message. I just don't understand why Jameson set off. Of course, he was worried that the Boers had discovered his position, that the civilians were in danger. But to disregard a direct order from you…'

Rhodes avoided Leroux's gaze and fidgeted another cigarette out. He lit the cigarette and coughed. 'There was a … a communications breakdown. He's ruined us all. It's a total disaster.'

Leroux looked at the gold sundial. Was that it? Had time run out for Rhodes? Had he just rolled the dice and hoped for the best?

'They've started digging out Maddox Deep,' Rhodes said. 'Well and truly buried, they say. I had no idea the scale of the illicit gold racket. I'll have to think about how to present that to the stockholders. And Scotland Yard is delighted to hear of the demise of Mr O'Connell. They could have caused havoc with all that money.'

'I saw Mrs Hammond outside. She looked distraught,' Leroux said.

'Hammond's not taking prison well. He's got dysentery. They're expecting the death sentence for all of them. The judge made a point of arriving with his black cap. We're pulling out all the stops.' Rhodes flicked his ash on the rug.

'Yes, sir.'

'The American Government is up in arms. They're putting a lot of diplomatic pressure on Kruger to release Hammond. Still, relations between Britain and the United States are improving. They've even asked London to intervene to help get Hammond out. Heaven knows why they think Kruger would want to do us any favours.'

THE END

HISTORICAL NOTE

President Kruger remained in office but was forced to flee South Africa as the Second Boer War turned against the Boers in 1900. His daughter-in-law died in a British concentration camp, and five sickly grandchildren passed away within days of being transferred from the concentration camp into the care of Kruger's wife, Gezina, who died two weeks later. Kruger outlived his nemesis, Cecil Rhodes, but remained in exile until he died in Switzerland in 1904. His body was returned to South Africa for a state funeral and buried in the Heroes' Acre, Pretoria.

Cecil Rhodes resigned as Prime Minister of the Cape Colony but escaped any real punishment. After he died in 1902, just before final victory in the Boer War, he was buried in the Matopos Hills in Rhodesia (modern-day Zimbabwe). Rhodes's dream of an imperial red line running from the Cape to Cairo became a reality when the League of Nations transferred German East Africa (modern-day Tanzania) to the British Empire as a mandate in 1920, although the railway was never built.

Frederic Kűrtze deserted from the German Navy after stealing a gold watch and seal from Captain Wilhelm von Veltheim. He subsequently styled himself as Baron Ludwig von Veltheim and financed his life through a series of bigamous marriages and blackmail. Kűrtze attempted to blackmail and then shot dead Woolf Joel, the nephew of Barney Barnato, a leading Randlord and the largest stockholder in De Beers. At the trial in 1898, Kűrtze claimed that Barnato, who had died in suspicious circumstances the previous year, had engaged him in a scheme to kidnap President Kruger.

Commandant-General Piet Joubert ran four times for President against Kruger. The third time in 1893 was close - 7,911 for Kruger and 7,246 for Joubert. It was suspected that Kruger's agents had altered the voting lists. On the 1st of December 1895, he made the unusual decision to go to Natal on holiday supposedly for two months. Kruger recalled him by telegram on the 26th. During the Jameson Raid, Judge E.J.P. Jorissen, a confidante of Kruger, accused Joubert of treachery and his son-in-law Malan of being in league with the Johannesburg rebels. Kruger, however, kept him close and he became Vice President in May 1896 until his death during the Boer War in 1900.

John Hays Hammond spent three years rehabilitating his reputation in London following his release from jail in Pretoria in June 1896. He returned to the United States where he continued a highly successful career in mining and was an unsuccessful nominee for Vice President to President Taft.

Dr Leander Starr Jameson only appears peripherally in the story, stuck out on the border, although the events are known in history as "The Jameson Raid". The British press lionised him in the wake of the 'Kruger telegram' and the subsequent wave of anti-German sentiment. The public felt he had been badly let down by the Government. The Boers handed the raiders over to the British for trial, and Jameson was sentenced to fifteen months which he served in Holloway. He then returned to South Africa and became Prime Minister of the Cape Colony in 1904 and is buried alongside Rhodes. Rudyard Kipling was inspired to write a poem, 'If'.

The Jameson Raid began on the afternoon of the 29th of December 1895 and was part of a plan concocted by Cecil Rhodes, John Hays Hammond and Doctor Leander Starr Jameson to annex the South African Republic for the British Empire. The Uitlanders would rise with Hammond in Johannesburg, armed with smuggled rifles, seize the armoury in Pretoria, and 'invite' Jameson to help protect them from Kruger's commandos. According to his autobiography, Hammond also considered kidnapping President Paul Kruger.

But the scheme was bedevilled by problems. The conspirators in Johannesburg failed to smuggle in enough rifles to arm the miners. Jameson's force numbered only six hundred instead of the hoped-for fifteen hundred. Support for the rebellion in Johannesburg was divided, particularly about fighting under the Union Jack. And the Boers discovered the force of American miners posted by Hammond at Irene, which withdrew to Johannesburg before it could be attacked.

When Jameson jumped the gun, the plot disintegrated. By the time the conspirators were aware of Jameson's move and debating what to do, the British Government had denounced the raiders, ordered them to turn back, and forbade British subjects from assisting them. Kruger cornered Jameson's force before it reached Johannesburg, captured them and then effectively used them as hostages to force the surrender of the Johannesburg rebels. The leaders were all arrested, and international condemnation rained down on Great Britain.

The German Foreign Secretary Baron Marschall dressed down the British ambassador, denounced the London Government for its failure to control their Cape officials, and declared the result would be an alliance of continental powers to oppose further aggression. On the 31st of December 1895, he instructed German Ambassador Hatzfeldt in London, "If you are of the opinion that this violation of international law is condoned you will ask for your passports," implying war would be declared.

The Kaiser wrote to Tsar Nicholas II of Russia on the 2nd of January to pursue the idea of a continental league against Great Britain.

Ambassador Hatzfeldt left a note for Prime Minister Salisbury stating that "Germany protests against this act and is unwilling to accept any alteration in the position of the South African Republic as defined in existing treaties." Salisbury had already retired for the day, and the note was left sealed at the Foreign Office. The following day, the 3rd of January, news of the failure of the raid came through, and Hatzfeldt was able to recover the note unopened before Salisbury saw it. Lord Salisbury had previously begged Hatzfeldt not to present any provocative demands which would make an already difficult position untenable.

On the 3rd the Kaiser sent the now infamous telegram to President Kruger which read, "I express to you my sincere congratulations that you and your people, without appealing to the help of friendly powers, have succeeded by your own energetic action against the armed bands which invaded your country as disturbers of the peace, in restoring peace and in maintaining the independence of the country against attack from without."

The Kaiser had wanted to take more extreme measures, but even as it was the "Kruger telegram" caused an explosion of anti-German sentiment in Britain and set Anglo-German relations on a course that would end in the catastrophe of World War One.

The French Government presented President Kruger with a ceremonial sword which glorified a heroic Boer strangling the imperial lion.

The Jameson Raid is now generally regarded as the opening shot of the Second Boer War, a colossal undertaking that strained the British Empire. It required over 400,000 imperial troops, concentration camps and scorched earth policies to overcome the guerrilla tactics employed by the Boers and led to the Union of South Africa.

The official explanation for Jameson jumping the gun is muddled between Dr Jameson acting on his own initiative and alleged miscommunication in telegrams. Perhaps this fudging is not surprising as the next person up the chain of command from Rhodes was Joseph Chamberlain, the British Colonial Secretary, who sat on the select committee of the parliamentary inquiry.

Rhodes was concerned about American influence, telling his friend, the journalist W.T. Stead: "It seemed to me quite certain that if I did not take a hand in the game the forces on the spot would soon make short work of President Kruger. Then I should be face to face with an American Republic - American in the sense of being intensely hostile to and jealous of Britain—an American Republic largely manned by Americans and Sydney Bulletin Australians who cared nothing for the [Union Jack]. They would have all the Rand at their disposal. The drawing power of the Outlander Republic would have collected round it all the other Colonies. They would have federated with it as a centre, and we should have lost South Africa. To avert this catastrophe, to rope in the Outlanders before it was too late, I did what I did."

Britain faced the real possibility of conflict with the United States and others, as the British High Commissioner in South Africa, Sir Hercules Robinson, noted on the 3rd of January 1896: "The difficulty coming at the present moment is very unfortunate as it is generally feared that the United States intends to go to war with us and that they will have the support of Russia and France. That is bad enough, but to have Germany likewise against us, would reduce us to having to fight for our very existence."

However, the Venezuela Crisis was resolved, and America's financial crisis abated, although the Democrats lost the November election. Britain assisted America in securing

Hammond's release, and Anglo-American relations began an upward path, the significance of which would play out twenty years later.

Along with the mystery surrounding Jameson's actions there is the question of why, on Friday 10th of January 1896, the day before learning that John Hays Hammond had been arrested, Alabama Senator, John T Morgan, Chairman of the Committee on Foreign Relations, put the following resolution to the Senate:

"The people of the United States of America, through their representatives in Congress assembled, convey to the President and people of the Republic of Transvaal their earnest congratulations upon their success in establishing free representative government, republican in form, and in their opposition to any foreign power that denies to them the full enjoyment of these rightful liberties."

Note the underlined text. The President's name is not specified. Kruger was President of the South African Republic; it was not officially called Transvaal. The American public did not regard the Government as being representative, as the Uitlanders, including many Americans, were not entitled to vote. Nor had it recently changed as 'success in establishing' implies.

The following day when it was reported that Hammond had been arrested, the resolution was passed to Senator Morgan's Foreign Affairs Committee where it was buried and never sent. Perhaps there was a conspiracy.

ACKNOWLEDGMENTS

The Rand Conspiracy is a work of fiction weaved into the historical events surrounding the Jameson Raid. I owe thanks to the fabulous British Library, a wonderful resource for research, and particularly to the author and historian Richard Hopton who read an early draft and provided valuable feedback. And most of all, to my family and friends for all their help and bearing with me.

ABOUT THE AUTHOR

Richard Westover was born in 1967 and lives with his wife and family in London. The Rand Conspiracy is his first novel.

Peter Leroux returns in
'The Ottoman Agenda' - Autumn 2022

Printed in Great Britain
by Amazon